with an unforgettable, high-caliber read!"

—*Heartland Critiques*

Iris

"Leigh Greenwood continues the standard of excellence that began with *Rose* and continued in *Fern. Iris* is a strong, multidimensional novel . . . The character depth and portrayal is nothing short of remarkable." —*Affair de Coeur*

Laurel

"Wow! What can I say but magnificent, superb, wonderful, and captivating. The characters are so true to life, I feel they are personal friends of mine!" —*Rendezvous*

"Each book in the memorable Randolph family saga is better than the one before and *Laurel* is no exception. Readers will eagerly await the next installment in this dynamic and exciting series!" —*Affaire de Coeur*

"Leigh Greenwood is riding high on this one. Encore! Encore!" —*Heartland Critiques*

"Leigh Greenwood is one of the finest writers in American romance today. *Laurel* beautifully evokes our heritage and captures our hearts." —*RT Book Reviews*

Daisy

"Fans of the Seven Brides series, as well as new readers, will find *Daisy* a not-to-be-missed keeper!" —*RT Book Reviews*

Violet

"Leigh Greenwood writes Americana at its best! Hold these books close to your heart." —*RT Book Reviews*

Lily

"If ever there was a happy-ending book, this is it. *Lily* has romance, intrigue, and especially humor with some very lovable characters. Its plot is simply wonderful. This book will capture readers' hearts, making them believe love is possible for everyone." —*Rawhide & Lace*

Untamed Love

"Do you have a liking for wildcats?" Laurel asked.

"If that's what you are, I guess I do," Hen said.

"You can get scratched up mighty bad."

"I have three brothers who married spitfires, and they've never been happier. Could be they know something I don't."

Laurel had accustomed herself to Hen's touch, his thoughtfulness, his gentle understanding. But she wasn't prepared when he took her in his arms and kissed her. This time there was nothing gentle or hesitant about it. It was hungry, hard, and hot. Laurel felt drained. At the same time she felt about to burst with a kind of energy that was one part excitement, one part anticipation, and one part disbelief. She didn't know what the other parts might be. She didn't care.

LEIGH GREENWOOD

Laurel

LEISURE BOOKS NEW YORK CITY

*To my family, who has seen too little of me, and
heard more than they wanted about the Randolphs.*

A LEISURE BOOK®

August 2010

Published by

Dorchester Publishing Co., Inc.
200 Madison Avenue
New York, NY 10016

ISBN 10: 0-8439-6435-9
ISBN 13: 978-0-8439-6435-6
E-ISBN: 978-1-4285-0920-7

Visit us online at www.dorchesterpub.com.

Seven Brides Series

William Henry Randolph (1816–1865)—Aurelia Pinckney Coleman (1823–1863)
m. 1841

George Washington
b. July 14, 1842
m.
Elizabeth Rose Thornton

James Madison
b. Feb. 14, 1845
m.
Fern Sproull

Thomas Jefferson
b. Nov. 12, 1843
m.
Violet Goodwin

Juliette Coleman
b. May 21, 1847
died in infancy

twins

James Monroe "Monty"
b. Sept. 16, 1849
m.
Iris Richmon

William Henry "Hen" Harrison
b. Sept. 16, 1849
m.
Laurel Simpson Blackthorne

John Tyler
b. June 17, 1853
m.
Daisy Singleton

Zachary Taylor
b. Aug. 2, 1859
m.
Lily Sterling

Chapter One

The shrill cry was out of place in this peaceful desert canyon filled with towering sycamores and a myriad of singing birds. Hen Randolph thought at first that the sound must have come from an eagle or some small animal. When it came a second time, he knew it was a woman's cry. Unsure where he was going or what lay ahead, he ran forward along the narrow path that hugged the canyon wall.

He didn't hear the deeper male voice until he rounded the bend. The canyon opened up into a small, boulder-free clearing on the steep incline of the creek. Back up against the sheer canyon wall, well away from the stream, Hen saw a small adobe house. In front of it, a man and a woman argued, lashing each other with their voices, striking out with open hands. Hen's steps slowed, then stopped. He had been told Laurel Blackthorne was unmarried, but this looked like a domestic quarrel. Just as he started to turn around, she cried out again in a voice that spoke to him of danger and desperation.

"Touch my child, and I swear I'll see you dead!"

The man shoved her aside, but she ran ahead of him.

"Adam, hide!" she screamed.

The man was faster and caught up. She threw herself at him, grabbing his arm to hold him back.

Hen started forward again.

The man seemed to be trying to get away from Laurel. Though she was much smaller, she held on tenaciously. Then he hit her. He simply drew back his fist and hit her in the face.

She fell to the ground.

Hen felt himself fill with hot rage. He had few principles, but he held to those with fierce tenacity. Among the most important was that a man should never strike a woman.

Hen drew his gun and would have shot the man right then. But even as the woman summoned the energy to shout one last warning, he disappeared inside the adobe. A moment later, he came out dragging a small boy.

"Let me go!" the child cried as he kicked and hit at the man.

Laurel struggled to her feet and tried to take the child from him. He hit her again. She staggered but refused to give up. She followed him as he tried to reach his horse.

Holstering his gun, Hen started forward as fast as he could run. He couldn't fire at the man and risk hurting the woman or child. Caught up in their struggle, they didn't hear Hen's approach.

"Let them go," he called out, still several yards away.

The man froze; the child continued to struggle; Laurel hit the man with her balled-up fist. He put his hand in her face and pushed her to her knees. Reaching him, Hen grabbed him by the arm, turned him around, and hit him so hard that he slumped to the ground, dazed. The child broke away and ran to his mother.

"Here, ma'am, let me help you up," Hen said and extended his hand.

The woman made no attempt to rise. As she leaned forward, holding herself off the ground with one hand, her other arm around her son, her body heaved in its struggle to fill her lungs. She lifted her head to look at him. Hen's stomach turned over and the rage inside him welled up more ferociously than before. Her face was covered with bruises. She had put up a good fight, but the man had beaten her unmercifully.

Turning, Hen found the bastard staggering to his feet.

"Only a coward hits a woman," Hen growled and back-handed the man so hard that he sprawled on the ground once more. Hen reached down and jerked him to his feet. "Only a rotten yellowbelly hurts a kid." A series of methodical blows rendered the man unable to stand, but Hen held him up so he wouldn't fall.

"If I ever find you here again, I'll put a bullet in you. Touch this woman or her child, and I'll kill you." A last backhand sent him to the ground. Hen kicked the gun lying near well out of the fallen man's reach. Then he took a rope from his saddle, rolled him over, shoved his face in the dust, and tied his hands behind him.

"I'll kill you," the man bellowed from between bloody lips.

"You might try," Hen said as he jerked the knot tight.

"Nobody touches a Blackthorne and lives."

Bending down, Hen spoke in his ear, low and menacing. "This nobody has a name. Randolph. Hen Randolph. Remember it. If you bother this woman again, I'll brand it on your forehead." Hen turned the man over. When he kicked at Hen and tried to scramble to his feet, Hen yanked on the rope and pulled the man's shoulders back until he screamed. Pushing him to his knees, Hen trussed him like a calf about to be branded.

He turned back to Laurel. She still sat on the ground, her arm protectively around her son.

"Let me help you up. We need to do something about those bruises."

"Who are you?" she asked.

"I'm the new sheriff of Sycamore Flats. I take it you're Laurel Blackthorne."

Laurel's gaze gripped him. "You realize you've signed your death warrant, don't you?"

Her tone was sharp and without a trace of appreciation for what he had done. It wasn't exactly the response he had expected.

"No, ma'am, I didn't. I thought I was helping you and your son. Didn't look to me like you were having a whole lot of fun."

"That's Damian Blackthorne." She still sounded stiff and ungrateful.

"So?"

"He's got at least two dozen brothers, cousins, and uncles."
Maybe she was too scared to show her real emotion.

"It figures. Trouble never shows its face but what it's got a whole lot of company."

Laurel continued to eye him. "Either you're crazy or you're a fool."

Hen smiled. "I've been accused of both. Now I'd better get started on your face. I was told you were a right pretty woman, but you don't look too pretty right now." He extended his hand once more, but she still didn't take it.

"At least you're nicer than the other gunmen who tried to be sheriff," Laurel said, continuing to stare at him. "I hope they give you a big funeral."

"Ma'am, being sheriff hasn't taken up a whole lot of my time so far, but if you don't get up off that ground soon, I expect I'll have Hope up here wondering why I'm late for dinner. Besides, all that blood's a lot easier to clean off before it dries."

Laurel finally accepted his help. Her hand felt rough and dry, not soft like those of the ladies he had known.

"This is my son, Adam," Laurel said as she got to her feet.

Adam continued to cling to his mother, apparently unsure of whether he could trust Hen.

"What was he doing here?" Hen asked, indicating Damian.

"None of your damned business," Damian shouted. "When I get free, I'm going to fill your ass so full of holes, the—"

Hen stuffed Damian's bandanna in his mouth. "That fella sure doesn't know how to talk in front of a lady," he said, turning his attention back to Laurel.

"Don't you ever get upset over anything?" Laurel asked.

"It's a waste of energy and doesn't change anything. Now let's see if I can do something about your face."

"I can take care of myself."

It upset him that she seemed afraid to let him touch her. "I'm sure you can, but you don't have to."

"I would prefer it."

"People don't always get what they prefer."

"Didn't anybody tell you that you were supposed to protect people, not bully them?"

"I guess they didn't get around to that. They seemed too anxious to pin the badge on me to say anything that might cause me to change my mind."

"That sounds like Sycamore Flats," Laurel said, disgust in her voice. "If they don't *see* anything wrong, there can't *be* anything wrong."

"A lot of people are like that. It's easier than doing something about it." He looked around until he saw a shallow pan. "I'm going to get some water. While I'm gone, see what kind of medicines you can rustle up."

As Laurel watched him go, she marveled at his confidence. Either he was a great fool, or he was more of a man than half a dozen Blackthornes rolled together. She felt a tiny shiver run down her spine, the same shiver she'd felt when he'd touched her.

From the way he'd handled Damian, she had no doubt that he was a man. But only a fool would try being sheriff of Sycamore Flats.

Laurel was inside the adobe when Hen returned. Adam stood by the door as if guarding his mother. He watched Hen uneasily, but he didn't shrink from him.

"Are you hurt?" Hen asked the boy.

"No."

"Damian wouldn't hurt another Blackthorne," Laurel said, coming outside. "Adam is his nephew," she explained, seeing Hen's confusion.

"Too bad he doesn't feel that way about you."

"He might if I'd given him what he wanted."

Hen moved a chair from next to the house to a spot where an opening in the canopy overhead offered the most light. "Sit."

Laurel didn't think she'd ever met anyone as coldly impassive. Or as incurious. "Aren't you going to ask what he wants?"

"I figure it's none of my business."

"It isn't, but Damian is going to make you his business." Laurel winced when Hen took her face and turned it toward the light.

"Don't talk."

Laurel sat absolutely still, trying to give no sign of how much her face hurt. By now the shock was wearing off, and the dull throbbing had become intensely painful. The cool, moist cloth Hen pressed to her face did little to ease the pain. Or remove the marks which would make her unfit to be seen in public for weeks.

"What did you find?" Hen asked.

"Yerba mansa," she replied.

Laurel handed Hen a small bottle. He passed it under his nose. Seemingly satisfied, he carefully cleaned the blood and dirt from one side of her face, then generously anointed it with the herbal tincture to disinfect the wound.

He worked in silence.

Laurel marveled at his gentleness. She had never met a man who would even consider caring for a woman. Women-folk had to take care of themselves. Neither had she imagined that a man tough enough to handle Damian would take such care not to hurt her. Yet beneath his easy touch, she sensed a hardness that seemed to go to the core of this man.

"What was all that about?" he asked at last.

"I thought you weren't interested." She didn't know why, but his failure to ask earlier irritated her.

"I'm not. The sheriff is."

"Is there a difference?"

"Sure."

She believed him. If anybody could divide himself in two, this man could. How else could his touch be so gentle and everything else about him seem so cold? Still the contrast intrigued her, as did the bluest eyes she'd ever seen.

"My husband died before Adam was born. None of his relatives paid any attention to him when he was a baby. But now he's six, and they think he ought to go live with them."

"I gather you disagree."

"Wouldn't you?" In her agitation, Laurel twisted in Hen's grasp. She winced.

"Keep still."

Gentle he might be, but there was no compassion in him. She was sure he would show more feeling for his horse.

"I know nothing about your situation," Hen said without taking his eyes off his work, "but in my experience, a boy who's around nobody but women is liable to grow up soft. That could get him killed."

Laurel jerked away from Hen. "Has your *experience* shown you what happens to boys who grow up like Damian?"

"They generally get themselves killed."

He acted as though he were talking of the weather instead of life and death.

"And you think Adam ought to grow up like *that?*" she snapped.

"I never like to see anybody get killed, not even those who deserve it." Hen took Laurel's face in his hands once more and resumed his work.

At least, Laurel thought, he didn't approve of killing. That was something. "I have no intention of letting Damian or any other Blackthorne get his hands on Adam. I don't want him growing up soft, but I mean to see he grows up with some principles."

"Nice if you can do it."

"You don't think I can?" Why did she care what he thought? She was mad at herself for asking.

"I don't know. You seem like a remarkably stubborn woman, but I don't know if you're any good at getting things done."

Laurel pulled away again. "I've gotten a lot done, including taking care of myself for nearly seven years."

"Weren't doing such a grand job a while back."

Hen turned her toward the light. She flinched when he touched her shoulder.

"You've got a bruise under your dress."

"I hit a rock when I fell."

"Let me see it."

"No."

"You afraid I'd try to take advantage of you?" His gaze was riveting, uncompromising.

"N-no."

"You think it would be indecent?"

"Of course not."

"Then let me see it."

No sensitivity either, Laurel thought to herself as she slipped the dress over her shoulder. He clearly didn't understand how humiliating it was to have to submit to his care.

When he touched her, she practically rose off the chair. His touch was too light to hurt. Rather, it seared her with a jolt of energy that left her feeling a little dazed. She forgot the pain in her face. She was aware only of his fingers on the warm flesh of her shoulder. She couldn't bring herself to look at him. She was suddenly, acutely, achingly aware that he was a man and she a woman.

Stop being a fool. You're only acting this way because you've been seven years without a man's touch.

Regardless of the reason, it was impossible to feel indifferent.

"The skin's not broken," Hen said. He pressed ever so slightly. Pain as sharp as a pin shot through her shoulder. He must have seen her wince, but he offered no apologies. "You're going to have to be very careful for a few days."

"Can I put my clothes back on now, doctor?"

He smiled. "Do you have any prickly pear around here?"

"Farther up the canyon," Laurel said as she righted her dress.

"I'll be right back." He headed off at a leisurely pace.

She was glad he was going. She needed time to calm down. She couldn't be calm, or she wouldn't be having this ridiculous reaction to him, this sense of not wanting him to touch her, yet somehow wanting him to. Of looking for comfort in a place she didn't expect to find it.

"Where's he going, Ma?" Adam asked. He hadn't left his mother's side the whole time.

"To find some prickly pears, though what he wants with them is a mystery."

But that mystery didn't interest her so much as why his touch had such a powerful effect on her. She had never enjoyed Carlin's caresses. Even in the beginning, when she was still wild and foolish and believed she was in love with him, she had found his nearness strangely unsatisfying. But with a single touch, this stranger had caused her body to ache and yearn, her skin to feel scorched, her nerves to become uncomfortably sensitive.

It must be the shock. Damian had been brutal. It would be days before she felt like herself again.

"Is anybody else going to come after me?" Adam asked. He looked scared.

Laurel had always been afraid the Blackthornes would come for Adam someday. She had expected it to be later. It had been a cruel shock when Damian showed up today.

"Maybe," Laurel said, "but we'll be ready next time."

She hadn't been ready today. Adam would be beyond her reach right this minute if it hadn't been for this unusual man. Okay, he was the sheriff and maybe protecting her was his job, but she didn't think she had ever met anybody remotely like him.

"He's coming back," Adam warned her.

Hen came down the canyon, his arms loaded with prickly pear fruit.

"Here, hold these," he said, and dropped the fruits in her lap. He took a knife from his pocket and sliced a fruit in half, then filleted it. "Do you have any cheesecloth?"

"Yes."

"Cut the rest of these just like this one. Then put them on your bruises and wrap your face in the cloth. You'll heal up twice as fast."

"I'll look like I'm being readied for burial," Laurel objected.

She broke off, staring at him. "Why did you come up here?" she asked.

"I wanted to ask you to do my laundry." He looked around. "I dropped it back there."

"I'll get it," Adam said and ran off. He had regained some of his confidence.

"I'm not sure when I can get to it," Laurel told him. "I've got a lot to do." She knew she ought to do his laundry first, out of gratitude if nothing else, but a feeling of disappointment, of irrational irritation, had taken hold of her. He seemed as immune to the fact that she was a woman as she was acutely aware that he was a man.

"You shouldn't do anything else today."

"Except pickle myself in cactus fruit."

"Except that."

She thought she saw a smile, a glint in those blue eyes, but maybe it was only a trick of the sun. She smiled back anyway. "I'll tell people to see you when they want to know why their laundry isn't done on time."

"Seems telling them to see Damian would be more appropriate."

The humor faded from her expression. "It wouldn't make any difference. The Blackthornes don't care what anybody else wants."

"You ought to see if you can work out a compromise. It won't do that boy any good to be caught between the two of you."

"You don't know anything about the situation," she said, her voice cold and sharp again.

"True, but you can't change who his father was."

"But I can see he grows up with some principles," she said stubbornly, "that he doesn't think it's okay to take what he wants just because he's bigger and willing to use a gun."

Adam came up, carrying a bag of clothes. He was a big boy for his age, and he handled the heavy bag well.

"You carry a lot of clothes with you," Laurel said when she saw the heavy bag.

"I'm a long way from home."

"Maybe you ought to consider going back." Even though he had made her angry, she meant it as a kindness. She didn't want to see him killed. No one had ever been this nice to her.

"You're going to consider letting that boy see his uncles once in a while?"

Laurel glared at him, all desire to be kind gone. "That's none of your concern."

"Neither is where I go yours."

"It is when you're on my property," she shot back. "I'll do your clothes, but I mean to see the back of you disappearing down that canyon before I stir from this spot."

"It'd be more to the point if you'd clap a couple of those cactus fruit to your face and lie down. You'll be a whole lot happier about what your mirror shows you tomorrow."

"Leave!" Laurel practically shouted. "And take your clothes with you."

"I'll be back tomorrow to see how you're doing," Hen said.

"I've got a shotgun."

"Good. A woman living alone needs to be able to protect herself." Hen turned to Adam. "Watch out for your ma, son. In her present frame of mind, she's liable to attack anything, including a panther. Poor old cat would be chewed to little bitty pieces before it could let out a screech. You'd have cat fur all over the yard. Take you the better part of a day to sweep it up."

Laurel had to struggle to preserve her frown. "I'd appreciate it if you'd go before you ruin my character with my own son."

"See, you *can* talk nice when you try," Hen said. There wasn't a trace of humor in his eyes. "I enjoyed the visit, too."

Hen walked over to Damian and untied his feet, then practically threw him into the saddle. Tipping his hat, Hen sauntered out of the yard leading Damian's horse.

"You forgot your clothes," Adam called.

Hen merely waved without looking around.

"Ma, he forgot his—"

"He didn't forget," Laurel said. "He had no intention of taking them."

"What are you going to do with them?"

She sighed. "Wash them, I guess."

"But you said you wouldn't."

"I know, but Mr. Sheriff doesn't seem to hear very well."

"He said his name was Mr. Randolph. I heard him."

"I know. Hen Randolph. What kind of name is that for a grown man? Hen. That's a chicken. It makes you think of something covered with feathers scratching in the dirt for worms and squawking for all she's worth when she's laid an egg in the bushes."

Adam was suddenly overcome with giggles. "He don't have no feathers, Ma. And he don't squawk."

"Doesn't squawk," Laurel corrected. "No, but he sure does talk a lot of nonsense."

"I like him. He beat up that man."

"Yes, he did, didn't he?" But violence frightened her, and Hen had been brutal.

"Do you think he'll come back?"

Laurel let her gaze linger on the spot where Hen had disappeared down the canyon. "I doubt we'll ever see him again."

"I didn't like him. If I had a gun, I'd shoot him if he came back."

"Oh, you mean Damian," Laurel said, jerked back to reality. "I'm afraid he will. And you will not shoot anybody. Now you'd better get some water and gather wood if I'm going to do Mr. Randolph's clothes."

"He told you to lie down."

"I know what he said, but you can be sure he expects to see his clothes done by tomorrow."

But as Laurel watched Adam heft the wooden bucket and head toward the stream, she wondered if Hen really did expect to have his clothes laundered by morning. She had never met a man like him. She really didn't know what he'd expect.

Except for her father, whom she could barely remember, every man she'd ever met believed a woman existed solely to provide for his comfort and pleasure.

Hen acted like that when he talked about Adam needing a man's influence. But when he cared for her bruises, his touch had been gentle.

Still, she hadn't missed the fury in his eyes when he systematically beat Damian into helplessness. That reminded her of her stepfather. She could still remember the blows raining down, the feeling of helplessness. She shivered. She had vowed never to tolerate that again. Yet despite what he had done to Damian, she felt sure Hen would never strike a woman.

"I'll need at least two more buckets," she said when Adam poured the first into the kettle. "He has an awful lot of clothes."

She watched her son return to the stream. He was a good child. She didn't care what Hen Randolph thought, she intended to keep Adam out of Blackthorne hands no matter what she had to do. And that included using the shotgun she kept by her bed. She didn't think Hen would approve of the Blackthornes, even though he felt Adam needed a man. But how could she know that? There was no law that said a man had to be good just because he was so good-looking it made a woman feel weak being near him.

She remembered white-blond hair showing under his hat, skin tanned to the color of new leather, lean features chiseled into an expression that gave no hint of his thoughts, and a tall, powerful body capable of knocking Damian Blackthorne to the ground with one blow.

But it was his eyes that had exercised the most powerful effect on her. As intensely blue as the sky, they showed no sign of warmth, amusement, or sadness. Nothing. Even though he had defended her, taken care of her, he appeared completely cold and unfeeling. But he couldn't be, could he? Not and risk his neck for her.

Stop acting like a fool. All this wondering is a waste of time.

*If you had spent half this much time thinking about Carlin be-
fore you married him, you wouldn't be in this mess now.*

Putting her former husband out of her mind, Laurel picked
up the bag of clothes and put them on the chair. Even that
effort caused the blood to rush to her face and her bruises to
ache. She leaned against the back of the chair. Maybe she
wasn't well enough to do any more work today.

She thought of the nearly bare cupboard inside and knew
she didn't have any choice. Not everyone in town was as careful to pay their bills as they were insistent that their laundry
be done on time.

"I wish we were closer to the creek," Adam said as he
poured the last bucket into the pot. His face was pink from
the exertion of lugging three buckets of water.

"I know, but then the creek would flood the house every
time it rained." Adam knew that, but she didn't mind his complaining a little. He did it so seldom.

Laurel opened the bag and began to pull out one shirt after
another. She was amazed that any man would use so many.
More than the number, she marveled at their quality. She
examined the fabric more closely. Fine linen, the best she had
ever seen. She inspected the needlework and tested the seams.
Better and more expensive than anything she got from town.
She kept pulling shirts out of the bag until she had twenty-
two. His underwear, pants, and socks were of the same quality. He even had a stiff collar. He must have a dress coat in his
wardrobe.

This man hadn't been a sheriff before. At least, not for very
long. A sheriff had to be calculating and careful. He had to
know who wielded the power. Hen seemed to be the kind of
man who did whatever he wanted and damned the consequences.

Laurel wondered if her life would have been any better if
she had married a man like Hen rather than Carlin.

She was certain Hen wouldn't have abandoned her for a
cheap whore, or gotten himself killed trying to steal a bull.

He would have married her in a church in a decent wedding instead of rustling some preacher out of bed in the middle of the night, a preacher she hadn't been able to locate in seven years. And he wouldn't have left her with a son to raise by herself and no means of support.

But she hadn't married a man like Hen. She had married Carlin Blackthorne and had spent the last six years raising her son alone. She didn't mean to give him up now. Neither did she mean to let him starve. She would wash this man's clothes. Then she would lie down. He would pay her. Then she could buy some food.

Chapter Two

Hen didn't feel the indifference he'd shown Laurel. Inside him simmered a dangerously hot anger toward Damian. Only remembering that he was now the sheriff had kept him from administering the brutal beating the son-of-a-bitch deserved, the beating he would get if he ever touched Laurel again. While Hen was sheriff, no man would get away with beating a woman.

He probably shouldn't have hit Damian more than once, maybe not at all. Well, that was too damned bad. He had hit him, and if Damian aggravated him any more, he'd do it again.

Hen knew that wasn't the right attitude. The very fact that it wasn't irritated him. He wasn't used to restrictions. He and Monty were used to delivering their own brand of justice and making it stick with guns and fists. It wasn't going to be easy to change his habits now.

Why the hell had he agreed to be sheriff anyway? Nobody paid two hundred and fifty dollars a month unless it was a job only a fool would take, or unless the last three sheriffs rested under six feet of desert sod. He ought to get the hell out and let them worry about their own hides.

But he couldn't do that, and he knew it. He might not like this damned job, he might wish he had never set foot in Sycamore Flats, but he couldn't back out until he'd done what he'd promised—cleaned out the rustlers. In the meantime, it was also his job to keep the peace, enforce the law, and protect the citizens.

And Damian Blackthorne was a citizen. But so was Laurel.

Hen didn't know what he *should* do about her any more than he knew what he *wanted* to do. She seemed ordinary enough, a bit sharp-tongued and short of temper, but no more than you'd expect of a young woman saddled with a kid and forced to make her living washing clothes. But it was the Laurel who had fought Damian Blackthorne with the determination of a lynx, the Laurel who never uttered a whimper of pain when he cleaned her wounds, who was so far from ordinary that she lingered in his thoughts.

She was a pretty woman. Not even the bruises and blood could hide that. She reminded him of a woman he once knew who claimed to be a gypsy. She had that same thick black hair and huge, dark brown eyes combined with skin the color of moonlight. She was unnaturally thin—probably from giving her son most of her food—but a lushness still clung to her. Maybe it was her sinuous movement. It certainly wasn't her seductive behavior. She had looked him square in the eye, challenging him, defying him.

Yet still a little frightened. No, unsure. Uneasy. He couldn't imagine Laurel Blackthorne being frightened of anyone. She might have been when she was younger, but then lots of people were different when they were younger.

He had been, but he didn't let himself think about that any more.

He didn't think Laurel had been prettier. She was the kind of woman who would grow more attractive as she matured, the kind whose beauty would benefit from well-chosen clothes and a proper setting, the kind who in her mid-thirties would make younger women look shallow and insignificant. Not that it mattered to him. He wasn't interested in women, young or old. They represented ties, responsibilities, restrictions—all the things he meant to avoid.

It wasn't that he disliked women, just that they were always demanding, expecting, wanting, needing. There was no end to it. They were always after something he didn't have to give. It wasn't that he didn't want to. He didn't have it. There was nothing to Hen Randolph but a shell.

He wondered if Laurel might not be the same.

"This is a good place to let me go. You can't see into this wash from town," Damian explained when Hen just stared at him.

"You're going to jail," Hen said.

"You're new here. I guess you don't know."

"Know what?"

"Blackthornes don't go to jail."

"Why?"

"It'll get you killed."

"Sounds like an empty threat."

"There's people who could advise you otherwise."

"I never take advice. It always seems to be for somebody else's comfort."

"You're a fool!"

"Maybe, but you're the one who's going to be sitting in jail."

Damian threw his leg over the saddle. He stumbled when he hit the ground, but tried to make a run for it. Hen pulled on the rope so hard that it nearly twisted Damian's arms out of their sockets.

"I'll kill you!" Damian managed to gasp from between clenched teeth. "I'll gut-shoot you and leave you to die."

"You'll have plenty of time to work out your plan," Hen said. He led Damian out of the wash and up to the back of the jail. Damian didn't say anything until Hen dragged him inside, shoved him into one of the cells, and locked the door.

"My family will get me out." The bruises from Hen's knuckles were beginning to show plainly on his face. "Then they'll kill you."

"Tell them to knock real loud," Hen said. "I'm a sound sleeper."

Passing into his office in the front part of the jail, Hen closed the door on Damian's profane response. The frame building had a door and two windows that faced the street. A desk sat to one side, a potbellied stove to the other. The floor was of local rough-hewn oak. It was a tiny building, but then, the sheriff didn't need much space. There wasn't much to do indoors.

Hen wondered what his brothers would say if they could see him now. He had sent George a telegram. He ought to know where to come in case he had to collect his body. Not that he expected to be killed. Or to stay here long. But it would give him something to do while he decided what the hell to do with the rest of his life.

He could have decided in Texas with George, in Wyoming with Monty, or in Colorado with Madison, but he was trying to avoid his family. No, he was running away from himself. He had accepted the job of sheriff because he thought if he kept busy, he might not be plagued by questions he couldn't answer.

The Widow Blackthorne offered him a problem to occupy his mind. Hen welcomed her intrusion into his life.

The office door flew open, and a grinning sprite of fourteen summers named Hope Worthy bounded in. Slim, of average height, with a smattering of freckles and red-brown hair that hung down to her waist, Hope moved with the energetic bounce of a puppet on strings. Her laughing brown eyes, ready smile, and breezy self-confidence guaranteed her welcome anywhere.

"I brought your lunch," she announced.

"You didn't have to. I can eat at the restaurant."

"You don't want to do that," Hope said. She kicked the door

closed with her foot, then placed the covered tray on his desk. "Keeps the flies away and the dust out," she announced as she removed the red-checked cloth.

"I imagine they're just as hungry as I am."

Hope looked up, startled, then giggled. "Mama said you were an old sobersides, but I told her you were just acting that way to keep all the fools in town from pestering you to death." Hope uncovered his plate and unwrapped his fork and knife from a white napkin.

"Are there many fools in Sycamore Flats?"

"Loads," Hope assured him. "Not much else, really. Papa says it's the heat. Mama says they didn't have any brains to start with."

"Could account for it," Hen said, as amused by the artless prattle as he was amazed at the amount of food the child seemed to think he required. He hadn't told her about Damian. It was just as well. Maybe missing a meal would take some of the starch out of him.

Hope smiled at Hen as though setting out his lunch was the one thing that made her happiest in the world. She poured out a cup of coffee and set the pot on the cold stove. "I hope this is enough."

"It'd be just right if I had three prisoners to feed," Hen said, eyeing the spread. He walked over to the desk and sat down.

"I thought men ate a lot," Hope said. She pulled a chair from against the wall and set it down next to the desk. "All the men I know do. Mama complains about it all the time." She straddled the chair backwards.

"Well, I don't want her complaining about me, especially when I've been here only a week. Why don't you have lunch with me?" Hen put a serving of the rich beef stew into the plate that had been used to cover his food.

"I can't."

He could tell she wanted to. "Why?"

"I can't eat stew with my fingers. It's not ladylike."

"Sure you can." Hen got up and walked over to his pack that lay in the corner. "Or slurp it out of the plate. I've done it lots of times." He delved inside his pack. "Of course, I carry my own kitchen for just such an occasion." He produced a plate, cup, and eating utensils. "Just so I can show I have good manners."

Hope grinned happily, pulled her chair closer, accepted the fork and spoon, and started eating with a very unfeminine appetite. "Mama's a good cook," she said, her mouth full of beef. "You won't want to eat anyplace else, especially none of the saloons. Hotel's not bad, but they charge too much."

"The town pays me well," Hen said. He sat down and tasted the stew. It wasn't up to Rose's standard. It certainly couldn't touch anything Tyler could do, but it beat his own cooking, and that's what he'd been eating the last while.

"You'll want to be saving your money."

"Why?"

"Mama says all sensible men save their money."

"What makes you think I'm sensible?"

"I just do. Papa says you got to be crazy to take this job, but I told him you took it because you believe in justice and freedom."

Hen still wasn't entirely certain why he had taken the job, but he did know that neither of those lofty concepts had entered into his decision.

"Besides, you been here a week and you haven't been gambling or drinking yet."

"Just getting the lay of the land, trying to see who serves watered-down whiskey and who likes to give Lady Luck a helping hand."

Hope giggled again. "You sure are a funny one. I bet your folks miss you. It must be real flat back home with you gone."

No one in Hen's family would recognize him from any description Hope Worthy might give. He wondered why she saw him as a jokester when everybody else saw him as a brooding, temperamental gunman.

"I don't have any family."

"Sure you do."

"How do you know?"

"You make room for people."

"What?"

"You don't crowd them, or expect all the attention yourself. I bet you got lots of brothers and sisters."

"No sisters. Six brothers."

"Really? Golly, wait until I tell Mama."

"Three sisters-in-law, four nephews, and two nieces, but don't tell anybody."

"Why?"

"I guess I don't think it's any of their business."

"Then why did you tell me?"

Why *had* he told her? He'd been chattering like a loose-lipped drunk. "Too many days in the saddle with nobody to talk to but my horse."

"They haven't talked about much else at the livery stable since he arrived."

"What's wrong with Brimstone?"

"Nothing, if you like being trampled to death."

Hen chuckled. "He is a mite ornery."

"That isn't what Jesse says."

Hen paused with a piece of beef halfway to his mouth. "What does Jesse say?"

"I couldn't repeat most of it without Mama skinning me."

"The part you can repeat."

Hope grinned. "He says you must be kin to the Devil because nobody but a devil could ride that horse. Jesse's always talking about devils and spooks. He says he can see them."

Hen smiled. If everybody was like Hope, stopping here might not be so bad. "Does Jesse really think I'm the Devil?"

"No, but he's sure you're his henchman." Hope's laughter filled the room. "I told him the Devil has sure got some handsome help."

"You can't expect him to lure people into evil with ugly bait."

"I hadn't thought about it like that. I guess that's why you never see an ugly soiled dove."

Hen's expression of amusement was only skin-deep. He thought of his own father. Handsome bait indeed. Never had so much beauty clothed such profound evil. He started to take a bite of his pie, but didn't feel hungry any more. Thinking of his pa did that. He threw down his napkin and got up to pour himself some more coffee. "Give your ma my compliments, but I'm too full to eat the pie. Next time bring about half as much."

"I think I ate more than you." Hope looked self-conscious.

"You'd never know. You're thin as a rail."

"I know," Hope said, not pleased with the compliment. "And nothing I do seems to make me any bigger." She started to place the dishes on the tray.

It took Hen a second to realize that she was talking about her breasts. Or rather, her lack of them.

"I wouldn't let that worry you. People develop quite suddenly at your age."

"I know. One minute Mary Parker looked like a boy. Then next thing you knew, every boy in town was following her around with his tongue hanging out."

"You wait. In a couple years, they'll be following you around."

"I don't want them to. I'm not interested in boys. They're too immature."

Hen had the sudden feeling that he was being stalked by a fourteen-year-old dying to be in heat. "Maybe," he said, keeping his distance, "but you could get them back for all the times they didn't notice you."

He could tell the idea appealed to Hope.

"By the way, I took your mother's suggestion and took my laundry to the Widow Blackthorne this morning. Rather a strange lady. What's she like?" Anything to keep from talking about Hope's lack of breasts.

"I don't know. She doesn't come to town very often."

"A woman who doesn't like coming to town?"

Hope grinned. "It's probably because of the way the men look at her."

"How's that?"

"She's very beautiful."

"And?"

"She has a little boy."

"So?"

"She doesn't have a husband."

"Being a widow isn't going to hurt her chances of finding another husband."

"She never had a husband."

Hen leveled an inquiring glance.

"She says she was married to Carlin Blackthorne, but his family denies it."

"What does Mr. Blackthorne have to say about it?"

"He's dead."

"Maybe I'd better ask somebody else to do my shirts."

"She needs the money."

Hen looked up.

"She's poor as can be. She lives up there in that canyon all by herself."

"I'll think about it. Now you'd better get this tray back to the restaurant. I bet your ma expected you back long ago."

"She won't mind," Hope said. "She says it's a shame any decent woman has to be in the same room with half the men in this town. Is it okay if I bring your dinner at six?"

"You really don't have to."

"I want to. Besides, it gets me out of work. It's hotter than hell in that kitchen." Hope stopped, and her hand flew to her mouth. "You won't tell, will you?"

"Tell what?"

"What I said?"

"What did you say? Oh that." Hen smiled. "No. I'll wait until you've been particularly loathsome."

"I knew you'd be ever so nice. I told everybody, but they kept going on about how you went around frowning and not talking and looking like you smelled something bad. I told them it was just your way."

Hen couldn't understand why this girl didn't see him the way everyone else did. He had to admit that he was glad she didn't.

Laurel wrung out the last shirt and sank back exhausted. She had washed all of Hen Randolph's shirts. She couldn't iron more than a few tonight, but she'd do some each day until she got them all done.

Her head ached fearfully. Her face throbbed with pain so intense it made her dizzy. Her hand instinctively went to her cheek only to encounter the cheesecloth that kept the cactus fruit pressed to her wounds. She couldn't help but smile. She must look like a mad woman. If anybody saw her, they would certainly think so. And she had done this because a stranger told her to. For all she knew, the cactus fruit would make her face worse.

But she believed Hen. He didn't seem to care enough about people to lie. Odd she should be attracted to a man who seemed devoid of passion.

She had married Carlin because of his unbridled emotions. Now she felt drawn to Hen Randolph because he was just the opposite. Had she become so fearful of emotion that she had given up on finding a man who could give her the warm, protective love she wanted so desperately?

No. But neither did she believe Hen was as cold as he seemed. A warm core lay somewhere deep within him, deeper even than the hardness she'd sensed earlier. It only needed someone who cared enough to bring it out. She dared not think she might be the one to do that.

Chapter Three

Hen got to his feet and walked to his office window. The street was nearly empty, the way it had been every afternoon since he got here. The hot September sun kept everyone indoors between noon and sundown. The horses in the corral, seeking relief from the heat and insects, stood end to end under the willows, their heads down, swishing tails keeping flies at bay. The silence was only occasionally broken by the sound of a rider or wagon coming into town.

Sycamores and oaks hung listlessly in the heat. Even the noisy cottonwoods down by the wash were silent. Buildings of unpainted, grey-weathered wood formed a stark contrast to the yellow and red of the surrounding rocks. It was a poor town, one without pride in itself, one that gave the passerby the feeling that it was merely a temporary stopping place.

Hen turned away from the window, his thoughts on Laurel. He wondered if she had taken his advice and lain down. Probably not. She didn't act like the kind of woman to take advice from anyone. Maybe he shouldn't have left his clothes. He could have taken them back another day.

He opened his desk and tossed some wanted posters on top. He'd go through them, maybe even memorize the pictures. It ought to come in handy someday. As he threw some old papers into the stove, he heard the sound of a muffled shot. It sounded as if it came from the other side of the street. Maybe in the wash behind town. It couldn't be the Blackthornes. He hadn't told anybody about Damian's arrest. He couldn't imagine why anybody else would be shooting that close to town, but he had learned that there was somebody fool enough to do just about anything.

Just then he heard second and third shots and knew it wasn't anybody in the wash. He picked up his gun belt and strapped it on, took his hat from the peg, and settled it on his head. He practically collided with Hope Worthy coming through the door.

"Finn Peterson's shooting up Elgin's Saloon," she managed to say, then stopped to gasp for breath. "He's crazy drunk." She grabbed a second breath. "What are you going to do?"

"I don't know yet."

"He'll kill you."

"I don't think so," Hen said, starting toward the saloon. "Most men don't take a chance on getting killed unless it's over something important."

But Hope wasn't in a philosophical mood. "Are you going to have a shootout in the street?"

"I can't say. Now you get back to the restaurant and keep your head inside the door."

"But I want to see." Hope seemed to be working up her courage to stand her ground, but just then another volley of shots erupted from the saloon, followed by two men throwing themselves through the door headfirst.

"Now!" Hen shouted, his order so curt and sharp, Hope jumped. "And keep your head down."

Hope threw Hen a hurt look, turned, and fled.

Hen headed for the saloon.

The street had cleared, as if by magic. Nothing moved. Even the horses seemed to have stilled for fear of drawing attention. Shots came at regular intervals now. Scott Elgin would have to get a new roof before winter. There ought to be enough holes in it by now for the customers to tell time by the stars.

As Hen drew closer to the saloon, he realized that he had no desire to shoot this man. The people had a right to expect him to defend their property and the peace of their town, as well as their lives, but that didn't mean it had to cost some harmless drunk his life. Hen paused on the porch of the saloon to let his eyes recover from the glare of the sun before he pushed inside.

It wasn't a big place, narrow and deep, with tables jammed close together. A bar, barely a dozen feet in length, ran across the back of the room. Hen couldn't tell how many customers were still in the saloon. They were all under the tables. The gunman was pouring himself another drink. He had his back to the door and didn't notice Hen.

"I think you've had enough," Hen said.

Finn Peterson turned so fast that he lost his balance and had to steady himself against the bar. Hen felt nauseated. He didn't draw on sloppy drunks. He didn't even talk to them if he could help it.

"I can have as many drinks as I want," Finn said, waving his gun at the extremely nervous bartender. His words were slurred, but it was clear he knew what he was saying.

"Maybe some other time. Now why don't you put that gun away and ride back where you belong. It's not fair to leave your riding partner with all the work."

"The son-of-a-bitch!" Finn exploded. He pulled himself around until he faced Hen. "He's left me by myself often enough. Let him see how he likes it."

A drunk shooting up the town because he was mad at his riding partner! Hen was too disgusted with the situation to talk any longer. He started forward.

Finn fired. The bullet went wide, shattering a window.

"You'd better come sleep it off in the jail," Hen said, unfazed by the bullet. "Your aim is rotten."

Hen realized that he wasn't handling this well. He ought to be talking softly, soothingly, trying to pacify Finn until he could disarm him. He was too impatient. He just wanted to get him out of the saloon and be done with him.

"Draw, dammit," Finn shouted, moving more quickly than Hen would have thought possible.

"Not in here. You might hurt somebody."

"Draw!" Finn shouted again, apparently furious that Hen didn't take his threat seriously.

"You've done enough damage to Mr. Elgin's saloon." He half turned toward the door, hoping Finn would follow.

"You can't walk away from me."

"I don't draw on drunk men."

"I'm not drunk." Finn leaned up against the wall and leveled his gun at Hen.

Hen's temper snapped. He drew and fired.

"Yeeoooow!" Finn's gun crashed to the floor; he shook his hand frantically.

"Stop yelling," Hen said dispassionately, as he holstered his own gun. "You're not hurt." He took Finn by the shoulder and shoved him through the door onto the boardwalk and then into the sunlit street.

"You shot my hand," Finn said, incredulous. "You shot my gunhand."

"I just shot your gun," Hen said, pushing the stunned man ahead of him. "The bullet didn't touch your hand."

"I can't move my fingers!"

"They'll be fine in a couple of hours. You'll be able to handle a rope as good as ever."

Finn stared at his hand in amazement. "Damian Blackthorne's my riding partner," he said. "When he finds out what you did, he'll ride in here and kill you where you stand."

"Thanks for the warning."

People started appearing in doorways, at windows, from alleys between buildings. Hope suddenly materialized at Hen's side.

"Why didn't you kill him?" she asked.

"I don't kill drunks," Hen said, guiding Finn toward the jail. "Besides, shooting up a saloon isn't much of an offense."

Hope looked disappointed. Hen wondered if the townspeople felt the same. They kept their distance as he pushed Finn along the street toward the jail.

"Get me the key out of the desk," Hen said to Hope as he pushed Finn through the front door. He propelled him through the office and the second door into the iron cage next to Damian.

"What the hell is Finn doing here?" Damian demanded.

"What are you doing here?" Finn demanded in return.

"You'll both have plenty of time to explain," Hen said, as he pushed Finn into the empty cell.

"I'll kill you," Damian shouted.

"You already said that." Hen locked the door into the office, cutting off the rest of Damian's threats.

"Is that Damian Blackthorne?" Hope asked. Her voice sank into a whisper, as though she didn't want Damian to hear her question.

"So he says."

"What did he do?"

"Tried to take Adam away from his mother. He hit her, too."

"What are you going to do with him?" Hope asked. Her eyes were bright with excitement.

"I'm not sure. Keep him here until I am."

Clearly Hope didn't find that exciting enough.

"What about his brothers?"

"What about them?"

"They'll come after you."

"I doubt it."

"They're terrible men," Hope told him, her eyes glistening with excitement. "They steal and kill and do awful things to women."

"I'm not a woman."

"You insulted one of them. They won't forget that. They'll ride in here from every direction, shooting down any man who tries to stop them. There'll be bodies everywhere, blood on the streets, widows and orphans crying into the night—"

Hen tried not to laugh at Hope's obvious desire for a general bloodbath. "If Damian is any example of his kin, I doubt they'll even care he's gone."

"They will," Hope assured him eagerly. "They'll come at a gallop."

"Well, you wake me up. I think I'll take a nap."

Hope looked stunned, apparently unable to believe Hen wasn't petrified of the Blackthorne clan and its thirst for vengeance.

"What about Mrs. Blackthorne and Adam? They'll be after her, too. They already did it once. Nobody stops a Blackthorne when they want something."

Hen might not take the threat to himself seriously, but he did believe the Blackthornes would try again to kidnap Adam. That angered him. It angered him even more that they would bother Laurel. She was a woman of courage and determination, but Hen knew she couldn't stand off several Blackthornes. She might hold them off for a while, but they would get the kid in the end.

It was up to him to do something about it. But what? She wouldn't welcome help. She had made it clear that she didn't want any from him. "I guess I'll have to send somebody to tell her. She ought to move into town where she'll be safe."

"She won't listen to anybody."

Hen had been afraid of that. "Well, she won't listen to me. Why don't you go? She'd probably—"

The door opened and Grace Worthy stepped into the office. "Here you are, Hope Worthy," she said, clearly out of patience with her daughter. "I should have known you'd be around trouble like a bee around a flower. Have you forgotten we start serving dinner in little more than an hour?"

Hope's excitement wilted before her mother's anger.

"I had to tell the sheriff about the Blackthornes," Hope explained. "He wouldn't know there are hundreds of them, all mean and ready to shoot anything that moves."

"I doubt they're eager to shoot honest citizens," Mrs. Worthy said, "but they are a thoroughly unsatisfactory family. You can be certain you haven't heard the last of them."

"See, I told you," Hope said.

"I'm more worried about Laurel Blackthorne," Hen said. "Damian says they'll keep trying until they get that boy."

"He's probably right."

"I need you or one of the other ladies to go up there and talk her into moving into town."

Mrs. Worthy didn't answer right away. Hope started to speak, but her mother silenced her with a single glance.

"I'd be happy to try, but I doubt she'll listen to me or anybody else."

"Why?"

"There's a good bit of hard feeling between her and the town. Unfortunately, the fault lies somewhat on both sides. She's a difficult young woman in a very difficult situation. Maybe you're the best person to speak to her."

"Why? She doesn't even know me."

"For that very reason."

"I'll go," Hope volunteered.

"You, young lady, are going back to work. And if you leave again without permission, you'll spend every night this week in your room."

That threat effectively cowed Hope, and she headed out the door ahead of her mother. Mrs. Worthy turned back.

"When Laurel first came here, some of our ladies condescended to offer her charity. Unfortunately, they didn't offer to believe she was married or allow her little boy to play with their own children. Laurel made it plain that she won't allow anyone to look down on her or her son. I'm afraid she has very little faith in the goodness of human nature. Maybe you can change that."

Hen stared after Mrs. Worthy. The woman might as well have broken his legs and left him to die. He had never been able to talk anybody into anything without using his gun. Why in hell did she think he could change Laurel Blackthorne's mind about anything? She didn't even like him.

He threw the keys in the desk drawer and slammed it shut, but the sharp noise did nothing to relieve the irritation that caused the muscles along his shoulders to knot. He didn't want to get involved with that woman. He would protect her, but he preferred to do it by having her move away from danger rather than his becoming directly involved.

Muttering a curse, he grabbed his hat and headed out the door. Despite the heat, the street was still full. He didn't want to talk to anybody, so he headed round the back of the jail toward the wash.

It wasn't the Blackthornes that bothered him. It was Laurel. He'd never known a woman who could get under his skin so quickly, and he'd only met her once. If he had to keep seeing her, it'd be worse than being covered with honey and tied to an anthill.

Of course, it wasn't her fault that he was jumpy and irritable and ready to bite anybody's head off. It wasn't her fault that he found himself obliged to do a job he disliked. It wasn't even her fault that she had a kid who needed the protection and guidance of a solid, dependable family man. It most especially wasn't her fault that she had the most beautiful black hair he'd ever seen, or that she moved with the grace of a gazelle.

He'd better stop thinking about her like that. Let her even suspect what was in his mind, and she'd probably throw his shirts at him.

He chuckled. She had spirit, but not much common sense. If she had, she'd have married the first man who asked her and moved as far away from Sycamore Flats as she could.

Of course, he didn't have any common sense either. He ought to be doing something useful with his time instead of wasting it baby-sitting this town and trying to figure out how to talk the most fiercely independent woman he'd ever met into giving up her mountain stronghold and moving down with the Philistines.

She'd never do it. He couldn't blame her either.

The streets of Sycamore Flats grew noisy after nine o'clock. Like most Western towns, it had more than its share of saloons.

There was a little mining in the area, so there was always a smattering of miners in town buying supplies, getting cleaned up from several months out on their claims, or just raising a little hell before they went back to the supremely boring task of trying to wrest a little wealth from the bowels of stingy Mother Earth.

The women had disappeared into their homes; but the excitement of the shooting had brought out every man in the area. They stood at bars in saloons, lounged around tables covered with cards and whiskey bottles, or stood in knots in the street or along the boardwalk. In every gathering, the shooting formed the main topic of conversation. Here and there some of the bigger boys, their curfew forgotten for the evening, tried to join their elders or took advantage of the break from routine to enjoy a few extra hours of unsupervised fun of their own.

Hen had never found any pleasure in the company of men who haunted saloons, but it helped to keep things relaxed to see the sheriff out and about. He stepped inside Elgin's Saloon. It wasn't the most popular, but you could find most of the respectable men of the town here sooner or later. He exchanged greetings with several men at the tables.

"Howdy, Sheriff," Elgin called, a smile of sincere welcome on his face. "Have a drink on me. Hell, after that shooting, you can have a drink any time you want."

"Thanks, but I don't drink." Hen leaned against the bar and let his gaze wander over the men in the room. He wasn't sure he liked the looks of one gambler, but the rest were good, solid citizens.

"Not ever?" Elgin asked, apparently unable to believe Hen wasn't simply trying to impress the citizens with his sobriety.

"It doesn't agree with me." Hen looked up. Stars winked through the holes in the ceiling. "Better get your roof fixed."

"Got plenty of time. The rainy season is months off."

Hen pushed away from the bar. "Best not to wait until the last minute." He headed toward the door.

"Want to play a hand, Sheriff?" Wally Regen asked as Hen walked by his table. The gambler Hen distrusted was seated at the same table. He didn't look as though he would welcome the sheriff's presence.

"I'm not much for cards." Hen eyed the pile of money in front of the gambler. "Generally ends up costing me more than I can afford."

Wally looked a little embarrassed. "Then sit a spell."

"Sure," Hen said, looking at the gambler rather than at Regen. "I got a whole evening to kill."

Wally pushed a chair toward Hen with his foot, and Hen sat down.

"Everybody's talking about that shot this morning."

"Everybody gets lucky once in a while."

Wally passed the whiskey bottle to Hen. He passed it on.

"That was no lucky shot."

"It was dead-eye shooting," the gambler said. "I don't know a gunman who could have done better."

"If a man can't shoot, he'd better not be sheriff," Hen replied.

"You know, Damian's brothers will be after you now for beating him," Wally warned. He was one of the men who'd hired Hen. He had been losing too many cows. Hen wondered if he had enough cows to satisfy the rustlers and the gambler.

"They're a rough bunch, the Blackthornes."

"What do you plan to do?" Wally asked.

"Make my rounds. Go to bed. Do the same thing tomorrow."

"You don't understand," Wally said. "There must be hundreds of Blackthornes scattered from Texas to California. Mexico, too."

"If they come, they'll take it out on the town," Norton said. "It'll be up to you to protect us."

Careful to keep the contempt he felt from his gaze, Hen eyed both men. "When they start gathering, you let me know. Until then, you can get on with your game."

Hen got up and started toward the door.

"What are you going to do about that woman?" a man at one of the other tables asked. Luke Tilghman. He had the look of a miner. Big, coarse, and contemptuous of rules.

Hen stopped and turned slowly. "What am I supposed to do about her?"

Luke grinned. "Nothing if you're not disposed. There's plenty others who'll be happy to do it for you."

"I take it you'd expect something in return."

"Nothing much. Leastways, nothing it would trouble her to give. With those Blackthornes on the warpath, maybe she won't be so standoffish."

"And if I'm interested?" Hen knew his gaze had turned positively glacial. Even Luke was no longer oblivious to the coldness that emanated from the depths of Hen's eyes.

"I don't notice her favoring you particular," Luke said defensively.

"I don't notice her favoring anybody," Hen replied. His gaze encompassed every man in the room before it narrowed once more on Luke. "It's my job to worry about Mrs. Blackthorne, not yours."

"Mrs. Blackthorne!" Luke repeated, laughing. "Why, she's no more a missus than I'm a—"

"A loud-mouthed fool," Hen finished for him.

Luke jumped to his feet. "No man calls me a fool."

"I did."

Luke stared at Hen's guns. Luke was unarmed. "You wouldn't say that if you weren't a gunfighter."

"But I am. Remember it." Knowing that his gaze had grown even colder, Hen looked around the room once more. "Anybody bothering Mrs. Blackthorne will answer to me. Good evening, gentlemen."

"Well I'll be hanged," Wally said. "I didn't know he was interested in that woman."

"He ain't," Horace Worthy said. "He went up there to see about getting his laundry done. That's when he found Damian trying to steal the kid. My girl, Hope, told me. She takes him his meals. Best I can tell, he ain't interested in any woman. Though from the looks of him, you'd think they'd be crowding around him like cows at a salt lick."

"I don't understand him," Norton said.

"I don't trust him," the gambler commented. Several heads turned in his direction. "There's something wrong with a man who won't take a drink or sit in on a friendly game of cards."

"Maybe he don't like losing his money," Wally said, eyeing the pile of bills in front of the gambler.

"Maybe he wants to keep a clear head in case the Blackthornes show up," Norton said.

"That still don't explain why he don't like women."

"We don't know he doesn't," Norton said, trying to be fair. "He hasn't been in town two weeks. You can't expect him to jump the first female he sees."

"Maybe he's not interested in women like her," Horace said. "Hope says he's mighty nice in his manners. Don't cuss around her, keeps that jail and the house neat as a pin."

"He sounds more peculiar by the minute," one listener added.

"I don't care what he's like as long as he can shoot like he did this morning," Scott Elgin said from behind the bar. "I'm paying him to protect me from drunks like Finn Peterson. I don't care about nothing else."

"You think he'll stand up to the Blackthornes?" Wally asked.

"He'll stand up to anybody."

The men looked up. Peter Collins had come in. He walked over to their table. It had been his recommendation that decided them to hire Hen.

"But there's a whole lot of Blackthornes, dozens at the last count," Wally said.

"As long as Hen Randolph is here, you're safe no matter how many Blackthornes gather. Now let's play cards." Collins took a seat and eyed the money the gambler had won. "I see a pile of bills just begging to fill my pocket."

"That's fine for you to say," Norton said as he shuffled the cards and began to deal. "You don't live in town. It's the townsfolk who'll suffer because Randolph put Damian in jail."

The room fell silent. Not everyone had heard of Damian's arrest. They turned toward Bill Norton.

"I thought it was Finn Peterson who shot up the place," someone said.

"It was, but he caught Damian beating up the Widow Blackthorne and trying to take her kid. According to Horace, he beat hell out of Damian, then threw him in jail. Didn't even offer him lunch."

"That's going to make his brothers mad as sidewinders with their tails tied to a post."

"They won't let him stay in jail. It would ruin their reputation."

"What can we do?"

"I don't know, but we gotta do something."

"You worry too much," Peter said, as he picked up his cards. "Leave everything to Hen. It's what he's paid for."

"It's my wife and kids I'm worried about, and the roof over my head."

"Either play cards or go home and sit up with a shotgun," Peter said. "Give me two cards. I'll raise you five dollars."

Hen told himself to forget what Luke had said, but he couldn't. Luke might be a loudmouth, but Hen knew he'd said what everyone else was thinking. It infuriated him that Luke, or anyone else, would think of Laurel as a way to satisfy his physical appetites. As far as Hen could see, she was a fine, upstanding, courageous woman, and the fact that she'd borne a child out of wedlock hadn't changed her basic nature. She was certainly a lot better than the men in the saloon. She might not measure up to the town's standard of what it took to be a lady, but he could see no reason why a single mistake should brand her for life. He was damned certain everybody in Sycamore

Flats had done at least one thing that wouldn't stand up under careful scrutiny.

He sure had.

He turned toward the house the town had built for a sheriff with a family of five. It was time he got some sleep. After a week of doing virtually nothing, he'd had a very active day.

The night hadn't brought any diminution in the restlessness or the feeling of irritation that rode Hen with the tenacity of a broncobuster. He had awakened at five. Rather than toss in bed, he had taken a long walk into the desert. The walk hadn't provided any solutions, but it had soothed his annoyance. He was almost calm when he reached the jail to find the back door standing open.

Hen could hardly believe his eyes. The door to the cells that had held Damian and Finn stood open as well. Somebody had let them out. The perpetrator had tossed the keys on the desk. Hen grabbed them up and stormed across the street to the bank. Bill Norton was just opening up.

"Who let Blackthorne and Peterson out?" Hen demanded.

Norton stared at him for a moment, then opened the bank door and signaled Hen to come inside. "I was afraid something like that might happen."

"And you didn't say anything?"

"I wasn't sure."

"I thought you hired me to get rid of the outlaws. You might as well send them a letter saying the townspeople are too spineless to stand up to them."

"People were afraid of what the Blackthornes might do to the town if you kept Damian in jail."

"So they let him go in hopes his family would leave them alone?"

"That's about it."

"Anybody ever tell you you're living in a town full of cowards and fools?" Hen snapped.

"Those are harsh words."

"And well deserved," Hen said, indifferent to Norton's anger. "I don't suppose I can expect your courageous citizens to stand behind me when the Blackthornes arrive or to make up a posse if I have to go after them."

Norton looked at the floor.

"How about you?"

"Of course I will, but—"

"Don't bother," Hen said. He unpinned the sheriff's badge from his shirt, but stopped himself in the act of handing it to Norton. "I think I'll keep this for a little while longer. But as of this minute, the understanding between me and this town is dissolved."

"You can't do that. You signed a contract."

Hen patted his gun. "This is the only contract that counts." He turned to leave.

"We've already paid you a month's wages."

Hen turned back around. "I think we're going to have to talk about a raise. It takes a whole lot more work to protect a town full of yellowbellies."

Chapter Four

Laurel loved the first hour after dawn. It was her favorite time of day. As she breathed in the cool stillness of the canyon, she could almost believe the past had been swallowed up by the night, that nothing threatened her son, that she would someday find a love so strong and enduring that it would wipe away the memory of the last fourteen years.

The reality of Adam helping her fill her baskets with clean laundry banished that daydream. Nothing had changed. Nothing ever would. She placed the baskets in a harness she had fashioned for her placid burro, and they headed down the canyon to Sycamore Flats.

She never failed to marvel at the beauty of her canyon. Even on the hottest day, it stayed cool, its air invigorating. Fed by a year-round flow of water from the mountains rising behind her, the canyon formed an oasis of life in the middle of the harsh desert. Birds filled the trees, their songs jubilantly announcing the arrival of each new day. Somewhere in the distance a woodpecker's rat-a-tat-tat echoed back and forth between the high canyon walls. A covey of Gambel's quail scurried across her path. A hummingbird darted hither and yon on silent winds, gathering nectar from a few late-flowering cactus. Small animals scratched out a living among the rocks and the eddies of the stream. It was a world complete in itself, and it made her feel the same.

All too soon they reached the end of the canyon. Laurel's sense of security, her feeling of well-being, disappeared almost as quickly as the life-giving water disappeared into the thirsty desert sand. She gave herself a mental jog. She had a living to earn and a son to support; she couldn't do it by hiding in the canyon.

Laurel went to town at this hour because she didn't want to meet anyone. The wives of Sycamore Flats had never accepted her, and they never let her forget it. Neither could she convince them she wasn't after their husbands. She didn't understand how a poor woman with a six-year-old son could cause so much uneasiness. Yet she had seen more than one woman pull her husband back inside the door when she saw Laurel approaching.

The men would have been only too happy to welcome Laurel, but on terms she found unacceptable. She found it easier to avoid trouble than to deal with it. So she came down just after dawn, while the women fixed breakfast and their husbands enjoyed their last few minutes of sleep.

For the last week, she had worn a thin piece of cloth over her face to hide the bruises which made her feel even less able to meet people. Traveling the lanes behind the houses, she hung back in the shadows while Adam set the baskets of freshly laundered clothes on porches and back steps, collected payment, and picked up the dirty clothes. Laurel made her rounds as quickly as possible with as little conversation as possible. It wasn't hard. Most women were too busy to talk to her even if they had wanted to.

Mrs. Worthy was different.

"What on earth are you doing wrapped up like a beekeeper?" Grace Worthy asked.

Laurel didn't know how to respond. Everybody knew Damian had attacked her, but she hadn't shown anyone her bruises.

Grace noticed her reluctance. "You don't have to tell me a thing you don't want to. Come in and have a cup of coffee," she said. She held the back door to the restaurant open, ignoring Laurel's reluctance to accept her invitation.

"You're busy."

"Not yet. People who eat breakfast at my place don't get up for a couple hours yet. You, too, son," Grace said to Adam. "I've got a piece a pie left over from yesterday that needs eating up."

Adam showed none of his mother's hesitation. Laurel followed reluctantly. As much as she tried to pretend otherwise, she missed female companionship. She hadn't had any since she ran away from home seven years ago, hardly any since her mother died. And while Mrs. Worthy hadn't tried to establish anything more than a casual friendship, she hadn't shown Laurel any of the superior attitude or downright contempt many of the other women had.

"I marvel that you can be up and about so early," Mrs. Worthy said as she set a large piece of apple pie before Adam and poured out two cups of coffee. "I'm surprised you don't get a few women angry at being pulled from their beds."

Laurel smiled and accepted the coffee. "Most are happy to leave the clothes and the money out so I don't have to bother them."

"I like to see who I'm doing business with," Mrs. Worthy said.

"You wouldn't if they looked down their noses at you, or looked at your little boy like they were afraid he was going to contaminate their own children."

"No, I wouldn't," Grace Worthy agreed. "I'm afraid I'd have some pretty sharp words."

"I've tried that. It's easier this way."

"I suppose so. A shame though. Eat the rest," she said to Adam, who was eyeing the last slice of pie.

"I suppose you're wondering what Damian did to me?" Laurel said.

Grace smiled, easy and friendly. "It did cross my mind."

Laurel untied the cloth and pulled it back from her face. Grace Worthy's expression of outrage told Laurel that the bruising was as bad as she feared.

"You should have seen it last week."

"But why would he do such a thing?"

"My husband's family has decided it's time they taught Adam to be a Blackthorne. When I wouldn't let Damian take him, he hit me."

"Why didn't you shoot him?"

"He took me by surprise. If the sheriff hadn't come along just then, he'd have taken Adam."

"Thank goodness you're safe."

"They'll come again."

"But surely . . ."

"Now that someone's let Damian out of jail, the Blackthornes know they have nothing to fear from the people of Sycamore Flats."

It was Grace's turn to look embarrassed. "There's the sheriff."

"What can one man do? I don't even know if he would stand up to them. What's he like?" She had tried not to ask, but curiosity about Hen was the real reason she had accepted Grace's invitation. "Sorry if I shouldn't ask," Laurel added quickly, "but I need to know."

"If I were in your place, I'd want to know everything I could about a man willing to stand between me and the Black-thornes."

"He did more than that. He took care of my wounds." Laurel chuckled unexpectedly. "He made me put prickly pear halves on my face. Even Adam laughed at me." She sobered. "The Blackthornes won't take this insult lightly. Somebody ought to tell him to leave town."

"Why don't you?"

"It wouldn't seem very grateful, especially after what he did for me."

"Well, I don't know if he'd leave town even if you told him. He's a gunfighter, and it's my experience that gunfighters don't run from a fight, even when they know they ought."

Laurel felt her stomach tighten. "What do you mean by gunfighter?" she asked.

"According to Horace, the ranchers chose Hen Randolph because he has a reputation for killing people who get in his way."

A killer! Hen Randolph was a killer!

Laurel felt her stomach heave. It seemed that no matter where she turned, she came up against another man who didn't mind killing any more than he minded sitting down to eat. She had been hoping that Hen Randolph was different. He was harsh and not particularly careful about her feelings, but he had been kind and gentle. She had been drawn to him more by his loneliness than his looks. She understood. She was lonely, too.

Laurel put her cup down and stood up. "Then I don't sup-pose I have to worry about him. He obviously can take care of himself."

"You don't think you ought to tell him about the Black-thornes?" Grace asked.

"If they hired him to chase cattle rustlers, I'm sure he al-ready knows." She put the scarf over her head and wrapped it so it covered most of her face. "We'd better be going. We've trespassed on your time too long already. Come along, Adam."

Grace followed them to the door. "You seem to have a very strong dislike of gunfighters."

Laurel turned back, a light in her coffee-brown eyes burning brightly. "My father was a peace-loving man, but he was killed in a gunfight. My husband *was* a gunfighter. He was killed five weeks after our marriage."

Grace opened her mouth to speak, then changed her mind.

"I know no one believes Carlin married me. Even his family denies it." Laurel turned away. "I'll try to have your clothes done by tomorrow, but I'm a little behind."

"Don't worry. The next day will be just as good."

Laurel left town by way of Sycamore Creek, a dry wash that filled with water only during the rainy season or after a cloudburst. Normally she loved the quiet walk through the oak and sycamore trees that shielded her from the heat as well as from prying eyes.

But today her mind was taken up with Hen Randolph.

He was a gunfighter! A killer!

"How could a man who would risk his own safety to drive off Damian be a callous, heartless killer?" she demanded of Adam. She couldn't reconcile Hen's gentleness with the gunfighters and killers who frequented her stepfather's saloon or with Carlin's family.

Adam ran ahead, kicking up sand with his bare feet and throwing stones into the trees to cause the birds to fly up. "He didn't kill nobody," he said.

Laurel was too preoccupied with her own thoughts to hear him. She didn't *want* Hen to be a killer. All week she had been hoping he was a man who didn't depend on a gun to do his talking for him.

"He's so strong and confident. He didn't swagger or posture or act like he thought he was better than anybody else. He didn't even act like he expected me to thank him. It was like it was just something he did, like currying his horse or saying 'ma'am' and 'excuse me' to ladies."

"I like him," Adam announced. He threw an acorn at a squirrel that chattered angrily at him.

Hen had acted like it was the most natural thing in the world to be concerned about her and Adam. He wasn't ashamed to know about herbs and how to use them. He was exactly the kind of man she'd been looking for all her life.

"But he's a gunfighter and a killer!" she said aloud.

"I like him," Adam said again as he climbed a tree.

But was he? Nobody had seen him use a gun.

"I'm just being foolish, grabbing at straws. Nobody but a fool tries to earn a reputation as a gunfighter without having skill and nerve. There are too many people looking to make a reputation by killing a famous gunman. Somebody will shoot him in the back like they did Wild Bill Hickok."

"Who's Wild Bill Hickok?" Adam asked. He swung on a limb and dropped to the ground.

No, she had to accept the truth and stay away from Hen Randolph. This man obviously had two sides to him, one that was remarkably kind and a second devoid of humanity. She couldn't trust a man like that.

She should have learned that with her stepfather.

And it didn't matter that he was so good-looking that his image kept popping up in her mind's eye. People like him used their attractiveness like a weapon. He had probably left a string of broken-hearted women across the better part of the Southwest.

Hen leaned back, his feet on his desk, his hat over his face.

What did sheriffs do to fill up the endless hours in the day? It was ironic that part of the reason he'd taken this job was boredom. He still had nothing to fill his time and only Laurel Blackthorne to fill his thoughts.

And fool that he was, he couldn't stop thinking about her.

Five shirts had appeared at his back door the day after he'd met her with a note to please leave the money and she would pick it up the next morning when she brought five more. His first inclination had been to take it to her, but he figured she wouldn't want him to see her face. He didn't know much about women, but he did know they didn't like to be seen at their worst, especially by men.

So he had put the money in an envelope, along with a note telling her of Damian's escape, and left it outside the back door. He was not a late sleeper. He was up when she came. Only it was Adam who delivered the shirts, while Laurel remained somewhere in the shadows. He caught a glimpse of her later, her head swathed in cheesecloth. He wondered what the townspeople were saying. He couldn't imagine she would receive anything but sympathy, especially once it was known her bruises had come at the hands of Damian Blackthorne.

Hen got to his feet. He had waited a week and still Adam delivered the clothes. Bruises or no bruises, he couldn't put it off any longer. It was time to talk to Laurel.

The midday heat wasn't oppressive in the wash. Ash, elm, oak, and cottonwood trees towered above the willows that grew along the bank of the dry creek bed. But nearly every other tree was a sycamore. The same trees surrounded the town before giving way to an unusually thick growth of mesquite, paloverde, and greasewood out in the desert. Subterranean irrigation kept everything green for nearly a half mile around, including Laurel's vegetable garden at the mouth of the canyon.

Hen climbed the narrow path up the canyon. A virtual forest of sycamores rose around him, their peeling cream-and-mauve trunks reaching skyward in an infinite variety of angles, their branches flung out like the limbs of deranged spirits. Their leaves, turned yellow by the sun, allowed only dappled sunlight to reach the ground. The creek gurgled happily from the mountains above, its water cold and pure.

Hen could understand why Laurel didn't want to leave her canyon. It was like a sanctuary.

She was standing at the tub when he reached the clearing.

Adam was feeding sticks into the fire under the wash pot. She looked up but didn't stop work. Adam stopped. She said something to him; he picked up a bucket and ran off toward the creek.

Hen realized that he hadn't noticed much when he was here before. The adobe looked smaller and meaner than he remembered, as if a bad rain could wash it away. The small clearing was empty of everything except wash pots and a pile of dry wood.

"What do you want?" Laurel asked. "I took you your clothes. There's no need for you to come here."

Her hands were red and chapped from all the washing. It must be worse in the winter. The cold must make her skin crack and bleed. He knew she wouldn't complain. Nor stop washing clothes.

She wore an old, low-necked dress of grey homespun, the sleeves pushed up past her elbows. Working over hot water had given a fine sheen of perspiration to her face, neck, and shoulders. Hen couldn't help but notice the white smoothness of her skin.

It formed a marked contrast to her hands and the discoloration of her face. She must have used the cactus pears. The tissue was no longer engorged with blood, but the bruises still showed. He was sorry he had come. Yet he didn't see embarrassment in her eyes, only caution and distrust. And dislike.

"I came to tell you Damian said they meant to have the boy."

"I already knew that," she said without looking up. She dropped another shirt into the rinse water.

"You'd better move into town."

Laurel wrung out another shirt and dropped it in the tub before she looked up at Hen. "What good will that do?"

"You'd be safer there."

"I'm as safe here as I'd be anywhere."

"I can't protect you here."

Laurel's hand froze in the act of reaching for another shirt. She looked Hen straight in the eye. "I can look after myself."

"You said that before."

"Besides, I have no place to go. You don't think I make enough money to live in the hotel, do you?"

"No, but—"

"I have to be close to water."

"There are wells in town."

"Nobody's going to let me use their well. I use more water in a day than half the town."

"You don't have to wash clothes. You could get another job."

Laurel stopped again. "What job do you have in mind?"

"There must be lots of things you can do."

"There are, but they won't let me do the things I might do. And I won't do what they want me to do."

Hen had no doubt what Laurel meant.

"You can't condemn the whole town just because some people haven't been very nice to you."

"How long have you been here?" Laurel demanded.

"A little more than two weeks."

"How many people do you know by name, their children, their relatives, their enemies?"

"A couple of families."

"I've been here for seven years. I know them all. I can condemn the whole town if I want. Maybe all of them haven't been hateful, but I'll stay in this canyon for the rest of my life before I let anybody look down on me and Adam."

Adam came up with the bucket of water.

"Fill the other tub," Laurel told him. She waited until he was out of hearing range. "I appreciate your trying to help, I really do, but I'm not moving. Now go back down there with the people who hired you."

"You could stay in the sheriff's house until you find a place."

"Aren't you living there?"

"Yes, but there's plenty of room."

Laurel looked at him like he was an idiot, but she only said,

"I'm fine where I am. Now if you don't mind, I have a lot of work to do."

"You know the Blackthornes will try again."

"Why are you so worried about me? I'm just the woman who does laundry."

"It's my job to protect everybody in Sycamore Flats."

"I don't live in Sycamore Flats, so you can stop worrying about me."

"Why are you so anxious to get rid of me?"

Laurel looked for a moment as if she wasn't going to answer him, then changed her mind. "I guess it'll save time and mis-understanding if I tell you straight out. Mrs. Worthy told me all about you, that the town hired you because you're a killer. That's fine for the town, but I don't want anything to do with gunfighters. Most especially I don't want Adam to even know about people like you. He's too young to understand why it's such a horrible thing. I haven't spent six years living by myself in this canyon to have it all ruined now. I don't even want him to remember your name. Now return to Sycamore Flats and don't come back."

Hen stared at Laurel, unable to believe his ears. He couldn't decide whether he was more stunned or furious until he felt the searing heat of rage scorch his brain and inflame his reason.

"I guess that's plain enough, even for a killer like me," he replied. He schooled his features into impassivity. "I asked Mrs. Worthy why the townspeople didn't like you. She said there was fault on both sides. She's probably right, but your tongue seems like reason enough to me. It's got me wonder-ing if you're a better influence on that boy than the Black-thornes."

Laurel felt as if Hen had struck her. But by the time she had recovered sufficiently from her shock and surprise to command her tongue, Hen had turned and walked away.

"You don't think I'm going to listen to the opinion of a gun-fighter, do you?" she called after him.

Hen stopped, turned slowly. "I'm still alive. That ought to count for something."

Rude, biting words rose to Laurel's tongue, but they remained unuttered. Waves of energy flowed from Hen's cold, hard, ice-blue eyes with the force of a flash flood down a mountain canyon. Struck dumb, she remained silent as he turned away. She could only stand watching as he strode across the yard and out of sight.

Anger warmed Laurel's cheeks long after Hen had disappeared down the canyon. That a common gunman, a killer, should have the nerve to criticize her seemed incredible. That he should compare her with the Blackthornes was infuriating. It was a good thing he had left or she would have been tempted to hit him.

One hand flew to her cheek. Hen had cleaned her wounds and cared for them. He had also been worried enough about her to warn her. He had even offered her his own house.

Laurel's hand slowly returned to her side. The heat of anger faded, leaving her feeling cold and empty. Nobody had ever done that much for her. Not her own family. Not her own husband.

She didn't think it was for the same reason other men were interested in her. She remembered the reflection of her face in the mirror. No, he wasn't after her body. Any cheap whore looked better than she did just now.

Again she lifted her hand to her face, but paused half way. She could still feel his fingers on her cheek, feel their gentleness. She could also remember his eyes. The most beautiful blue eyes she had ever seen, deep and clear. And empty. No emotion. As though he were only a shell.

His words had been equally harsh. She didn't know why she should have been surprised that he thought she wasn't any better than the Blackthornes. He had already told her that he thought boys brought up by women were soft. He must have been brought up by a cougar. She had never seen anybody so harsh and unyielding in her life.

Then she remembered his touch. It was the touch of someone who cared, the same kind of touch a man would give his son—strong, gentle, firm, healing, comforting.

A gunfighter wouldn't have bothered to care for a woman. Neither would a killer. Yet he had.

Why?

Chapter Five

"Is the sheriff gone?"

Laurel had been so caught up in her thoughts that she hadn't noticed Adam's return from the creek. "Yes," she said, turning once more to the wash tub.

Adam poured the water in a rinse tub. "Are we going to move to town?"

"You were listening."

"I could hear you all the way to the creek. Are we?"

"No. We'll be fine here."

"I know. The sheriff shot the other man."

Laurel's hands stopped, and she stared at her son. "How do you know what the sheriff did?"

Adam shifted his weight nervously, but he didn't avoid his mother's gaze. "I saw."

"I told you never to go into town without me."

"I didn't," Adam said, "not exactly. I was watering the garden when I heard the shooting. I ran around the back of the building and peeked in the saloon window. I didn't go in the street."

"What did you see?" Laurel could have bitten her tongue off. She didn't want to encourage Adam to talk about Hen Randolph, but she couldn't help herself. She had to know what had happened.

"A man was shooting holes in the saloon. He called the sheriff a coward. They both drew, but the sheriff was faster."

A shiver of fear ran through Laurel. "If the man he shot was a Blackthorne, every one of his kin within a hundred miles will be here when they bury him. Then they'll come up here."

"The sheriff put him in jail."

Laurel stopped. "He's not dead?"

"The sheriff shot his gun. That man was jumping around and yelling and holding his arm."

Hen hadn't killed the drunk, even though the man had drawn on him. Laurel didn't trust the feeling of relief, the surge of excitement, she felt.

"Mr. Elgin said it was the best shooting he'd ever seen," Adam said.

Maybe he wasn't a killer. Grace Worthy hadn't said anybody had seen him actually kill someone.

"Do you think he could shoot as good as Pa?" Adam asked.

Laurel's train of thought ended abruptly. "I don't know. Probably."

"Can I ask him to teach me to use a gun? I want to be like Pa when I grow up."

"No!" she said, far more sharply than she intended. "You're too young." Laurel felt a sharp stab of panic every time Adam mentioned guns. And he mentioned them more and more frequently these days.

"Danny Elgin has a gun, and he's only seven."

She had known the time would come when he would begin to question her decisions, to argue, to disobey. She had also known he would need more companionship, but she hadn't expected that time to come so soon. She was afraid of what he would pick up from the boys in town. She had meant to keep him away from them as long as possible, but obviously she couldn't any longer. She could only try to influence his opinion of what he learned.

"I'm sure the older boys have guns, but you're still too young."

"When can I have my own gun?"

Never! But she knew that wasn't possible. It wasn't even

right or fair. "You don't need a gun. We don't have to hunt for food, and we're not in danger."

"The sheriff said more people will come after me. If I had a gun, I could kill them."

Laurel felt the props go out from under her. She had done everything she could to shield Adam from that kind of thinking, yet his first response to danger was to kill. Carlin had been a man of weak character and bad training, but she had tried hard to teach Adam to be different. She wondered if killing was bred into men along with beards and tracking mud into the house. She wondered if women had to care so much because men cared so little.

"You don't have to shoot people just because you don't want to do what they want you to do," she told Adam. "There are other ways to protect yourself."

"How?"

That was something else about men. They never took anything on faith. They always wanted chapter and verse. Even then, they weren't convinced half the time. "We'll talk about that later. Right now I have to finish these clothes."

"You don't want me to have a gun." Adam didn't look defiant—not yet—but he did look angry.

"No, I don't. Your father was killed by a gun. I begged him not to wear one, but he wouldn't listen. Men who wear guns die by them."

"Maybe if Pa had been as good as the sheriff, he wouldn't have been killed."

Laurel fought down a feeling of panic. "Some men are born to kill and be killed. The sheriff is one of them. You're going to be different," Laurel said.

"But you said Pa was good, that he was protecting people, like the sheriff. Is it bad to protect people?"

Laurel wondered for the thousandth time if she had done the right thing in lying to Adam about his father. It would be so much easier if he knew the truth. "It's not wrong, but it's dangerous. Sooner or later, somebody is going to shoot you before you can shoot them."

"Not if I'm as fast as the sheriff. Mr. Elgin said he was the fastest gun he'd ever seen. He said—"

"I don't care what Mr. Elgin said." Frustration made her sharp. She had to control her temper. It wouldn't help if she yelled at Adam. He wouldn't understand. "We'll talk about it tomorrow," Laurel said, desperate to gain some time. "Now I want you to go down to the garden and get something for dinner."

"What do you want?"

"I don't care. Anything that's ready to eat."

How could she think about food when her son was turning into a gun-crazy child right before her eyes? It would only get worse as he grew older. But she refused to have him watching Hen Randolph, admiring him, wanting to be like him.

It was obvious that she couldn't keep him in the canyon. She didn't really want to. He needed to play with other boys, to develop friends, to learn how to get along, to like people, to try to understand them rather than want to shoot them when he didn't get what he wanted.

But it wasn't the companionship of boys that he needed most. Adam needed a father, a man he could admire, look up to, try to emulate. Every boy deserved that. But it would have to be someone who could help him develop a strong character, who could teach him sound values. It had to be just the right man, or she would have no man at all.

Once more Hen Randolph's image pushed into her mind. She had never seen a man more carefully fashioned by nature to appeal to a woman. Even though she told herself he was the last man on earth she wanted to see again, he had haunted her dreams for the last several nights. He was impossible to forget.

And not just in her mind. Her body held its own quivering memory of his touch. She could still close her eyes and remember, just as if he were close to her right now. The touch of his fingertips on her shoulder would be with her always.

Laurel opened her eyes and plunged her hands into the water. She worked furiously to rinse the shirts and get to the next batch. *This* was her reality. She would work as hard as she must until she found a man who wanted her and her child, a man who would not depend on guns, a man who understood that life was a much more powerful force than death.

That obviously didn't include Hen Randolph, no matter how much she was tempted to think otherwise.

But where would she find such a man? Not here. If she hadn't found one in seven years, she wasn't likely to find one now. She would have to leave Sycamore Flats. But she didn't have the money to move. She could barely feed and clothe the two of them now. Besides, the Blackthornes wouldn't let her leave.

Perhaps Hen *would* stop them.

But she couldn't depend on Hen Randolph or any other man. If she was going to make a better future for Adam and herself, she had to do it herself. She could still remember the happy years before her father was killed, but she would not marry for protection as her mother did. She was tired of isolation and worn down by hard work, but despite her yearning for love and acceptance, she'd live alone rather than ever be a man's victim.

Adam came into view by the creek. "Beans was all I could find," he said when he reached his mother. "Same as always."

Hen had left the canyon, traversed the wash, and walked well beyond the town before the fury in his brain cooled enough for him to have a coherent thought.

He was furious that Laurel had called him a killer and thrown him off her land. *No one* had ever done that to him. No one had dared. Yet she had rejected him, personally, so completely that she didn't even want her son around him.

Who the hell did she think she was, anyway?

She was a nobody, some silly woman who had let herself be sweet-talked into running off with a no-account who left her with no ring and a kid to raise by herself. He didn't have to help her. He sure as hell wasn't interested in her. He was just trying to make sure she didn't get her face bashed in and her boy stolen.

She didn't have to be thankful. But she didn't have to act as if he were something to scrape off her boots. She didn't know a thing about him or the men he had been forced to kill.

He wasn't a killer.

The town hired you because you're a killer.

That's what she had said. Hen wondered if other people thought of him as a gunfighter, a killer. Things people had said over the years, fragments of conversations, actions, reactions, flooded his mind in a series of lightning vignettes—men backing away from him, refusing to look him in the eye, women avoiding him, whispering, staring.

All these years he'd thought he was avoiding people, but maybe *they* had been avoiding *him*.

It didn't matter. He didn't care what people thought. He didn't need them. He didn't want them. He just wanted to be left alone.

He thought again of that day when, at fourteen, he had come upon the two rustlers who had captured Monty. They had had his hands tied, a rope around his neck. One of the men brought a quirt down across the rump of Monty's horse. The animal bounded forward and Monty hung from the rope, his tongue out of his mouth, his body jerking convulsively. There was no time for thought. Hen had fired five shots—three for the rope and one for each rustler.

The scars left by the rope were still visible on Monty's neck. The scars left by the shooting were still on Hen's soul, even though they weren't visible to anybody but himself.

He'd had no choice. He had no choice the other times either. He couldn't help it if he was good with a gun and others weren't, that people depended on him to protect them. That's just the way things were. Someone had to be the soldier. Someone else the farmer, the philosopher. Only Hen wore no uniform to legitimize what he did.

He didn't need anybody's approval, certainly not Laurel Blackthorne's. Her slate was rather badly smudged as it was. She'd better look to herself and stop coming over pious on him.

But as he turned back toward the town, he couldn't forget her words. Somewhere deep inside him, they had caught on a snag, some painful splinter, some unsmoothed roughness. And the question flapped noisily in the storm gale that battered his soul.

Was he a killer?

Two days later, Laurel's accusation still rankled.

"Tell me about Mrs. Blackthorne," Hen said when Hope started to lay out his lunch.

"What do you want to know?"

He scowled. "Everything."

"There's not much to tell." Hope set out a second plate and started dividing the food. She regularly ate her meals with Hen now. "She came here just after the town got started and moved into that canyon. She's done washing and cleaning ever since. Keeps to herself, her and that little boy. That's about all I know."

"Does she have any friends?"

"No."

"Why not?"

"She says she was married to Carlin Blackthorne. She insists that everybody call her Mrs. Blackthorne. Some of the ladies won't do that. They say it's an insult to the women who are married."

"Surely she's got a marriage certificate or something."

"Not that I ever heard of. The Blackthornes swear Carlin never married her."

That explained a lot. He knew enough about wives to know they held themselves strictly apart from fallen women.

Hope set out the last dish and put the tray to one side. She pulled up a chair and sat down. "She avoids men, too."

"Why?" Hen wasn't particularly hungry. As usual, Hope ate as if she were starving.

"Ma says it's not good for a woman in Mrs. Blackthorne's position to be that pretty. It just causes trouble for her and everybody else."

Hen put a few beans in his mouth. They were tasteless, and he set down his fork. He took a swallow of his coffee, but it was too bitter. He watched Hope fork down mouthful after mouthful and wondered how she could possibly eat so much and remain as skinny as a boy.

He wondered how a woman like Laurel could have taken up with a man like Carlin Blackthorne without the benefit of marriage. He didn't care what the women of Sycamore Flats thought—Laurel had as much character, honesty, and dignity as anybody.

"How old was she when she ran off with Carlin?" he asked.

"Sixteen," Hope answered. "Ma said she was old enough to know better."

Maybe, but he could remember himself at sixteen. If George hadn't been there to jerk him up every now and then, no telling what would have become of him and Monty. If George hadn't married Rose, they might have gone to ruin anyway. They had taken a lot of straightening out.

At least Monty had. He wasn't straight yet.

He wondered what Laurel's parents had been like. Had they wanted her to refuse Carlin, or had they thought sixteen was time to get married and out of the house?

Hen got up and walked to the window. The sun blazed down as it did every day, forcing shadows to stay close to the walls. The street was quiet. Probably everybody was eating lunch. That's what he ought to be doing instead of worrying over Laurel. If he had any sense, he'd mind his own business. She could take care of herself. No, if he had any sense, he'd have handed his badge to Bill Norton the minute he discovered someone had released Damian.

But he wouldn't leave. Not yet. Not until he knew Laurel was safe.

"Don't you like the food?" Hope asked.

"I'm not hungry."

"Ma's not happy with it either. She's looking for a new cook. She says a restaurant can't expect to keep going if people don't like the food."

"Can Mrs. Blackthorne cook?"

"She'd have to, wouldn't she? I mean, she doesn't ever eat in town."

"Come on," Hen said as he started stacking the plates back on the tray. "I need to talk to your ma."

The strain was obvious on Mrs. Worthy's face. "I'd like to help, sheriff, but even if I knew she could cook—and I don't know she can boil water without burning it—I couldn't hire her."

Hen had known the answer the minute he explained what he had in mind. He could see it in Mrs. Worthy's eyes. He could hear it in her voice when she sent Hope away. He controlled his anger. Long practice had enabled him to eliminate any outward sign of his feelings.

"Personally, I would like to do something for her. I probably will, if she'll let me, but hiring her to cook would be the wrong thing."

"She needs someplace to stay where she'll be safe," Hen said. "She can't afford to move into town unless she has a job."

"I'm sorry. Whether I like it or not, people disapprove of her. They wouldn't come to the restaurant if I hired her."

"Why? They let her do their laundry."

"I can't tell you why. I just know what would happen. As much as I'd like to help Mrs. Blackthorne, I have to think of my family first. It wouldn't help her to have us lose our business to the saloons and the hotel."

"You call her Mrs. Blackthorne? Do you believe she was married?"

"I know nothing of it," Grace Worthy said. "If she says she was married, then she's Mrs. Blackthorne to me."

"Even though his family disputes it?"

"I never take the word of a Blackthorne for anything."

Hen felt the knot inside him loosen just a little.

"Maybe you could speak to the women about her, try to get them to include . . . What is it?"

Her face had gone rigid again.

"The ladies won't accept her. I know, because I've tried. The men get improper thoughts whenever she's around."

"That's not her fault."

"It doesn't matter. Women aren't going to welcome a woman into their midst whom they feel is a threat."

"They ought to talk to their husbands."

"Mr. Randolph, apparently you were raised to have very high ideals and to expect other people to come up to them. I wish everybody had been raised that way. But they weren't. You can say what ought to be all you want, but that isn't going to change what is. If you're going to be any good as a sheriff, you'd better learn that real soon."

Hen stared at Mrs. Worthy, shocked.

"The ladies of Sycamore Flats believe Laurel Blackthorne ran away with Carlin and never got married. So do the men. She's twice as pretty as their daughters, four times as pretty as any of them. They're afraid of her. They don't want their daughters to take up with her any more than they want their husbands or sons to. You may not like it any more than I do, but that's the way it is. If you want to help Laurel, you'd better understand that."

Chapter Six

Hen would probably have been grateful for Mrs. Worthy's candor if he hadn't met Mrs. Norton on leaving the restaurant. She was accompanied by a young woman Hen didn't know and an even younger one who was obviously her daughter. As the banker's wife, Mrs. Norton had immense influence in Sycamore Flats. If she decided to accept Laurel, most of the other women would follow her lead.

"Good day, Sheriff," Mrs. Norton said. She smiled benignly. "I've been meaning to tell you how impressed I was with the way you handled that young hoodlum. William tells me it will be some time before he's able to hold a gun again."

Hen smiled to himself. Nobody else in town called Bill Norton William. "I'm glad you mentioned that," he said. "There's something I'd like to ask you."

"Certainly, Sheriff. Anything I can do to help."

"I've been trying to convince Laurel Blackthorne to move into town."

The smile disappeared from Mrs. Norton's face as though wiped off by a wet cloth. Her entire demeanor changed from affability to annoyance.

"The Blackthornes have threatened to steal her son," Hen continued. "She's not safe in that canyon. She needs a job and a place to stay."

Mrs. Norton's expression grew stern, as though she had come face to face with something as unsavory as it was unavoidable. "I have tried several times to extend Christian charity to that woman."

"We're not talking about charity. We're talking about a job and shelter for a woman and child who are in danger."

"Then let her ask for it."

"Do you think she will?"

"No."

"Then it's not very Christian to lay on such a restriction."

Mrs. Norton turned red.

"I'll talk to her," the young woman said.

"You'll do nothing of the kind!" Mrs. Norton stated emphatically. "I won't have a niece of mine consorting with that woman."

The young woman smiled. Hen thought it was an absolutely charming smile. "Talking isn't consorting, Aunt Ruth."

"Miranda Trescott, your mother would never have forgiven me."

"Probably not, but Mama and I didn't agree on a lot of things. I'll be happy to talk to her, Sheriff. How do you suggest I go about it?"

"Maybe you ought to talk to Hope Worthy, or her mother. They can help you better than I can."

"Grace Worthy is always taking in some person better left alone," Mrs. Norton said.

"Thank you, Miss Trescott. I'm glad someone is willing to set a proper example in Sycamore Flats."

Mrs. Norton turned crimson.

"Let me know the results of your talk."

Hen walked off. If he had stayed a minute longer, he would have told Ruth Norton exactly what he thought of her and her Christian charity. That wouldn't have done anybody any good, especially Laurel.

"I'm sorry I couldn't be more help," Miranda Trescott said to Hen. "She refuses to consider moving."

Hen had never expected Miss Trescott to come to the jail. He had jumped up when she entered. A jail was no place for a lady.

"No, thank you," Miranda said when Hen offered her his chair. "I can't stay. I just came to report my dismal failure."

"I appreciate your trying."

"Oh, I haven't given up. I'm hoping a few more visits will persuade her of our genuine desire to help."

"Have you been in Sycamore Flats long?" Hen asked.

"Less than six months. I came to live with my Aunt Ruth after my mother died. I grew up in Kentucky." She started to the door.

"Let me know what happens," Hen said.

She turned back. "I will. Good day."

Hen felt himself sweating. He walked back to his desk and slowly sank into the chair. He didn't know why he was acting like this. Miranda Trescott was a perfectly charming woman, the epitome of a lady.

Maybe that was why he was sweating. He wasn't used to being around women like her. Their purity and innocence made him nervous. He didn't know how to act or what to say, but he'd better learn. She was the only woman willing to help Laurel.

Laurel wasn't in sight when Hen reached the house. No sound came from the adobe, and no one answered his knock. He looked around at this tiny island in a canyon filled with crumbling rock and wondered what could have driven Laurel to stay here for so long. Seeing the canyon without the humanizing effect of her presence gave him a better understanding of her determination to bring up her son her own way. It would take a lot of convincing to change the mind of a woman willing to make herself a prisoner in this place.

Hen walked over to the stream. He wondered if Laurel was in any danger from wild animals living higher in the mountains. He doubted they would need to come down this far to drink or hunt, but he decided to check for signs just in case. That was when he found the trail going up the canyon. Footprints showed it was well-used. He decided to see where it led. About fifteen minutes later, he came to a small meadow where he found Adam trying to saddle a horse that was far too big and spirited for him.

"That's a mighty big animal you got there, son," Hen said. "Why don't you try a smaller one?"

"This is the only one I got," Adam said.

"Where did you get him?" Hen asked. It was a fine horse, much too fine for anyone in Laurel's position to be able to afford. Besides, Hen didn't believe she'd be crazy enough to buy an animal like that for Adam. The boy needed a pony until he developed more size and strength.

"My grandpa gave it to me. He said it was from my pa."

So Damian wasn't the first Blackthorne to take an interest in Adam. Laurel hadn't said anything about that.

"Let me see if I can help," Hen said. Adam handed him the reins. Hen petted the horse and spoke softly to him until he calmed down. "What's his name?"

"Sandy."

"Okay, Sandy, it's about time we had a talk."

Adam laughed. "You can't talk to a horse."

"Sure you can. I talk to Brimstone all the time."

"Jesse's afraid of Brimstone."

"Jesse ought to be, but Brimstone won't hurt you any more than this big fella. He just doesn't know what you want him to do."

"I want to ride him."

"Then tell him. Pat his head and tell him what you're going to do."

Adam reached up and Sandy threw up his head. Hen held it still. "You need a little help." He picked the boy up and held him in one arm. "Now look him straight in the eye."

Adam looked as if he wasn't quite sure about this, but he petted Sandy and started talking to him.

"See, he's calmer already. Now I'm going to put you on his back."

Adam's body stiffened when Hen set him on Sandy's back. He looked small perched up on the huge horse. He kept his arm about the child.

"It'll be a lot better when you get a saddle, but you can hold on to his mane and grip with your knees. Indians never used saddles, and they didn't fall off."

Adam's body relaxed slightly. "Can you ride without a saddle?" he asked.

"Sure. My brother and I used to do it all the time to show off."

"I wish I had a brother," Adam said.

Hen walked the big horse around the clearing, talking to Adam about whatever came into his mind and giving him instructions when he needed them. It wasn't until he'd been doing it for nearly half an hour that he realized the tension had gone out of his own body. He felt more relaxed and happy than he had in months.

He figured it must be the canyon. There was a wonderful sense of quiet and peace and solitude here. It wasn't surprising that Laurel didn't want to leave. He wouldn't either. Well, no, he really preferred the open plains. He liked to see the horizon disappear in the distance. Still, he could get used to this canyon. Here was privacy, a feeling of sanctuary, a place he might relax the control he had exercised over himself for as long as he could remember.

Maybe some of this sense of peace stemmed from Adam. He liked the boy and enjoyed helping him with his horse. He guessed he liked kids. Maybe it was their innocence, their blend of unquestioning, uncritical acceptance. Whatever it was, he felt more human today than he had in a long time.

But children came with mothers, this one with one mother in particular. Hen admitted he was curious about Laurel, but who wouldn't be attracted to a lovely woman with white skin and abundant black hair?

He remembered her eyes most, nearly black, huge and lustrous. They had looked at him with distrust. Or maybe weary acceptance stemming from years of disappointment. But there was more. Hope, expectation, or was it merely a question? He didn't know, but she had touched something in him, asked some question he had to answer. She might be a difficult woman, but she held the key to a puzzle about himself that he had to solve.

Laurel knew she had no business standing back in the trees watching Adam and Hen. She ought to march out there, send Hen on his way, and chain Adam to a tree. She had told him to stay away from Hen, yet here he was looking happier than he'd been in months. She had told him to stay away from that horse, but there he was perched on an animal almost too big for her. She had told Adam he would have to wait until he was bigger to ride that horse. After today, there was no way she could keep him off.

She didn't like the way Adam was looking at Hen, as if he were some kind of god. She knew Adam needed a father, but until now she hadn't known just how much. She had tried to be both father and mother to him, but she couldn't handle that horse the way Hen did. She cursed the Blackthornes for giving it to Adam. She cursed the people of the town for refusing to buy it from her. She should have taken it out of the desert and let it go.

But she hadn't. She couldn't afford to buy such a beautiful horse for Adam, but Adam deserved a horse like that. He just needed a man to teach him how to ride it.

She needed a man, too.

The thought shocked her. She'd never considered remarrying, not for Adam's sake or her own. Laurel wiped the thought from her mind. She didn't need a man. She didn't even want one.

Then she had no business looking at Hen Randolph as if he were the answer to a maiden's prayer. Her body shouldn't come to quivering life every time he came around. Her thoughts shouldn't linger over his handsome face or his powerful thighs. She shouldn't be obsessed with the curve and power of his backside.

But she was.

She didn't like blond men. There was something about their fairness that made them seem devious. Maybe it was the disappearing eyebrows or the pathetic-looking mustache. Hen was clean shaven. There was nothing devious about him. He walked with complete confidence in himself, a man so strong he wouldn't even notice the added responsibilities of a woman and child.

Laurel couldn't deny a desire to lean on such a strong pair of shoulders. She had been alone since the day Carlin left her, had been forced to accept menial work to support them, to hold herself apart from the community. She might as well have resigned from life.

What would she do when Adam was old enough to be on his own? Life would have passed her by. Looking at Hen, she couldn't shake the feeling that this was her last chance to taste life before she grew too old.

They had stopped now. Hen lifted Adam off the horse. For a minute, he stood with Adam in his arms—the child almost dwarfed by the man—talking to him, letting him pet the horse, letting them each become more familiar with the other.

Quite unexpectedly, Laurel's eyes filled with tears. As a young girl, she had dreamed of the man she would marry, the children she would bear, the life they would lead in some enchanted corner of the world. She had forgotten her dream until just now. This tableau, with the evening light fading in the canyon, the man and boy side by side with a horse, the peace and solitude of the setting, was the essence of her dreams.

She attempted to tell herself it couldn't be, not if Hen were in the picture, but her heart would have none of it. She beheld perfection. She could never have, nor hope to find, anything more.

When Hen set Adam on the ground, put his hand on Adam's shoulder, and started toward the trail, she felt a lump in her throat. Damn Carlin! This was how things could have been for them.

As she watched Hen and Adam walk toward her, so much like father and son, it was almost impossible to believe a gunfighter could take so much time, so much effort, over a small thing like teaching a boy to ride a horse. Effortlessly, he drew Adam to him, the way a flower drew a bee.

He had drawn her just as easily. What was there about him that appealed to her so powerfully?

His caring.

He had cared enough about her to tend her wounds, to warn her that the Blackthornes would come again, to ask her to move to Sycamore Flats so he could protect her. He had cared enough about Adam to spend an hour of his time teaching him what to do with a horse. Hen had acted as if spending time with Adam was more important than anything else he had to do.

His caring must be genuine. What could he have to gain?

They were close enough now that she could see his eyes. They looked different. He looked different. There was no openness, no invitation, no uncomplicated joy of life, but there was a subtle difference, as though he had allowed some protective shield to slip ever so slightly. He looked almost human, as if he had a heart and soul and conscience like everyone else.

Maybe Adam had brought this about. Maybe with a child he could be more himself.

They had almost reached her hiding place. She had to step out of the shadows and go to meet them or let him know she had been watching him from concealment.

He looked up when he heard the sound of her footsteps, his body tense, his hand poised near his gun.

The instinctive reaction of a gunfighter. She felt the warmth inside her chill.

"It's only me," she said stepping forward. She looked into his eyes. They were the same as before—brilliant blue, hard, and empty. He was like a shell, a verdant landscape concealing an arid desert. The body of a man and the soul of a killer.

"Ma," Adam called as he ran forward, "the sheriff's been teaching me and Sandy."

Laurel enfolded her son in her arms and gave him a hug. She hated to feel so antagonistic toward a man who had helped her son. She didn't approve of him, but she could let him know she appreciated what he had done for Adam.

"I know the horse is much too big. I had planned to wait until Adam was bigger."

"I learned to ride before I finished learning to walk."

Nothing about Hen's expression changed. He might have been talking to the banker or a rancher or a town matron. She might have been anybody for all the impact she seemed to have on him. She felt her female vanity respond to the slight. The implied criticism in Hen's words stung her. She controlled her temper. Her posture became ever so slightly more erect, her movements more stiff.

"Run ahead and get some water from the creek," she told Adam. "I have to start supper."

"You never needed water before," Adam said, perplexed.

"I do tonight."

She watched Adam stalk away, reluctant to go, irritated with her for sending him, and added that to the list of Hen's transgressions. "I don't care when you learned to ride," she said, turning to him as soon as she thought Adam was out of hearing range. "That has nothing to do with my son."

She tried to ignore the physical response he kindled in her, but it was a hopeless battle. His presence always caused her to feel much more feminine, more alive, more physically aware of herself. His ignoring her only aggravated the situation.

"I grew up on a plantation in Virginia. Out here, boys need to ride even sooner."

He didn't look anything like her conception of a Southern aristocrat. He was clean and neat, but he looked as much like a man of the West as anybody in Sycamore Flats. Maybe that explained some of the contradictions. Southerners were raised to protect their women. They were also taught how to shoot the eyes out of a snake.

"As long as we live in this canyon, Adam doesn't need to ride."

She wondered when Hen had started killing. He looked too young to have fought in the war, but it was hard to tell. Years in the sun and wind had taken the softness from his skin. He could be anywhere from twenty-five to forty. Maybe he had fought Indians in the army. Maybe he'd been a lawman in other towns.

"You can't coddle that boy. If he's going to grow up to be a man, you've got to start treating him like one."

"He's only six," Laurel snapped. "What do you want me to do, give him spurs and a gun?"

"You ought to give him a pony instead of that horse."

Laurel wondered why he felt so free to criticize her. She wondered, too, why he thought he knew more about how to raise her son than she did. He might be a man, but that didn't qualify him for anything except being hard-headed and insensitive.

"His grandfather gave Adam that horse."

She expected some show of surprise. She got nothing. Those empty eyes just stared at her.

"I tried to give him back, but he wouldn't take him. I tried to sell him, to trade him for a pony, but nobody would take him. You're right, I couldn't afford a horse like that. I can't even afford to buy a pony."

She hated him for forcing her to admit she was incapable of such a small thing as buying a proper horse for her son.

"I'll trade him for you."

"No, you won't," Laurel said. "I won't have you ingratiating yourself with him. I don't want him growing up thinking guns make a man."

"He ought to have his own gun," Hen said. "He ought to know how to use it, too."

Laurel fought for words. It was bad enough that Hen had come into her life upsetting her feelings and questioning her beliefs. It was worse that Adam was beginning to look up to him. But it was absolutely unforgivable that he should expect her not only to give her child, *her baby*, a gun, but to teach him how to use it as well.

"Adam will not have a gun for many years. When I do permit him to have one, he's only going to use it for hunting."

Hen stared at her as though he was trying to make up his mind about something. "You don't *look* stupid."

"What?" Laurel gasped, stunned.

"But you sure act it where that boy's concerned."

"How dare you! Just because I don't agree that men ought to go around killing each other every time they can't agree on something—"

"I guess you just don't want to see the truth," Hen said interrupting. "That's generally not as bad as being stupid. But sometimes it's worse."

Many things had happened to Laurel during her twenty-three years, but no one had ever treated her like an idiot. Yet this man had waltzed into her life and proceeded to tell her that everything she thought and did was wrong.

"I can understand your wanting to protect your little boy," Hen continued. "I don't agree with it, but I can understand it."

"Thank you so much," Laurel said, sarcastically.

"But it won't do you any good to ignore reality. He's all boy, and he's going to want to grow up all man. If he doesn't, somebody's going to take everything he's got, including his self-respect, and then they're going to kill him."

The adobe came into view. Laurel was so furious that she could hardly see straight, but she stopped arguing with him. She didn't want Adam to hear what she was going to say.

"Why are you always sending the boy away or talking where he can't hear?" Hen asked. "Do you think by protecting him, you're going to make him any better prepared to take his place in the world?"

"Yes, I do!"

Laurel took a deep breath and forced herself to be calm. She would never get anywhere by shouting at this man. In a way, he was even worse than Carlin. He represented everything she hated and feared. Yet he gave the appearance of being everything she ever wanted in a man. It was a cruel, heartrending joke, and she wanted to hate him for it.

She tried to wipe from her mind everything he had ever done for her. She concentrated on remembering her stepfather, Carlin, the Blackthornes, the men of Sycamore Flats.

"Adam is going to be a gentleman," she told him, her body shaking from the intensity of her emotions. "He's going to have compassion and understanding. He's going to value beauty and despise cruelty. He's going to learn that women are human beings to be prized and cherished, to be cared for and loved. He's going to be taught to treat others with patience and tolerance. But most particularly, he is *not* going to have his self-esteem tied to his ability to kill another human being."

"You sure do read a lot into a fella's words."

"But you said—"

"A man can be all that without putting on a petticoat."

Chapter Seven

"I'm not putting Adam in a petticoat."

"You already got him washing clothes and tending the garden. You might as well start teaching him how to cook and clean."

"And what's wrong with that?"

Hen took one of her hands and held it up to the light. "It ruins your hands, for one thing."

Stunned, Laurel tried to snatch her hand back, but he wouldn't loosen his grip.

"Your hands ought to be soft and white. You ought to live in a big house and have closets full of beautiful dresses with someone to wash them for you."

Bemused, Laurel felt incapable of resisting.

"You ought to have flowers in your hair and go dancing every night."

Forcing herself to close her ears and heart to his words, Laurel recovered her hand. "I might have, if my husband hadn't been a gunfighter who got himself killed a month after we were married." She shook off the remnants of the spell cast by his words. "Which is all the more reason Adam will never learn to love guns."

"No man should love guns any more than he should like to kill, but a gun is a tool, a necessary one out here. Without it, and the knowledge of how and when to use it, a man is at the mercy of thieves, brutes, and murderers."

"Is that how you excuse your killings?"

Laurel hadn't meant to be cruel, but his scorn for the way she was raising her son angered her. She also couldn't be entirely sure he wasn't mocking her. The possibility hurt.

"I haven't killed anyone here," Hen said. Then he walked away. He didn't excuse himself or say good-bye. He just turned and left.

Laurel felt dismissed, discounted, forgotten.

And that made her furious. The colossal gall of the man, the incredible conceit, to think he had answers to everything! That he only had to open his mouth and she would fall all over herself to abandon the principles of a lifetime.

She watched him as he walked across the clearing, and she felt the shiver in her belly again. His backside would be her undoing. All he had to do to reduce her to a quivering, helpless ball of nerves was to walk away, his tight pants hugging the curves of his bottom, his powerful thighs straining the seams of his pants, his broad shoulders moving with apparently effortless power.

Laurel was shocked to feel a vague sense of warmth in a part of her body she had nearly forgotten belonged to her. In seven years, no one had aroused even a mild response. Yet even after Hen Randolph had insulted her, she only had to look at his backside and feel desire curl through her like wisps of smoke from a fire.

Laurel averted her gaze. She would not allow him to dictate to her or taunt her. He was a totally unsuitable companion for Adam. He wasn't the kind of man she admired.

Yet even as she told herself that, she looked up to catch a final glimpse before he disappeared around the bend in the canyon wall and felt her resolution waver. He had been born on a plantation in Virginia. He must have been raised a gentleman, the kind of man she wanted Adam to become.

She started across the yard as Adam came up from the creek with the water. "I won't need that much. Why don't you take it to Sandy? Some grass, too, if you can find some."

"He can get grass and water by himself."

"I know, but it will help you gentle him."

Adam gave her an appraising look. "Are you going to let me ride him?"

"If I feel you're strong enough to handle him."

"The sheriff let me ride him."

"He was with you the whole time."

"He said I had good hands. He said I had a natural seat," Adam told his mother proudly. "He said he'd come back tomorrow."

It was on the tip of Laurel's tongue to tell Adam that Hen was never coming back, but she bit her tongue. Whatever her problems with Hen, she didn't want them to come between her and Adam.

"You'd better run if you're going to feed Sandy. I'll have dinner ready in a jiffy."

But Laurel wasn't thinking about dinner as she watched Adam trudge off to find his horse. She was thinking of a tall blond man who had entered her life with the force of exploding dynamite. He had ripped her world apart, and she couldn't put it back together again.

Worse than that, he had kindled hope in her heart that he was somehow different from the other men she had known.

Despite the evidence to the contrary, she still looked for signs that underneath that hard facade there was some lingering softness, some humanity. She searched those empty eyes for the reason he had become so unfeeling.

During the endless, mind-numbing hours when she washed clothes, she invented a hundred reasons why a caring, decent man should change into a monster of inhumanity. Her imagination was just as fertile in picturing the kind of person he would become when his hard exterior was finally peeled away.

Thoughts of Hen invaded her empty hours the way mist from the stream invaded every niche and cranny in the canyon. She fought it but lost. Hen had aroused a need in her that had been sleeping for years, a yearning she was helpless to control. Something about him communicated with something in her more primitive than thought. She responded despite all her efforts to ignore him.

The question was, did she want to take the time to look for the man she knew must be locked away inside Hen Randolph? It was a risk. The safety of her heart was at stake. Already she could feel the tug. If he stayed, she could win so very much. If he left, she could lose everything.

The sound of scuffling didn't immediately draw Hen's attention. Boys did a lot of that, especially during a long summer afternoon. But something about the grunts didn't sound quite right. They seemed to be coming from behind his house, but when Hen stepped outside, he found that they were coming from the wash. As he entered the stand of trees that lined the creek, he saw two boys tumbling in the dry streambed. Coming closer, he recognized Adam. A bigger boy on top seemed to be holding Adam down rather than fighting.

Deciding that things had gone far enough, Hen seized the boy by his collar and lifted him off Adam. Adam scrambled to his feet, murder in his eyes, and came at the other child.

"Whoa!" Hen said as he held Adam back. "I think this has gone far enough."

"He said my pa was a bad man!" Adam shouted, trying to break loose. "He said he was shot dead for a thief!"

Adam struggled with all his might to attack the larger boy, but Hen kept his grip.

"What's your name?" Hen asked the boy.

"What's it to you?"

"Very little as yet. Some manners would be a good start."

The kid glared back at Hen.

"He's Jordy McGinnis," Adam said. "He's an orphan."

"I don't see how you can hold that against him. It's none of his doing."

Jordy's stare became a little less defiant.

"I want to talk to you. Will you wait here?"

Jordy hesitated a moment before he nodded.

"You won't run away?"

"I said I'd wait, didn't I?"

"Yes, you did. Come along with me," Hen said to Adam.

"But Jordy said—"

"You can tell me what he said while I get you cleaned up," Hen said. "Your mother would have a fit if she saw you like this."

"No, she won't. I'll tell her I fell down. I tell her I fall down a lot."

Adam walked to the house with a defiant swagger, but as soon as they got inside, he seemed to deflate. Hen poured some water into a basin and wet a cloth. "Now tell me what this is all about." Hen positioned the child in the light so he could see better.

"He said my pa was a two-bit thief. He said he was killed trying to rustle some cows."

Hen wiped the dirt off Adam's face. He had a couple of red spots, but the skin wasn't broken. He might not have any bruises.

"What did your mother say?"

"Ma said Pa was killed trying to stop some thieves. Ma said he was a good man, like you."

Hen's body tensed, his senses sharpened. Could Laurel have changed her mind about him?

"Did your mother say I was a good man?"

"No."

He hadn't thought so. He felt disappointed, and that surprised him. He never cared what people thought of him. Why should he start now?

"Do you get in fights very often?"

"Some," Adam said, hanging his head.

"Over what the boys say about your pa?"

"It's not true," Adam flashed. "Pa was a good man. Ma said so."

"Then why were you fighting Jordy?"

"He said Pa was a thief."

"You've got to learn to ignore people when they bait you. They don't care what they say. They're only trying to get you mad."

Adam hung his head. "That's what Ma says."

"She's right. Now you'd better go home. I imagine she's missing you."

Adam walked to the wash with Hen. The minute Adam saw Jordy, his walk changed to a swagger. He made a face and ran off toward the canyon. Jordy was waiting where they had left him. He had occupied his time by drawing lines in the soft dirt. Hen eyed him for a moment. The boy squirmed under his relentless stare.

"Why did you say his pa was a thief?"

"Because he was." Jordy didn't look up, just kept making lines in the dirt. "Everybody knows he was killed trying to steal a bull. I don't know why Adam don't believe it."

Because his mother has told him a different tale, trying to make Adam feel better about himself.

"Why did you fight him? You're bigger than he is."

Jordy's head snapped up. "He jumped me."

"Wouldn't you jump him if he called your pa a killer and a thief?"

Jordy's gaze fell to the ground again. "It's the truth. Everybody knows it."

Hen picked out a small boulder at the edge of the wash and sat down. "My pa was a killer, too. And a thief, I suppose."

"I don't believe it," Jordy said.

"Everybody knew it. It got so bad, people ran us out of Virginia all the way to Texas."

"How'd you get to be sheriff?"

"People don't know."

"You think they'll take your badge away if they find out?"

"Who's going to tell them? Nobody knows but you." Hen looked over at Jordy, rather casually.

Jordy's eyes grew wide. "You ain't told nobody but me?"

"Nope."

"Not even Adam?"

Hen shook his head.

"Ain't you afraid I'll tell on you?"

"I was sort of figuring we ought to stick together. You, Adam, and me."

"Why? Nobody picks on me," Jordy said rather proudly. "I'd bust their face in."

"Adam said you were an orphan."

Jordy turned sulky. "I shoulda hit him for that."

"Where do you live?"

"Here and there." The boy squirmed under Hen's gaze. "Sometimes I sleep over the livery stable."

"Where do you eat?"

"I get along."

"Do you steal?"

"No!" He lowered his gaze. "Mrs. Worthy feeds me."

He was clearly ashamed of having to depend on the charity of others.

"Well, I'd like it if you sort of kept an eye on Adam, kept the bigger boys from picking on him."

"Why should I?"

"I'll make it your job. In exchange, you can sleep in my

house. I've got two whole rooms nobody uses. I also need somebody to keep my things straight. I'll pay you a dollar a day."

"A dollar!"

"That's not enough?"

Jordy quickly reined in his surprise. "It will be in the beginning," he said, "but if I do a good job, I'll expect a raise. And I get fifty cents extra if I get in a fight on account of Adam."

"Fair enough. Now why don't you get your things."

Jordy drew some more lines in the ground. "My pa got caught stealing gold." He raised his gaze. "What did your pa do?"

Hen had spent years refusing to even think about his father. Now, even before he could say a single word, he felt the fury bubbling up inside him, as hot and destructive as ever. Years of hate, rage, and shame struggled to escape through the tiny crack that opened in his soul.

"I don't know all the things he did," Hen said, his voice suddenly thick. He saw the beginnings of skepticism in Jordy's eyes. He wasn't going to believe Hen unless he was as honest as he expected Jordy to be. "I do know he killed his best friend after he seduced the man's sister."

"Geez!"

"Then he brought his family to Texas and deserted us."

Hen could see his father as clearly as if he'd been standing here. Big and handsome, untouched by the anguish and misery he left in his wake. He could remember the day he left for the war, the shock of his sudden departure. His mother's will to live had died that afternoon. It had taken her body two agonizing years to catch up.

Hen stood up. "No more questions, okay?"

Jordy nodded.

"Now go get your things. You got a lot of work to do. My place is a mess."

A wintry smile twisted Hen's lips as he watched Jordy scamper off in the direction of the livery stable. Poor kids. It was impossible for Jordy and Adam to feel good about themselves as long as the world kept saddling them with the sins of their fathers. So they struggled to find excuses for what their fathers had done. The only alternative was to hate them. And themselves.

Which was exactly what he'd been doing his whole life.

Hen sat back down, his mind numb with the shock of discovery. How long had he been hating himself? Since he killed those rustlers? Before that? Maybe that was part of the reason he had taken this job. Killing had compromised his integrity in his own mind, but other people admired him for it.

The thought that he could have fallen for such a stupid line of reasoning embarrassed him. Even Laurel didn't need to trick herself into thinking well of herself. She was strong enough to set her own standards, believe she was right, and go her way regardless of what anyone else thought about it. If a woman was strong enough to look her past in the face and dare it to touch her, he could too.

But as Hen got to his feet, he found it wasn't so easy to shake the demons of a lifetime. Their hold went deep, all the way to the center of his being.

"Where's the sheriff?" Hope asked when she found the office empty except for Jordy.

"Out on business," Jordy said.

Hope thought he was acting a little cocky. "Do you know when he'll be back? I brought his dinner."

"He's gone looking for rustlers. He ain't likely coming back tonight. He said I was to have his dinner."

Hope didn't like that. She didn't much like Jordy, either. He was usually too ready to take offense at anything she said, but he didn't act like that tonight.

"What are you doing here?" Hope asked.

"I live here now," Jordy announced.

"You do not."

"I do too."

"Since when?"

"Since this afternoon."

Hope paused to digest that bit of information. "Why should the sheriff let you live here?"

"Because I work for him. I'm going to keep his place straight. And we have other deals." Jordy's manner told Hope he had no intention of explaining further.

Hope set the tray down and began to get out the plates. "I usually eat with the sheriff."

"I know. He told me to look out for you while you were here."

Hope started to tell him she didn't need any grubby nine-year-old to look out for her, but she stopped. "Why?"

"We got an understanding."

"Well we got an understanding, too. And I don't know that I want any dirty-nosed urchin horning in on it."

"I'm not dirty-nosed. He made me wash." Jordy looked as if he wished he hadn't told her that last bit.

"So he did," Hope said, checking his face and ears.

Jordy pushed her away.

"Well, I guess you can eat with me, but you got to mind your manners."

"I can behave as good as you."

"Maybe, but you don't talk as well."

"The sheriff's going to teach me to talk good, too."

They sat there eyeing each other over the food.

"What's your deal?" Hope asked.

"I won't tell."

"I'll take the dinner back."

Jordy eyed the food. "Let's eat first, then I'll tell you."

"Half," Hope bargained.

"Okay," Jordy said, grabbing a chair for himself. Suddenly he remembered and grabbed one for Hope, too. "But you got to swear on your mama's grave, you won't tell a soul."

"My mama doesn't have a grave."

"Your grandmama then," Jordy said, disgusted.

"That's childish."

"Then I won't tell you."

"Okay," Hope said, capitulating, "but if it's all a hoax, I'll give you a fat lip."

"And I'll break your face."

These preliminaries over, the two settled down to a hearty meal and a cozy chat.

Chapter Eight

Laurel walked quickly along the boardwalk. She wasn't used to being in town this late in the morning. She wasn't used to seeing the streets filled with people. She wasn't used to being stared at either. She pulled her flat-crowned hat lower over her eyes. The bruises still showed.

But reaching her destination didn't ease the tension. She paused a moment outside the door of Reed's Bakery, took a deep breath to bolster her courage, opened the door, and stepped inside.

The wonderful aroma of fresh-baked bread caused her mouth to water. Cakes and pastries of all kinds rested behind glass covers on both sides of the shop. From behind the counter, Estelle Reed eyed Laurel frostily.

Estelle's bosom was tightly encased in a black cotton dress that covered her throat to her chin and her arms to her wrists. She had pulled her hair back in a bun so tight that it nearly caused her eyes to slant. She had put on an enormous white apron to protect her dress from the sugar and flour.

"What are you doing here?" Estelle demanded.

Nothing could make Laurel as mad as being spoken to in such a contemptuous manner. She marched up to the counter and planted herself directly in front of Estelle.

"I've come for my money. You haven't set anything outside your door in more than two weeks."

"I can't be leaving money lying about," Estelle said. "You never know who might make off with it."

"The other women do, or they meet me at the door with it."

"I can't be sticking my head out of doors at all kinds of hours just because you insist upon coming around before decent folks are out of bed."

"Well, I've come at a decent hour this time. You're out of bed, and if anybody steals my money between here and the canyon, it's none of your concern. You owe me nine dollars. I'd like it now."

"You'll get it when I'm ready to give it to you," Estelle said, anger making her eyes as hard as agates.

"I'll take it now."

"I don't have it to spare."

"You've got it in that drawer. I saw you counting it when I came in."

"How dare you spy on me."

"I wasn't spying. You didn't hide it until you saw me enter the store."

"I don't trust you."

Laurel felt a hot flash of rage, but she told herself that Estelle was a mean, tight-fisted, greedy woman. Laurel doubted she would have trusted St. Peter with her cash drawer.

"Besides, you haven't brought my clothes for two days now."

"I won't until I'm paid."

"Strumpet!" Estelle barked angrily. "I should have suspected a woman brazen enough to go around pushing her love child forward like he was a respectable little boy would do something like that."

Laurel raised the counter, stepped through, and walked right up to Estelle, their faces only inches apart.

"If you ever say anything like that again, I'll slap you so hard you'll have a permanent crook in your neck."

"Don't you threaten me," Estelle said, backing up.

"That's no threat." Laurel pulled open the cash drawer and pointed to the contents. "Pay me."

"I won't pay anybody who threatens me."

"Maybe you would like me to do some talking," Laurel said, moving closer to Estelle.

"I'm not afraid of anything the likes of you can say. My life is an open book."

"Then I guess you wouldn't mind everybody knowing your husband sneaks around to the Leghorn Saloon every night about nine-thirty? I understand he's real friendly with a girl who goes by the name of Toothsome Tilly."

Estelle turned deathly white. "You breathe a word of that, and I'll kill you, if I have to do it with my bare hands."

"Give me my money, and you'll have nothing to worry about."

"I won't pay you until I get my clothes."

"Suppose we lay the entire matter before the sheriff. He ought to be mighty interested in why a prosperous merchant is unable to pay her laundry bill."

Estelle clearly didn't like the idea of her stinginess being made public. "I'll pay you to get out of my shop," she said. She pulled open the drawer and snatched up a handful of money. She counted out four-fifty. "You'll get the rest when I get my clothes."

"I'll get the rest now, or I'll put up a line and hang your undergarments across the middle of the street."

Estelle swelled with outrage, but she counted out the rest of the money. "There, and you needn't come back after you return my laundry! I shall find someone else to do my washing."

"You won't find anyone to do it so well and so cheaply."

"Get out."

"And a good morning to you, too." Laurel turned to see Hope Worthy standing in the doorway, her mouth open. Before she could speak to the child, Hope turned and ran down the street.

Laurel hoped she wasn't going to tell everybody in Sycamore Flats what she'd just overheard. The women didn't think much of her now. They would be horrified when they knew she had threatened to spread a rumor about Frank Reed. She had made the threat to scare Estelle, but she didn't think anybody would believe that. Oh well, it didn't matter. No one believed anything she said anyway.

She looked up and down the street. Even more people were out and about. She looked toward the mountains and her canyon. Seven saloons stood between her and the end of town, every one of them filled with men. She wasn't about to run that gauntlet. She would slip behind the sheriff's office and follow the wash back to the canyon. She had crossed the street and turned down the alley between the buildings when she heard a door open. Her heart missed a beat when Hen stepped out the back door of the jail.

"It was nice of you to drop by to see me, but you don't have to use the back door. You're allowed to visit the sheriff in his office."

"I wasn't coming to see you and you know it," Laurel said. "I'm on my way home."

"This isn't the way." He took her arm and turned her around. "It'll take you twice as long if you go along the wash."

"I want to take twice as long," Laurel said. "I have a whole afternoon to waste."

"Then we'll see about getting you a customer to replace Mrs. Reed."

"Hope told you, didn't she?"

"She couldn't wait."

"I wish she'd mind her own business."

"I wish I could have seen Mrs. Reed's face. What did you tell her? Hope couldn't quite hear."

"Something I don't mean to repeat. Now let me pass. I really do need to get back to Adam."

"You just said you had the whole afternoon to waste."

"I lied. Now are you satisfied?"

"Not as long as you go skulking back along the wash."

"I'm not skulking."

"You most certainly were. I saw you. There's a very definite look to a skulk. You were doing it perfectly."

A smile banished Laurel's frown. "Are you always so ridiculous? I imagine your family was always trying to get you to be serious."

He looked startled. "My family never got what they wanted. If they had, they wouldn't have known what to do with it."

"What a terrible thing to say."

"We're not a nice family. Now, you and I are going back the way you came. There are still a few people in Sycamore Flats I don't know, and I'm depending on you to introduce me to them."

Laurel pulled back. "I don't want to go that way."

"And we've got to talk about finding you a job so you can move down from that canyon."

Laurel dug in her heels. "Why are you so determined to drag me out of the canyon?"

"Because I don't want to be tramping up there every five minutes to make sure you're all right. If you were in town, everybody could watch you. Besides, I don't think the Blackthornes would bother you down here. Now come along."

"No."

Hen looked as if he were humoring a child. She hated it when he did that. It made her feel brainless.

"You've got to stop running away from people, if not for yourself, at least for Adam."

His perceptiveness shocked her. She had told herself that she wasn't running away, that she was merely avoiding an unpleasant situation. Sneaking out of town through the wash had always left a bad taste in her mouth. Hen's pointing it out only made it taste worse.

"Are you ashamed of yourself or your son?"

"Neither."

"I didn't think you were, but you're letting your fears make you act like you are."

"Where do you get off telling me what to do?"

"I know. I'm a nasty killer, but I'm not so twisted and evil that I don't understand about pride. You've survived by isolating yourself, but you're strong and courageous. You don't need to hide anymore. I want you to walk down the boardwalk and speak to every woman you meet. I also mean for you to walk past the saloons and dare any man to make a suggestive remark."

"I've done that until I'm tired. It hasn't changed anything."

"Keep on doing it. Stop slinking into town at dawn—"

"I do *not* slink!"

"—sneaking through alleys, creeping down the wash, or hiding in your canyon."

"I don't hide because I'm afraid. I do it because I'm tired of beating my head against a brick wall."

"You have to tell them every day that you're stronger than they are and you're just as good. Then show them you believe it."

"I tried."

"So you're going to give up and let them think you're a whore and Adam's a bastard?"

Laurel slapped him. Before either of them knew what was happening, her hand had sailed through the air and crashed into his cheek. "I won't allow anybody to call me that."

Hen looked completely unfazed, as if he was slapped by enraged females every day. "Good. Now walk down the street thinking the same thing."

Laurel was so mad at him, and at herself, that she turned and marched back down the alley toward the street. "Okay," she said when she reached the street, "what do we do now?"

"We walk down the street like we are having a friendly conversation, and we speak to everybody we meet. If I don't know them, you introduce me and tell me something about them."

"How can I act friendly when I'm mad enough to hit you?"

"Pretend. We're both good at that."

Laurel started off at a rapid clip.

"And walk slowly. At that speed, you'll run past people before they get a look at your face."

Laurel turned and came back to where he still stood. "Any more instructions?"

"Smile. Look like you're having a good time. Give them half a chance, and most people will meet you halfway."

Thus began the longest walk of Laurel's life. Sycamore Flats wasn't more than two hundred yards from end to end, but it seemed like two hundred miles.

She was conscious of the sound of the boardwalk under her feet, the angle of the sun, the stillness of the morning. She had never noticed how rundown Sycamore Flats looked. Even the buildings looked faded and wearied by the heat.

The first introduction was awkward. When it was over, Laurel wanted to hit Hen again. But the second was easier. The third easier still. It helped to be walking with the sheriff. He drew people's attention. It couldn't, be otherwise. When a tall, good-looking man walked down a street as if he owned it, people just naturally took notice. Laurel couldn't help but admire his composure. She could ignore people. Hen could make them feel they were invisible.

But what intrigued her most was the way women looked at Hen, then at her. With an animal heat in their gazes. More than one woman allowed her eyes to linger on parts of Hen's body other than his handsome face or broad shoulders. This obvious attention merely reinforced what Laurel already knew. Hen was a dangerously attractive man.

But still more surprising was their look of envy. It was obvious that several women would have jumped at the chance to change places with her. That stunned her. She had been so busy thinking of him as the kind of man she wanted to avoid at all costs, she hadn't realized other women might not feel the same way. Even women who didn't want to be married to a gunman any more than she did. Did they see something in him she couldn't?

She was intensely aware of his presence. The air was charged with his energy. When he touched her elbow to help her up or down the boardwalk steps, her body received a shot of adrenalin. Even the hem of her dress seemed to become charged when it brushed against his boots. She moved away to put a little space between them.

"Have you thought about what kind of work you can do?"

Hen's question jerked Laurel back to the present. "We've already discussed that," she answered. "I don't really mind washing clothes. It allows me to be by myself. It gives me time with Adam."

"But it also keeps you exposed to the Blackthornes."

"Why do you care about what happens to Adam and me? Are you trying to make me like you?"

"Could I?"

How could any female not like him when he acted as if she were the center of his universe? People had ignored her for years, demeaned her and her son. Hen had shown more attention to her than to any woman in Sycamore Flats. She could easily lose her head entirely.

"Maybe, but that's not why they hired you."

"It's my job to protect the citizens."

"Of Sycamore Flats, not Sycamore Canyon."

"I can't stand by and see a woman abused."

"You're not in Virginia any longer."

"You need a new job. Bending over that tub must give you a crick in your back."

She couldn't deny that. She had lain awake more than one night unable to sleep because of the pain in her back and shoulders.

"People look down on you because of the work you do. You're too good for that."

Laurel found it hard not to stop and stare. Nobody had ever said she was too good for anything. Just the reverse. She couldn't believe Hen really meant what he said. He was probably just trying to make her feel better after her brush with Estelle Reed. She appreciated that, but she could handle Estelle. What she couldn't handle was his being so considerate when she didn't believe he actually felt that way. No matter how sensible she tried to be, she couldn't help but hope he meant what he said.

"Good morning, Mrs. Blackthorne."

Startled at the genuine warmth in the greeting, Laurel turned to see Miranda Trescott coming toward her. She and her aunt had just emerged from Loyal's Dry Goods.

"Good morning," Laurel said, her gaze slipping past Miranda to Mrs. Norton.

"Good morning, Sheriff," Miranda said, turning her warm smile on Hen. "I don't recall seeing either of you about so early in the morning."

"I have trouble finding time away from my work," Laurel mumbled.

"It's the best time of day for doing errands. Aunt Ruth always drags us out before it gets too hot."

"It's always cool in the canyon." Laurel doubted anybody was interested in the canyon, but she was at a loss as to what else to say.

"We're having an informal tea on Thursday," Miranda said to Laurel. "We'd love to have you come."

Shock held Laurel silent. It had been years since she'd been invited anywhere, and never with such obvious sincerity.

"I don't know . . ."

"Don't refuse just yet. It's nothing formal, just friends getting together to visit."

"I can't leave Adam alone."

"I'll see to him," Hen offered. "It's about time he had another riding lesson."

Laurel thought of her dress. She didn't have anything she could wear to a party. They might call it a tea, but it was really a party. Then there were her hands. They were chapped and red, and she had no gloves to hide them.

"I have a lot of work. I don't know if I can spare the time."

She couldn't go. She'd be uncomfortable, and she'd make

everybody else uncomfortable. She wouldn't know what to say. She'd feel out of place."

"Do try," Miranda said.

"Miranda, dear, if she doesn't feel she can come, it's not fair to press her." Mrs. Norton's face was expressionless.

"I'm sorry," Miranda said, "but I'm still new in town. And there's nobody my age to talk to."

"I have to confess I'd feel a little uncomfortable," Laurel said, deciding the truth was best for everyone. "I don't have anything fit to wear. Besides, I don't imagine your friends want to sit down to tea with the washer woman."

"That would make absolutely no difference."

"I'm sure you'd try, but it would." Until now Laurel had never felt genuinely welcomed by anybody except Mrs. Worthy. She was sorry she couldn't take advantage of this invitation.

"Maybe you would feel more comfortable with just Miranda and myself," Mrs. Norton offered.

Laurel felt as if her wits were paralyzed. This couldn't be happening to her. She couldn't be standing on the street in broad daylight being invited to tea by the banker's wife.

"Yes, I would."

Laurel and Mrs. Norton stared at each other, neither seeming to know exactly what to do next. The situation had moved beyond the expectations of either of them.

"Then we will expect to see you on Tuesday of next week," Miranda said, smiling with genuine pleasure.

Laurel felt the words of refusal rise to her lips. She also felt the pressure of Hen's presence, his challenge to show everyone she respected herself. It would be easier to refuse, to stay in her safe canyon, but she knew it was time to come out. For Adam's sake, she must.

And for her own. She didn't really care whether she had tea with Mrs. Norton or not. She did care that the other woman thought her good enough to be invited. It made Laurel feel good, and she hadn't felt good about herself in a long time.

"Thank you. I'll be pleased to accept."

"Don't bother to dress up," Miranda said. "I promise there won't be anybody there but my aunt and myself."

"I can't believe I let her talk me into going to that house," Laurel said after Mrs. Norton and her niece moved on.

"You should have done so long ago."

Laurel wanted to argue with him, to defend herself, but they were approaching the saloon district. Her attention was distracted by the men who lounged outside. The people who congregated at this end of the street weren't at all like those who confined themselves to the other end.

"It's time you stopped allowing other people to think they're better than you."

"I never *allowed* it," Laurel said, her nervous gaze settling on a group of men just ahead. "Like you said, nobody invites the laundry woman to Sunday lunch."

One of the men stepped back to let Laurel and Hen pass. "Morning, Miz Blackthorne," he said.

"Good morning," Laurel said, struggling to keep her wits from deserting her completely.

"Howdy, Sheriff."

The scene repeated itself at the next two saloons.

"I know what you're going to say," Laurel said, turning to Hen as they reached the end of the street and headed toward the canyon, "but that never happened to me before. Those very same men would have said something entirely different."

"Then forget what they might have said. Tomorrow you walk right back by here and expect the same treatment you got this morning."

"But—"

"You say good morning to them, and I guarantee they'll say good morning to you. And nothing more."

Laurel started to argue, but her ankle twisted on the rocky soil, and she leaned into Hen. All thoughts of argument banished from her mind, Laurel righted herself and pulled away from Hen. She hoped he didn't notice her flushed features. Her face felt as hot as fire. Quite suddenly, she felt terribly vulnerable. She looked toward the canyon and hurried her steps.

While they had been in town, she had been too preoccupied to think of anything except the next encounter. But now the town was behind her. The safety of her canyon was at least a hundred yards away, and she was alone with Hen.

The fact of his physical presence was extremely distracting. It would have been overwhelming if Laurel had not been dazed by what Hen had done. He had not merely forced her on the town, he had forced her to look at herself in a different light. He had refused to let anyone, including herself, think of her as anything except the equal of anybody in town, *from the banker's wife on down!*

And he had gotten away with it.

In one fifteen-minute amble through town, he had achieved what she had been unable to do in seven years.

Why? The question would not go away. He couldn't think of her as his equal, not a man who had been born on a Virginia plantation and whose undergarments were made of finer linen than those of the richest people in town. It was obvious that he had grown up with the habit of command. He probably didn't see it—it had been with him his entire life—and he probably would deny it, but he had been born a member of the ruling class. What could he possibly see in her—the daughter of an itinerant miner, the widow of a cattle thief, the mother of a six-year-old boy—to interest him for more than a few weeks at most?

Fortunately, before she could torture herself too much, they reached the stand of sycamores that shaded the streambed where the creek slowly disappeared into the desert floor. She turned to Hen and extended her hand.

"Thank you for what you did today. I was angry at the time, but I'm grateful now."

Hen took her hand in his and started forward.

Laurel didn't move.

"I'm going up with you. I want to see how Adam's getting along with Sandy."

A whole new set of emotions arose that were in direct conflict with her personal feelings about Hen. "I'd rather we parted here," she said.

"Why?" Hen asked, his eyes searching.

"I've already told you. I don't want you to have anything to do with Adam."

Chapter Nine

Laurel quailed before the look of rage that blazed in Hen's eyes. There was nothing cold and vacant about them now. She felt scorched by their fury. If she had ever had any doubt about his aristocratic birth, she had none now.

"Do you mind explaining that," Hen said with barely restrained fury.

Laurel recovered quickly. After all the trouble he'd gone to for her, she was sorry she had to be so blunt, but Adam's future was more important than Hen's feelings.

"I don't want Adam to start depending on you. I don't know why you came here, but you won't stay. I've washed your clothes. I've heard you talk, seen the way you keep to yourself. You'll never be part of this community. You'll leave within a year. Then Adam will have to make his way on his own without depending on you."

Laurel didn't like the way Hen was looking at her. It was impossible not to remember her stepfather's eyes when he beat her and her mother until he had exhausted the fury in him. Hen had beat Damian—methodically, systematically, brutally.

"You might as well stop looking at me like you want to wring my neck. I asked you to stay away from us that very first day. The next time you came, I told you I didn't approve of gunfighters and didn't want you around Adam. You came anyway. Well, you can't go around ignoring people's wishes and not expect to get your toes stepped on once in a while."

"Saying you don't think me fit company for your son is more than stepping on my toes."

"I guess it is, but going around killing people is serious too."

"I don't *go around killing people*," Hen said. "I never shot anybody who didn't try to kill me first."

"Maybe you had reasons for what you did, I don't know, but that's not the point. I hate what guns can do, and I don't want Adam admiring anyone who uses them. Being a boy, he's particularly susceptible."

"Especially since you lied to him about his father."

His accusation was so unexpected that Laurel lost her composure. She had always dreaded having anyone find out what she had done. "How do you know that?" She could have kicked herself. Her words were a virtual admission.

"It doesn't matter how I know. What matters is that you're so damned afraid that Adam might kill somebody someday that you're lying about the past *and* about the future. What you don't see is that you're making it dead certain somebody will kill him."

"I don't think we have anything more to say to each other."

"I have plenty more to say," Hen shot back. He grabbed her as she tried to turn away. "Only problem is, you're not doing any listening. It's okay for you if you want to do something stupid, but it's not fair to the boy. He deserves a chance. And if you don't have any faith in the advice of a *killer*—and it's obvious you don't—why don't you ask one of those women when you go to tea. Hell, even Hope could set you straight."

With that, he turned and left her standing alone. Again.

At that moment, Laurel was prey to contradictory emotions, but above all she felt guilty about her lie to Adam. She always had. For some reason, Hen's knowing made it worse than ever.

She also felt guilty about the way she had treated Hen. He had been so kind and thoughtful to her and Adam. There had to be a lot of good in him. She didn't question that any longer. It was that good that had made it impossible to stick to her resolve to have nothing to do with him.

But it was his willingness to kill that stopped her. His anger, too. Her stepfather would beat her the way Hen had beaten Damian when he was angry. She couldn't, *wouldn't*, subject herself to that again. Nor Adam. Neither would she live with a gunfighter. Sooner or later, somebody would kill him.

Then she would be alone again.

She would not be left again. She wouldn't allow her heart and her dreams to be shattered by the crack of a gunshot. She had to push him away now, before she and Adam began to depend on him.

As Laurel turned and entered the canyon, she realized that she had come perilously close to letting herself become attached to Hen. She liked him. She had to admit that. How could she not? Everything he had done since that first day had given her a better feeling about herself. For the first time in years, she felt like a desirable woman.

She had forgotten how good that felt, how much it changed her entire outlook on life. She had forgotten that it gave her hope. A wonderful, but very dangerous thing—hope.

She climbed the trail slowly, hardly aware of the rapid drop in temperature under the sycamores, the noisy scratching of a mouse among dry leaves, or the rattlesnake that slithered across the path in front of her. She didn't even notice the multi-colored layers of rock in the canyon walls, the shafts of sunlight that penetrated the dimness under the trees, or the cheerful babble of the creek as it tumbled over and darted around the boulders which tried to block its path.

She thought only of Hen Randolph.

He was the best-looking man she had ever seen. Her breath still caught in her throat every time she saw him. It was as though he had been sent to torture her, to show her everything she couldn't have. His physical appeal was like a rope pulling her toward him against her will, like a wind at her back, blowing her where she didn't want to go. When he touched her, it was all she could do to remember he was a gunslinger.

He had an air of competence that was wonderfully reassuring. When she was with him, she was keenly aware of a feeling that he could handle anything that might arise, solve any problem, answer any question. The weight she had carried by herself for so many years was lighter.

But it was pointless to dwell on what she liked about him. He was not the kind of man to stay in Sycamore Flats. She had only attracted his interest momentarily, and not very strongly at that. He seemed more interested in teaching Adam to ride. And use a gun.

Laurel reached the adobe, but Adam didn't answer her call. She hoped he was in the meadow with Sandy. She had given him strict instructions not to go to town again. She headed on up the canyon.

She didn't know why Hen thought Adam should know how to use a gun now. He could learn after he became an adult. She didn't want him to grow up thinking of a gun as a way out of difficulties. That was how Carlin had been raised, and it had gotten him killed.

She interrupted a squirrel in the process of gathering seeds. He darted to the top of a nearby rock and chattered shrilly at her as she walked past.

Laurel laughed.

If she and Adam could only stay in this canyon forever, they wouldn't have to worry about guns or social acceptance or being abandoned by people they loved.

But even as she thought of how easy that would be, she knew she wouldn't keep Adam here even if she could. He deserved his chance to see the world. As for her, she had retreated here in self-defense. She had never asked herself if she wanted to stay.

What if Hen asked her to leave?

Laurel was angry at herself for even thinking of that question. She wasn't going to waste her time coming up with an answer. It would never happen. They had nothing in common.

When she reached the meadow, she found Adam with Sandy. Things weren't going quite as well as they had with Hen, even though Adam was obviously trying to do everything Hen had told him. Adam walked Sandy over to his mother.

"He won't let me ride him."

"Maybe you ought to wait," Laurel said, uneasy with the thought of her son perched atop the big horse.

"I want to show the sheriff how good I can do." Adam led Sandy to a large rock. "Hold him while I get on."

Laurel took hold of Sandy's halter. "It'll be easier when you're bigger."

"I'm not a baby. The sheriff said I ought to be riding all by myself."

"The sheriff doesn't know everything," Laurel snapped.

"He does about horses."

Adam seemed a little unsure of himself as he climbed onto Sandy's back, but he mounted the horse anyway. Laurel was proud of her son's courage and determination, but she wasn't pleased that her influence had been supplanted by Hen's.

"You ought to have a saddle," Laurel said as Adam grabbed a handful of Sandy's mane.

"The sheriff said he'd get me one, but he said every boy ought to be able to ride bareback. You can let go now."

"You can't ride Sandy by yourself."

"The sheriff said all I had to do was guide him with my knees."

"Maybe you can do that when you're bigger, but not now."

"The sheriff said—"

"I don't care what he said," Laurel exploded. "I'm not going to let you ride without a saddle and a bridle."

"But I want to show him what I can do. He said he'd come back real soon."

She had to tell him now. It wasn't fair to put it off. Besides, the sooner he knew, the sooner he would get over it and things would return to normal.

"He's not coming back."

"He said he would. He promised. He said—"

"I told him not to."

Adam stared at his mother for a moment. "Why?" It was a long, anguished wail, a cry of protest from a little boy who desperately needed what he had found with Hen.

"He's not a nice man. He—"

"He is!" Adam cried. "He is! He is!"

"He's a gunslinger," Laurel told her son. "He kills people."

"I don't care," Adam cried. He shook his head from side to side, his eyes closed as tears began to appear in the tightly squeezed corners.

"I don't want you to have anything to do with people like that," Laurel said. "I don't want you to learn to think of guns as a way—"

"I don't care about guns," Adam cried. "I liked him. You had no right to make him go away."

Adam let go of Sandy's mane and slid off. He fell to the ground rather than landing on his feet.

Adam headed across the meadow at a stumbling run. "I'm going to tell him I like him."

"Adam Blackthorne, you come back here this minute," Laurel called, but Adam didn't slow his stride. Laurel let go of Sandy's halter and headed after her son, but she had no hope of catching him. He might be only six, but he was quick and strong.

"Adam, come back!" she cried, but she didn't expect him to obey her. She stopped. As she stood there, her breath coming in gasps, biting the knuckle of her clenched fist, she watched him disappear down the canyon.

She had lost her son.

She had to get him back. Adam was all she had in the

world. Without him, she had nothing to live for. Much to her horror, Laurel found herself thinking of Hen. How could she let a man who stood for everything she hated work his way into her affections? And he had done exactly that. Even when she was telling Adam that Hen was bad, something inside her sprang up to deny her own words.

This was the same way she had acted with Carlin. She had been a foolish girl then, desperate to get away from a brutal stepfather, but she should have had enough sense to realize that the wild look in Carlin's eye, his thumbing his nose at authority, his recklessness, his willingness to let his head and heart be ruled by his senses would make him a terrible husband.

But she hadn't. She had seen only the excitement of being with a man who feared nothing, who threatened to kill her stepfather if he ever touched her again, a man willing to run away with her and never look back.

She seemed to be showing the same lack of judgment with Hen. She had to find a way to leave Sycamore Flats. Adam wasn't strong enough to stand against Hen's fascination, and neither was she. Safety lay in never seeing him again.

But she had nowhere to go, and no way to get there. She could only stay and face her problems.

A week later, Hen was still so angry that people crossed the street to avoid his intimidating gaze. Hope fell unnaturally silent during meals. Jordy was subdued.

After eating lunch in total silence, Hen decided that he needed to get away for a little while. He'd never been the center of attention, but his foul moods were attracting the notice of the curious. He had no intention of telling anyone the source of his ill temper, but knowing he was becoming the subject of gossip and speculation further worsened his mood.

"I think I'll take a ride," he told Hope. "Jordy can have my lunch."

Hope blocked Jordy's hand when he reached for Hen's plate.

"He eats too much," she said.

"I do not," Jordy exclaimed indignantly. He tried for the plate and missed again.

"He's just trying to make up for the years when he didn't have enough," Hen said.

"Does he have to do it all in one month?"

The hint of a smile curved Hen's lips. "Little boys do that."

Jordy snared the plate with a diving catch that caught Hope off guard.

Hen's flash of good humor vanished. Speaking of little boys made him think of Adam. He turned away so Hope wouldn't see the hardening of his features.

"You going looking for rustlers again?" Hope asked.

"Yes. Peter Collins has been losing stock."

"Then you ought to head toward Cienega Wash."

"What would I find in a marsh?"

"If you're looking for rustlers, you're looking for Blackthornes. A bunch of them stay over that way."

Hen grabbed his hat and headed toward the livery stable through nearly empty streets. Apparently no one else had finished lunch so quickly.

Hen didn't know why Laurel's opinion of him rankled so. People had disapproved of him all his life, including his family. Hell, Jeff still couldn't say a civil word to him, but it didn't bother him. He and Monty argued as often as they agreed. Even Rose thought he was making a mess of his life and told him so.

"Good morning, Sheriff."

Hen came out of his reverie long enough to speak to two ladies coming out of Estelle Reed's bake shop. Apparently not everyone was eating lunch just yet. One of the ladies smiled and laughed nervously. Hen sped past. He could recognize a female on the prowl at a hundred yards. He wanted no permanent ties, especially not that kind.

So why did Laurel's opinion bother him so much? Because it cut him off from Adam?

He didn't care much for adults, never had, but he had a soft spot for kids. He knew how much that boy needed the attention and approval of a man. He had spent the better part of his youth looking for a man he could admire, could pattern himself after. He hadn't found one. Maybe that was why he was such a foul-tempered misfit. If Adam didn't find someone, he could end up the same way.

Hen didn't want that. A life like his took its toll. You couldn't be wide-eyed and innocent. You couldn't look for the best in people, learn to love them, to depend on them, to put down roots. He had to distrust everyone, keep his distance, keep moving.

"Making rounds early?" Scott Elgin asked when Hen reached his saloon.

"I want to see if I can find out what's happening to Peter's cows. Hope tells me I ought to ride toward Cienega Wash."

Elgin's easy smile vanished. "The Blackthornes consider that their personal stomping grounds."

"According to Hope, that's why I ought to look it over."

"I know you're good with that gun, but you watch out. We need a sheriff like you around here. I don't want to be burying you."

"I'll give it some thought," Hen said as he moved on. "Never liked the idea of dirt in my face."

If the people of Sycamore Flats could appreciate him for his ability with a gun, why couldn't Laurel? What right did she have to pass judgment on what he did or the way he lived his life? You'd think she could at least see that if he hadn't been willing to use his gun and his fists, she wouldn't still have her son.

She did see that. She had told him so, but she still disapproved of him. That made it even more hopeless. She saw the good and still rejected him.

"Fork out Brimstone," Hen said to Jesse McCafferty, the

handyman at Chuck Wilson's Livery Stable. It was a running joke. Nobody would touch Brimstone.

"Fork him out yourself if you want him," Jesse said. "I ain't touched that horse since you been here, and I ain't going to start now."

"You two ought to be best friends by now," Hen said as he picked up his saddle and headed toward where Brimstone stood munching marsh hay.

"Him and the Devil, maybe," Jesse said. "Don't know why he lets you get close to him when he nearbout kills anybody else."

"Maybe I'm the Devil." Hen placed the saddle blanket on Brimstone, then the saddle. The white horse kicked with his hind foot. A sharp slap on the hindquarters seemed to make him feel better. He only tried to bite Hen after that.

"Don't see why you put up with him," Jesse said.

"Because he's the best horse I ever rode."

"And the meanest."

"That, too." Hen led Brimstone outside and mounted up. "When I'm out in the desert, I don't care if the horse is nice, just as long as he can get me back safely."

A man always had to be ready to face danger, to know where to look, what to avoid, when to face it down. This was something Laurel knew nothing about. It wasn't the same for a woman. Even though she had had a rough time, being a woman offered her a kind of protection a man didn't have.

A man was expected to follow a different code of behavior. That was something Laurel couldn't teach Adam. It didn't matter if she agreed with it or not. Men would expect it. Women too. Sometimes they were the worst. A man might forgive another man a weakness. A woman never would. Maybe it was because they were so vulnerable and needed a strong man to protect them. Maybe it was because, even though they might be weak physically, emotionally they were stronger than most men. He didn't know. He just knew women could be right hard on a man.

Laurel was and didn't even know it.

* * *

About a half mile from town, Hen rode out of the belt of trees
that surrounded Sycamore Flats and into the desert. The
tangle of mesquite and paloverde, rarely more than a few feet
high, stretched into the distance where it finally gave way to
an area dominated by cactus. Some miles past that, the land
fell away toward the Cienega Wash, an area of towering cottonwoods and still ponds. More than seventy miles away, a range
of mountains drew a jagged line across the horizon.

Hen kicked Brimstone into a canter. He was in a hurry.

No, he was just irritable, and the horse seemed to be catching his mood. He made several attempts to bite Hen, something he rarely did after Hen mounted up.

"Knock it off," Hen said. "I always could think of worse
things than you could."

Apparently the horse remembered at least one example. He
settled into a ground-eating stride. Despite Brimstone's foul
temperament, Hen had never considered buying another
horse. He couldn't find a better companion when it came time
to leave.

Hen had always known Sycamore Flats was a temporary
stop. Laurel was right. Neither she nor Adam could depend
on him. He was here only until something drew him away,
until the emptiness inside drove him on. Running from everything, toward nothing. He was the kind of man he didn't want
Adam to be.

He had once heard it said that women were the civilizers
of mankind. He didn't know about that, but they sure had a
habit of putting down roots and sticking close to their kind. If
you saw one woman, you could be sure there were more of
them about.

Women didn't leave real well, and they didn't like other
people doing it either. They had a way of latching on to things—
people, land, towns—and expecting them to be in the same
place for the rest of their lives. And they hated change almost
as much as leaving.

Staying around Laurel and Adam wouldn't be so bad if he were the settling type. He would like watching Adam grow up. The boy might have a worthless, no-account for a pa, but he was a good kid. All he needed was some guidance.

Not that Laurel was a bad influence. She just didn't understand men. She had got it into her head that men only looked at her with lust in their hearts. She didn't understand that no man could look at her with indifference. He expected there were several men in town who would have been quite willing to settle down and be a father to Adam if she had just given them a chance to say so.

She was a good-looking woman. No red-blooded man could look at her without thinking things he'd be ashamed to say. He had, and he'd spent years teaching himself how to look at women and feel nothing. Even with her face cut up and bruised, he'd found her attractive. Now, with her face practically healed, he found her even more disturbing. He wondered what she'd say if he told her he had dreamed of them together.

It would probably shock her as much as it shocked him. He wasn't used to such dreams. They were like something Monty would have done before he got married. Just thinking about them caused Hen's body to tighten.

Cattle tracks! Hen pulled Brimstone to an abrupt stop. He dropped from the saddle to study the tracks on his knees. A half-dozen cattle had come this way. So had two shod horses, herding the cattle away from Peter Collins's ranch.

Hen mounted up and followed the tracks.

Who did Laurel think was going to teach Adam how to be a rancher, to trail his own stolen cattle, to take his stand against rustlers? The Blackthornes could teach him, but she wouldn't let them near him. He could teach him, but she didn't want him near Adam either. She didn't like what he was.

Why should she? He didn't. He never had. That's why he had been on the move. He was running from himself.

The thought annoyed him so much, he almost missed the

piece of charred mesquite. He dismounted. Standing to one side, he carefully studied the opening in the desert. This had been the scene of considerable activity with cows and horses. Brushing the sand and gravel off a small mound, Hen uncovered the remains of a small fire.

Somebody had branded cattle here. Most likely, they had been altering the brand to fit one of their own. So he had proof there was rustling going on. Now he had to find out who was doing it.

But when Hen swung back into the saddle and pointed Brimstone for home, he wasn't thinking of rustlers. He was thinking of Laurel Blackthorne. One way or another, he was going to prove to her that he was more than a gunman. He just might prove it to himself at the same time.

Chapter Ten

"What did you find?" Wally Regen asked Hen. Hen had stopped by the Regen ranch on his way back to town.

"I found signs of branding cattle."

"I knew it!"

"I also found signs of a sloppy ranching operation."

"What?" Regen responded, shocked.

"You can't just turn your cows loose and forget about them. If Monty and I had done that, there wouldn't have been a single longhorn on the Circle-7 when George and Jeff got home from the war." Hen followed Wally inside the house and accepted a cup of coffee.

"What do you suggest I do?" Wally asked, eyes glittering angrily.

"First, you and Peter ought to get all the ranchers together, find out who's having the most trouble, where the rustlers seem to be striking most often. Then organize your hands into pairs and send them out on regular patrols. If all the ranchers cooperate and share information, you'll be able to cover twice the ground with half the men. You need to clean out your water holes and keep the cattle closer for better control."

Wally didn't look pleased at the criticism. "That won't stop all the rustling."

"No, but it will stop all but those determined to stick their necks in a noose. I'll catch them sooner or later."

"I don't know how much longer I can keep taking these losses."

"Not long if you keep playing cards with that gambler."

Wally flushed. "Don't tell me what to do with my money."

"I'm not telling you anything," Hen said, setting down the cup. "It's your money and your cows. I'd see Peter tonight if I were you. Let me know what you decide."

Hen didn't know if Wally would take his advice. He looked exactly the kind of stubborn, independent man who would reject good advice just to show he could. That was okay. Peter would make sure he followed it to the letter.

Laurel hadn't seen Hen for ten days. But rather than feel relieved, she found herself thinking about him more and more. Everywhere she turned, something made her think of Hen.

It was the same with Adam. The child refused to forget that long, sunny afternoon in the meadow. It stood between Laurel and her son. And that gap got worse every day. Adam still did his chores, but he spent most of his time with his horse. He held everything Hen told him as gospel. The more success he had with his horse, the more he resented his mother sending Hen away.

Laurel looked up from her washing to see Adam coming up the canyon. She could tell from his walk that he had been in town. It was defiant and too energetic; he held his head too high. He was prepared for an argument.

Laurel tried to shrug off the feeling of defeat. She tried instead to be angry with Hen. It was all his fault. Adam had never defied her until he came preaching his credo of guns and independence from the influence of women, of little boys having to learn to act like men. Now he had disappeared, leaving her to wrestle with the results of his meddling.

"I need water," Laurel said even before Adam reached her. "And I need more wood for the fire."

She could tell that Adam was surprised she didn't ask him where he had been, fuss at him for doing what she had told him not to do, but she knew by now that she would have to find a different way to reach Adam.

"Who did you play with today?" she asked as Adam picked up the bucket and headed toward the creek.

"Jordy McGinnis."

Laurel bit her lip. Jordy was an orphan, the son of a man killed trying to jump another man's claim. He was always in trouble with somebody, mostly for stealing. Laurel imagined that he only stole to keep body and soul together, but he wasn't the kind of boy she wanted Adam to have for a companion. She ran through a list of the boys without finding one she liked better. Either she didn't approve of them, or their parents wouldn't want them playing with Adam.

"Is there anybody else you like to play with?" she asked when Adam returned.

"Danny Elgin, but he likes Shorty Baker, and I hate Shorty." The sons of a saloon owner and a bullwacker.

"Jordy's got a job. He says he'll pay me if I help him."

"Who would give Jordy a job?" Laurel demanded.

"The sheriff." He threw the words at her, using them like a whip.

"Hen Randolph?"

"Jordy keeps the sheriff's house straight and sweeps out his office, and the sheriff pays him. He lets Jordy sleep at his house. And eat his lunch, too."

"What are you talking about?"

"The sheriff's never hungry. Hope says he hardly ever eats nothing no more."

"Anything anymore. He lets Jordy stay at his house?"

"Jordy likes the sheriff. Says he's the best sheriff there ever was. He gave Shorty a nosebleed when he said the sheriff was afraid of the Blackthornes. They got some kind of deal. Jordy won't tell me. Hope don't know neither."

"Doesn't know," Laurel corrected automatically, but Adam had already gone off, leaving her to wonder again if she hadn't misjudged Hen. It was one thing to give Jordy McGinnis a job. Still another to take him in. But to get the little demon to regard him as a demi-god, well that took another kind of talent. The same kind of talent that had captivated her own son— genuine interest.

Hen took one look at the meal Hope spread out on his desk and knew something was wrong.

"Where'd you get that?" he demanded.

"At the restaurant. Where else?"

"Who cooked it?"

"The new cook, I guess. Why?"

Jordy looked at the food closely. "It doesn't look right." He tasted some of the sauce poured over the meat. His eyes popped with surprise. "But it sure tastes great."

"I knew it," Hen said. He grabbed his hat and hurried out the door.

"What's wrong with him?" Hope asked. "It's beef like always. I thought he'd liked it."

"Don't mind him," Jordy said, his mouth full. "He'll like it just fine when he gets over what's eating him."

"If there's anything left to eat," Hope said, as she watched Jordy fork the food into his mouth as fast as he could swallow.

Hen charged across the street and headed straight for the restaurant. It hadn't taken him more than one look to know who had cooked that meal. The crowd in the restaurant seemed bigger than usual. The patrons were eating with Jordy's enthusiasm. Hen's brow furrowed more deeply.

"I hear you got a new cook?" Hen said when Mrs. Worthy came through the door with three plates.

"It's wonderful," she said, beaming. "We haven't been able to keep up with the orders since breakfast."

"Is he a tall, skinny, ugly drink of water?"

"He is thin and quite tall, but I think he's very nice-looking. Reminds me something of you, come to think of it."

"Hellfire and damnation!" Ignoring Mrs. Worthy's look of astonishment, Hen burst into the kitchen.

As he had expected, he saw Tyler at the stove filling a batch of plates. Ignoring the astonished Horace Worthy, Hen strode up to his brother.

"What the hell are you doing here?"

Tyler didn't even look up. "It's nice to see you, too, brother. Thanks for coming over to give me such a warm welcome."

"Don't try any of your sarcasm on me," Hen snapped. "I want to know what you're doing here."

"I'm cooking," Tyler said without slowing his work. "They had a job, and I took it."

"You don't want me hanging around you any more than I want you traipsing around behind me."

"What makes you think I came here because of you?"

"This man is your brother?" Horace Worthy asked.

"Yeah, and you're going to have to get yourself another cook."

"He's the best we've ever had," Mrs. Worthy said, entering the kitchen. "We'll keep him if we have to double his wages."

"The money's okay with me," Tyler said.

"You're leaving as soon as you finish that batch you got on the stove."

"I think you'd better put a sign on the door saying customers aren't allowed in the kitchen," Tyler said. "It would make things go smoother."

Mr. and Mrs. Worthy looked from one brother to the other.

"Where'd you come from?" Hen asked after a moment of silence.

"New Mexico. I've been prospecting."

"You don't know anything about prospecting except how to feed miners," Hen said scornfully.

"You don't know anything about being a sheriff except how to pull a trigger," Tyler replied, as calmly as ever. "But I didn't come charging into your office telling you to get out of town."

"Why did you come?" Hen asked. "And don't tell me you heard about this job all the way in New Mexico."

Tyler looked up from his work. His expression never changed. "There's a call going around for all men by the name of Blackthorne."

"If you've started listening to rumors, you're going—"

"They're supposed to collect at Tubac. It seems they mean to get rid of a certain sheriff and punish the town that hired him."

Color drained from the Worthys' faces.

"Don't tell me you came hot-footing it all this way to protect me."

Tyler's face still bore no expression. "I thought I'd see the fight was fair. A couple of Blackthornes have a reputation for shooting people in the back."

"I can take care of myself."

"Then I guess I'll just watch."

"Go back," Hen said.

"I like it here," Tyler said. "The Worthys appreciate my cooking."

"I can throw you out of town."

Tyler turned back to his cooking. "It'll take more than a badge to move me."

"I got more than a badge."

"There's a rumor to that effect going around."

"Damn you!" Hen turned to go.

"I telegraphed George."

Tyler had spoken softly, but the effect on Hen was electric. He stopped in his tracks and turned slowly. "Why!"

"He'd never forgive you if he didn't know. He has a right."

Hen stormed out of the kitchen with a stream of curses so virulent they turned Grace Worthy's ears pink.

"Are you two really brothers?" Grace asked in disbelief.

"None of us ever did get along too well with Hen," Tyler explained. "He hates to have anybody looking over his shoulder."

"Are the Blackthornes really coming after the sheriff?"

"I expect so. They don't seem the type to go in for reunions."

Hen didn't go back to the office. He didn't go for a ride either. If Brimstone caught his mood, he was liable to throw him and eat him alive. He strode off down to the wash behind town, but that wasn't a happy choice either. The wash made him think of the stream, and the stream made him think of the canyon. That made him think of Laurel.

He should be worried about the town. He should be thinking of his own safety. But all he could think about was Laurel. And Adam. There would be no safety for them if the Blackthornes descended on Sycamore Flats. After they finished with him and the town, they would turn to the canyon. At the very least, they would take Adam. Hen knew they'd have to kill Laurel before she'd let them do that. She had closed everything else out of her life except that kid.

He hadn't taken the Blackthorne threat seriously—Damian hadn't given him a very good impression of their courage—but it must be real. Tyler might have come alone if he wasn't sure, but he wouldn't have telegraphed George. Because George would come. They both knew that.

Hen cursed. He would have to talk to Laurel again. She had to leave Sycamore Canyon. But how would he get her to go? She had no money, and he knew she wouldn't accept any from him. Hen wondered if he could kidnap Adam. She'd follow him. That stupid idea showed how desperate he was becoming. He couldn't put Laurel through that kind of pain. Besides, knowing how stubborn she was, she'd probably turn right around and go back to the canyon once she reclaimed Adam.

Hen cursed again. He was supposed to be a killer, a gun-slinger, a man who solved every problem with his guns. Well, his guns weren't any good now. He had to solve this without them.

Fire!

After the cry of *Indians*!, it was probably the most dreaded word in the West.

"It's the livery stable," Jordy hollered. He entered Hen's room and ran to the window. "It's going up like dry kindling."

Even though the livery stable was at the other end of town, Hen could see the flames through the window and hear the screams of the horses. Brimstone! He was in the stable. They kept him in a stall because nobody would go in the corral with him.

"Do they have a bucket brigade?" Hen asked as he jumped out of bed and jammed his legs into his pants. He grabbed his boots and shirt and ran out the door.

"Yeah," Jordy gasped, trying to keep up with Hen, "but it ain't doing no good."

A mild breeze rustled the leaves of the sycamores. The flames cast the pale light of the moon and stars into insignificance. Against the hot orange tongues of fire, people moved like black, featureless shadows as they formed lines to throw buckets of water on the fire.

Horses in the nearby corral screamed in fright and lunged against the far side of the corral. The poles grunted and sagged from the impact, but they held. A quick glance told Hen that Brimstone was still inside the stable.

It seemed the entire town had turned out, buckets in hand. In a matter of minutes, they had formed one line to the water tank behind the livery stable. Another line stretched a hundred feet to the well behind the saloon. The fire had already gotten a good hold on the straw and hay.

Hen heard a scream and turned to see Jesse McCafferty leading a pinto gelding from the stable.

"Where's Brimstone?" Hen yelled over the din of the fire and people shouting to each other.

"I couldn't get near him," Jesse said. "He tried to kill me."

"How many horses left?" Hen asked.

"Yours and that yella horse that belongs to the kid up the canyon."

Adam's horse! What was Sandy doing in the livery stable? Hen ran to the water tank, soaked his shirt, and headed back to the stable.

"You be careful," Jesse shouted. "The whole loft is ablaze."

"It's just the front of the stable," Hen said.

"Not anymore. It was falling on me when I was getting—"

"Adam!"

Jesse broke off as a child emerged from the night and headed straight for the stable. Hen saw Laurel burst from the darkness. He grabbed her to keep her from following Adam into the stable.

"Adam!" she screamed again.

"Hold her," Hen said to Jesse. "Hold her tight, or she'll get away."

Hen ran into the barn. The heat was intense. The fire hadn't yet gotten hold on the part of the stable where the last two horses were stalled, but the burning hay and straw was making them crazy. Hen managed to grab Adam before he dashed into the stall with the fear-crazed dun. He could have been trampled under the horse's hooves.

"I've got to save Sandy!" Adam shouted, trying to get loose.

"I'll get him," Hen said. "Right now he's too scared not to hurt you."

Hen entered the stall, slipped around the frantic horse, and grabbed him by the bridle. Sandy fought, but Hen quickly tied the wet shirt over his eyes. Prevented from seeing the fire that frightened him so, Sandy stopped rearing, but he still fought when Hen tried to lead him from the stall.

"Take that whip and get behind him," Hen shouted at Adam. "When I tell you, cut him across the rump." Fighting Sandy all the way, Hen managed to get him out of the stall and turned in the direction of the doorway. "Now!" he shouted.

Adam struck Sandy with all his might, and the dun lunged for the doorway. Hen let go of the bridle, and the horse plunged to safety. Hen picked up Adam and hurried from the building.

Laurel fell on her son, sobbing.

Someone had caught Sandy. Hen untied the shirt and turned back to the barn.

"You can't go in there," the man shouted.

"Brimstone is still inside."

The temperature was much hotter now. All around him, the air was filled with pieces of hay and straw floating from above. Fragments of wood exploded into the air as the timbers in the loft caught fire. It was almost impossible to breathe. Hen tied his wet handkerchief over his nose and mouth. Brimstone was crazy with fear. He slipped into the stall with the frantic stallion, narrowly avoiding a vicious kick from a rear hoof. He grabbed hold of the bridle, but Brimstone fought with all his strength.

"Stop it, you fool," Hen grunted, "I'm trying to help you."

Brimstone showed no signs of recognizing his master. Finally, Hen managed to tie the shirt over Brimstone's eyes. He could then turn the horse and lead him out of his stall. One of the timbers overhead cracked with the sharpness of a rifle shot. Brimstone dug in his heels and refused to move.

The fire was approaching the doorway. In a few moments, they would be trapped inside. Hen threw himself on Brimstone's back. Simultaneously he jabbed his heels into his flanks, brought his open palm down on his quivering flanks, and let out a yell that would have raised the dead.

The big horse burst through the doorway before the floor above burned through and a fiery cascade of straw filled the opening with tongues of hungry flame.

Hen saw Laurel standing in the middle of the yard, Adam

clutched in her arms, staring toward the barn with haunted eyes. He could see the relief when he emerged from the barn.

Hen told himself that he should still be angry with her—he'd been telling himself that for two weeks—but his heart skipped a beat, then started beating a little too fast. He felt a kind of excitement that had nothing to do with the fire or the danger to the town. Just seeing Laurel had the power to send fire racing through his veins, buzzing along every nerve in his body until he felt like a simmering, smoldering mass of banked energy. Knowing she had feared for his safety caused it to erupt into flame.

Hen hurried to put Brimstone in the corral.

When he returned, Laurel still stood where he had left her, her arms wrapped around Adam, her body trembling worse than if she'd fallen into an icy stream. She appeared to be too stunned to move. Hen took her by the shoulders and guided her to a bench under a huge sycamore. Still holding tightly to Adam, Laurel sank to the bench.

"What are you doing down here?" Hen asked.

"I s-saw the fire f-from the canyon," Laurel stammered. "I knew they'd need help. I didn't know S-Sandy was in the stable until Adam ran into the flames." Still shaking, she clutched her son tighter. "I wanted to thank you, to tell you how much—"

"Anybody would have done what I did."

"But you did it, not somebody else. I'll never forget that."

Hen wondered if he was now good enough to teach her son to ride. Probably not. If he remembered the old Puritan principle, fire had to burn a person to a crisp before he was purified. If that was the only cure, he'd just as soon remain defiled.

"The water's gone! There ain't no more water!" With that shout went any hope of being able to save the building.

The tank behind the livery stable was empty, and the well was down to mud. People shifted to the next nearest wells, but the lines were longer, the buckets slower, and the water gave out even sooner. All they could do was try to keep the fire from spreading to the rest of town.

Fortunately, the livery stable was separated from the rest of the town by nearly a hundred feet. A few sparks floated down on other buildings, but they were put out without difficulty. The townspeople stood in silence as they watched the flames engulf the livery stable. The fire would burn for hours yet. It would smolder through most of the next day.

"It's a shame the creek dies when it hits the desert. We could have saved the stable with that water," Hen said, grateful that his voice did not betray the sudden wildness inside him. He realized how much he had missed talking to Laurel, how much he had missed seeing her, how much he didn't want to go another two weeks without seeing her. "Why did you bring your horse to the livery stable?" he asked Adam.

The boy wiggled out of his mother's arms, but he didn't try to run away.

"Nobody's going to fuss at you," Hen assured him. "I just want to know why you didn't leave the horse in the meadow."

"Ma said you wasn't coming there anymore."

"That doesn't explain—"

Adam looked up. "You helped Jordy." It was almost like an accusation of betrayal.

"That's part of our deal. Jordy works for me, and I teach him how to ride."

"I been helping Jordy," Adam said. "Can you teach me, too?"

Hen turned his gaze to Laurel, but she was staring at her son. He wondered if she had known what Adam was doing with his time. He shouldn't have to sneak behind her back to get somebody to teach him how to ride.

"Did your ma say you could bring Sandy down here?" Hen asked.

Adam shook his head.

"Did you ask her?"

He shook it again.

"A fella ought to do what his ma says," Hen said.

"She didn't say I couldn't."

"You didn't ask because you knew she'd say no, right?"

Adam nodded.

Hen could remember how impatient he had been with his mother's restrictions, so impatient that he and Monty had ignored them. He knew how much their disobedience had hurt her. He didn't want Adam to fall into the same habit.

"I think you ought to tell her you're sorry and beg her pardon."

"But she said you weren't coming to see us no more. She said she didn't want me around you. But you kill bad people just like my pa did. Why are you bad?"

Chapter Eleven

"You'll have to ask your ma about that," Hen said. Laurel had told Adam that Hen was bad. She'd have to be the one to explain why he wasn't quite so terrible anymore. "Not everybody sees things the same way. Could be your ma doesn't want you to take after your pa or me."

Laurel didn't seem to understand the dangers of living in the Arizona territory any more than his mother had understood Texas.

"But—"

"If you want me to teach you how to ride, you got to act like a man. Don't sneak around behind your ma's back. Face up to her and ask."

That's what he and Monty ought to have done. Ma wouldn't have understood. She wouldn't have believed them, not when Pa said they'd be perfectly safe. She always believed Pa no matter how little sense he made—but they ought to have tried.

"But I already asked her."

"Ask her again. Your ma can change her mind just like the rest of us."

He hoped Laurel was beginning to understand that a boy

started learning how to be a man long before his voice dropped or he started noticing girls.

"Can the sheriff teach me how to ride?" Adam asked Laurel. His gaze was once again on the ground.

"Look her in the eye," Hen said. "Only cowards look at the ground when they're talking to somebody."

"I ain't no coward," Adam said, glaring angrily at Hen.

"I didn't think you were. You just need someone to give you a hint now and then."

He wished Laurel could understand how hard Adam was trying to grow up, how important it was to him to be a man *in a man's eyes*. As much as he loved his mother, her opinion would never be the final one in this matter. If she didn't understand that, he would keep on defying her. It would break her heart if she lost that special love that had always existed between her and her son.

"Can I, Ma?" he asked.

"If the sheriff will agree to come to the canyon," Laurel said. "You will have to keep Sandy in the meadow."

"But Jordy—"

"Maybe I'll let you bring Sandy down after Mr. Wilson rebuilds. You'd have nowhere to keep him now."

They all looked at the stable. The flames were beginning to die down. The fire had consumed the straw and hay and most of the framework, but the support timbers were too thick to burn.

"You sure you want me around?" Hen asked when Adam moved away to join Jordy.

"I haven't changed my mind about killing," Laurel said, "but it's clear Adam needs a lot of things I can't give him."

Her words touched the old anger, and his temper flared. "Riding lessons can't fix that. You ought to look about for a husband for yourself and a father for the boy."

He might as well have touched a match to dry kindling. Laurel practically exploded. He had never seen her look quite so furious.

"I'm never going to get married again," Laurel declared. "Never! I'll be grateful if you can help Adam, but I don't share his need of a man."

Hen could hear deep anger in her voice. Fear as well. He wondered what Carlin Blackthorne had done to her. It had to be more than taking her virtue without benefit of marriage.

He wondered if any other man had been able to touch her heart. He doubted it. She had wrapped herself up in the boy to the exclusion of all else. That wasn't good for her or Adam. He'd have to do something about that, but helping women come out of a shell wasn't exactly his specialty.

"You may have been hired by the town to protect it," Laurel said, "but that doesn't mean you have to start giving personal advice."

"I won't do it again," Hen said. "Now I'd better see if there's anything I can do for Chuck. I'll be around in a few days."

After he'd had time to think. No woman as fiery and tempestuous as Laurel Blackthorne was meant to live alone. She might reject him—she wouldn't be the first—but she shouldn't be rejecting men in general. There was something Laurel wasn't telling, and Hen was determined to find out what it was.

"We got to have more water," Scott Elgin was saying. "If there had been a wind, we could have lost every building in town." The townspeople had gathered in his saloon to discuss what to do in case of another fire.

"But there ain't no more water, not when it ain't raining," Chuck Wilson said. "I got the biggest water tank in town, and it was used up in no time flat."

"We could dig more wells."

"We could dig a ring of wells around the town, and it still wouldn't be enough if we had a big fire," Bill Norton said.

"Well, I don't mean to stand by and let my bakery burn to the ground," Estelle Reed said. "Frank and I mean to do something about it."

"What?" Elgin asked.

"We ain't figured that out yet," Frank Reed admitted.

"There's water in the canyon," Estelle said. "Plenty of it."

"But that's half a mile away. We can't carry it that far."

"Who said anything about carrying it? Build a chute. It's downhill all the way."

"It would take a lot of work."

"But we'd have plenty of water. The stream flows year 'round."

"Who's going to build it?"

"All of us. It's our town."

"Who's going to pay for it?"

"We'll put a levy on every building."

"When can we start?"

"As soon as we get the lumber."

"How long will that take?"

Hen got to his feet. "Haven't you forgotten something?"

"What?"

"That water belongs to Laurel Blackthorne."

"That water doesn't belong to anybody. It's there for the taking."

"Mrs. Blackthorne homesteaded that canyon," Hen said. "She has deeded ownership from just this side of where the water disappears into the desert to well past the high meadow."

"I don't believe it. Nobody would homestead that canyon."

"She did. I looked it up."

There was dead silence.

"I guess we'll have to talk to her."

"That won't do no good. She hates the whole town."

"We got to have that water no matter whether she likes us or not."

"If the town needs it, we can take it."

"Nobody will take anything," Hen said.

"Who's to stop us?"

"I'll stop you," Hen said.

"But you're our sheriff. You're supposed to do what we say."

"I'm here to uphold the law and protect the property of every citizen. That includes Laurel Blackthorne."

"We'll fire you and get another sheriff."

"We'll run her out of that canyon."

"You won't have to fire the sheriff or force me off my land. I'll sell you the water."

The entire gathering turned around. Laurel had entered the saloon without their knowing. She walked forward to stand next to Hen. Their gazes met briefly before she turned to face the crowd.

"The sheriff is correct. I do own the canyon."

"Where did you get the money?" Estelle demanded. The inference was so pointed that several people colored in embarrassment.

"Not by refusing to pay my bills," Laurel replied.

It was Estelle's turn to flush crimson.

"You may begin the chute as soon as you like," Laurel said, turning back to the others. "I have just two requirements. You must begin the chute outside the sycamores. I don't want half the town stomping up and down my canyon."

"What's the other?"

"Sheriff Randolph has to be in charge of the project."

"Why him?"

"How much is it going to cost?" Estelle demanded.

"Five dollars a day to be paid in gold on the first of each month."

"But we don't need it all the time. Just when the wash is dry."

"Five dollars a day all year long, or you can't build your chute."

"But that's a hundred and fifty dollars a month!"

"You can't do that. Why, we—"

"You've heard Mrs. Blackthorne's offer," Hen said. "Now I suggest you discuss it among yourselves. When you're done, see if you can find someone among you who knows how to talk to a lady. If you can, send him to see Mrs. Blackthorne."

There was stunned silence while Hen escorted Laurel from the room.

"Sorry you had to hear all that," Hen said when they reached the street.

"Do you think they'll buy the water?"

"Sure. Is it so important?"

"With that money, I can take Adam and leave this town."

"Leave!" Hen had never thought in terms of Laurel leaving. "Are you that afraid of the Blackthornes?"

"Not just them. Myself as well."

Laurel turned away, leaving Hen more puzzled than ever.

And excited. She wouldn't be afraid of herself unless she were unsure of her reaction to him. After the way she had treated him, he wouldn't mind seeing her squirm a little.

But he had to be careful of his own feelings. It was all right to be attracted to Laurel—she was a beautiful woman—as long as he remembered he was not cut out for a permanent relationship. That was all too easy to forget when he was around Laurel Blackthorne.

Laurel walked back toward the canyon, her feet barely touching the ground. For the first time in her life, she would have some money. She would be able to give her son more than just the bare essentials. And after a time, they would be able to leave Sycamore Flats. She could go somewhere where justice wasn't determined by a gun, where men knew how to treat a woman without hitting her, where a woman unfortunate enough to have been abandoned by her husband wasn't treated like a soiled dove. She didn't know exactly where that was, but she'd find out.

Her first thought was to ask Hen. He must have traveled all over the West. He would know exactly the kind of place.

She wondered where he had spent the years of his adulthood, what kind of women he had known. Had he ever been in love with one of them?

She didn't know why she bothered thinking about him. She

had told him the truth. She didn't want a husband. She didn't want anyone else in her life. Adam was enough. As soon as she moved away, Carlin, the Blackthornes, and Sycamore Flats would all be forgotten.

But she didn't think she would ever forget Hen.

The late September sun beat down on Hen with merciless intensity. He was grateful to reach the shade of the trees along the wash. The sycamores seemed to stand still, holding their breath, waiting for the first rains. The willows hung just as listless in the gentle breeze, but the leaves of the cottonwoods rattled like dry seedpods. The parched soil of the stream bed crunched under his feet. It would take more than one heavy rain to start this stream flowing again.

Hen's boots crunched on a smattering of dry leaves as he entered the sycamore grove at the base of the mountains where the canyon walls rose three hundred feet into the air. Even though the long, dry summer had caused many plants to droop, their leaves coated with several months' worth of dust, the steady flow of the creek kept everything green, and the leafy canopy overhead was always thick and full.

He had come to talk to Laurel about building the chute. He was also going to ask her if she could keep Brimstone until Chuck Wilson rebuilt the livery stable. The big stallion followed behind him, sniffing the air curiously.

Hen was very much aware that this would be the first time Laurel welcomed his presence since he'd come to Sycamore Flats. He felt an increase in tension inside himself. Maybe she was welcoming *him*, not just his help. It hadn't felt like that when she invited him, but he hoped it was. He liked Laurel Blackthorne, and he wanted her to like him.

He didn't understand that. Most of the time, he preferred that people dislike him. That way they kept their distance. Even his family left him alone most of the time. He'd better watch himself, or he'd get more involved than he wanted.

He'd felt safe in the beginning because she kept driving him away. But she wasn't doing that now.

Laurel looked up when he rounded the bend in the canyon. Her eyes grew wide when she saw him leading the stallion. He wondered why just seeing her made him feel better. Maybe not better exactly, but different. He felt things more—enjoyed them more, too. And for the first time in his life, he was drawn toward someone, not repelled. Quite simply, he liked being around Laurel and Adam.

"Adam is off somewhere," she said, her eyes never leaving the stallion. Brimstone had a fearful reputation, one Hen reluctantly admitted was well-earned. He had been broken to saddle by being beaten. But rather than breaking his spirit, the brutal treatment had made him savage. It had taken Hen a year to win his confidence. Brimstone still distrusted men, but he was always well-behaved with women and children. He seemed to have nothing but curiosity toward Laurel.

"I know. He's with Jordy."

He had known her invitation was just for him to teach Adam. But he wanted to find out if her change of heart included him as well.

"I'm a little bit worried about that."

"Why?"

"Jordy is so big. And he's terribly rough. I've heard people say—" Laurel caught herself. "I'm sorry. I'm doing the same thing to Jordy that people do to Adam, judging him because of what his father did."

"People say all kinds of things about a kid with no pa and no place to call home." Hen felt a tinge of irritation. She didn't seem to have a thought that didn't have Adam at its center. It was as if nobody else existed.

"It's a good thing Jordy wasn't sleeping in the livery stable last night."

"He'd have gotten out. His kind always survives. Just like you."

She didn't seem to know how to take that remark, but he meant exactly what he said. Laurel would do what she must to survive. She was strong, indomitable, courageous. Only she had to learn not to use her strength to shield Adam. He must grow as strong and courageous as she, and he couldn't do that if she protected him from every difficulty.

His parents hadn't shielded them—their ma because she was too weak and their pa because he was too indifferent. That treatment had been rough on the Randolph boys, but it toughened them. There wasn't one of them who couldn't handle his own trouble.

"If you knew Adam wasn't here, why did you bring your horse?" Laurel asked.

"I wanted to ask if I could leave him here until Wilson rebuilds his stable."

"I've heard terrible things about him."

"He likes women and children." Hen suddenly chuckled. "But he'll go after Zac every chance he gets."

"Zac?" Laurel said, all at sea.

"My youngest brother," Hen explained. "Brimstone doesn't like him one bit. Good judge of character."

"What a terrible thing to say about your brother."

"Wait until you meet Zac."

"I doubt I ever shall meet any of your family."

He started to tell her about Tyler, but changed his mind. He was still angry at Tyler for coming. He didn't need anybody's protection. For years, rustlers had avoided the Circle-7 because they feared him. Now to have Tyler—Tyler! of all people, a soft-spoken loner who felt more at home with herbs and spices than he did with people—thinking he could protect Hen hurt the older brother's ego.

"Here, let Brimstone smell you."

Laurel extended her hand. Brimstone threw up his head and snorted, but when he didn't scare Laurel, he reached out to nibble her sleeve. Laurel smiled.

"He's testing me, isn't he?"

"She's seen through your disguise, old boy. Guess you'll have to behave now." She was testing him, too. He didn't know exactly how, but she was measuring his every response.

Still, she was different when she wasn't trying to get rid of him. She smiled at Brimstone with more than just her lips. Her eyes held humor, understanding, appreciation for an animal who tested people to see how far they'd let him push them. She didn't mind about Brimstone. Why couldn't she be as understanding with him?

"You sure he won't hurt Adam?"

"Jordy handles him all the time. Do you still think you could learn to like me?"

"W-what?" The abruptness of his question startled her.

"The other day in town you said maybe. I just wondered if you'd made up your mind one way or the other." He was aware of holding his breath. He couldn't believe anybody's acceptance was this important to him. It had never been before.

"I like you," Laurel said, her gaze on the ground. "You're kind and thoughtful and good-looking and concerned for our welfare." She raised her gaze to meet his. "It would be rude to dislike you."

"I don't want you to feel like it's a duty."

"I don't. I mean, it would be if I didn't like you already, but I do, so it isn't."

"Does that mean I can come up here not only to teach Adam how to ride?"

Laurel looked flustered.

"I'll need to keep you up to date on the chute."

"That'll be fine," she said, apparently relieved.

He wondered if she was worried about gossip or about him. She looked uncomfortable, but not as if she wanted him to go. Instead, it seemed she didn't know what to do next.

Neither did he.

"Sheriff Randolph! Sheriff Randolph."

Hen turned to see Jordy and Adam running toward them. He couldn't help feeling irritated. This was the first time Laurel hadn't acted as if he were a viper, and the two rascals had to come breaking in on them after less than ten minutes.

"Mr. Collins is in town," Jordy said, between gasps for breath, "and he's mad as fire."

"Rustlers!" Adam managed to squeeze in.

"Hundreds of 'em," Jordy said. "They've taken all his cows, and he wants you to get them back."

Leave it to Peter. He never had known when to stand back and keep quiet.

"You go back and tell him I'll be along in a little while. I promised to help Adam with his horse."

"He wants you to come now," Jordy said. "Old Mr. Regen is with him. They went and got Mr. Norton, and he—"

"How many of them are there?" Hen asked.

"Six. They're tearing around your office like a bunch of caged cats."

There wasn't any help for it. Jordy was going to dance around him until he left. He liked the boy, but Jordy had started to stick to him like a shadow. Hen was discovering that a shadow could get in the way.

"I'd better go," Hen said to Laurel. "You think you can show Adam how to take care of Brimstone?" Hen asked Jordy.

"Sure. There ain't nothing to it."

Jordy took the reins from Hen. The big stallion snorted and half-reared.

"Don't you go getting smart with me," Jordy said, not the least bit intimidated by the stallion's show of temper. "You keep it up, and I'll tie you where you can't get no grass or water."

"Can I lead him?" Adam asked.

Laurel started to object, but Hen touched her arm. He shook his head when she turned toward him.

"Maybe tomorrow," Jordy said. "I better do it till he gets used to you. He don't cotton to strangers."

"I ain't no stranger," Adam said as he walked off at Jordy's side. "I seen him lots of times."

Hen watched the two boys walk off—Adam, so young, trying to act so big; Jordy, short and stocky, but as tough as the land that bred him. Two fatherless boys who seemed to think he held the key to something they needed. He wondered what would become of them after he left.

"Are you sure he won't hurt them?" Laurel asked.

"Don't try to steal him or ride him, and you'll be just fine."

"Are you going after the rustlers?"

"That's why they hired me."

"Be careful. The Blackthornes are bound to be mixed up in it. Damian has three brothers and a father who's mean as a snake."

"Do you care?"

She looked defensive, as if he'd attacked her and she was scrambling to find a defense. He shouldn't have asked that question. Curiosity was not a valid reason to expect her to share a confidence. As long as he expected people to contain their curiosity about what he might be feeling, he should do the same.

But it was different with Laurel. He wanted to know. It mattered.

"The father hates all Texans," she said. "It was a Texan who killed Carlin. And watch out for Allison. He's hunting a name as a gunfighter."

"I won't be going alone."

"They've been known to ambush a posse."

"I'll keep that in mind. I'll let you know before I go. I'll have to come get my horse."

Hen felt reluctant to leave. He had something to say but wasn't sure quite what. He sensed Laurel had similar feelings. It was an odd experience for him. He had always been so positive about everything. Even when he changed his mind.

"You can send Jordy along in half an hour. That ought to be enough time for Brimstone to settle down."

"When will you leave?"

"First thing in the morning. It's never good to let things like this drag on."

"Would you like something to eat?"

"No. I'll just head out without waking anybody."

"You're sure?"

"Yes."

He couldn't think of anything else to say, so he left, but he felt odd, as though he had come away and missed the whole purpose of his visit.

"I don't mean to go alone," Hen was saying. "But if we go down there with a dozen riders, we'll scare everybody off. I've got to catch them in the act. So far, we don't even know who we're chasing."

"What do you propose we do?" Peter Collins demanded. "We did what you suggested, but if I keep losing stock like this, I'll be reduced to a thirty-dollar-a-month hand inside a year."

"I'll take you and Wally," Hen said. "It's your ranches that have been hardest hit, and you know the land. Won't be more than one or two of them working together anyway. Either they're branding them and running them in with someone's herd, or they're gathering them in a canyon somewhere until they're ready to sell them."

"What do you want the rest of us to do?" Bill Norton asked.

"Go about your business as usual. If we need a posse, we'll let you know."

"You think it's Blackthornes behind it?"

"Could be."

"You won't get no posse," Peter said. "This town is scared to death."

"Now wait a minute—"

"You know they are. All you have to do is say Blackthorne and everybody starts to shake."

"That's a lie. There ain't—"

"We'll have time to thrash this out later," Hen said. "Get some sleep. I intend to leave an hour before dawn."

* * *

"The sheriff is going after the rustlers, and he's taking Wally and Peter with him," Horace Worthy told his wife.

"He'd probably have an easier time of it alone," Grace said. "I don't know much about Peter, but Wally can't get out of his own way."

Grace had a few more trenchant remarks to make, but the dinner hour arrived and she lost interest in rustlers.

"When is he leaving?" Tyler asked Mr. Worthy when his wife left to serve meals.

"First thing in the morning."

"Where's he going?"

"Over toward Cienega Wash."

"I won't be here to cook breakfast."

"I sorta thought you might not. You going to follow him?"

"Somebody has to watch his back. He won't."

Chapter Twelve

Laurel woke up with a start.

She had been dreaming of Hen. She had brazenly thrown herself at his feet. She had followed him, offering herself without shame, taking the crumbs he offered, hanging around him like a whipped dog when he ignored her.

Laurel blushed at the memory of such a dream. She would die before she'd let any man treat her like that. Not that she expected Hen would. Still, it was embarrassing to be dreaming of him. It was bad enough that thoughts of him filled her waking hours.

She hadn't been able to stop thinking of him since he left in the afternoon. He had been different. Usually he acted confident, businesslike, brisk, even impatient. But today he seemed reluctant to leave. Something had changed, something that made him more human, more approachable. She was sorry Jordy had come to tell him about the rustlers.

Then maybe she had it all wrong. Maybe she couldn't get him out of her mind because his horse was tethered less than a hundred feet from her front door.

Thinking of Brimstone made her remember what woke her. Brimstone was acting up. She didn't know how he usually behaved, but in her experience horses were quiet at night. He was stamping his feet and snorting, as though he smelled a cougar. There were no cats in the canyon.

She remembered something Carlin had said when they were in the midst of their mad ride along the Mexican border. He had said they could sleep soundly because his horse was better than a watchdog. Maybe Brimstone was like that. Hen had said he didn't like men. Maybe that was what he had smelled.

Laurel sat up in the bed and snatched up her shotgun from where it lay next to the bed. Moving quickly across the room, she raised her head carefully until she could look out the window without being seen.

At first she couldn't make out anything in the dark except Brimstone's milky-white coat. He was dancing about, his ears laid back. Something was very close, and he didn't like it.

Then she saw them. One, two, three, four men silently approaching the abode. It had to be the Blackthornes. Laurel dashed across the room and shook her son. "Wake up!" she whispered urgently. "The Blackthornes are here! Get the ammunition."

Laurel took down a rifle and a pistol and hurried back to the window. The men were halfway to the house. Laurel set the rifle against the wall and eased the shotgun barrel through the window.

"Don't come any closer," she called out. "I've got a shotgun."

"We just want the boy," Damian shouted back. "We don't want to hurt you."

Damian again. Would he never give up?

"Not if I have to kill every one of you."

"He's a Blackthorne. We mean to see he's raised one."

Laurel's reply was to empty the first barrel of the shotgun into the darkened yard. She had the satisfaction of hearing a yelp of pain. She knew the shotgun wouldn't kill anybody at this distance, but it could do a lot of damage.

"I've also got a rifle and a pistol," she called out just before she emptied the second barrel of the shotgun. She heard Brimstone scream. She hoped it was in fury rather than pain. Hen would never forgive her if she hurt his horse, but Brimstone would have to take care of himself. She had to protect Adam no matter what the cost. She hurriedly shucked the empty shells and dropped two new ones into the chambers.

"Dammit, Laurel, why can't you just hand over the kid?" Damian demanded.

"Why do you want him so much?"

"He's my brother's brat, dammit. Pa already gave him that horse."

"You can have the horse," Laurel called back, "but you can't have Adam."

"He can't take Sandy!" Adam protested, starting up from the corner.

"Keep down!" Laurel ordered. "I'm just trying to fool him."

She had to be careful what she said. Adam would risk his own safety for that horse. She didn't understand that, but she'd bet her shotgun Hen would.

Brimstone screamed again. He seemed to be fighting something.

"If we don't get Adam tonight, we will come again," Damian called out. "We'll have him in the end."

"Not if you're dead." Laurel emptied another barrel. She was tempted to reach for the rifle, but the men spread out, moving toward the canyon walls. They didn't realize that the house was built into the rock. The only way in was through the front door or the one front window.

"Are they still out there, Ma?" Adam asked in a frightened whisper.

"Yes."

"I don't hear nothing. What are they doing?"

"They're trying to get in and steal you."

"I don't want to be stolen."

"Don't worry. I won't let them touch you."

"Will the sheriff come?"

Laurel was ashamed to admit she'd been wondering the same thing, but she had dismissed the possibility. The canyon walls were very high. She doubted Hen could hear the shotgun in town even if he were awake. She had to depend on herself.

"He'd blast 'em," Adam said with a child's complete confidence in his hero.

"I can *blast 'em* myself," Laurel said, irritated that Adam should think so little of her ability to defend him. "And I will if they come any closer."

The men seemed to be in a quandary. Having failed to find a way to scale the nearly perpendicular canyon walls, they seemed to be trying to decide on a new method of attack. Behind them Brimstone had quieted, but every now and then he would snort and rear at a tree.

Laurel's gaze was drawn back to the four men still spread out across the yard. She couldn't cover them with her shotgun if they rushed her. She might get two of them, but two of them would probably reach the house before she could reload.

"Keep that rifle ready," she told Adam.

"This is your last chance," Damian called out. "Give us the boy and we won't bother you."

"No."

"We warned you."

The men started forward, balanced on the balls of their feet, ready to sprint forward at the first sound of gunfire.

"Drop your guns."

The voice came out of the night, cold and heavy with menace. The Blackthornes spun around, but the inky shadows cast by the sycamores hid the speaker. They searched in vain for a target.

"You've got just ten seconds, or you die where you stand."

A bullet whizzed by just inches from Damian's cheek. The four men froze.

"It's the sheriff," Adam crowed. Laurel had to grab him, or he would have run out the front door.

"You can forget about your lookout," Hen called. "My horse has him up a tree." There was a moment's silence. "It's a spindly tree. It could break any minute."

Laurel counted nine dull thuds as rifles and guns hit the ground.

"Your gun belts, too."

"We ain't done nothing," Damian Blackthorne said. "We were just trying to talk to Laurel."

"I heard three shots."

"All hers," Damian said.

"Is that true?" Hen called out

"Yes," Laurel answered.

Hen materialized from the shadows. "I'm waiting for your gun belts."

The men grumbled, but they unbuckled their belts and let them fall to the ground.

"Now you can go."

"You can't take our guns!" one of the other men exclaimed. "We ain't done nothing."

"I call threatening a woman and trying to steal her kid doing a lot."

"You can't prove that."

"I don't have to. I'm the one with the gun. Of course, if you'd like to try for one, go ahead."

"With you drawing down on us!" Damian exclaimed. "We wouldn't have a chance."

"About as much as you intended to give Laurel. Now you've got five seconds to get out of my sight, or I'm arresting the lot of you."

"What about Ephraim?"

"I'm arresting him for trying to steal my horse."

"We'll come back and get you," Damian said.

"You know where I live. In the meantime, you're keeping Mrs. Blackthorne up past her bedtime. Unless you want to do her washing for her, I suggest you hightail it out of here. There's a couple of fellas waiting at the bottom of the canyon to escort you out of town. I'll send someone with your horses tomorrow."

"It's nearly five miles," one of the men said.

"Be glad it's not farther. Get going."

Laurel watched as the Blackthornes departed in silence.

"Adam," Hen called, "collect these guns. I want to see to the man in the tree."

Adam was out the door and halfway across the clearing before Laurel could put her guns away and step out into the coolness of the night. She took the four gun belts from Adam. Ephraim was out of the tree with his hands tied behind him by the time she reached them.

"I wasn't trying to steal that horse," he protested. "He came after me. He's a killer."

"Hello, Ephraim," Laurel said.

Ephraim ignored Laurel. "You sure played hob this time," he told Hen. "Avery will come next time. He'll shoot you as soon as look at you."

Hen ignored Ephraim. He took the gun belts from Laurel and dropped them around Ephraim's neck. "I might as well take Brimstone along with me now. Save waking you in the morning."

"It seems like I'm always thanking you for saving me," Laurel said to Hen.

"That's what I'm here for," Hen said.

"You wouldn't have gotten past me if that damned horse hadn't nearly killed me," Ephraim said.

"Don't count on it," Hen advised. "Now get moving. Watch him, Brimstone."

Much to Ephraim's horror, the big white stallion started down the canyon behind him.

"He'll kill me," Ephraim said, trying to get beyond the reach of Brimstone's big, strong teeth.

"Then make sure you don't do anything he doesn't understand. You all right?" Hen asked Laurel.

"Yes."

Hen ruffled Adam's hair. "Looks like you got an experienced gun handler for a ma. It's not every woman who can handle a shotgun without ending up with a broken shoulder."

Laurel was thankful for the darkness. She felt herself blush with shame. Everything she'd said about Hen being a gunfighter came back to make her look like a hypocrite. She could only be thankful he was kind enough not to point that out.

"You'd better look after your prisoner."

"Can I help you take him in?" Adam asked.

"I'd rather you stay here and protect your ma." He turned to Laurel. "I want you to move to the sheriff's house while I'm gone."

"We'll be fine here."

"At least spend the night in town."

"They won't come back for a while." She sounded calm, but her mind was reeling.

He must have awakened with her first shot, then run all the way to get here so quickly. That was more than a man doing his duty. It was a man who had only one thing on his mind—so much so that when he awoke to the sound of distant gunfire, he could come to only one conclusion. He had come not knowing how many people he might be facing, oblivious to any danger to himself.

Now he was insisting that she stay in his house. She felt the familiar excitement that consumed her every time he came around. Only this time there was also a sense of amazement. He must care for her, at least a little bit. If not, he would never have thought of offering her his own house. She tried to tell herself to take some time to think, but she was fast discovering that hope wasn't a biddable beast. It leaped past all obstacles, ignored reason, crushed common sense underfoot, and needed only the slightest encouragement to embrace utterly impossible possibilities.

But Laurel knew that as nice as it might be to build harmless castles in the air while she washed the endless pieces of clothing that filled her laundry tub, hope had the power to hurt. And she had been hurt already.

"I'm not leaving until you promise," Hen said. "You can hold them off with that shotgun, but you can't drive them away. They could keep you holed up here until you starved."

"Not with you around."

"That's just it. I won't be around for a while. You're to spend every night I'm gone in the sheriff's house."

Laurel could feel her resolution failing. She wanted so badly to believe someone cared that she was almost willing to forget caution. Almost.

"I told you I'd be all right."

"If you won't go, I'll bring Sycamore Flats to you."

"What do you mean?"

"I'll deputize a dozen fellas. Three or four of them can take turns camping out in your yard."

"You're not serious."

"Name some men you trust."

"I don't trust anybody." She couldn't tell whether he was joking. He didn't act like it, but what he'd said was absurd. But if he was serious . . .

"Don't worry. I'll leave Jordy here to keep them in line."

Laurel couldn't help but laugh, a confused, somewhat distracted sound. This whole conversation was ridiculous.

"You can't really expect me to sleep in your house."

"Yes, I do."

"What will people say?"

"When they see what good care I take of you, they'll know I'll take care of them too. They don't have to know there's more to it than that."

"Is there more?"

"I hope so."

Laurel's heart beat so loudly that she was sure Hen could hear it. "Suppose I agree, then stay here." My God, her resolution had failed; she was giving in. Nothing felt right. Everything was in a jumble. She couldn't tell what she was doing anymore. She could only go where she felt she must.

"You won't. You'll keep your word to me."

Yes, she would. Even if she didn't want to. "Okay, but we're coming back here the minute you return."

"I sure hope so. I'd have to camp out by the wash if you didn't. Good night."

Hen didn't leave at daylight. The attack on Laurel caused him to postpone his departure. He doubted Peter and Wally would be happy, but he considered Laurel's safety more important than a few rustled cows.

"I'm letting you go back to your family," Hen told Ephraim after the man had eaten breakfast. "You can return their horses and guns. You can also take them a message."

"They won't be listening to any message from you," Ephraim said, still furious at being cornered by a horse and forced to spend the night in jail.

"You tell them I said to leave Laurel Blackthorne alone," Hen said. "They can steal every cow they can get their hands on, and I won't touch anybody I don't catch in the act. But if you harm that woman or her child, I'll burn you out and leave you dead to rot in the street."

"That's a mighty big boast for one man."

"I figure I can handle a hundred men who can't do better than attack a woman and a child under cover of night," Hen said, contempt in his voice. "Now get out. I'm sick of the sight of you."

Ephraim was hardly out of the office before Hen had forgotten him. He had a bigger problem to solve. He had made up his mind to convince Laurel to move down from the canyon. With the money she would receive for her water, she could live anywhere she wanted. But until she overcame her distrust of men, especially him, she wasn't likely to budge.

"You wouldn't think the Blackthornes would want the boy," Hope was saying as she laid out lunch. "They must have dozens of their own."

In her effort to be more like her hero, Hope had started to borrow from her brother's wardrobe. She wore a checkered shirt, boots, and a flat-crowned hat. Hen figured she would have worn pants if her mother had let her.

"Some people are clannish like that. They like to keep all the family together in one place."

"Why don't they want his mother, too?"

"I guess because she doesn't seem to like them very much."

"I didn't mean that. She's so beautiful, you'd think one of them would want to marry her."

That idea gave Hen an odd feeling. Laurel would never marry one of the Blackthornes. But why should he care if she did? It would solve one of his most pressing problems.

"I can't answer that."

"Maybe she'll marry somebody else. Maybe if Adam had a father, they won't want to take him away."

"Why are you so sure she'll get married?"

"She has money now. She doesn't have to stay in Sycamore Flats. She could go to Tucson or Casa Grande or some place like that. Lots of men will want to marry her. Mama says she's never seen a more beautiful woman. I think Miranda Trescott is just as pretty, but Papa says men would pick Laurel Blackthorne over Miranda any time. I don't understand that. Do you?"

Yes, he understood. Miranda's beauty could be likened to that of a porcelain figurine, perfect and fragile, not for touching. On the other hand, it was impossible to think of Laurel without wanting to touch her. The deep, rich colors of her hair and lips, the brilliance of her eyes, the creamy texture of her skin, the fullness of her slender figure—everything about her had a quality that fed the senses.

Yes, he understood all too well.

"I guess men and women like different things," Hope said.

"I guess so."

"What kind of man do you think she will marry?"

The thought startled Hen. Ever since Damian's attack, he'd had some hazy notion that she ought to marry for her own protection and to give Adam a father. He hadn't been thinking of her marrying anybody in particular. In fact, now that he thought of it, he realized he'd been thinking of protecting her himself. Of helping with Adam.

For as long as he was in Sycamore Flats.

He hadn't really thought about what would happen after he left. He supposed he'd have to see about talking her into moving somewhere where her lack of a wedding ring wasn't common knowledge. There were lots of good, upstanding men, who wouldn't care that she had made a mistake if it wasn't thrown in their faces every day.

"Mama says she won't find anybody she likes around here. If she was going to, she'd have found him already."

"Sounds logical."

Hope looked at him speculatively. "Mama says it's about time you thought about getting married yourself."

Hen flinched instinctively. "I'm not the marrying kind."

"Why not?"

"I don't know. Some people like staying in one place, having a nice home to come to each night, staying around people they like, knowing what they're going to do tomorrow and the day after that. That sort of life never appealed to me."

"What does appeal to you?"

He didn't think he'd ever asked himself that question. He'd been so busy running from things he didn't like, he'd never had time to ask himself where he wanted to end up. Stupid. Nobody ever got where they wanted to go by accident. "I don't know that anything appeals to me in particular. Right now, I just want to keep moving."

But he wasn't sure that was true any more. He didn't plan

to stay in Sycamore Flats, and he didn't plan to go back home to the Circle-7. But he didn't mean to keep roaming the rest of his life. He just hadn't found a place he liked well enough to stay.

Or a woman to stay with him.

He hadn't considered that. In all his thinking about the future, he'd never visualized himself as married. He supposed it was because Rose was the only woman who had ever won his unqualified admiration, but admiration was not a warm emotion.

"What kind of woman would you marry if you decided to settle down?" Hope asked. She almost seemed embarrassed by the forwardness of her question, but it was clear that she was vitally interested in his answer.

"I don't really know."

"Mama says every man knows exactly what he's looking for in a woman. He may not find it, but it doesn't stop him looking."

He wasn't looking. He never had. He didn't want to. "If I had to marry, I suppose I'd look for someone like Miranda Trescott—someone young, pure, and innocent."

But the words were no sooner out of his mouth than he knew they weren't true. He'd never thought of Miranda until just now. The one time she'd been in his office, he'd practically broken out in a cold sweat.

"I didn't know you'd talked to her more than once or twice," Hope said, obviously not pleased to see another woman find such favor in his eyes.

"I didn't say I wanted to marry her, but she is the type of woman a man can admire."

"You made it sound like you were nutty on her." Hope still looked petulant, but a little more hopeful.

"Don't you dare go tell her what I said."

"I'd never do that," Hope said. She jumped to her feet. "I'd better get back. Mama will be over here after me if I don't." She started to gather up the plates.

Although it seemed that his ideal woman had ceased to interest Hope, Hen found it nagging at him. He had always thought he wanted somebody like his mother, but now he knew he didn't. She had been a beautiful, gentle creature, and he'd loved her dearly, but she wasn't strong. He had assumed he could love somebody like Rose. She was strong, determined, and full of common sense, but somehow that didn't excite him. No man in his right mind would ignore a woman like Miranda Trescott, yet he'd never once thought of her as his wife. Now that he had, it didn't fit.

But he did think of Laurel, not as his wife, but as someone who interested him. Several times he had found himself wondering where she would be in several years, what Adam would be like, and every time he had found himself there also. Was that the kind of feeling that led to wanting to marry somebody?

It wasn't like that with Monty. He couldn't think about a woman without wanting to make love to her. Hen admitted that he found Laurel attractive that way. His dreams were all the proof he needed of that, but other feelings were stronger, especially the desire to protect her, to take care of her. He wondered what George would say.

Well, he could ask him. After Tyler's telegram, he was bound to be here sooner or later.

"You won't have to do this again for a while," Hen said to Hope as she was leaving. "I'll be gone several days."

"Will it be dangerous?"

"It depends on what we find."

"Everybody says the Blackthornes are vicious killers. If you get in their way, they'll shoot you dead."

"I expect I'll get in their way sooner or later."

"You already have. People are saying you'll be the first one they come after when they come to town."

"Is everybody expecting them?"

"Sure. Pa told me how your horse chased Ephraim down the canyon. He'll never forgive you for that. You'd better start watching your back. A bullet can't tell when a coward's pulling the trigger."

"I'll stay healthy," Hen promised. "If I get myself shot, I'm liable to have another brother show up."

"You sure Tyler's your brother?" Hope asked.

"Why do you ask?"

"He's not a thing like you. He spends all his time cooking and reading. The only exercise he gets is those rides he takes."

Hen knew he should have kept an eye on Tyler. He might have known he'd get up to something.

"Where does he go?"

"You'll have to ask Pa. That's who he talks to."

What the hell did Tyler think he was doing? Trying to be the hero? Hen didn't need protecting. He'd have to have a talk with his little brother when he got back. He'd never allowed anybody to dog his trail all these years, and he didn't mean to start now.

Chapter Thirteen

"What do you want me to do?" Mrs. Worthy asked Hen. "She won't listen to me any more than she does to anyone else."

"She's already promised to sleep in town," Hen said. "I just want you to make sure she doesn't change her mind."

"You think she might?"

"She didn't want to come."

"Then why did she agree?"

"Because I practically forced her." Mrs. Worthy's scrutiny made Hen uncomfortable. "I couldn't go after rustlers and leave her up there alone, not after two attacks. They could take an army up that canyon and half this town would never know."

"You knew."

"It's my job."

"Is that the only reason?"

"It doesn't matter whether it is or not," Hen said, annoyed that Mrs. Worthy seemed more concerned with his motives than Laurel's safety. "She likes you more than anybody else."

"I'll do what I can. I always did feel sorry for her, but she seems determined to see the worst in everyone."

"I wouldn't know about that. I just want her and the boy safe while I'm gone. Jordy will be staying with them. I've told him to come to you if anything goes wrong."

"Everybody's talking about how you've turned that boy around."

"Anybody could have done it if they'd taken the trouble."

"People don't always know what to do until somebody shows them."

Hen had the feeling that Mrs. Worthy wanted to talk about something else, and he was determined not to be drawn in.

"Maybe you could ask Miss Trescott to stop by and see her."

"I didn't know they knew each other."

"Well enough for her to get invited to tea."

Mrs. Worthy arched an eyebrow. "I'll do that." She smiled to herself, as though enjoying a private joke. "I wonder what Ruth Norton made of that."

"She was the one who extended the invitation."

Grace Worthy's other eyebrow rose. "If Laurel has conquered that citadel, she has nothing to worry about."

"Good. Now I'd better be going, or Peter Collins will be telling everybody I've dilly-dallied until the rustlers ruined him."

"Mr. Collins complains too much if you ask me. He ought to do more of his own work."

"That's what they pay me for."

"Perhaps you should think about that. The day might come when you won't be glad of the reputation."

"What do you mean by that?"

"Men don't usually remain gunfighters for long. Either they get themselves killed, or they give it up for some settled job."

"You sound like you've been talking to Laurel."

"I imagine all women feel pretty much the same. Now go catch your rustlers. Just don't do anything you won't want to have to explain to a son of yours fifteen or twenty years from now."

"I don't plan on having any sons."

"A lot of men don't, but they have them anyway."

Hen decided it was a good deal safer chasing outlaws than dealing with women. It seemed that no matter what he did, they wanted him to do something else. He should have told Hope that the ideal woman would accept him as he was.

"I just don't feel right about it," Laurel said to Mrs. Worthy. "If I hadn't given my word, I'd march myself right back up to the canyon."

"You don't want to do that. I'd have to go up there and stay with you." Mrs. Worthy chuckled. "I'd be so out of breath by the time I got to the top, I wouldn't be able to sleep. Then you'd have to sit up with me."

Laurel smiled, but it was a weak effort. Despite her promise to Hen, she had almost made up her mind to stay in the canyon. If it hadn't been for Adam's excitement at the prospect of spending the night with Jordy, she probably would have stayed, despite her promise.

The sheriff's unpainted frame house stood two doors away from the jail. It had three rooms up and three down and walls of painted board gone grimy with dust and age. The bare wood floors creaked. The lack of pictures and curtains gave the house an uninhabited look despite the serviceable furniture.

"You can stay with us if you don't feel comfortable here," Mrs. Worthy said. She looked around the sparsely furnished room. "I know it's not much, but men don't care as long as they've got a bed and a comfortable chair. And the town isn't going to spend any money it don't have to."

Laurel's uneasiness had nothing to do with the house or its furnishings. It had to do with the fact this was Hen's house, and she felt as though she was moving in with him. She knew Hen was miles away, but that made no difference.

"If it comes to that, it's better than my own house," Laurel said.

"With the money you'll be getting for the water, you'll be able to do something about that."

"I guess so." Laurel wasn't about to tell Mrs. Worthy that she would be saving her money so she could leave Sycamore Canyon.

"Hope will be over with your breakfast about seven o'clock."

"We can't—really we can't."

"We're contracted to provide the sheriff his meals. With him gone, somebody has to eat them."

"Give it to Jordy. I imagine he can eat as much as Hen."

Mrs. Worthy chuckled. "Twice as much, according to Hope. Now you get those boys settled and stop worrying. The sheriff will be back in a couple of days, and things will be back just like they always were." Mrs. Worthy turned toward the door. "Be sure to give me a call if you need anything. I'm just three houses away."

"I will. And thanks for being so kind."

"No trouble at all. I'm glad to know you're out of that canyon. I couldn't get a wink of sleep up there myself."

"I miss it already."

"I'm sure it's fine for those who like that sort of thing," Mrs. Worthy said, unconvinced. "Me, I like knowing I got people around me. There's cats in those mountains."

"They never come down the canyon."

"Never say never," warned Mrs. Worthy as she opened the door in preparation for her departure. "It's just tempting Fate."

Laurel listened to the sound of Mrs. Worthy's fading footsteps on the boardwalk with mixed feelings. She was relieved to have her privacy restored. At the same time, she didn't feel quite ready to be left alone with the overwhelming sense of Hen's presence. Agreeing to sleep in his house meant taking a step deeper into a relationship she knew was doomed from the beginning.

All day she had told herself she had only agreed because of the Blackthornes. If they were determined to take Adam, she was going to have to leave the canyon sooner or later. Adam would like it. Jordy was his first real friend. But as she climbed the stairs to break up the wrestling match she heard going on, she admitted that she had come because it made her feel nearer to Hen. Being nearer him made her feel safe and protected, a feeling she had grown to like.

Laurel got up, rinsed her coffee cup, and placed it on the shelf. It was time to go to bed. She couldn't put it off any longer. She picked up the lamp and began to climb the stairs. There was no sound from the boys' room. She held the light up as she stood in the doorway of Hen's room. It took an act of will to enter, to walk over to the bed, set the lamp down on the night stand, and sit down on the edge of the bed. She had to steel herself to keep from jumping up again.

This is stupid. You're a grown woman. It's foolish to act like you're getting into bed with a ghost.

She might not have minded a ghost. Hen's presence seemed real and concrete.

If Laurel hadn't known she'd be faced with explanations she'd be too embarrassed to make, she'd have gotten dressed and gone back to the canyon then and there. Never had she been so acutely conscious of a man's presence in her life. He could hardly have been more real if he had been in the room with her. Plucking up her resolution, Laurel managed to dispel some of the unnerving feeling, but this evening had made one thing crystal clear.

Her feeling for Hen had moved beyond friendship.

Laurel forced herself to pull back the sheet and get into bed. But as soon as she did, a new set of sensations assaulted her. She became intensely aware that her body was touching the same spots that Hen's body had touched just hours earlier. She felt herself stiffen, her muscles clamp down and become rigid.

By a concentrated effort, she forced her body to relax. But as her muscles loosened and she felt some of the tension melt away, she became aware of a feeling deep in her belly that she hadn't felt in years.

Her relationship with Carlin had lasted only a few weeks and had been very unsatisfactory, but she could remember that first night and the anticipation of giving herself to a man she thought she loved with all her heart. She felt some of that now—the sensations that radiated out to all parts of her body, the shivers that had nothing to do with cold, the feeling that something terribly exciting and very wonderful was about to happen.

She could smell a faint trace of Hen.

She could imagine him lying in this bed, his head on this pillow, the weight of his body causing the bed to emit soft protests, his long limbs reaching to the end of the bed. The image of him as he walked away from her sprang into her mind sharp and clear, his trim body encased in pants almost too tight for comfort. The spiraling sensation in her belly became more intense, her limbs more tense.

Did he sleep naked? She couldn't block out the mental image of his lean body brushing against the sheets, the same sheets that now rubbed against her arms and legs. Almost instinctively, her body settled more deeply into the bed. The vision of his long, powerful legs caressed by the sheet became more powerful, more vivid.

Laurel was startled to find her nipples beginning to harden. Her entire body was in a state of physical arousal just thinking about Hen Randolph.

Once again she struggled to force her body to relax, to ignore the roughness of the sheets that made her think of hands running over her skin, to ignore the chill of anticipation, to ignore the desire that had lain untapped within her for so long, to ignore the feeling that only Hen could soothe this deepening ache.

She forced herself to go over the list of things she had to do the next day. When the image of Hen intruded too powerfully, she spoke out loud. When she could think of no more tasks, she started to inventory the pieces of clothing to be washed, the pieces that required extra boiling, the pieces that required extra soap and scrubbing, the people who wore their clothes until the dirt was ground into the fibers, the people who wore everything only once before having it laundered.

Gradually Laurel relaxed enough to grow sleepy. Whenever thoughts of Hen threatened to disturb her hard-won calm, she concentrated even more fiercely on her work. Gradually the fatigue of a long day preceded by a virtually sleepless night caught up with her, and she sank into an uneasy slumber.

Hen haunted her dreams just as completely as he had her waking hours.

Avery Blackthorne pulled his horse to a stop in front of the livery stable. Already the charred remains had been removed, and a new building of freshly cut lumber was rising on the same spot. He rode a poor horse, wore dusty clothes, and slumped in the saddle. No one would know his name, but he had the look of a Blackthorne. If his tall stature and distinctly Spanish features didn't attract attention, his eyes would. They looked like cat's eyes, yellow and tawny, and were a stark contrast to his dark skin and black hair. They were also hard and cruel, something he normally used to his advantage. Today, however, he kept the brim of his high-crowned hat pulled low over his face to avoid recognition.

He had come to town to kill Hen Randolph.

"Where can a man stable a horse?" he asked one of the men cutting a piece of lumber to length.

"Try over the blacksmith's place," the man said without looking up from his work. "He's got a small corral."

"And where can I find the blacksmith?"

"Right over there," the man said, pointing to the next building. "You can hear the hammering from here."

Avery dismounted and led his horse the short distance to where the blacksmith worked on a wagon hitch.

"I was told you might be able to put up my horse," Avery said.

The blacksmith looked up from his work. "Long enough for Wilson to finish his new stable, but you'll have to talk to him about feed."

Avery walked his horse over to the corral and began to strip the saddle from his back. "When did the livery burn?"

"More than a week ago. The new one ought to be finished in a couple of days."

Avery lifted the saddle from the horse's back and placed it on the corral fence. He put the blanket beside it. "How did it start?"

"Probably one of those damned cowpokes who don't pay no attention where they drop their cigarettes when they're drunk."

Avery slid back the bars and hazed his horse into the corral. "You're lucky nothing else caught fire." He looked at the collection of wooden buildings that made up the town. "Could have burned the whole place down."

"That's why we're building a chute to the creek in the canyon up yonder," the blacksmith told him. "We mean to start on it as soon as the sheriff gets back."

Avery leaned against the corral fence. "I heard you got a new one."

"Nobody stays long."

"I hear this man's different."

The blacksmith paused to look up from his work. "He seems capable."

"How long does he mean to be gone?"

"Can't say."

Avery took the time to roll a cigarette. He took a few puffs, drawing the smoke deep into his lungs before he exhaled. "Where can I get something to eat?"

"Over at the Worthys' restaurant. You can't miss it. With that new cook they got, people can't stay out of the place."

"Thanks," Avery said and ambled down the street. He hadn't seen Sycamore Flats in nearly eight years. The place had grown. He'd have to give that some thought. There might be some real possibilities here.

He had no trouble finding the restaurant. The aromas of fresh bread and seasoned beef were impossible to miss. From the number of people inside, he gathered no one had tried.

Avery sat down at the only empty table. "I'll be with you in a minute," the woman said when she came to collect the dishes left by the last customers.

"No hurry," Avery assured her, but she was back quickly.

"We have only one thing today," she said.

"Then dish me up a plate."

The food arrived in a few minutes. Avery studied the people in the restaurant as he ate his food.

"Who owns this place?" he asked when the woman came to bring his pie.

"I do. I'm Mrs. Worthy."

"My compliments to the cook," he said. He waited until she had refilled his coffee cup and turned back to the kitchen. "Could you tell me where I can find Laurel Simpson?"

Mrs. Worthy's expression froze. "I don't know anybody by that name."

"I think she goes by Blackthorne now."

Mrs. Worthy's gaze narrowed and became more intense. "If that's who you want, why didn't you say so?"

"I didn't want to give her a name she doesn't have a right to."

"As to that, there seems to be a difference of opinion."

"I don't guess it matters what I call her."

"It will if you call her the wrong name."

Avery's eyebrows bunched. He wasn't used to opposition

from women. In fact, he wasn't used to opposition at all. It was with some difficulty that he controlled his temper.

"How should I ask after her?"

"If you must ask for her—and I'd advise you to do some thinking on that question before you make up your mind—you'd better call her Mrs. Blackthorne. Then everybody will know who you're referring to."

"You don't act very friendly."

"I'm never friendly to people trying to stir up trouble."

"What makes you think I'm doing that?"

Mrs. Worthy gave him a hard stare. "If there's nothing else you want, I have other customers."

Avery sat quietly until his anger subsided. Then he ate his pie, drank his coffee, tossed some money on the table, and left. He reckoned that not everybody in town would be quite so stingy with their information. In less than thirty minutes, he found several people only too happy to tell him where to find Laurel Blackthorne and delighted to learn her maiden name, the only name they felt she had a right to. Avery also learned that Adam was spending most of his time out of the canyon. Avery found him riding his horse back and forth, teaching him to turn with the pressure of a knee.

"That's a mighty big horse you've got there," Avery said, stepping from behind a paloverde tree. "Who taught you to ride like that?"

"The sheriff."

Avery's face tightened. He had heard more about this sheriff than he liked. "He must be a good rider."

"He's good at everything."

Avery decided it was about time he did something about Hen Randolph. "You ought to be careful of strangers. You never can tell what they're up to."

"The sheriff ain't no stranger. He's been here for weeks and weeks."

"I heard he beat your uncle and threw him in jail."

Adam pulled his horse to a halt. "He tried to steal me. He hurt Ma."

"He only wanted to take you to your family. He didn't mean to hurt your ma."

Adam glared at Avery. "Yes, he did. He hit her."

Avery decided he had to take a different tack if he was going to get anywhere with this child. "He shouldn't have done that. It's not right to hit a boy's ma."

Adam looked a little less defensive.

"It's not right to depend on strangers when you've got family."

"Ma says I don't got any family except her."

"Sure you do. You got three uncles and a grandfather who gave you that horse. If you don't treat him nice, maybe he'll take it back."

"No!" Adam jerked on the reins as if he was about to run away.

Avery sensed that he had finally found a weak spot. Adam obviously loved his horse. "Wait!"

"Ma says I'm not supposed to talk to strangers."

"I'm not a stranger. I'm your grandfather."

"I don't believe you," Adam said stubbornly. "I don't know you."

"If you let me talk to you, you'll know me. Then maybe you'll like me."

"Are you going to try to steal me?"

"No. I want us to become friends. I want you to help me against the sheriff."

"No. He's a good man like my pa."

Avery paused. Obviously Laurel hadn't told the boy how Carlin had died. Maybe this was the wedge he needed. "You love your pa, don't you?"

Adam nodded.

"You think he was a fine man."

Adam nodded again.

"Do you think your pa would like you siding with some

stranger against his family?" Avery immediately knew he had hit Adam where he was most vulnerable. "Do you think he'd be proud of a son who helped a sheriff hurt his brother?"

"I didn't help him," Adam said.

"You didn't stop him."

Adam looked confused. "I'm too little."

"You could help me punish him."

"He didn't do anything wrong."

"He hurt your father's brother. He's out right now looking to hurt some more."

"He's looking for rustlers."

"That's what he said, but he's looking to kill Blackthornes. What kind of boy would you be if you helped a stranger shoot your uncles?"

Adam's chin held its stubborn jut, but Avery could see he'd planted a seed of doubt. He was satisfied with his progress for the day. "I just want you to help me keep him from hurting any more of your father's brothers. Will you do that?"

Adam didn't answer.

"You won't be much of a man if you let people go around hurting your family. People will start to think you're yella."

"I'm not yella!" Adam shouted.

"I know you're not. No Blackthorne is yella, but other people might think different. You think about what I said. We'll talk again tomorrow."

"I'll tell my ma."

"This is men's business," Avery said, looking hard at Adam. "Only a sissy would talk to his ma about men's business."

"I ain't no sissy."

Avery smiled. "You think about what I said. You got nice hands, a good feel for a horse. You'll make a top rider one of these days."

"It sure has been quiet the last couple days," Horace Worthy said to his wife. "I hate to criticize your cooking, but it ain't up to Tyler's."

"You're not hurting my feelings," Grace said. "I'd rather eat his cooking any time."

"You think he'll be back?"

"Not until his brother returns."

"You think he can do any good? After all, he's just a cook."

"He's not just a cook. He's a *man* who can cook."

Laurel had kept her mind off Hen all day, but the moment she started washing his clothes, that became impossible. Every thought she had tried to push aside, every feeling she had denied, every hope she had ignored rushed in upon her like an incoming wave. Hen had been gone three days, and she had been conscious of each passing minute.

Sleeping in his bed every night had made the pressure to think of him overwhelming. But after three days of trying to think of anything but Hen, she was finally forced to admit that she was incapable of common sense where he was concerned.

She couldn't avoid the question that had begun to haunt her. Did he care for her, or was he just a particularly gallant sheriff with a weakness for single widows and fatherless boys? Common sense told her his letting her spend her nights in his house was merely part of his duty. But her heart wouldn't let her believe it. She didn't *want* to believe it.

She would miss him if he never came around again. She looked forward to his visits. Well, maybe not exactly looked forward, because they were never regular, but she couldn't deny her excitement and pleasure when he did come.

That was a terribly hard admission to make. It went against everything she wanted. But she had to be honest. No matter what kind of man he might be, she liked him better than any man she'd ever met.

She scrubbed a little harder on the shirt, wrung it out, put it in the rinse water, and started on another.

She smiled to herself. Hen was something of a dandy, at least by Sycamore Flats standards. He was so tall and slim.

The crisp contrast of the black and white he wore created a startling impression, especially in a hot, dusty town like Sycamore Flats. Every day he put on a clean shirt, which he wore with a string tie, dark vest, and black pants. He wore nothing more than once. Laurel wondered if all rich Virginians were accustomed to such extravagance.

It was getting harder and harder to remember that he was a gunfighter. She even wondered if he was quite the gunman everybody thought he was.

She hoped not.

But if he wasn't, he was in grave danger. Any rustling within a hundred miles probably involved the Blackthornes. They *were* killers.

Adam came running into the yard. "The sheriff's back," he shouted, "and he's got two rustlers."

Laurel wrung out the shirt, dropped it into the rinse water, and ran after Adam, drying her hands on her apron as she went.

Chapter Fourteen

The crowded streets gave the town a festive atmosphere. Everyone wanted to see whom Hen was bringing in. Women who had completed their shopping and men and boys who ignored their chores milled about gossiping and speculating. Laurel caught a final glimpse of Adam as he ran off with Jordy. He'd been given so much freedom lately that she no longer expected him to stay by her side.

"A lot of people seem to have found reason to be in the street," Grace Worthy observed.

Laurel turned in surprise. She had been so intent on watching for Hen, she hadn't seen Grace approach. "I suppose they're hoping this will mean an end to the rustling."

"Nobody cares about rustlers except Peter and Wally. They're anxious to see who he caught."

"Why?" Miranda Trescott asked. She had come up just after Grace.

Laurel almost cringed. Being around Miranda reinforced all her feelings of inferiority. Laurel knew she was prettier than Miranda, that her breasts were fuller, her curves more rounded and alluring, yet she felt almost ugly standing next to the other woman. Miranda was young and pretty, beautifully dressed, self-possessed, friendly, and good-natured. She was as kind as she was unfailingly cheerful, and she looked every inch a lady. Laurel no longer denied that she hoped for more than friendship from Hen, but being around Miranda made her realize how farfetched such dreams were.

"They're hoping he caught Blackthornes," Grace Worthy said. "And they're hoping he didn't."

"That doesn't make sense," Miranda said.

"It does when you know the town. People suspect the Blackthornes are behind the rustling. Maybe some of them are, but they all stick together. If we try to hang any of them, the rest will take it out on the town."

"But that's against the law," Miranda said.

"There's the law out here," Grace said, pointing to Hen as he rode into town.

"Surely the townspeople—"

"The town hired Hen Randolph to do what it couldn't," Grace said.

Grace Worthy's words struck Laurel with blinding force. She had thought only of the harm guns could do, of Carlin's death, of the kind of people who used guns for selfish gain. She had forgotten that unless men like Hen were willing to use a gun, lawless men would rob and kill at will.

Hen had told her that, but she had been so blinded by her determination that Adam would never have anything to do with guns, by her own fear of being abandoned again, she couldn't see it. Good people had to use guns, even if they didn't want to, because evil people would.

The crowd tightened up as Hen came down the street. Two men rode behind him, their hands tied behind them, their feet tied under the saddle. Peter Collins and Wally Regen brought up the rear, smiles on their faces.

"William says this may not stop the rustling, but it ought to slow them down for a while," Ruth Norton said, no more immune to curiosity than anyone else.

"Depending on how the town reacts," Grace said.

"What do you mean?" Miranda asked.

"Someone let Damian Blackthorne out of jail after he attacked Laurel," Grace said. "If the town feels the same way about these men, there won't be anybody but Peter and Wally standing behind the sheriff."

"And William," Ruth said. "How could his own children be safe if he doesn't?"

Laurel was forced to admit that somebody had to stand up against the Blackthornes. She couldn't do it herself. The townspeople probably felt the same way. But she didn't know why Hen had to be the one. There must be plenty of other men willing to use their guns for two hundred and fifty dollars a month.

"Are those men Blackthornes?" Miranda asked.

"They're Carlin's cousins," Laurel said. "Corbet and Doyle."

"How do you know?" Grace asked.

"You forget I was married to a Blackthorne. I spent a month with them before—"

She stopped. She had never told anyone what Carlin had done to her. She wasn't about to start now.

"—before I left."

"Will the Blackthornes take their side?"

"They won't have to if somebody lets them out of jail," Grace said.

"But this isn't the same. Not that attacking you wasn't a

terrible thing," Miranda hastened to assure Laurel. "But this is stealing cows."

Grace chuckled. "You're learning fast. Yes, cows are more important than women. That just might make the difference."

Tyler rode in an hour later. He passed behind the town, keeping in the wash until he reached the livery stable. Jesse wasn't about, so Chuck Wilson came to take his horse.

"Give him some oats," Tyler said.

"He looks rode hard," Wilson commented.

"He was."

"See anything?"

"Yes. The Blackthornes are behind the rustlers."

"You going to tell the sheriff?"

"I think I'll keep it to myself for a bit. The sheriff and I aren't getting along too well at present."

"He don't like taking advice from his little brother, eh?"

A hint of a smile broke the solemnity of Tyler's expression. "Something like that."

"I don't know who he is, but I'd swear on my grandmother's honor he's a Blackthorne," Grace told Hen. "He had the look of one, especially those nasty yellow eyes."

"And he didn't do anything but eat his dinner and leave?"

"Not that I saw, but you can bet there's others that saw more. That man's not here for no reason."

"No, not if he's a Blackthorne," Hen agreed. "I guess I'd better look into it."

"I guess you'd better if you want to keep your head on your shoulders—and that little boy in his mama's arms."

"You think he's after Adam?"

"I don't know why this Blackthorne should be any different from the rest."

"Yeah, I saw Avery," the blacksmith said. He was fixing a broken trace for the stagecoach. "He left his horse here a bit."

"Did you see where he went?"

"He asked about a job. I told him to see Phil Baker, the bullwacker. He always needs help."

"You ever seen any other Blackthornes on your stage?" Hen asked Sam Overton, the stage driver, who was keeping an eye on the blacksmith.

"A few times. Didn't pay much attention."

"I'd appreciate it if both of you would keep your eyes open for strangers about," Hen said.

"You expecting trouble, Sheriff?"

"Hoping it won't come, but I mean to be ready if it does."

"I want everybody to understand the rules before we start," Hen said. "If you don't stick to them, we can't build the chute."

"What's so important about rules?" someone asked.

"Nothing, if you don't break them," Hen replied.

About twenty men had gathered at the livery stable. They had loaded several wagons with freshly cut lumber from the pile that had been collecting behind the stable over the last several days. Armed with hammers, saws, and nails, they were about to begin the chute to bring water from Sycamore Canyon.

"How long is this going to take?" one man asked. "I got work of my own to be doing."

"Months," another replied. "That damned canyon is at least half a mile from here."

"We'll need a million pieces of lumber."

"That'll cost a fortune."

"It won't cost as much as it would to rebuild the town," Hen said. "Let's get going. Just remember. No one is to go past the mouth of the canyon."

Laurel watched the procession approach the canyon with mixed emotions. She was pleased that construction had finally begun. The sooner they finished, the sooner they got their water and she got her money.

The anticipation of that day was delicious. She had felt so helpless, so desperate, for so long that the prospect of the freedom to do as she pleased, go where she wanted, was almost too wonderful to believe. She knew nothing of the outside world. Her imaginings might have no foundation in reality, but they were wonderful because in her dreams nobody questioned her about her marriage or regarded her son from narrowed eyes. She and Adam would be just like everybody else.

It made her uneasy to see the men in her sanctuary. But even though Hen made her more nervous than all the rest, she was pleased to have him near. She had given up trying to pretend that she didn't like him, that she didn't think about him nearly all the time. She had stopped telling herself that she hoped he didn't care about her. She had stopped saying he was a terrible model for Adam. She had stopped pretending she wasn't on the verge of falling in love with him.

But she wasn't foolish enough to think he was in love with her.

Adam ran by. Laurel grabbed him by the collar. "It's time to get back to work," she said. "We still have a lot of clothes to get done today."

"Can't I watch?"

"You've seen enough. After you've done your chores, maybe you can ride your horse with Jordy."

"Okay."

He gave in too easily. Something was bothering him. She didn't know what. Half the time she thought she was imagining things, but every once in a while he would look withdrawn and remote, as if he were puzzling over something. He looked like that now.

"Do you think Pa would want me to help his brothers against the sheriff?" Adam asked.

The question was so unexpected that Laurel had no ready answer. What on earth could have gotten him to thinking about something like that? "Your father wasn't like his brothers," Laurel said.

"Wouldn't he want me to help my uncles?"

"It's wrong to help anyone who hurts other people, even if they are family."

Laurel was relieved to see that her response seemed to have answered Adam's question. His expression lightened, and he ran on ahead.

"It won't take me a minute to fill the tubs," he shouted as he entered the wash. "I'll be done before you can make it up the canyon."

Laurel laughed, her mood lighter.

Hen noticed Adam watching from among the sycamores. "You want to come down where you can see?" he asked, surprised the boy hadn't been at his elbow all morning.

Adam shook his head. "Ma said I was to stay out of the way."

Hen wasn't surprised at Laurel's order, but he was surprised that Adam had obeyed. "She won't mind as long as you stick with me."

Adam stayed among the sycamores.

Hen gathered some lumber, put it on a small hand cart, and started up the trail.

"Ma said you weren't going to build it in the canyon," Adam said.

"This is something special."

"What is it?" Adam asked, unable to control his curiosity now.

"Come with me, and I'll show you."

Adam followed without a backward glance.

Laurel looked up, startled, when Hen pushed the cart of lumber into the clearing. She felt her heart leap into her throat. She never saw Hen any more without feeling that rush of excitement, the dizzying sensation that made it hard to breathe. He looked the same as always—white shirt, black vest and pants, and flat-crowned hat. Devastating. Laurel didn't know how she had ever thought she could ignore him, how she could ever have imagined going through the rest of her life and never seeing him again. He was already part of it.

Her brow knitted as she realized that the cart was loaded with lumber. They weren't supposed to do any building here. She glanced down the trail, but no one followed Hen. What was he meaning to do?

"We started building the chute today," he said as he set the cart down. "You shouldn't be bothered by the hammering once they move away from the mouth of the canyon."

Laurel could hear a steady rat-a-tat-tat of several hammers, but the sound was muffled.

"What are you going to do with that lumber?" she asked.

"Build a chute from the creek."

Laurel had never thought of asking for a chute of her own. It certainly never occurred to her to ask Hen to build it. He was a gunfighter. What did he know about building?

"I don't need a chute."

"I'll bet Adam would appreciate not having to carry all that water day after day."

"Let him, Ma," Adam begged.

"I'm afraid I can't afford to pay for it."

"It won't cost you anything. Consider it a goodwill gesture."

"But they're already paying me for the water."

"This is for offering. You want to help?" Hen asked Adam.

Once more Laurel was aware of a change in Adam's attitude toward Hen. He didn't seem at all anxious to help, and Laurel knew it wasn't because he was lazy. Whatever had been said about helping the sheriff against his father's brothers had upset him. Laurel wondered if Shorty Baker had said it. She knew it wasn't Jordy. He worshipped Hen.

"I really don't need a chute."

"I'm going to build it anyway."

Laurel smiled in spite of herself. Hen smiled back. "I knew you would. You've never done a single thing I asked you."

Hen looked startled by that remark. "I'm just doing—"

"You're just doing what you think is best for me," Laurel

finished for him. "Every man I ever knew did the same. I survived the rest, so I suppose I'll survive you."

"I was hoping we could get along a little better than that."

Why did he have to look at her with just a trace of a teasing smile on his lips? It made her want to do something extremely foolish, like throw her arms around his neck and kiss him hard and fast. She wouldn't, but she'd been wanting to for days. Ever since he came back from hunting rustlers.

She tried to ignore that feeling, but it wouldn't go away. "Maybe we can. I'll try very hard not to mind having my wishes ignored."

"And I'll try not to remember I'm a bad influence."

Laurel flushed. "I'm sorry I said that. I was wrong."

"You approve of gunfighters?" Hen asked in apparent disbelief.

"No. But when you brought in those rustlers, I realized there's a difference between gunmen and an officer of the law. Somebody has to do your job, and I'm glad it's you." She could tell he wanted to explore the issue further, but she didn't feel she was on firm ground. "I've got to get back to work. If you're going to build Adam's chute, you'd better get started."

She watched them go down to the creek, Adam acting much like his old self again, full of questions and dancing around Hen as if he were the center of the universe. That made Laurel feel better. Already she was coming to depend on Hen to help with Adam. It hurt her to know he could do things with her son she couldn't, but she told herself to stop wasting time complaining about what couldn't be changed. Instead, she ought to be glad Adam had someone like Hen to model himself on.

She didn't want to admit it, but she was becoming too dependent on Hen, too. Their need scared her.

I hope he's going to stay. If he's not, I wish he would leave right now.

As she watched him work, she reminded herself that he hadn't said a word about liking her. She could be reading too much into his actions. Yet there was something different about the way he did things. She could feel it. Something very personal, as if he were doing it especially for her.

Laurel liked that feeling. He might be rude and overbearing and ignore her wishes, but he could be kind and thoughtful too. He worried about her and cared about the way people treated her. He worried about her safety. She loved the feeling so much that she was even jealous of the time he spent with Adam, the attention he lavished on her son. But she had only herself to blame if Hen spent time with other people. She pushed him away every time he came around.

She picked up a dress and pushed it into the hot, soapy water. As the material soaked up the water, making the dress almost too heavy to be lifted out again, she made up her mind not to drive Hen away anymore. She would allow Adam to go down to Sycamore Flats to see Hen any time he chose. She wanted her son to be as much like this strange man as possible.

She watched in surprise as the chute began to take shape. Hen might be a gunfighter, but he obviously knew how to handle a hammer as well as a gun. She hoped he knew how to handle her heart. She feared it was permanently in his keeping.

Hen was surprised that neither Laurel nor Adam were at the house when he arrived the next day. They must have finished their work for the day and gone off together. He hoped they hadn't gone far. He headed toward the meadow. He didn't consider going back to the men working below. The chute was progressing rapidly. It was still a long way from town, but once they left the rocky part of the canyon, they could practically build the chute on the ground.

Adam was riding Sandy when Hen reached the meadow. He was proud of the boy's progress. Hen had to look harder before he saw Laurel. She had found a depression in the rock that formed a shallow cave. It allowed her to remain out of the sun and have a complete view of the meadow at the same time.

"Mind if I join you?" he called out as he climbed up the jumble of rocks which gave access to the cave.

"If you think the men can get along without you."

"They prefer it," Hen said, as he reached the rock shelf that formed the base of the cave. "I'm still an outsider here."

"Come join two more. Are you hungry?"

Laurel had spread a blanket over the rough, cold surface of the rock. From a small hamper she offered him bread and cold ham.

"No, thank you," Hen said. "Hope did her best to fatten me up already."

"She didn't succeed."

Laurel looked away, but not before Hen glimpsed a look in her eyes that caused excitement to leap within him. Gone were anger, disdain, disapproval, disgust, irritation, annoyance or any other look that said she wished he would go away. Instead this was a look of such longing, such need, such naked hunger, Hen couldn't be certain he had interpreted it correctly. He had never thought of Laurel as a cold woman, but until now he had felt only the cold shoulder of her rejection.

He had never understood why some man hadn't marched his way into the canyon and into Laurel's heart. She was a beautiful woman. The stunning contrast of her black hair and clear white skin was dominated by her luminous dark-brown eyes. Surely someone had longed to caress her cheek and run his fingers through the silky luxuriance of her hair. Surely at least one man had wanted to lose himself in the depths of those eyes. There must have been at least one who could see she was a woman to be cherished.

Hen dropped down next to Laurel. Her gaze was fixed on Adam. She didn't move away. He felt the tension escalate inside him, felt a stinging heat slowly eddy into every part of his body. He hadn't touched Laurel since that first day. His fingers itched to touch her again.

Laurel turned to him. "Where were you before you came here?" she asked unexpectedly. "You don't belong in this place.

I'd swear you've never been a sheriff before." Her expression showed nothing of what she might be feeling. Even her eyes were shuttered.

"Am I that bad?"

"No. You're just not like the other sheriffs we've had. You've got a reputation as a gunfighter, but you haven't killed anyone. You're rude, almost brutal to people, yet you've taken Jordy into your own house. Everybody in town knows you don't drink, gamble, or womanize."

"Is it so important to understand me?"

He shouldn't have asked that question. As long as he didn't care what anyone thought, he was in control of his life. Yet even though he felt uneasy—like a man stepping on ground that might prove to be quicksand—he couldn't turn back.

"Yes, it is important."

With a sigh, he yielded the information. "I was born in Virginia, but we moved to Texas when I was eleven. For the last twelve years I've traveled all over. I don't suppose I come from anywhere anymore."

"Is that all?"

"You want to know how I got started with a gun." She didn't have to blush or nod her head or even look embarrassed. He knew what she wanted. "I came upon two rustlers about to hang my brother. They already had the rope around his neck. I had about one second to make up my mind."

"Why didn't you stop after that?"

"People kept wanting what we had, and they were willing to kill to get it. Somebody had to protect the family. It sort of fell to me."

"So you've got a family." Why was everybody so surprised he had a family? Hen wondered.

"I've got six brothers."

"No sisters? I suppose that's why you dislike women."

Hen couldn't have been any more shocked if she had struck him. "I don't dislike women."

"It's nothing to be ashamed of. Lots of men do."

He opened his mouth to deny her charge, but let it close again. He didn't dislike women. He had simply distrusted them his whole life. "My mother was blinded by her obsession for my father. She died when he left her. Monty and I were thirteen, Tyler and Zac a lot younger. I never forgave her for that."

He had never told anyone that. He had never even admitted it to himself. Yet even though he felt guilty for feeling that way, he was relieved. He had hated her for not loving them enough to find the strength to go on living, for their sake if not for her own, and he had taken it out on every woman he had met since. Rose was different, but she hadn't been able to eradicate the anger or teach him how to love.

"Not all women are like that," Laurel said softly.

"I know."

He wanted to make Laurel understand that he didn't want to be this way. He just was, and he couldn't do anything about it.

Chapter Fifteen

"Doesn't that make any difference to you?" Laurel asked.

"Maybe."

She was leaning on her hand. It was only a few inches from his. He traced a vein with his fingertip. She jumped.

"Why did you do that?"

"What?" She was suddenly defensive.

"Jump like that."

"It surprised me. You haven't touched me before."

"You haven't let me."

Laurel sat up, pulling away from Hen. Hen reached out and took her hand. She felt terribly uncomfortable. She desperately wanted to take her hand back, but couldn't figure out a polite way to do it.

"Are you afraid of me?" Hen asked.

"No."

"You act like it."

"I guess I don't like being touched very much."

When she had welcomed him to sit with her, she'd never suspected their conversation would become so personal, nor wander to such painful subjects. She was probably the one to blame. She'd asked him first.

But as she sat there, Hen holding her hand, waiting, she realized that she *was* a little afraid of him, just as she was of all men. Deep down, she was afraid he would be like her stepfather and Carlin. She pulled her hand out of his grasp and moved away.

"You said you didn't think of me as a gunfighter anymore."

"I don't."

"Then why are you afraid to let me touch you?"

"I'm not."

"Then don't move away."

He moved closer and ran his fingers along her arm. Laurel sat still, struggling to decipher the feelings that rushed through her like a herd of stampeding longhorns. There was the chill his touch caused in her. That was easy to identify. It was the same coldness she had felt with Carlin after he had hit her that first time. There was the same desire to run away she had felt when her stepfather started drinking.

But along with this, she felt the warmth she remembered from that day when Hen took care of her bruises and cuts. He had such a wonderfully gentle touch. It comforted and reassured her. It was so smooth, as if his fingertips were covered with silk. Carlin's touch had been rough.

She also felt a tingling excitement that radiated all over her body from the point where he touched her. That unfamiliar feeling had begun churning in her belly again. It made her want to move closer to Hen, want to touch him, want him to touch her.

"What happened?" Hen asked.

"Nothing."

"Who hit you?"

It wasn't the question. He had seen past her defenses. The sound of his voice carried understanding and sympathy. It was like absolution wiping away ten years' accumulation of resentment, the bottled-up rage, the stifling fear that had virtually held her prisoner in her canyon.

Her resistance collapsed. She wanted to tell him. She *needed* to tell somebody. All the years of keeping it to herself had weighed too heavily for too long. The hard core of anger was breaking up. She had to let go.

"My stepfather used to beat me," she said.

She pulled away from him. Her hands moved nervously within each other. Hen took them and held them in his hands. She felt some of his calm flow into her.

"He used to get drunk. I learned to hide. When I got older, I would leave the house. I'd sleep anywhere I could until he sobered up."

"What about your father?"

"He was killed when I was five. My mother had to marry somebody. She chose my stepfather."

"What happened to her?"

"She died when I was nine."

She could remember the years she had spent waiting for her stepfather to come home, yet being afraid once he did.

"I married Carlin to get away from him." She tensed, expecting Hen to say something, but he continued to sit quietly, holding her hands, giving her comfort. "I was sixteen. He was twenty-two. He was so handsome and exciting. He rode a beautiful horse with a silver-mounted saddle and was forever laughing. When he came courting me instead of one of the older girls, I lost my head. After he told my stepfather he'd kill him if he ever touched me again, I'd have followed him to the end of the earth."

She nearly had. She would never forget the rides from one village to another, always looking for fun.

"He got drunk. He hit me when I complained. Finally, when I wouldn't ride with him anymore, he left me for one of the older women. He was killed a few weeks later trying to steal a valuable bull from a Mexican rancher."

She felt the pressure on her hands increase.

"I didn't find out I was going to have a baby until two months later. My stepfather threw me out. I haven't heard from him since."

She felt hot tears pool in her eyes. She wasn't crying because these two men left her. She was crying for herself, all the years she had lost, all the dreams that had died so long ago. She sniffed and turned to look into Hen's eyes.

"Carlin married me."

Laurel didn't know why it was so important that Hen believe her. She didn't even know why she tried. If her own stepfather couldn't trust her, how could she expect a stranger to?

"I'm sure he did," Hen said.

"No one else believes me, not even his family. Why should you?"

"I've only known you to lie once, and that was to protect Adam."

Laurel had to take her hand away long enough to dab tears that began to flow like spring rain. The doubt surrounding her marriage had been a barrier that separated her from the town. She wouldn't allow anybody to call Adam a bastard. Nor would she allow anybody to treat her like a whore. Hen's blind faith in her meant far more than any acceptance the town could offer. Because of that, she wanted to explain to him. She wanted him to know. She wanted him to understand.

"I told Carlin I wouldn't make love to him until we were married. He spent a week dragging me all over the territory before he gave in. I don't know where we were. We had been riding all day and arrived after dark. He found a minister who was trying to make it as a farmer. His wife and brother-in-law acted as witnesses. I've tried to find them ever since, but I can't."

"Don't worry about it," Hen advised.

"I can't stop. You don't know what it's like to be an outcast. As long as people don't believe I was married, they won't accept me or Adam."

"I've been an outcast my whole life."

"But you've got a family, brothers—"

"You can be as alone in the middle of your family as in a strange town." Hen moved closer to Laurel. She didn't object when he put his arm around her. "You don't have to fight everybody. Just concentrate on what makes you happy."

"It's not that easy."

"I never said it was. Somehow the right things always seem to be the hardest. You can't change that, so don't worry about it. You're a fine woman. You've raised a fine boy. You've supported the two of you all these years without help from anyone else. You even managed to homestead this canyon. I don't know any other woman who can say as much."

His words were balm to her soul. She had fought for so long to force people to give her the respect she deserved that it was absolutely wonderful to find Hen ready to give that and more. Laurel felt a warm glow of happiness spread through her. For the first time in years, she felt like a real human being. Even though she was poor, she felt equal to any woman in Sycamore Flats. They might not believe her, but Hen did.

Yet it wasn't enough. She wanted more. She *needed* more. She had held herself aloof from everyone for so long that she hadn't realized how vulnerable she would be when she finally let down the barriers. Without the hard shell of anger and defiance that had supported her all these years, she felt defenseless. She needed Hen's strength to lean on when the hurt came.

But he hadn't offered that. She would have to stand alone. But could she? She fought against a pressing need to cry, but she lost the battle. Silent tears rolled down her cheeks.

"I'm sorry," she said, wiping her cheeks with a napkin. "I never cry."

Hen took the napkin from her and dried her tears. "Maybe that's why you're crying now."

She stared at him. "How can you understand so much and—"

"And still be a gunfighter?"

She averted her eyes rather than give an answer she was ashamed of the moment the words formed themselves in her thoughts. "Don't you like people?" she asked.

"I like you and Adam."

Laurel forgot other people. "Adam likes you, too."

"How about you?"

She couldn't look him in the eyes. She was afraid she would see the same emptiness she had seen before. How could he care for her or Adam and look at them with empty eyes?

"Are you still afraid of me?"

"Not anymore. Maybe I never was. I didn't know you very well at first."

"Do you know me now?"

She turned to face him. His eyes were softer. She couldn't see what was in them, but they were no longer empty. "No," she whispered. "I don't know you at all."

"Do you want to?"

"Adam would like to."

"I asked about you." He put his fingers under her chin and raised her head until she had to look at him.

"Yes," Laurel said.

She was surprised how hard it was to say that single word. It was as if her ability to express love had been shelved for so long that each word had to be taken down and dusted off one at a time.

"You won't send me away if I come to see you instead of Adam?"

"No."

She wouldn't send him away ever again. He had beaten down the last of her resistance. With it had gone the defenses that had enabled her to stand alone for so long. She needed his strength. She wasn't sure she could survive without it.

She was in love with him.

That thought should have shocked her, but it didn't. It seemed too natural.

Hen's lips brushed her own. The effect was electric. It was the merest touch, almost too gentle to feel, but not even Carlin's most passionate kisses had affected her so profoundly.

"Did anyone ever tell you you're beautiful?" he asked as he kissed her again.

"Not in a long time."

"They should have. Even Hope says you're the loveliest woman in town."

Laurel didn't see how he could think her lovelier than Miranda Trescott, but she didn't feel the slightest need to argue with his opinion.

"I thought so that first day in the canyon."

"I distinctly remember you saying I wasn't looking my best."

"You were still lovely."

Laurel feared she would melt. He might be cold and heartless with others, but he knew what to say to her. "Did you really think that? Did you really like me even then?"

"I liked the way you fought Damian, the way you got up after he hit you. But I guess what I liked best was the way you looked at me." Hen chuckled softly. "I knew if I put a foot wrong, you'd tear into me just as fiercely."

"Do you have a liking for wildcats?"

"If that's what you are, I guess I do."

"You can get scratched up mighty bad."

"I have three brothers who married spitfires, and they've never been happier. Could be they know something I don't."

Laurel had accustomed herself to Hen's touch, his thoughtfulness, his gentle understanding. But she wasn't prepared when he took her in his arms and kissed her. This time there was nothing gentle or hesitant about it. It was hungry, hard, and hot. Laurel felt drained. At the same time, she felt about to burst with a kind of energy that was one part excitement, one part anticipation, and one part disbelief. She didn't know what the other parts might be. She didn't care.

She threw her arms around Hen and gave herself up to his embrace. It was impossible to think of reality or consult reason when he held her in his arms. She thought she had put away all the dreams that died with Carlin, but Hen had brought them to life again. Only now they were even more vibrant, even more extravagant. Being in Hen's arms wasn't the fulfillment of her dreams. It was the creation of a new one.

"Let go of my ma!"

Adam's cry of protest was like a bucket of cold water in the face, jerking Laurel back to reality with dizzying force. Adam was pulling on Hen, beating his arm, trying to force him to release his mother.

Laurel removed herself from Hen's embrace. "It's all right," she said, taking the child in her arms. "He's not hurting me."

"Go away," Adam said. "I don't like you."

Laurel flushed with embarrassment. "Adam, you don't mean that. Apologize to the sheriff."

"I do mean it," Adam insisted. "I want him to go away."

"Okay," Hen said, backing away from Laurel a little. "I'll go away, but I mean to come back. I still haven't finished teaching you how to ride a horse."

"I don't want you to teach me anymore."

"I don't know what's gotten into him," Laurel said. "He's never been like this." She felt herself blush. "Maybe he thought you were hurting me. He's never seen anyone kiss me."

"Or maybe he's jealous."

"I suppose that's it," Laurel said, unsure, hoping such a simple explanation could account for this startling change in her son. Adam climbed into Laurel's lap and threw his arms around her neck as though he were shielding her from Hen.

"Okay if I come back tomorrow?"

"Yes."

"Maybe you'll feel a little different," Hen said to Adam. He smiled at the child, but the boy failed to respond to his warmth.

"I don't understand—" Laurel began.

"Don't worry about it," Hen said, getting to his feet. "I'll come by tomorrow to let you know how things are going." He paused. "I meant what I said about that first day."

Laurel watched, bemused, as he headed out of the meadow and down the canyon. Only thirty minutes had passed, but nothing was the same as when Hen had appeared in her meadow. So many impossibilities had been transformed into bright, shining hopes. So many barriers had vanished as though they had never existed. For the first time since her father died, she wasn't afraid of the future. As long as Hen was part of it, she would be safe.

She felt Adam release his hold on her and start to pull away. "And now, young man, suppose you tell me why you behaved so badly to a man who has done nothing but be kind to you from the moment he set eyes on you."

To Laurel's surprise, Adam burst into tears, turned, and ran away. She stood there, mystified by the bewildering changes in her world.

Hen wasn't nearly as in control of his emotions as he wanted Laurel to believe. He had known he was drawn to her, but the strength of that attraction had surprised him. He had never expected to start kissing her, yet the moment their lips touched, he felt he had waited his whole life for that moment. He could count on one hand the women he had kissed. In no case had he found the experiment worth repeating.

That wasn't so with Laurel. His fingers itched to caress her again. He wanted to hold her in his arms, even if he could do no more than that. It calmed a restlessness in him, soothed a deep-seated irritation. Somehow the emptiness inside didn't seem quite so profound, nor the ache quite so painful.

Funny thing about that ache. It had always been there. He had assumed all men felt that way, sort of empty, separated from others, emotionally cut off. He figured it was part of being able to stand alone without depending on others.

Now he knew it had nothing to do with that. His soul was like a desert, dry and cracked. Laurel and her son had brought a little moisture, a little caring, and the soft green of new-budded life.

It felt good.

He wasn't sure that would be enough, but neither was he sure how much he wanted—how much he dared let himself want. Until he could decide, he'd concentrate on seeing that Laurel was safe. He had to convince her to move into town. When his job here was done, he'd have to convince her to leave Sycamore Flats altogether. There were hundreds of other towns. It shouldn't be too difficult for her to find suitable work elsewhere.

Of course she ought to find a husband and get married again.

Hen didn't find that solution—the perfect one, he admitted—to his liking. How could he be certain the man would treat her as he ought?

He'd have to be careful who courted Laurel, but it shouldn't take long. She was a lovely woman. Given the right clothes, she would be breath-taking. There was no reason why she should settle for some farmer. If he took her to San Antonio or Austin, she could find herself a rich husband.

But his sense of satisfaction was short-lived. As soon as he reached town, Jordy caught sight of him. When the boy came running toward him, an ear-to-ear grin on his face, Hen remembered the change in Adam. He didn't understand it. Obviously something had happened, but what? Maybe Jordy would know.

"His name's Avery Blackthorne," Jesse McCafferty told Hen. "He's staying a couple of miles out of town. Drives the route to Tucson for Phil Baker."

"Does he hang around town?"

"No more'n he'd have to for his job."

That didn't make Hen feel any better. He couldn't see any reason for a Blackthorne to be in the area unless it had to do with Adam. He must not be trying to steal him. He'd had plenty of time to try that already. What was he up to?

"You ever seen him around Adam?"

"Naw. Not likely, either. That kid's as skittish as a puma."

"You know when he starts a run?"

"Sure. He's got to come here for his horses."

"Let me know next time you're expecting him? I want to get a good look at him."

Chapter Sixteen

Laurel mounted the steps to the Norton home, but even her most determined effort could not make her use the knocker right away. She had very mixed feelings about this visit.

Hen Randolph's arrival in Sycamore Flats had made her realize that she was tired of being alone, of being a recluse, of never laughing or having friends, of never being invited to join any gathering. She no longer wanted to stand alone against the world. She doubted she had anything in common with the Nortons, but she intended to accept Miranda Trescott's offer of friendship.

She lifted her hand and knocked.

Seeing her rough, chapped, red hands resurrected her feeling of inferiority. She hid them in the folds of her dress. That only made her miserably aware that her clothes were poor by anybody's standard. The dress was old, one she had made that first week of marriage when Carlin was pleased enough to give her some money. It didn't fit very well anymore. Her body was no longer so unformed.

Miranda opened the door. "I was afraid you might not come."

Laurel smiled despite the tension that made her face feel like a frozen mask. "I was tempted," she admitted as she stepped inside.

"Come on in. Aunt Ruth will be down in a minute."

The Nortons owned the biggest two-story house in Sycamore Flats. One glance convinced Laurel that it must also be the most elegantly furnished. The brightly painted walls were covered with pictures; curtains hung at every window. Upholstered chairs filled the rooms, and rugs covered most of the wood floors. The table was set with blue-tinted china and a painted tea pitcher. Laurel felt completely out of place. But even as she was feeling small and insignificant and fervently wishing she could slink back to her canyon and never come out again, she remembered what Hen had said.

You've supported the two of you all these years without help from anyone else. You ought to be very proud of that. She couldn't have so little faith in herself when he had so much.

"Could I offer you some tea?" Miranda asked.

"Please."

"Sugar and cream?"

Laurel nodded. She had no idea what it would taste like. People she knew drank only black coffee. Sugar and cream sounded wonderfully rich and decadent.

Mrs. Norton came in bearing a plate of sandwiches, which she set down in front of Laurel. "I'm putting them close to you so I won't be tempted," she said with a slightly stiff smile as she seated herself across the room. "You're far too thin. I'm not."

Laurel took one of the sandwiches and bit into it. Chicken. In a land where beef and bacon were virtually the only meats, it was a delight to taste this light, well-seasoned meat. The tea was hot, sweet, and rich from the generous helping of cream. But the best thing about the food to Laurel was that she hadn't had to fix it. She could hardly remember eating anything she hadn't prepared. The conversation proceeded at a leisurely pace. Grace Worthy's arrival was a welcome addition, and Laurel gradually felt more comfortable.

"I'm glad to see the sheriff has been looking after you," Grace said. "It's about time somebody did."

The effect of her words on the gathering could hardly have been more startling if someone had thrown a sidewinder into their midst. Ruth Norton stared at Grace Worthy. Miranda stared at Laurel. Laurel stared at the sandwich in her hands. Grace Worthy stared at everybody and smiled with satisfaction.

"I told him he had to talk you into moving into town. You're not safe in the canyon by yourself."

Now that the conversation was on safe ground, the tension in the room relaxed.

"No woman should live in such an isolated place by herself," Ruth Norton said. "It isn't proper."

"Proper or not, it's all I have," Laurel said. "And I have been safe up until now."

"Why aren't you safe now?" Miranda asked.

Laurel felt as if she were in a frying pan and each lady was adding wood to the fire beneath her. She wished Grace Worthy hadn't introduced the subject, but she guessed she was trying to force her to do something for her own good. She knew Miranda's interest was genuine. She was certain Ruth Norton still disapproved of her, but she had to admit there was a certain fairness in the woman, a sense of humanity hidden most of the time by her very stiff exterior. Laurel wondered whether Ruth Norton might not have her own insecurities. Maybe she felt intimidated by a younger and more beautiful woman.

That thought made Laurel feel so much better that she almost didn't mind explaining things that weren't anybody else's business.

"Carlin Blackthorne was my husband. Adam is his son. The Blackthornes want to take him away from me."

"That's disgraceful," Miranda exclaimed. "We can't allow anyone to steal a child from his mother."

"We agree," Grace Worthy said. "That's why I'm trying to get Laurel to move out of that canyon. The sheriff doesn't strike me as the kind of man to stay here forever. Even if he did, Laurel can't go on depending on him. There's already talk about the attention he's paying her."

"Goodness me, what could people be saying?" Miranda asked. "Isn't the sheriff supposed to protect the citizens?"

"Sure he is," Grace Worthy replied, "but any time a man pays attention to a pretty woman, you're going to get talk."

"I don't think you can say he's *paying attention* to me," Laurel protested.

"Doesn't he go up to see you every day?"

"He comes to tell me about the progress of the chute."

"You could see that for yourself, couldn't you?"

"I prefer to stay in the canyon."

"I imagine the kind of attention she'd receive from those men would be quite unwelcome," Ruth Norton commented. "But you must acknowledge, my dear, people are going to wonder. Mr. Randolph is an extremely handsome man. People will always be curious about anything he does."

"Let them stay curious," Laurel said, pique causing her to speak sharply. "They never believed the truth before. I don't expect they will start now."

Mrs. Norton didn't seem very pleased with Laurel's answer. "There are other reputations involved," she said, her tone and manner a reprimand. "It would never do for people to think Mr. Randolph a philanderer. His discredit would harm the reputation of any young woman to whom he showed special attention." Mrs. North eyed her niece with special meaning.

"Don't be ridiculous, Aunt Ruth. The sheriff hasn't shown any partiality for me."

"You can't expect him to show any *pronounced* partiality in such a short time," Mrs. Norton replied, at her most formal, "but you can't deny he has been very nice in his attentions."

"He's nice to everyone."

"But that niceness takes on a special meaning when an eligible bachelor is paying attention to a single young woman."

Not being one to beat about the bush, Grace Worthy asked point-blank, "Are you saying the sheriff has intentions toward your niece?"

"I would never presume to speak for the sheriff or my niece," Ruth said, as coy as a woman of her age and disposition could be, "but he's from a very wealthy Virginia family that's positively bristling with important people. Did you know the Confederate General Robert E. Lee is a member of his family?"

"It could be some other Randolphs," Miranda said.

"I asked him," Ruth said, looking almost smug. "He's related to a president and a chief justice of the Supreme Court as well. I ask you, who in this town is more suitable to become his wife than Miranda? I don't think she would be averse to his attentions."

Miranda blushed.

"It's news to me that he's looking for a wife," Grace Worthy said, her tone sharp. "In fact, the gossip seems to be that he's given every female except Laurel a wide berth."

"His behavior has been extremely proper. It's easy to tell he was born a Virginia gentleman."

"It's been my experience that men go straight to what they want," Grace said, impatient with Ruth's pretensions, "especially when it's a woman. I don't think you should go building any great expectations," she said to Miranda. "Men who've reached the sheriff's age without marrying are remarkably slippery characters, especially if they're also rich and good-looking. If he's all your aunt says, there must have been dozens of females chasing after him with nets."

Ruth laughed. "I doubt they would go that far, but you've got a point. He's not going to be easy to catch."

"I don't mean to *catch* anybody," Miranda said. "I like the sheriff very much—how could I not?—but I have no romantic interest in him. Nor he in me."

"Well, time will tell," her aunt said. "In the meantime, I think we ought to consider some additions to your wardrobe. The seasons here are nothing like Kentucky."

"Not in the least," Grace Worthy agreed. "You won't believe . . ."

Laurel's mind was numb. The rest of the conversation faded into an indistinct murmur. Hen was from a wealthy, aristocratic family. She was nothing but the stepdaughter of one petty thief, the doubtful wife of another. He couldn't possibly fall in love with her. She ought to be grateful he was interested in protecting her.

She looked at Miranda—cool, stately, perfectly dressed, always knowing exactly what to do. That was the kind of wife a man like Hen Randolph should have. Even if he did like Laurel, he would never think of marriage. Men like that didn't. A little dalliance maybe, something more if she was willing, but nothing permanent.

Laurel stumbled to her feet. "I must go," she said, trying desperately to appear calm. "I don't like to leave Adam alone too long."

"That's all the more reason you ought to think about moving down here," Grace Worthy said. "With a whole town to watch him, you wouldn't have to worry as much."

"I'll think about it." Anything to get out of that house.

"You'll have to come again," Miranda said. "Soon."

"I don't know. I'm awfully busy."

"You'll have more time once you get the money for the water," Ruth Norton said.

"Of course. I hadn't thought of that," Laurel said. "I'm used to having to work all the time."

Laurel didn't want to be rude or seem ungrateful, but if she didn't get out of that house in about two seconds, she was going to start screaming. "I'll let you know. I really do have to go."

She turned and fled.

People who spoke to her as she hurried down the street were clearly startled when she didn't answer, but she didn't dare stop. They expected her to be rude. That would be old news before dinner time. If she started crying in the middle of the street, they'd be talking about it for days.

"Going home already? I thought you ladies would have your heads together half the afternoon."

Hen!

Laurel's heart thumped painfully in her chest. Her body seemed incapable of movement. She felt heat burn her skin. He was the one person she didn't want to meet, the one she was least prepared to face. She couldn't look up, at least not yet. If she did, she might faint dead away.

Hen fell into step beside her. "Did they say anything about your moving into town?"

"Yes."

"Are you going to?"

"Not yet."

She wanted to scream she would never move into town, where she would have to come face-to-face with him a dozen times a day, especially if he married Miranda. She had to get as far away from him as possible. Her world had started to fall apart the moment he came to Sycamore Flats.

"When?" Hen asked.

"I don't know."

"Will you think about it?"

"Yes." Never! But she'd tell him anything just to get him to leave her alone.

"Why are you in such a hurry? Are you upset?"

"No."

"Look at me," Hen said, but Laurel kept walking. He kept up with her and asked in a softer voice, "What's wrong?"

"Nothing."

"I know you."

"Nobody knows me. I don't even know myself anymore."

They had reached the wash behind town. Hen took her hand and forced her to turn and face him. "Did one of the women say something to hurt your feelings?"

"No. They were extremely kind, especially Miranda."

They had been. At least they had tried to be. Ruth Norton had no idea she had virtually plunged a knife into Laurel's heart. She thought only of her niece, a wonderful girl who fully deserved a husband as rich and kind as Hen Randolph.

"Then what's wrong?"

"I guess I'm tired of people trying to run my life for me," Laurel said, lashing out in her pain. "I'm tired of people telling me where to live, what to do, what to think, when to do it, who I should be afraid of, what I should wear, what kind of job I should have, what I should do with my money."

"They're only doing it because they're worried about you."

"Well they can stop. You can tell yourself I'm fine. I'm going to be fine. I've always been fine. Now I've got work to do. I'm sure you must have rustlers to catch."

"I caught them."

"Then go throw some drunks into jail."

"The saloons haven't been open long enough."

"Then go talk to Miranda Trescott. I've got work to do. And please don't walk me home. I can find my way."

"I'll be up in the morning. I hope you'll be feeling better by then."

"I'm sure I will be," Laurel said with a sniff as she stalked off. Then she stopped and turned back. "Thanks for being worried about me." She turned and almost ran from Hen. She knew she wasn't being fair, but she couldn't take any more. She had to be alone.

Laurel set her basket down and leaned against the tree. It seemed she had picked up more laundry today than any other day in her life. She had already sent Adam back up the canyon with all the burro would carry. She had so much left over that she had to stop and catch her breath. She was uncharacteristically tired because she hadn't gotten any sleep last night.

She couldn't help but glance toward the sheriff's house. She knew he would come up to the canyon today. After spending the whole night trying to decide what to say to him, she had finally decided not to say anything. How can you tell a man you really don't mind if he falls in love with another woman, that you'll get over your broken heart somehow?

You couldn't. She couldn't.

She would try to pretend nothing had happened. She didn't know if she could do it, but she would try. In the meantime, she might as well get going. The laundry wouldn't walk up the canyon by itself.

She heard the sound of hoofbeats as she bent over to pick up the clothes. She looked up to see a horseman ride out of town, cross the wash, and head out toward the desert.

Avery Blackthorne. What was he doing in town?

We'll come back and get you. And when we're done, we'll tear this town apart.

She remembered every word of Damian's threat. If Avery was around, it meant they were getting ready. Her first thought was for Adam. She relaxed when she remembered that she had already sent him up the canyon. But he couldn't run free any more, not with Avery around.

She had to tell Hen. Maybe Avery meant to lie in wait for Hen, to shoot him in the back. Laurel picked up her basket and headed toward the sheriff's house. She was startled when Hen came to the door, fully dressed and ready to ride.

"I thought you'd still be in bed."

Hen stepped outside. "Jordy is. I don't like to wake him."

What kind of man would leave his own house so a nine-year-old scamp could sleep late? She didn't think she would ever understand him.

"Avery Blackthorne is in town."

"Did you know you look particularly lovely in the morning?"

His response nearly rendered her speechless. It was the last thing she expected him to say. She blinked.

"I said Avery Blackthorne is in town."

"It guess it's the morning light. It makes your skin almost translucent. I never knew skin could look like that."

Laurel wondered if he had gone crazy or if she had. Here she was trying to tell him that his life was in danger, and he was talking about her skin. The worst part was, she *wanted* him to talk about her skin. She wanted to simply stand there drinking in every wonderful word he said.

She pulled herself together with a jerk. She had to make Hen understand. Avery had come to Sycamore Flats to kill him.

"Avery is the oldest. He's the leader."

Hen turned toward the east. The sky was light, but the sun had yet to rise above the horizon. "It has a wondrous effect on your hair as well. It's so rich and black."

"Will you listen to me and stop talking about my skin and hair!" Aware that she had practically shouted the words, Laurel forced herself to calm down. "I just saw Avery ride out of town. He wouldn't be here unless he's come to kill you."

"Why don't you want me to talk about your hair?"

"Avery Blackthorne means to kill you. Doesn't that mean anything to you?"

"He's been here about a week now."

Laurel could hardly believe her ears. "You've known all that time?"

Hen nodded.

"And you haven't done anything?"

"What am I supposed to do? He hasn't broken any law. He has as much right to be here as I do."

"There must be something you can do. You can't just let him go anywhere he pleases until he kills you. Or steals Adam."

"I don't think he means to do that, but keep Adam at home for a while." Hen put his fingers under Laurel's chin and lifted it to the light. "I can't get over how black your eyes are this morning. There's not even a hint of brown."

In frustration, Laurel slapped his hand away.

"Don't you understand? Avery means to kill you!"

"You should always be seen in morning light. You can't believe how vivid you are."

"All right, don't listen to me. Ignore Avery. Get yourself killed. But don't tell anybody you weren't warned. You're just too crazy to listen."

"I won't ignore him."

"Then why won't you do something?"

"What do you want me to do?"

"Quit. Go to another town."

"If a man starts running from the Avery Blackthornes of this world, he'll be running all his life. He's got to stay and face them if he wants to call himself a man."

"Spoken like a true gunfighter," Laurel shot at him. "Don't use your head. Just your guns."

"Have you ever seen me kill anybody?"

"No, but Avery will try to kill you. It's all he knows."

"Then I'll be ready for him."

"You can't be ready for somebody like Avery. He would shoot you in the back."

"Then I won't turn my back on him."

"Don't be so pigheaded. It won't do you any good to be a dead hero. You act like you're not even worried."

"No point in worrying about something that may never happen. May as well take things easy. Then if trouble does show up, you won't be all tense and liable to do something you shouldn't."

Laurel grabbed her basket of clothes.

"Okay, *take things easy*. And plan your funeral while you're at it. Don't expect me to have anything to do with it. I wouldn't lift a finger to bury a man who doesn't have the sense to try to save himself."

Laurel headed up the wash unconscious of the weight of the

full basket. Stubborn, conceited, hard-headed Hen Randolph was determined to get himself killed. She didn't know whether he thought she was a silly woman worrying about things that didn't concern her, or whether he thought Avery Blackthorne was an overrated gunman. Whatever the reason, he wasn't going to do anything to save himself.

She had to help him. She might be so mad at him she could hit him, but she couldn't stand by and let him get killed, even if he didn't love her. She ought to go wake up Mrs. Norton. If she was so anxious to have Hen marry Miranda, let her get gray hair worrying over him.

But she knew she wouldn't do it. Hen had gotten into this trouble because of her. She would have to do something.

Only she didn't know what.

Laurel handed her letters to the postmistress.

"What can you want sending so many letters to preachers?" the woman asked, looking at the addresses. "The whole tribe is nothing but a lot of trouble."

"Just send them off," Laurel said. "And make sure you let me know the minute I get an answer."

"You must have had a hundred already. It's five or six years you've been sending these off regular as clockwork."

"There'll be another batch next month," Laurel said.

And every month after that until she got the answer she wanted.

Chapter Seventeen

Laurel almost bumped into Hope as the girl came out of the restaurant.

"You're looking very pretty today," Laurel said. Hope had always been attractive, but recently she had started to wear some very masculine clothes. Today, however, she wore a bright yellow dress with a yellow ribbon in her hair. "Who's the lucky boy?"

"I'm not interested in boys," Hope said as she fell into step next to Laurel. "All they think about is horses and guns."

"Sometimes," Laurel agreed. "But they usually get serious enough when they meet the right girl."

"I haven't got time to wait for them to get serious."

"You're rather young to be in such a hurry to get married."

"I'm fourteen," Hope said, as though that made her a grown woman. "Lots of girls get married at my age. Corrin Anderson is only a year older, and she already has a baby."

"I got married when I was sixteen and had a baby when I was seventeen. That was definitely too young." Too young to get married, too young to understand the consequences, too young to take on the responsibilities. "Most girls your age are thinking about having fun, not marriage."

"I've got to start thinking about it so I'll be prepared when someone asks me." They walked a few steps in silence, then Hope stopped and turned to Laurel. "Do you think I'd make a suitable bride for the sheriff?"

The question so stunned Laurel that she couldn't think of an answer. Was every unattached female in Sycamore Flats hoping to marry Hen? What had he done to make Hope think he might marry her? Did Mrs. Worthy know what was going on in her daughter's mind?

"I really can't say," Laurel finally managed to answer. "I'm not sure I think it's wise for a girl to marry a man twice her age."

"But I'd be exactly the kind of wife he wants."

"How do you know?"

"I asked him."

Laurel stared at Hope, dumbfounded. "You asked him?"

"Sure. How else was I going to find out?"

Nonplussed, Laurel asked, "What did he say?" She knew she shouldn't have asked, but she had never shown any common sense when it came to Hen. It was useless to think she would develop any at this point.

"He said he wanted someone young, innocent, and pure. If that's what he really wants, don't you think he might like me?"

Young, innocent, and pure.

Laurel knew Hen hadn't meant that description to fit her. It proved what she had feared for some time. No matter how much Hen liked her, how frequently he thought of her, how strongly attracted he might be to her, he would never think of marrying her.

She wasn't the kind of woman men wanted for a wife. Her black hair and white skin might excite their senses, but they only thought of her in a carnal way. For a wife, the mother of their children, the chatelaine of their homes, they wanted someone young, and pure, and innocent—someone they could respect, someone they would worship.

"He mentioned Miranda. Do you think he could like me better than her?"

Laurel collected her wandering thoughts. In her own misery, she had forgotten about Hope. She ought to feel sorry for the child. This was probably her first taste of love. Unless Laurel misjudged the situation, the taste would be bitter.

"No man could find anything wrong with you. You'll make someone a wonderful wife. But if you'll take some advice from an old woman, you'll wait a little longer and look for someone closer to your own age."

"You're not an old woman," Hope said. "You're still beautiful."

Laurel gave Hope a hug. "I've got to go. No telling what mischief Adam will get into if I'm gone too long."

"He's playing with Jordy. I just saw them."

"That's even worse. Two little boys can think up four times as much trouble as one."

But Laurel's thoughts were far away from Adam and Jordy as she hurried to the wash and made her way toward the canyon. This was one more blow to her hope that Hen would love her so much that he would overlook her background. All along she had known she was allowing hope to crowd out common sense. But now common sense had received reinforcement from Mrs. Norton and Hope. Hen might like her, but he would never marry her. If she insisted upon going on with this relationship, she might as well do it with her eyes open. When he left, it wouldn't be a surprise.

Could she live with that? Could she endure the days, the hours, the minutes, knowing they would come to an end and leave her with nothing?

She didn't know. She couldn't imagine life without him. She had already failed to drive him away. She didn't know if she could keep seeing him, knowing there was no possibility of a future for them together.

No man—father, stepfather, or husband—had been part of her life for very long. Even Adam would leave her someday. But she had hoped Hen would be different.

"What did you say to Mrs. Blackthorne?" Miranda asked Hope.

"Why?" Hope asked. She had been studying a blue-and-white dress in the window of Bailey's Wholesale.

"She went by me looking like someone had died. She didn't even see me. I spoke to her most clearly."

"We were just talking about the kind of wife the sheriff would choose."

"And how would you know anything about that?"

"I asked him."

Miranda's eyes grew almost twice their normal size. "No respectable female would do anything like that."

"Why not?" Hope demanded, nettled.

"Men don't know what they want. They certainly don't know what's good for them."

"Well, the sheriff knows. He wants a wife who's young, pure, and innocent."

"That just proves my point."

"How?"

"Well, normally I wouldn't breathe a word of something like this. It's too much like gossiping. But considering what you've already done, I feel I must speak before you do something else frightful."

"I am not frightful."

"As you are well aware," Miranda said, ignoring Hope's indignation, "the sheriff has been very concerned about Mrs. Blackthorne's safety. He even went so far as to allow her to use his house while he was gone."

"Everybody knows that."

"What you don't know is there's considerable speculation that these attentions might be of a serious nature."

"But she's nothing like what he said he wants."

"That's exactly my point," Miranda said. "Men say one thing, but they invariably do something else."

"You're more like what he wants than she is."

"Don't ever repeat that remark to a living soul," Miranda said in a severe voice. "There's a very good chance you've hurt Mrs. Blackthorne's feelings very badly as it is."

"I didn't."

"You did if she likes Mr. Randolph. Now, I suggest you stop meddling in things which can only cause trouble and go see if your mother needs help in the kitchen. If you must fall in love with somebody older than you, why don't you consider your mother's cook? He's a Randolph, too, and he's much closer to your age."

With that severe reprimand, Miranda turned and walked away down the boardwalk.

Hope simmered angrily, despite a guilty feeling that Miranda might be right. Coming to a sudden and defiant decision, she headed toward the sheriff's office. Hen was sitting behind his desk, his feet on top, when she entered.

"It's not lunch time yet, is it?"

"Do you like Mrs. Blackthorne?" Hope blurted out. "Are you in love with her?"

Hen's feet fell off the desk with a crash, and he sat bolt upright.

"You get right to the point, don't you?"

"Miranda—I mean, Miss Trescott—says people are thinking you're sweet on her. They're saying you wouldn't be paying her so much attention if you weren't."

Hen swallowed. Obviously he hadn't been as circumspect as he thought. It might be too late, but he had to do his best to stop the rumors. "People will say just about anything. I've been trying to get Laurel to move into town. I'm worried the Blackthornes might try to take Adam again."

"Then you're not thinking about marrying her?"

"I'm not thinking about marrying anybody."

That was true, but much to Hen's surprise, the idea didn't fill him with dread as it usually did. He still wasn't interested in getting married. No, he definitely wasn't going to get married. But if he did—well, he wouldn't mind a wife like Laurel.

"You've got to marry somebody someday."

Hen jerked his attention back to Hope. "Some men aren't cut out to marry."

"I thought everybody wanted to get married."

"Maybe they do, but not everybody can."

"I don't understand."

Neither did he. He had always thought he did, but he didn't.

Laurel wrung the sheet out and tossed it into the rinse water. She was furious when she missed and the tail of the sheet fell on the ground. She rinsed the dirt from the sheet and poured the now dirty water on the ground. She didn't need Adam's help to fetch water now. She only had to swing the chute over to the tub, lower it, and allow the water to pour into the tub. The chute held more than enough water to do her morning washing. All Adam had to do was collect enough wood to keep the fire going. He spent most of his time with Jordy and Sandy.

She missed Adam and the companionship of their mornings together. The work went faster, seemed easier when he was around working, playing, asking questions, being the center of her universe. She couldn't keep him at her side anymore. Not since Hen. Everything was different since he came to the canyon. The chute was a mute reminder of the changes he had wrought in her life. Not that she needed any.

Young, pure, and innocent.

The words rang in her ears like a mocking chant. They haunted her like an evil spirit. They lurked around every corner, pounced on her when she was least prepared, taunted her, punctured every good mood. They were like a death sentence. Only she didn't die. She had to go on living, go on facing them.

She had made up her mind to leave Sycamore Canyon. At first she tried to tell herself she was running away to protect Adam, but she couldn't keep up the pretense. She was running away because of Hen, and she might as well face the truth. She had been living in a dream world far too long.

She wrung out the next sheet and tossed it into the rinse water. She didn't know where she was going, but she was sure of one thing. She was never going to wash another thing that didn't belong to her or Adam as long as she lived.

Avery had waited in the wash, out of sight behind a large cottonwood tree, until Jordy headed off to do his chores and Adam started back to the canyon.

"I don't want to talk to you," Adam said when he caught sight of Avery.

"You should always want to talk to your grandfather."

"I don't like you."

"But you like the sheriff."

Adam squirmed. "I don't like him either."

"I saw him helping you with your horse yesterday. You don't drive him away when he goes to see your mother."

"He's too big. Besides, he's nice," Adam said, finally getting up his courage to say what he really felt. "He brings me things.

He helps Ma. He even let us sleep in his house so you couldn't steal me."

"I could steal you right now if I wanted."

Adam backed away.

"I could have stolen you any number of times, but I haven't. I want you to want to come live with us."

"I want to stay with my ma."

"Even if she marries the sheriff?"

"She's not going to marry anybody."

"When they get married, the sheriff might not want some other man's little boy around."

"That's not true. The sheriff likes me. He told me so."

"He especially won't like it when he has little boys of his own. He won't want your ma doing things for anybody but his kids."

"I don't believe you."

Avery could tell that Adam didn't want to believe him, but he had planted a seed of doubt in the boy's mind. "I can make him go away if you'll help me."

"How?"

"He's very good with his guns, isn't he?"

"He's the best. Everybody says so."

Avery noticed that Adam took pride in that. His loyalty still remained with Hen. "Your pa wouldn't want you admiring a man like that."

"The sheriff is a good man, just like my pa. Ma said so."

Avery felt a spurt of temper. It would serve the kid right if he snatched him now. He could always come back and get Hen later. But reality cooled his anger. He was no match for Hen in a gunfight and he knew it. None of the Blackthornes were. If any one of them touched that boy, they'd have Hen down their throats faster than an Apache arrow. No, he had to figure out how to kill Hen first. Then there'd be nothing to stop him from taking Adam any time he wanted.

A thought occurred to him. "Did your ma tell you who killed your father?"

"Some bad man."

"It was Hen Randolph."

"That's not true." Adam threw the words at Avery like one last, desperate spear thrust. "Ma didn't say nothing like that."

"Your ma doesn't know. I didn't know for a long time. Why do you think I didn't do anything about it? But now I know, and I've come to kill him."

"I don't believe you!" Adam shouted. His face crumpled as he backed away. "He's faster than you. Danny Elgin's pa says he's the best ever. He'll kill you."

"That's why I need your help," Avery said. "Your father would want you to help me."

"I won't do it. I don't believe you!" Adam cried. He turned and ran down the wash as fast as he could.

Avery smiled when he saw Adam stumble, get to his feet, and run again. It would take him a while to accept it, but he would soon believe the lie even if he didn't want to. When he did, he would be ready to do anything Avery wanted.

Avery hated all lawmen, especially those from Texas. Lawmen had run his family out of Tennessee. A Texas lawman had given him a wound in his hip that still pained him whenever he rode. A retired Texas Ranger had caught Carlin trying to steal his prize bull and shot him. Worst of all, Avery's wife had run off with a Texas sheriff.

Avery harbored a special hatred for Hen Randolph. Hen had embarrassed his sons, damaged his family's reputation, and stolen his son's widow. Laurel was Carlin's woman. She had no business taking up with another man.

Hen had come between Avery and his grandson, too. It was bitter gall to realize that Adam thought more of Hen than he did of his own flesh and blood. Avery prized family loyalty above everything. It was the source of his power. Hen threatened that power, and Avery meant to destroy him.

Avery turned and started back toward the town. After he finished with that sheriff, he meant to take care of Laurel. All this was her fault. He meant to make the bitch pay for it.

* * *

The sound of Hen's footsteps on the boardwalk reverberated in the night. Most of the buildings were dark, their owners having closed up and gone home several hours ago. Light shone from the windows of most houses, but silence reigned in this end of town.

At the end of town toward the canyon, light poured into the street from seven saloons. They wouldn't close up for at least another hour.

Hen walked slowly. He loved this time of night. After even the hottest day, the desert turned cool during the evening. Now, as he made his rounds, listening to the sound of his footsteps echo down the empty street, he enjoyed the cool breeze as it wafted in off the desert. But his thoughts were on the canyon, where still cooler breezes flowed down from the mountains.

Laurel's canyon. She had rarely left his thoughts since Hope asked him if he was in love with her. He wasn't, was he?

Much to his surprise, he discovered that he had no idea what it felt like to be in love. He didn't even know how to love. He wondered about his feelings for George, Monty, and the rest of his family. He had always assumed he loved Monty. After all, he was his twin.

He checked the door to the Worthys' restaurant. It was locked. It was dark and quiet inside. He moved on.

Did he love his family? Or were his feelings nothing more than loyalty, a feeling of comfortable familiarity because he'd known them all his life? Maybe he'd never loved anybody. Maybe he couldn't love anybody.

That thought frightened him. He was a loner by choice, but for the first time in his life, he didn't like the idea of facing the future by himself. He wanted to face it with Laurel. Did that mean he was in love or just that he was lonely and wanted company?

He thought about Adam. He wanted to be around when the boy saddled his first horse, had his first crush—when he became a man. Was that love, or was it sympathy for a father-less boy who felt confused and angry?

The way he had felt after his mother died.

He stepped off the boardwalk and started down the narrow alley between two buildings. Shadows dominated the open space behind the buildings and where it ran down to meet the scrub growth and boulders that marked the beginning of the mountains rising in the distance. Nothing moved. No sound disturbed the silence.

He returned to the street and the boardwalk.

He hadn't seen Laurel all day. He'd need a new excuse to go see her when the chute was finished, but he wasn't sure he should look for one. Her welcome the last few times had been forced. That confused him. He knew she liked him. At times he would surprise her looking at him with a longing so intense that it made her face seem pinched and gaunt. Surely no woman looked at a man like that unless she liked him a lot. Yet her words and actions denied the warmth in her gaze, the closeness of that afternoon before Adam turned on him.

He ought to give up. He shouldn't keep going back when he was unsure of his welcome. He had never done anything like that before. One rebuff and he was gone. Forever.

He stopped at the bank. Light from a rear window cast an amber glow on the ground behind. He rounded the building and knocked on the back door. Moments later, Bill Norton unlocked it.

"You're up late tonight," Hen said.

"I had several deposits late in the day. Miners. They struck a new pocket of color."

"Do you expect an influx of prospectors?"

"Not enough to do the town much good."

"But enough to cause me trouble," Hen said as he waved good night. He returned to the street, and his thoughts returned to Laurel.

Why did he keep thinking about her? Because he wanted to be around her. He had to know she was safe. He didn't understand how she had become so important to him. He had known more beautiful women, but Laurel was the first one to draw him back to her time and time again. She had been the only one to invade his dreams so often that she left room for nothing else.

She had been the one to awaken the physical desire that had lain like a dead thing within him for all these years.

As he neared Chuck Wilson's new livery stable, Hen wondered at the change in himself. For years he had condemned Monty's insatiable appetite for women. He couldn't understand how his twin could separate his need from the women who satisfied it. For Hen, the connection was crucial. Any passion, any physical need, died when the woman who had awakened it proved unworthy. He could not understand a joining of bodies unless there was a joining of hearts and minds.

Now, for the first time in his life, all three had come together in a single person. Laurel.

Hen stopped at the huge water tank the town had built behind the livery stable. It was waiting to be filled with fresh, cool water from the canyon. They planned to ring the town with tanks like it. He smiled to himself as he noted the light coming from a small window in the stable. Jesse McCafferty's lamp. He wouldn't stay anywhere at night without it. He believed only the lamp kept the spooks at bay.

Hen returned to the street. Several horses stood in front of Scott Elgin's saloon, their heads hanging, a hind foot lifted off the ground, bored with the hours of forced immobility, waiting to be taken home and turned loose in the corral. A man wandered out of the saloon and turned toward the dark part of town.

"'Night, sheriff," he said, then turned his unsteady steps homeward.

"'Night," Hen said as he approached the next saloon. It was quiet. Everyone inside seemed to be concentrating on cards and whiskey. The next saloon was noisy enough to make up for both the others. A couple of women moved among the patrons singing a bawdy song and evading grasping hands.

Occasionally a squeeze brought a playful rebuke from the woman and an excited flush to the face of the man.

Hen passed on without entering.

He reached the end of town. He had completed his last round for the evening. He had nothing left to do but go home and make sure Jordy washed his feet and legs before getting into bed. A boy who had spent most of his life sleeping in hay or on the ground wasn't quick to understand the importance of cleanliness.

Neither was Adam. He smiled, thinking of Adam's efforts to imitate Jordy. He had had a difficult time talking Laurel into letting Adam spend the night with his friend, but he knew it was important for Adam. It was also the first time in days that Adam had been close to friendly.

But Hen was too restless to go home. He didn't care if Jordy's dirty feet turned the sheets gray. He had to find some answer to the building pressure within him. He knew the only one who could help him was Laurel.

He glanced toward the canyon. It was too late. She would have been in bed hours ago. He started to turn back toward his house, but his feet wouldn't move. He had to see Laurel.

Chapter Eighteen

It was as dark as midnight under the trees. With the moon a mere sliver against the sky, only familiarity enabled Hen to keep to the trail. It would be virtually impossible for Laurel to see anyone approaching the house.

Hen hesitated when he reached the clearing. He shouldn't be here. If anybody saw him, the rumors would be all over town before morning. Yet he couldn't turn back. He had to see her. He had reached a personal crisis.

"Laurel," he called from a safe distance from the adobe. He

had seen the shotgun. He didn't want her firing at him by mistake. "Laurel, it's Hen. I need to talk to you."

The chute from the creek lay across the yard like a huge black snake. The pots and tubs resembled large mushrooms sprouting from the canyon floor. The simple adobe was a black mass huddled against the dull orange of the canyon walls. The terrible poverty of the scene bespoke years of back-breaking work just to afford necessities. Days when she was sick, when Adam was sick, days when she was too exhausted to leave her bed. Days when she must have longed for the sound of another adult's voice, the sight of a friendly smile. Yet on all these days the laundry had to be done.

Their lives depended on it.

There must have been times when she felt just as empty as he did when his mother died. She must have felt just as alone as when his father abandoned them. Yet she hadn't let it defeat her. She had grown strong and self-sufficient.

What had he done? He had turned in on himself, refused to let the love of those around him nourish his soul, refused to let their wisdom guide his footsteps, or let any emotion touch his heart. Until something about this woman coaxed him out of his shell. Against his will, he had been drawn into her life until he had become part of it. Now he had to know what it meant.

"Laurel, are you in there?"

Surely she heard him. She couldn't sleep that soundly. No mother could. Still no sound came from the house. He approached the door and knocked. Still no sound. Something must be wrong. Surely she couldn't have fallen sick.

"Laurel, are you all right? I'm coming in."

Almost immediately, he knew there was no one in the adobe. There was no sign of a struggle. She must have left on her own. She wouldn't go to the town at night. The only other place was the meadow.

He couldn't imagine why she would be wandering about at midnight, but he had to know she was safe. Hen began to climb the narrow path that snaked its way between boulders. He had never been in this part of the canyon at night, but he could understand the feeling of security Laurel felt living in this narrow, rock-walled fortress.

The meadow lay still, hazy in the sparse light. Five white-tailed deer grazed about fifty yards away. A big buck lifted his head when Hen emerged from the shadows. He stood sentinel, the small band of does continuing to eat, secure in the knowledge that the buck watched over them.

Hen's gaze searched for Laurel, but he saw nothing. He was about to turn back when he remembered the cave. Staying within the shadows to keep from frightening the deer, he soon reached the path that led to the ledge. He had climbed only half way up when he saw her seated, staring out over the meadow.

"Do you mind some company, or is this a private meditation?"

Startled, she turned toward him. The scant moonlight illuminated a smile he had waited for his whole life.

"I'd like that."

Such a simple invitation, yet it reached all the way to the bottom of him, to an emptiness far beyond his reach. "What brought you up here?" he asked as he settled down beside her.

"I couldn't sleep." She turned toward him, her face in shadow. "Do you realize, I've never gone to bed without Adam close to me?"

"Is that the only reason you can't sleep?"

"Isn't it enough?"

No, not for him. He had to be part of her restlessness. He had to be part of the unanswered questions that disturbed her peace.

"Why aren't you in bed?" she asked. "Can you trust two little boys not to tear your house apart while you're gone?"

"Jordy would have to put it back together again."

She laughed softly. "I forgot. Leave the houseboy in charge of the house. You always were clever."

"Not clever enough to figure out what Hope understood in a flash."

"What's that?"

"Can't you guess?"

"No. I can never guess about you."

"I think I love you. I didn't figure it out until I discovered you weren't in your house."

Laurel felt the breath still in her body. For a moment, nothing in the universe moved. Then her heart lurched in her breast, and everything started moving too fast.

Hen loved her!

She forgot about the Blackthornes and the way the people in the town had treated her. She forgot that Adam had turned against Hen. She forgot that Hen was from a rich, aristocratic family. She forgot that he wanted a young, pure, and innocent wife. She even forgot the word *"think."*

Hen loved her.

"Don't you have anything to say? I've never known you to be speechless before."

"You caught me by surprise."

But that wasn't the reason. She had hours of questions to ask, days of things she wanted to say to him. She was speechless because of the intensity of the emotion that nearly choked her. She felt as though some huge bubble had been released inside her and was unable to force its way out. Only when it escaped, taking away the surprise and shock, could she know her real feelings. Right now she could do no more than take deep breaths and stare foolishly into his eyes.

Hen reached over and took her hand. "You don't dislike it, do you?"

"No."

"You seem so quiet and solemn. I thought women were supposed to shriek or swoon."

She smiled. "Probably most do."

"Why didn't you?"

"I still have trouble believing it."

"Why?"

"When you spend a long time wanting something you're convinced you'll never have, it's a shock when it's suddenly thrust into your lap."

Hen grasped her other hand, his tightly controlled intensity showing signs of snapping. "Are you saying you wanted me to love you, that you're in love with me?"

He sounded surprised. Why did he think she had been staring at him like a moonstruck idiot for the last several weeks? Why did he think she had abandoned every principle of her life and allowed herself to be talked into doing things she didn't want to do? Did the adorable fool think she did that for just anybody?

"I've loved you for a long time."

"Even though you hate gunfighters?"

"I never hated you."

Hen took her by the shoulders and pulled her to him. He kissed her roughly, without finesse. "You gave a pretty good imitation."

"I was afraid. I still am. The Blackthornes—"

Hen kissed her into silence. "This evening is just for us," he whispered, their lips still touching. "The Blackthornes, Sycamore Flats, everything else is for tomorrow." He kissed her again. "Put it out of your mind. All of it. Just think of me. Of us."

He could have no idea how much she longed to do just that. All her life she had had to plan and worry. Out of habit, questions hammered at the back door of her mind, but she firmly closed it against them. She *would* put it off until tomorrow. In the privacy of this canyon, in the quiet, the solitude, nothing could disturb them. She would have these few hours just for herself.

"When did you know you loved me?" he asked.

Laurel snuggled in the crook of Hen's arm. "I'm not sure I'm going to tell you. I don't want you gloating because I fell for you so fast."

Hen held her away from him so he could look her in the eye. "But you hated me."

"I hated what I thought you were. I think I fell in love when you told me to pack my face in cactus fruit."

Hen's smile was weak. "Is that what love means to you?"

"It's part of it."

"Tell me what it feels like."

She turned in his embrace to gaze into his eyes. "Why?"

"Because I've never been in love. I want to be sure I am now. I don't feel strange. I haven't gone around making a fool of myself like Monty did. I don't feel crazy. I don't even feel unwell."

"What makes you think you love me?"

"I once asked Rose how she knew she loved George. She said she knew when she couldn't imagine going through life without him. That's how I feel about you, but it doesn't make any sense. I got along without you for twenty-eight years. Why should I now feel I can't make it through the next day?"

Laurel tried to caution herself against hoping for too much, but her heart wouldn't listen. She *wanted* Hen to love her. Maybe if she hoped hard enough, he would. "Because you don't want to."

"Such a simple answer. Why couldn't I think of that?"

"Men always look for something earth-shaking."

"That's how it's affected me. I never wanted to sit in the moonlight with a woman, holding her in my arms, kissing her. Now I don't want the night to end."

"It doesn't have to for a while yet."

Laurel couldn't believe she was so brazen. After years of keeping men at a distance, she was practically inviting Hen to do with her as he wished. Something inside urged her to put aside caution. This was her chance for the kind of love she had always dreamed about. If she held back now, she might lose it forever.

She didn't pretend to resist when Hen took her in his arms. She didn't coyly avoid his lips when he tried to kiss her. She entered his embrace like a familiar lover and returned his kiss with an intensity that made the night grow warm. He didn't kiss like a practiced lover, but he had all the vigor of an honest one. She loved the feel of his arms around her. Their strength was as heady as Indian whiskey. She felt wrapped in a cocoon of warmth. She felt secure. Safe.

She also felt cared for. Not the way Carlin cared for her, or even her parents. This feeling went beyond anything she had ever experienced. Or expected. For the first time, she knew what it would feel like to be free of worry, to know she rested safe in the arms of a man who could, and would, care for her.

Hen held her close to his chest and kissed the top of her head. "You ever thought of getting married again?" he asked.

Laurel felt her body tense. "I suppose every woman thinks of getting married."

"I'm not interested in every woman. Just you."

What should she tell him? He didn't seem like a man who scared easily, but there had to be a reason anyone this rich and good-looking was still single.

"I have thought of it often. It's not easy for a woman to bring up a son alone."

"What about you? What do you want for yourself?"

What about her? What did she expect? If there were no missing marriage certificate, no poverty, no fear, what would she want? "I want someone who will love me and my son and take care of us."

"Is that all?"

"It's more than enough."

But it wasn't enough now, not anymore. She wanted him to love her as no man had ever loved a woman, so much that she would be consumed by his passion. Anything less would be famine.

Suddenly Laurel felt the earth shake. A terrible explosion shattered the night and echoed up and down the canyon. The deer jerked their heads out of the grass, then disappeared into the night, their white tails the only sign of their departure.

"What was that?" Laurel cried, clinging to Hen.

"An explosion."

"Where?"

"Down the canyon."

Their romantic mood shattered and nearly forgotten, they hurried out of the meadow. Clouds of dust filled the air when they reached the clearing. Rocks and small boulders littered a yard that only an hour ago had been clear and flat. As the dust began to settle, Hen could see that half the chute had been destroyed, the washtubs buried. When the dust finally cleared, there was only a hole in the ground where Laurel's adobe had stood.

"My God!" Laurel exclaimed. "What could have done that?"

"Dynamite," Hen said. "Lots of it."

"But why? No one would want to kill me."

"Not even the Blackthornes?"

Laurel looked at him, her eyes wide with shock. "No. If they had, they could have done it long ago."

"Maybe they knew you weren't here. Maybe they only wanted to drive you out of the canyon."

A shiver of cold fear arced along Laurel's spine. If whoever did this knew she wasn't in her house, then they were spying on her and she didn't even know it. If they thought she was in the adobe, they were trying to kill her. Either way, she was no longer safe in the canyon.

Adam! Was he safe? Could someone be after him?

They saw the reflection of lights on the canyon walls before they heard the noise of several people coming up the trail from town. Moments later several men emerged from the dark.

"What happened?" Scott Elgin asked. "I was just about to close up the saloon when I heard the explosion."

"Did you see anybody when you were coming up the trail?" Hen asked.

"No."

"Did anyone stable a horse at the livery stable within the last hour?" he asked Chuck Wilson.

"Jesse, did anybody stable a horse?"

"Ain't had no horse brought to that stable for the last hour," Jesse said.

"Someone threw dynamite into Mrs. Blackthorne's house," Hen told them. "He might still be around. Let's have a look."

"I'll stay with Mrs. Blackthorne," Jesse offered; "Can't have her left by herself. Could be something out here besides men," Jesse mumbled under his breath.

"There're no spooks here," Laurel told him. "I've lived here for seven years. I know."

"You can't always see spooks if they don't want you to," Jesse confided.

"Well if there's a spook up here, he must be a good spook. I was up at the meadow when this happened."

"You mean there's more places up here where things can hide?"

"Lots of them," Laurel said, smiling despite the apprehension she felt at being left by Hen. "Caves too."

Jesse shivered.

"I don't see anybody," Hen said, returning from an inspection. "Whoever did this was probably lost among the mesquite before anybody in town could get their pants on. But with half the town having tramped up the path, there's no way to tell."

"What happened? What happened?" Hope cried, bursting out of the night barely ahead of Jordy. Adam ran straight to his mother's arms, fear having banished all desire to act like a big boy. Laurel crushed the boy to her bosom, relief making her tremble.

"Someone threw dynamite inside our house," Laurel told Hope.

"There's nothing there," Hope said.

Only then did Laurel realize the full enormity of what had happened. She and Adam had nothing but the clothes on their backs. They had no place to live. They were destitute.

"Merciful heavens," Grace Worthy said, gasping for breath

as she reached the yard. "To think you used to climb that trail a dozen times a day. You must be as strong as an ox." She stared at the hole in the canyon wall. "Dear God! Was that your house?"

Laurel nodded. She was too numb to speak. She had never had much, but the realization that everything she owned in the world had been destroyed overwhelmed her.

"They can stay with me," Hen said. "I've got plenty of room."

"Adam can stay with you," Grace Worthy said, "but Laurel will stay with us."

"I couldn't do that," Laurel said.

"It's me or move in with Ruth Norton."

Laurel wondered if she was dreaming. People were actually arguing over the chance to help her. It felt strange. It also felt good. "I'll be grateful if I can stay with you until I can make some arrangements," she said.

"Adam can stay with Jordy and me," Hen offered. "Why don't you let Tommy come over for a few days," he said to Grace. "That ought to make things a little easier on you."

"I couldn't do that."

"Sure you can. I'm never home, and the town will rebuild the house if they burn it down."

Grace chuckled. "Come along with me," she said to Laurel. "Let the men worry over this mess. That's what they're for anyway."

Laurel hesitated. The loss of her possessions made her feel terribly vulnerable. Only Hen could provide the feeling of safety she needed.

"Go on," Hen said. "I'll drop by later."

"You'll do nothing of the sort," Grace said. "There's not a thing you have to tell her that can't wait until morning. I intend to see she goes straight to bed, and I won't have you upsetting her again tonight."

Laurel felt as if she had been scooped up and swept away on a benevolent tide.

"Can I stay?" Jordy asked.

"You'd better go back with Adam. He's got to have some man to stay with him."

Jordy swelled with pride. At that moment he was the biggest little nine-year-old in the Arizona Territory.

Laurel cast a forlorn glance at Hen as Grace Worthy led her away. Hen smiled as reassuringly as he could. He would rather have had Laurel stay with him, but he saw the sense of Grace's arrangements.

"You think it was a Blackthorne?" Elgin asked after the ladies had gone.

"Can't be nobody else," Chuck Wilson said. "I wonder if they're the ones who set my livery stable afire."

"I'm not so much worried about who did it as whether they thought Laurel was in the house," Hen said.

"Where was she?" Chuck asked.

"In the meadow where they keep Adam's horse."

"Where were you?"

"I'd come up to let her know Adam was all right," Hen said. That wasn't his only reason, but he didn't figure anybody else needed to know that. "I didn't see anybody when I reached the house."

"Probably came up after you," Chuck said. "What are you going to do?"

"I'll come back in the morning. There's nothing we can do tonight. Everybody might as well go home."

But Hen remained after everyone else had gone. He was still uneasy in his mind. Did the man who did this know Laurel was gone, or did he think she and Adam were in the house? The possibility was chilling. He didn't know much about the Blackthornes, but if they were capable of that, maybe the people of Sycamore Flats had reason to be afraid.

Another thought occurred to him. Suppose it had been someone from town, someone who knew Laurel wasn't in the house and was trying to scare her away in hopes the Blackthornes would leave Sycamore Flats alone. No one had heard the sound of a horse galloping across the desert or seen anyone running away. Was it possible the perpetrator was even now in their midst?

That didn't seem likely, but Hen had no clues, no ideas he liked. He intended to keep an open mind to all possibilities.

"What did you find out?"

Tyler dipped a wooden spoon into a sauce he had simmering in a large pot. He blew on the hot liquid, tasted it, blew and tasted again. He put a dash of seasoning into the mixture and stirred slowly. Only then did he look up at his brother. "It took you long enough to ask."

"Let's not go into my personal failings."

"Good idea. We wouldn't get done with that for a least a couple days."

Hen wondered why his brothers always tried to make him mad.

"It was your idea to come sticking your nose in where it doesn't belong, riding God-only-knows-where, trying to get yourself shot. Ever think I might be worried?"

"No."

"Well, I was."

"I'm glad you were careful to keep it from showing."

Hen had a strong desire to empty Tyler's precious sauce out in the corral and let the horses trample in it. At least that might shake his perpetual self-control. "We're not going to get anywhere arguing. I know you've been scouting the Blackthornes. What did you find out?"

"Why didn't you ask me sooner?"

"Dammit to hell, Tyler! You know why."

"Tell me."

"The hell I will!"

Tyler almost grinned. "It was worth a try."

"You keep trying to wind me up and I'll . . ." What could he do? Tyler was his brother. And even if he was the most aggravating human in the entire universe—after Jeff, who had developed aggravation into an art form—he had come here because he was worried about him. "What did you find out? It'll help me decide what to do." Hen would have sworn Tyler looked disappointed that he had backed down. "Then after you tell me, I'm going to feed your precious sauce to the dogs, tie you to your pack mule, and point it toward the Rio Grande."

Tyler grinned, his faith in his brother apparently restored.

"The call did go out."

"I know that. What I want to know is how many answered it."

"Not as many as the old man hoped. Maybe a dozen. A few more might come in later."

Tyler tasted, added another seasoning, stirred, and tasted again.

"The old man hates you, but some of the family have settled down to ranching. They'd rather tend to their cows than start a war."

"You think Avery can stir them up?"

"He might."

"I know he *might*," Hen snapped. "They *might* all move to Canada and raise sheep."

Tyler grinned.

"I want to know if you think Avery can stir them up enough to attack this town."

"Yes, but not all of them will follow."

"How many?"

"Too many. At least two dozen."

"How did you learn so much?"

Hen was certain that Tyler smiled. "Not all the women in Tubac prefer Blackthorne men. If you like, I'll ride out again."

"No, you've done enough. Thanks."

Tyler's head spun around, a look of disbelief on his face.

"That's right, I said *thanks*," Hen snapped. "But you'd better remember it. It'll be a cold day in hell before I say it again."

But it hadn't been as hard to say as he'd expected. He wasn't even in a bad mood. In fact, he felt good.

Hell, being in love was ruining him.

Chapter Nineteen

Avery caught Adam as he started down the alley between the two buildings. The child tried to pull away, but Avery took a firm hold. Adam seemed afraid of him.

"I see you're living with that man now. What would your pa say about that?"

"I got no place to stay," Adam shot back, trying to twist free. "Somebody blowed our house up."

"Why aren't you staying with your ma?"

"I ain't staying with a bunch of females," Adam scoffed. "There's three of us staying with the sheriff. Yesterday we beat up Danny Elgin and Shorty Baker."

It was obvious that the boy desperately wanted to see himself as a young tough. Avery wondered how he could use that to his advantage.

"Maybe it's a good thing you're staying with the sheriff. You can help me better there."

"I won't help you."

"Yes, you will."

"Jordy says only cowards shoot people in the back."

Avery's grip tightened and his expression became menacing. "You calling me a coward?"

"Jordy said it," Adam said, bravely sticking to his position. "Ma told me the sheriff was a good man, just like my pa."

"Did you tell them about me?"

"No. I didn't tell nobody you want to kill the sheriff. He would come shoot you between the eyes. He's not afraid."

Avery backhanded the boy. Adam stumbled to the ground, but his eyes remained defiant. "You're a traitor to your pa," Avery growled, so angry that his breaths came in short gasps.

"You're letting that killer lord it over everybody like he's somebody special while your pa lies cold in his grave."

Adam glared at Avery.

"Every minute you don't help me, you're letting a killer live while your pa lies rotted in the ground."

"I ain't letting him do nothing," Adam protested.

"I told you the sheriff killed your pa, you little fool—shot him in the back from ambush so he could have a big name for killing a Blackthorne."

"That's not true," Adam said, stubbornly refusing to believe him.

"Why do you think I've been so determined to see him dead? That man killed my son. I'd be a coward if I didn't try to kill him. So will you if you don't help me."

"I won't."

"He's a killer. Why do you think the town hired him? To kill more Blackthornes, that's why."

"Ma said pa was killed by bad men."

"She's right. He was killed by Hen Randolph."

"I don't believe you."

"She didn't tell you because she's in love with that killer. She wants to marry him. And when she does, they're not going to want you anymore. You're going to be thrown out of your own house by your pa's killer. What kind of coward does that make you?"

"It's not true." Adam jumped to his feet and ran off toward the wash. "You're lying!" he shouted back. But his voice broke. "You're lying," he repeated between broken sobs as he disappeared into the mesquite beyond the wash.

Hen was standing in front of the bank talking to Bill Norton when George rode into town. Hen's virulent curses caused Bill to stare in surprise.

"What's wrong?" Norton asked. He looked at the well-dressed rider, then back at Hen. "He looks like a respectable businessman to me. Probably a family man from the look of him."

"That's exactly what he is," Hen replied, his voice tight with anger. "He has no business getting in the middle of this. I'll strangle Tyler yet."

Leaving the banker thoroughly confused and a little alarmed by his outburst, Hen headed after his brother. At least George had had the good sense to leave Rose at home.

George was talking to the clerk when Hen entered the hotel. "He doesn't need a room," Hen said to the clerk. "He'll be staying with me." Hen picked up George's suitcase. "That way you can ride out again first thing in the morning."

"I'll take that room," George said to the clerk. "That way, if I don't want to leave, I won't find myself without a roof over my head."

The clerk looked apprehensive at being caught between the two men, but George's air of quiet authority convinced him to push the open register toward him.

"I suppose you believe that cock-and-bull story Tyler told you," Hen said.

"I made some inquiries of my own," George replied. He signed the register and accepted his key from the clerk. "There are at least forty adult male Blackthornes scattered from Mexico to Canada. I sent a telegram to Jeff in Denver."

"At least he won't be rushing to my rescue."

"We'll see. Now, if I could have my bag?"

"Go home, George. You have no business here. Rose and the children need you."

"That reminds me, Rose wanted me to tell you she's expecting you home soon."

"That's your home, not mine. You ought to be there right now enjoying your family, not here chasing shadows."

"You're my family, too, or have you forgotten? Sometimes I think you try."

George took his suitcase from Hen's hand. "I hear the Blackthornes are gathering in Tubac."

"Tyler told me."

"What do you plan to do about it?"

"I'm waiting to see how things develop."

"That's what I plan to do."

Hen grabbed George's arm as he started to turn away. "Go home, George."

George faced his brother, Hen's fierce determination mirrored in his eyes. "I can't cure the anger that drives you away from everybody who loves you. I can't even keep you from getting yourself killed. But I'll be damned if I'll let the Blackthornes do it. Now, where can I get something to eat? I'm starved."

Hen regained possession of George's suitcase and handed it to the clerk. "Tyler is holding forth at the Worthys' restaurant. You can plot how to keep me alive while you fill that hole in your stomach."

Hen was surprised to find he wasn't nearly as angry at George as he'd expected. He shouldn't have come, and he'd break Tyler's head yet for sending him that telegram, but George was the closest thing he'd ever had to a father. Even though he couldn't live with him and Rose, he always felt a little better when George was around. In fact, if he was really honest with himself, he was sort of glad George was here.

They walked down the boardwalk together.

"If you want to do something useful while you're here," Hen said, "you can talk Tyler out of this prospecting business. He's liable to go charging into somebody's camp to teach him how to cook a decent dinner and get himself shot for claim jumping."

"Do you like the sheriff?" Adam asked his mother.

Laurel stopped scrubbing the chemise she had in hot water. She had set up her wash tubs at the base of the canyon. Grace Worthy refused to let her pay for staying at her house, but Laurel insisted upon paying for their meals. "Of course I like the sheriff. Everybody likes him."

Adam stirred the coals under the wash pot. "Are you going to marry him?"

Laurel rinsed her hands and dried them on her apron. "Why do you ask?"

"Are you?"

"He hasn't asked me."

"Will you if he does?"

Laurel couldn't understand why Adam was asking these questions. Boys his age didn't think about marriages and falling in love. It was all guns and horses. Somebody had been talking to him. Probably Hope or Jordy. Most likely they only repeated things they had heard, but she wished they wouldn't relate them to Adam.

"It would depend on a lot of things."

"What things?"

What did it depend on? She loved Hen, and she was certain he loved her even though he might never ask her to marry him. "I don't know. Whether he still wants to be a sheriff. Whether you like him."

"I hate him. I don't want you to marry him."

Adam's response shocked and upset Laurel. She had noticed the cooling in his feelings for Hen, but she had decided it was jealousy and hadn't taken it too seriously. It had never occurred to her that Adam might really not want her to marry Hen. The shock intensified. No matter how many barriers stood between them, she had never given up hope that someday, somehow she would marry Hen. But Adam's reaction was like a slamming door. She couldn't marry a man her son hated.

She refused to acknowledge the end of hope. There must be a misunderstanding. Adam couldn't hate Hen. He couldn't!

"Why? You used to beg me to let you see Hen."

"I hate him," Adam insisted. "And don't call him Hen!"

"You can't dislike somebody for no reason. It's not fair. You wouldn't want somebody to do that to you."

"He doesn't want me."

"What do you mean?"

"You'll have his babies. You won't love me anymore."

Laurel's old anger at the cruelty of people flared up. Some

child had been teasing Adam. Maybe they hadn't meant to upset him, maybe they were just talking the way children do, but they had hurt him.

"Come here and sit next to me," Laurel said. She sat down on a bench and patted the place next to her.

Adam came slowly, reluctantly. When he sat down, Laurel put her arm around him and drew him to her. He resisted for a moment, then suddenly put both his arms tight around her middle.

"I'll always want you," she said. "Even after you're a man and go to live in your own house, I'll miss you and worry about you."

"I'll never go live in my own house," Adam said. "I'll live with you."

"And you can be sure I would never marry anybody who didn't love you as much as I do."

Adam squeezed her tighter, and Laurel returned the pressure with one arm as she brushed away a tear with the other. Since his birth, Adam had been the most important person in her life. Yet she had become so wrapped up in Hen that she hadn't noticed something serious was bothering her son. She had to find a way to heal this rift. Her happiness depended on it.

But what if Hen didn't like Adam? Not all men could accept another man's son, especially the son of an outlaw, especially if he thought he was illegitimate. His family would be furious. Could Hen's love for her endure if his family turned their backs on him?

Some more of the joy that had been born that night in the meadow died. It seemed there were too many bars to their happiness, too many chasms to keep them apart. One thing was certain. She would stop daydreaming about a future with Hen and think more about her son.

Adam was holding one of the guns Hen kept in his desk when he entered the office. "Never play with a loaded gun," Hen warned as he took the gun from Adam.

"I want you to teach me how to use it," Adam said. He

sounded unnatural, as if he were reciting something he had memorized.

"Why?"

"Danny Elgin's pa says you're the best. He says if you want to learn something right, you got to learn from the best."

Hen didn't like the fact that Adam wouldn't look him in the eye. The boy was still angry at him. "Does your ma know what you want me to do?"

"No."

"Do you think I ought to do something your ma won't like?"

Adam's expression turned stubborn. "A man ought to know about guns."

"You're a little young."

Adam drew himself up to his full height. "I'm going on seven. Danny Elgin is only seven, and he has his own rifle."

"Why didn't you ask your ma about this?"

"She'll just say I'm too little."

Hen agreed with her, in principle, but he could see that knowing something about guns was important to Adam. It was also practical. A gun was a necessary tool in the West. A man who didn't know how to use one here might as well order his tombstone.

"Okay, I'll teach you a few things, but I'll have to talk to your ma before I let you shoot one."

Hen emptied the gun of its bullets. "Hold it. See how it feels. You got to work with a gun until it feels like it's part of your hand. That's the only way you'll be able to use it quickly and accurately."

For the next thirty minutes, Hen explained how to take a gun apart, how each part worked. "It's very important to keep your gun clean at all times. It's as important as your horse. Take care of your gun and your horse, and they'll always take care of you."

The whole time he worked with Adam, Hen looked for a change in the boy's expression, a sign that the anger was growing weaker. But Adam watched stony-eyed and listened without his usual flurry of questions.

"How do you load it and fire it?" Adam asked.

Hen wondered if he was doing the right thing. There was something unsettling about Adam's attitude.

"The most important thing about a gun is to know when to use it," Hen said.

"I already know when to shoot it," Adam said.

Hen was alone when Laurel burst into his office. She had tried to find him earlier, but he was out on one of his mysterious rides. Waiting had only caused her anger to build. She was furious at him for teaching Adam how to use a gun. She was also scared. Adam had become more and more withdrawn. At first, it only seemed to affect his relationship with Hen. But during these last few days, he had turned his anger against her as well. That was how she had learned about the guns.

"I know how to use a gun!" he had shouted at her when she punished him for staying away too long without permission. "The sheriff taught me. I can take care of myself now."

A wall of fear and anger separated her from Adam, and it was breaking her heart. She had always been afraid she would lose Hen. It would kill her to lose Adam, too.

"What do you mean teaching Adam to use a gun behind my back?" she demanded the minute she stepped through the door.

Hen paused for a moment, staring at her in surprise. Then he jumped to his feet and pulled a chair from against the wall so she could sit down. "You sure look mighty pretty in that dress."

"I don't want to sit down," she said, waving away the chair and her curiosity about the way he looked at her. "I want you to tell me what you were doing—"

"I never did think brown was a good color for you. I like red much better. It makes your eyes look darker, your skin whiter."

"I didn't come here to talk about my skin or my clothes. I demand to know—"

"I never guessed Mrs. Worthy had any dresses like that."

"Miranda lent me this dress, but—"

"That explains it," Hen said. "I didn't think you'd find clothes like that in Sycamore Flats."

"You're the most infuriating man. I can't even carry on a normal conversation with you." She could see the admiration in his eyes, the look of hunger that was no longer carefully shielded. She had forgotten she had on a dress Miranda had given her. Hen was clearly having difficulty adjusting to her transformation from a washer woman to a fashion plate.

"It's a waste of time fussing at me for showing Adam how a gun works when I want to tell you how pretty you look. I never realized how really lovely you are. I never told you, did I?"

"No, you didn't," Laurel replied, so thoroughly sidetracked that she despaired of ever getting her anger worked up again.

Hen took her by the hands and pulled her toward him. "Shall I begin?"

Laurel tried to hold him at arm's length. "You know, Hope has been trying to tell me what a funny man you are. I told her she was crazy. Now I think you are."

"You make me crazy. I've never felt this way before. I never talked this way either. It must be the beginning of a fever."

"How dare you compare falling in love with me to a fever."

"Monty said it was like a sickness."

"You tell Monty he's wrong."

"George and Madison said the same thing."

"They're all wrong. It should be the most wonderful feeling in all the world."

"A wonderful sickness."

Laurel forced herself to concentrate. "There's no use talking to you. Why did you let Adam touch that gun?"

Hen pulled her close and planted a kiss on her forehead. "Every boy needs to know about guns, for his self-respect if nothing else. It was time Adam learned."

"But you know I disapprove of guns."

"So do I, but they're necessary." He tried to kiss her lips.

She averted her face. He settled for her cheek and a nibble on her ear.

"You know, I used to wonder how Monty could spend so much time kissing Iris. Never could see anything in it. I suppose it's just a matter of who you're kissing."

It was impossible to be angry at Hen when his kisses drove everything else from her head. It was even harder to recall that she couldn't marry him until she found out what was wrong between him and Adam.

"You're not the least bit sorry, are you?" she asked. Her body leaned against him despite her efforts.

"I'm sorry I waited so long to find out how much I like kissing you."

"You're always going to do exactly what you want no matter what anybody says."

He wasn't listening, but it didn't matter. His nearness had turned her brain to mush. Her breasts brushed against his chest, setting her body on fire. The feel of his hands on her arms, his lips on her neck—she could only think of what she wanted to do, not what she should do. But before she could give in to the desire to throw herself into Hen's arms and damn the consequences, a rough clearing of the throat behind them caused her to break away from Hen's embrace.

"I doubt you'll find this of much importance, sheriff," Mrs. Worthy announced, "but your brothers have requested that you join them for dinner this evening."

"Damn my brothers!" Hen cursed, much less embarrassed than Laurel. "I didn't ask them to come here. They can eat by themselves."

"Of course you'll go," Laurel said, struggling to regain her composure and not turn mortified eyes toward Grace Worthy.

"You have been invited to dinner at the Nortons'," Grace told Laurel. "Would you like me to help you pick out something to wear?"

Laurel knew there was nothing to pick out. She also

knew Grace didn't intend to leave the office until Laurel left with her.

"I'm still angry with you," she said to Hen as she prepared to leave. "Next time consult me before you decide what's best for my child."

"You call that anger?" Grace marveled to Laurel as they left the sheriff's office. "Lord help you, child, if you two ever decide to make up."

As Hen made his way to the livery stable, he wondered what had come over him. He'd never talked to a woman the way he talked to Laurel. He sounded like a kid who'd fallen in love for the first time. Not even Monty talked like that around Iris.

He found Sam Overton at the livery stable checking out the horses Jesse meant to harness to the stage.

"Hear about any more Blackthornes?"

"Maybe one or two."

"Thanks. Keep your eyes open. We'll pull through this yet."

"I hope so. This place has the makings of a right nice little town. I don't want that one," Sam yelled at a zebra-striped gelding Jesse was leading out. "He pulls something awful. Give me that little sorrel."

Hen didn't pay any attention to the scuffling sound until he realized it was drawing close to the office. He got up from his desk and looked out the door. Jordy was headed his way dragging Adam behind him. The child fought every step, but Jordy was too strong for him.

"What's going on?" Hen asked as Adam almost broke loose. Jordy pounced on him, picked him up bodily, and deposited him inside the office. He slammed the door and leaned against it, barring Adam's escape.

"Tell him what you've been doing," Jordy ordered.

Adam charged Jordy, ready to attack him again. Hen caught him by the back straps of his pants.

"That's enough fighting. How about telling me what's gotten into you two? You've always been such good buddies."

"I don't have sneaks for buddies," Jordy said. "I don't go around trying to shoot people in the back."

"That's a pretty serious accusation, Jordy," Hen said. "I hope you got something to back it up."

"I caught him," Jordy said, pointing an accusing finger at Adam. "I caught him dead to rights."

"Caught him doing what?"

"You tell him, you yellow-bellied double-crosser," Jordy shouted.

The two boys tried to get at each other again, but Hen held them apart.

"Whoa! Slow down! Now I want to know what's going on here, or I'll put you both in jail until you're ready to talk."

"Tell him if you've got the guts," Jordy taunted.

"Tell me what?" Hen asked Adam, but the boy wouldn't even look at him.

"Tell him you've been hanging around that cross-eyed piece of crow bait, Avery Blackthorne. Tell him I caught you twice."

Hen looked at Adam. The boy's gaze remained on the floor.

"Is this true, Adam?"

"Of course it's true. Ask Tommy Worthy if you don't believe me. He saw them, too."

"Why were you seeing this man, Adam? Don't you realize he's one of the people who wants to take you away from your mother?"

"He's my grandpa. He loves me," Adam cried.

"He might love you, but he's not interested in what's best for you if he's trying to steal you from your mother."

"He doesn't want to get rid of me," Adam flung at Hen. "He wants me to go live with him."

"Nobody wants to get rid of you. Jordy and I are your friends."

"You can count me out," Jordy declared, glaring at Adam. "I ain't friends with nobody that hangs out with somebody trying to kill you, Hen. I'd have to go back to sleeping in the livery stable if you was dead. I might get burned up."

"I'm still your friend," Hen told Adam. "I guess I can't blame a fella for wanting to see something of his grandpa."

"I can," Jordy declared. "I ain't having nothing to do with a two-bit, four-flushing piece of mule-meat like Avery Black-thorne."

"He's not mule-meat!" Adam shouted. He was so upset that he was near tears. But Hen knew he would let himself be cut into little pieces before he cried in front of Jordy. "He wants to teach me how to grow up to be like my pa!"

"What do you want to be like that jail-bait for?" Jordy asked.

Adam nearly tore his clothes trying to get at Jordy.

"He wasn't jail-bait! Ma said he was good. And you killed him!" he shouted, turning on Hen. "You shot him in the back and killed him."

"Who told you that?" Hen asked, stunned at the accusation.

"Killer! Killer!"

"Let me at him," Jordy said. "I'll teach him to call you a murderer."

"No, let him talk."

But just then Hope came through the back door with the lunch tray.

"I hate you!" Adam shouted. "I hate you!" He ran past a very startled Hope and out the back door.

"I'll catch him and bring him back," Jordy promised.

Hen caught Jordy by the shoulders. "Let him go. He's too upset to listen to anything I have to say just now. Apparently Avery has told him I killed his father."

"Everybody knows that ain't true," Jordy said.

"Everybody except Adam."

Chapter Twenty

The shot sounded in Hen's ears like the crack of doom.

Hell, somebody else was trying to shoot up the town. He wondered if everybody in Arizona did the same thing when they got angry or bored. He hadn't taken this job to spend his time disarming a bunch of drunken malcontents. He had pushed back his chair and unlocked the rifle rack when Jordy burst into the office.

"Allison Blackthorne is down at Elgin's Saloon," he announced, his eyes glistening with excitement. "He says he's going to kill you for what you did to his pa. You going to have a shootout in the street?"

"Not if I can help it. You stay here until I get back."

Adam rushed to the window. "What's happening, Ma?"

"It sounds like someone is shooting up the town," Laurel said as she looked out the window over her son's head. She felt her heart lurch when she saw Hen coming down the street. If she married him, this was what she would go through every time she heard gunfire.

Adam started for the door.

"Stop," Laurel cried. "You're not to leave this room until I say so."

"But I want to see."

"You'll have to see from here. The sheriff will take care of it."

Laurel prayed someone would take care of Hen.

Hen headed for the saloon. Here and there a man stood inside a doorway, his gun ready, but all the women and children had disappeared from sight.

As Hen drew closer to the saloon, he realized that he had no desire to face Allison. He wasn't the least bit interested in whether he shot up Elgin's Saloon. He didn't care whether the citizens were able to sleep in their beds without being waked up by crazy cowboys or trigger-happy drunks. In fact, he didn't care about Sycamore Flats at all.

Except for Laurel and Adam. And Jordy and Hope. And her family. And Miranda and the Nortons. And a few others. Without realizing it, he had come to know the whole town. And care about them. They were no longer a collection of unknown faces. He knew Jesse McCafferty had an obsession about spooks, but the old man was a genius with horses. He could recognize Ruth Norton's silhouette at a hundred yards, Grace Worthy's voice at a thousand, the sound of Hope's footsteps on the boardwalk or the thud of Jordy's feet as he raced down the stairs.

They were just as real to him as his own family.

George stepped out of the hotel as Hen approached. He wore his guns. "What's going on?"

"One of the Blackthornes is shooting up the saloon. I can handle it."

"You sure there's only one? Maybe they've set a trap for you."

"You've been listening to Tyler again."

George smiled, a little grimly. "At least he talks to me."

Hen felt guilty about refusing to see George—he had refused even to speak to Tyler—but he hadn't wanted them here.

"Just stay here. I don't want to have to explain to Rose why she's a widow."

"When did I ever need you to protect me?"

"Never. It was you who always protected us," Hen admitted. "But this is gun business. I'll do better alone."

"I'll wait outside," George said, falling into step beside Hen.

"You always were too damned stubborn for your own good."

George chuckled. "Look who's talking."

They hadn't gone six steps before Hen saw Tyler emerge from the back door of the restaurant. "Hell!" he cursed. "I should have known Tyler couldn't keep his nose in the kitchen."

Tyler was crossing the street to join his brothers.

"I don't know what he's doing here," Hen said. "He never cared two hoots about anybody."

"If you knew him at all, you'd know better than that."

"I'm finding out I don't know anybody, including myself."

George and Tyler waited in the street as Hen mounted the steps of the boardwalk in front of the saloon. Approaching the door with caution, he paused on the porch to let his eyes recover from the glare of the sun. He didn't know anything about Allison Blackthorne. The man could be waiting to shoot him the minute he stepped through the batwing doors. Taking care that his boots made no noise on the boardwalk, Hen approached one of the windows. He inched forward until he could see inside.

All the customers had taken cover. Allison stood at the bar, his back to the door. He leaned on the bar with one elbow, leaving his other arm free to handle the whiskey glass. He wore a single gun. He seemed unaware, or unconcerned, that someone might sneak up on him while his back was turned. Still Hen moved with care. A mirror hung on the wall in front of Allison. He only had to look up to see the entire room.

Hen unholstered his gun and pushed through the door into the saloon.

"Hello, Allison."

Allison froze. He looked at Hen in the mirror, then turned slowly.

Hen could see he'd been drinking. Disgusted, he holstered his gun.

"I'm going to kill you," Allison said. His words were slurred, but it was clear he knew what he was saying.

Hen had a sick feeling in the pit of his stomach. Allison was just a kid. He couldn't be more than sixteen. He had probably started drinking to bolster his nerve. Now he had drunk too much to realize that he was in no shape for a gunfight.

From the well of memory, a picture rose before Hen's eyes, a picture of himself when he saw the rustlers about to hang Monty. He could remember no feeling, no thoughts, no reluctance when he shot those men. He still flinched when he remembered burying them, throwing dirt in the face of that first man.

The rustlers had been about his own age. Just boys.

He would do it over again, but it still haunted him. All the gun battles since hadn't been able to make the memory any less painful, the image any less vivid. That day had changed him forever. It had destroyed his innocence, denied him peace of mind, and forced him into a role he still found alien.

Now he was facing another kid.

"Why don't you go home and sleep it off," Hen said. He tried to make his voice sound impersonal, free of condescension or pity. This must be Allison's first gunfight. Otherwise he wouldn't have had to get drunk.

"I can hold my liquor," Allison insisted. He attempted a fast draw, but the gun caught on a cartridge loop in his belt. He snatched it free. He waved his gun around the room. The men who had started to get up when Hen entered dived for a table or hit the floor and lay flat.

"Maybe, but it won't improve your aim."

Hen searched for a way to convince Allison to holster his gun and go home, but he'd never tried to avoid a fight before. He didn't know what to do.

"I'm going to kill you," Allison said again.

"Sure, when you can decide which one of me you're going to shoot first. Now why don't you put that gun away and ride on back where you belong."

Allison fired into the ceiling. "I'm going to kill you," he said for the third time.

Hen didn't think Allison was a killer. Not yet. He looked scared, not excited. He had come to prove something to himself and the rest of his family. If Hen could stop him now, maybe he wouldn't become a killer. If he couldn't, it would be too late. For both of them. He didn't want this boy's death on his conscience. Hen wished he could talk to George. He had commanded dozens of youngsters like Allison during the war. He would know what to do, what to say.

"I've got no quarrel with you," Hen said. "Why don't you go back home, sober up, and give yourself time to think this over."

"I'm going to kill you for what you did to my pa."

"I don't know your pa."

"You set a horse to watch him. People will never stop laughing at him."

So Allison was Ephraim's son. Hen wondered if Ephraim had sent him to get revenge. Probably. The Blackthornes didn't seem to put a very high value on life, even the lives of their own kin.

"If your pa's got an argument with me, tell him to come himself."

"I'm here in his place."

"Then you're wasting your time. Go back home. If you start now, you won't be late for dinner." Hen turned and started toward the door.

"Don't walk away from me, dammit," Allison shouted. "I'll kill you."

"Then you'll have to shoot me in the back," Hen said without turning around.

A bullet shattered one of the saloon windows. The concussion felt as if it would break Hen's eardrums. He kept walking, through the door, across the boardwalk, and into the street.

At the sound of more gunshots, Laurel felt her throat constrict, her heart thump erratically and painfully in her chest.

"There's the sheriff," Adam exclaimed the instant he saw Hen walk into the street. "Where's the other man?"

Laurel's hope that Hen had killed the gunman expired almost immediately when she saw a man follow Hen into the street. She didn't know his name, but she could tell from the cast of his features that yet another Blackthorne had come after Hen. And all because of her.

"Draw, dammit," Allison shouted as he rushed out of the saloon behind Hen. "I'm going to kill you. Draw!" he shouted, too furious that Hen didn't take his threat seriously to realize he'd been given a chance to escape with his pride intact.

"Go home," Hen shouted over his shoulder.

A shot whizzed past Hen, but he kept walking.

"You're a coward," Allison shouted. "You're afraid to face me like a man."

Hen headed toward the other end of town. Another shot whizzed past, but he kept walking.

"Turn and face me!" It sounded like a cry from a boy who didn't understand why the game wasn't being played the way he had expected.

Hen stopped and turned back. "I don't draw on drunks, and I don't shoot boys. The fun's over. Everybody's going to stay inside until you're gone. You may as well go home."

"There's two men over there," Allison said, pointing to George and Tyler. "I can shoot them."

"You're too drunk."

"I'll show you I'm not drunk," Allison shouted. "I'll show all of you cowards." He aimed shots at several windows. The sound of breaking glass seemed to fuel his excitement. "See, I told you." He aimed a shot at Tyler, who was standing in front of the restaurant. Even Allison looked surprised when he fired the shot.

Tyler's hand flew to his cheek.

A window shattered.

Someone screamed.

Laurel gasped. Why didn't Hen do something? Why was he just standing there?

"Shoot him!" she shouted into the street. "Shoot him before he shoots you."

Laurel didn't have time to worry that she was imploring Hen to shoot this unknown gunman. She only worried that he was too far away to hear her voice. She could worry about this shocking change in herself once she knew Hen was safe.

Hen watched Tyler draw his hand away covered with blood.

Hen's temper snapped. That fool kid had almost killed his brother. He drew and fired almost before he knew what he was doing. Allison yelled, and the gun flew out of his hand. A red furrow appeared from his wrist to his elbow. Allison grasped his arm, grimacing in pain.

"You think it's fun to play with guns, do you?" Hen said, his voice full of menace.

This kid was just like all the rest. He thought a gun made him somebody. It made him feel like a big man to see people afraid of him, to know he could hurt them, could make them beg. Well, he would find out what it felt like to be the victim. Then let him decide if it was such great fun.

Hen fired again and Allison's hat flew from his head. He advanced toward the boy, who was now thoroughly frightened. "You think it's fun to ride into a town and shoot up the place. You think it's fun to scare people who've done nothing to you."

Allison turned, half backing away from Hen, half running.

Hen fired again, twice. The heels disappeared from Allison's boots. He stumbled and got to his feet. He staggered unsteadily, too afraid of Hen to turn his back and run.

"That's enough. Let him alone." George was at his side, but Hen didn't heed him.

"You shot my brother. Did you know that? A little more of your drunken wobbling and you could have killed him. Did you think of that, or were you just trying to make me mad enough to draw on you? Is that how you think of people, as *things* to use any way you need them?"

He fired and the shoulder of Allison's shirt tugged.

"Stand still, you damned-fool puppy. I'm going to give you a crease along your cheek. See how you like it."

"That's enough," George said.

Hen didn't pause. "You'd better stand still. It's not an easy shot. I'd hate to shoot off half your face."

Allison stood stock still, petrified with fear.

"I'll try not to make it a very big scar. No bigger than the one you gave Tyler."

Allison held up one hand to ward off the shot. "Don't. Please don't."

"You don't think it's fun anymore?" Hen fired two quick shots into the ground on either side of Allison's boots. The boy jumped and fell backwards. He lay there.

"The fun's only started. Maybe I'll give you matching scars. Then I might crease your ribs. I've always wanted to see if I could do it."

"Stop it, Hen. You're being cruel."

"Stay out of this, George. He came in here planning to kill me. I mean to see he understands what it's all about."

"I think he understands."

"Not yet, he doesn't. Maybe I'll notch your ears instead," Hen threatened.

Allison turned dead white. Notched ears would brand him a coward for life.

Hen came to a halt about five feet from Allison. "Now stay real still." He raised his gun.

"He's only a kid," George said.

The gun held steady.

Laurel's breath stilled in her lungs. She saw the gun lift and waited for the sound of the shot that would end the young man's life. A feeling of nausea surged through her, forcing her to lean on the window sill for support.

"Is he going to shoot him?" Adam asked.

"I don't know," Laurel replied, her voice hoarse and unsteady.

Please, no, she implored silently. *I didn't mean it. Don't kill him. I'll never be able to look at you without seeing his face.*

Laurel couldn't understand her reversal of feeling, but she knew it was true. If Hen killed that boy, her love would die.

"Are you enjoying this, kid? Is this what you were going to do to me? It's not much fun knowing you can die, is it?"

Hen dropped his gun, strode forward, and jerked Allison to his feet. "You can decide whether you like being a gunman while you're in jail."

Hen could hear the pent-up breath escape George's lungs. He wondered if George had actually thought he would shoot the kid. Probably. He hadn't given him reason to think anything else.

"You'd better send for a doctor," George said. "His arm needs attention."

"He can wait until after the doctor looks at Tyler's cheek," Hen said, pushing Allison before him.

Laurel sagged against the window, her body almost too weak to stand.

"What's he going to do now?" Adam asked.

"Take him to jail," Laurel replied. She closed her eyes to offer a prayer of thanksgiving. She loved Hen Randolph more desperately than ever.

But even before Hen reached the jail, he saw Doc Everson and Tyler hurrying toward the restaurant.

"Why didn't you ask him to look at your face?" Hen said when the doctor went inside and Tyler stayed behind.

"The doc came to see Hope. One of the bullets hit her."

Hen felt something inside him cave in. Only now did he identify the sound of crying among the confused sounds coming from inside the restaurant. Without realizing that he took Allison with him, Hen pushed inside. Hope lay on the floor next to the window, a bloody hole torn in the front of her dress. Oblivious to the pieces of broken glass scattered all around, a sobbing Grace Worthy worked on her knees to save her daughter. Her husband struggled to pull her away to make room for the doctor.

One look told Hen there was no chance. Hope would be dead by morning.

He had never seen a young woman die, not one he knew and cared for. The shock was devastating. He expected to feel fury, ungovernable rage. Instead he felt the inside of him drain away, leaving nothing but dry ashes.

"How did it happen?" he managed to ask.

"She wanted to watch," her father answered. "We thought she'd be safe inside."

Grace turned her tear-stained face to Hen. "It's your fault. Why didn't you kill him?"

"He's just a boy. I couldn't just shoot—"

A scream sliced through Hen's sentence. Recognizing Allison, Grace Worthy attacked him with all the fury of a mother whose child has been brutally murdered. She tore at his face with hands curved into talons. She attacked his body with fists weighted with the lead of grief. It took George and her husband together to drag her away.

"Kill him!" she screamed through her sobs. "Kill him! Why should he live when he's killed my daughter?"

Dazed, Hen dragged Allison from the restaurant. Propelling him through the streets at a stumbling run, he pushed him through the door of the sheriff's office. He rummaged in the desk for the keys. Opening the door to the jail, he shoved him into a cell.

Allison collapsed on the cot. "Is she going to die?" he asked.

He sounded liked a scared kid, not a gunman, but the question caused Hen's anger to explode with the force of gunpowder. He couldn't feel even a shred of sympathy for Allison. He whipped around, his face distorted by the black anger that poured forth from every corner of his soul.

"Do you care? Does it make any difference to you Black-thornes who you beat or kill? A woman struggling to support her child, a young girl barely old enough to have her first boy-friend? Or do you prefer a man with a family to support? Why didn't you kill me?" he said, stabbing a finger into the small piece of tin pinned to his shirt. Hen jerked the door open and stormed into the cell.

"I wear a badge," he shouted at the cowering Allison. "Sheriffs are your favorite targets, aren't they? Every Blackthorne ought to get himself one."

Allison shrank deeper into the corner.

"What do they teach you in that family of yours? When are you told it's your right to take anything you want? How soon do you start believing you can beat or murder anyone who gets in your way?"

Hen grabbed Allison by the front of his shirt and lifted him off the cot. Still using only one arm, he slammed the boy into the iron bars of the cell.

"Who told you this whole damned territory belonged to the Blackthornes to plunder at will?"

He smashed Allison's body against the bars again.

"It's going to stop if I have to kill every one of your damned tribe myself."

"Hen."

Hen barely heard his brother's voice. "You've terrorized your last female. You've shot up your last town. You've killed your last innocent child."

Hen slammed Allison into the wall with such force that the boy nearly passed out.

"Stop it, Hen."

"I'm going to kill you," Hen growled. "Then I'm going into Tubac and wipe out the rest of your scurvy relatives."

George laid a restraining hand on Hen's shoulder. "Put him down. If you hurt him now, you'll be just as bad as he is."

Hen shrugged off George's hand. But despite the rage burn-ing in his gut like hot lava, despite a groaning desire to make good on every threat, he knew he couldn't take it out on the boy. He tossed him into the corner and walked out of the cell.

"How is Hope?" he asked as he locked the cell.

"I don't know. I left Tyler to see if he could be of any help. I came after you."

Hen slammed the door into the jail and locked it. "Being well acquainted with my notorious temper, you came to make sure I didn't hurt the kid."

"I came to make sure you didn't do anything to hurt yourself."

"It's too late for that," Hen said, starting for the door. "If there was anything of me left to protect, I lost it today."

"Where are you going?" George asked as Hen headed out the door.

"To see how Hope's getting along."

"You can't do anything right now. Why don't you—"

"I've got to go. I've got to know what's happening to her. She got shot because of me."

"It's not your fault."

"Don't try to explain it away," Hen said, heading for the restaurant at a fast walk. "You're awfully good at it, but I'm a big boy now. I don't believe everything I hear."

"It's no good blaming yourself."

"Who else do you want me to blame? I'd love to find somebody. I may be a hardened gunfighter and a merciless killer, but there's just enough of a human being left in me to feel like hell when a kid gets killed."

Hen entered the restaurant just as the doctor stood up. "There's nothing I can do for her. Do what you can to make her comfortable."

Mrs. Worthy's gaze settled on Hen, and she gave an agonizing cry. "You killed her!" she cried, breaking from her husband's arms and staggering toward Hen. "You and that horrible boy, as sure as if you'd held the gun and fired it yourself. If you hadn't encouraged her to hang around you and gotten her excited by all your talk of gunfighters, she'd have been in the kitchen where she belonged, not standing at the window."

Grace's blotched face glistened with tears of grief. Some of her hair had come undone and had fallen over the right side of her face. She didn't look like anybody Hen knew.

"Get out. I don't ever want to see you again. You're a killer. You poison everything around you." Her eyes stared at him, wide with impotent rage, wet with unquenchable despair. "I hope Laurel doesn't marry you. You'll ruin her life, too."

Horace Worthy tried to stem his wife's torrent of angry words. Before she could shake him off, Miranda and Ruth Norton entered the restaurant. Miranda offered to see Hope moved to her own bed. Ruth Norton tried to help Horace quiet Grace's hysterics.

George took the opportunity to hustle Hen outside.

Laurel came down the street at a run. She noticed people peering in through the shattered restaurant window. "What's wrong?"

"One of the bullets hit Hope."

"How is she?"

Hen was unable to answer.

"Oh, my God!" Laurel said.

"See what you can do," Hen said. "Mrs. Worthy is hysterical."

Laurel hesitated, then hurried inside.

Tyler remained in front of the restaurant. The blood on his cheek had dried.

"Are you all right?" Hen asked.

"It's just a graze," Tyler replied, his expression blank.

"It could have been more."

"But it wasn't."

Hen stared at his brother. He didn't know what to say. He didn't really know what he felt. Tyler was even a more determined loner than himself. Yet he had come to Sycamore Flats to see that nothing happened to Hen. He had gotten shot in the face for his pains.

"It wouldn't have happened if you'd stayed where you belonged."

That wasn't what he wanted to say, but no other words would come out. They were caught in his throat, a log-jam of unidentifiable sentiments, locked in by their unfamiliarity. For a moment, Hen stared at his brother, feeling helpless to express what he was only dimly aware of himself.

Abruptly he turned toward the street, the buildings, the people who walked by casting inquiring glances toward the restaurant.

Without a word Hen headed back toward the jail. But rather than enter, he turned into the alley and headed for the wash.

George followed.

Laurel came to the restaurant window in time to see Hen disappear behind the jail. She desperately wanted to go to him. She knew he shouldn't be alone. He would blame himself for what had happened.

But she couldn't go. The Worthys needed her. Besides, George had followed. She felt cut off, as though George had suddenly come between them. She told herself not to be foolish. He had always been there.

Chapter Twenty-one

"It won't do any good to hold yourself responsible for what happened," George said.

Hen turned an angry face to his brother. "Who should I blame?"

"Everybody. Nobody."

"If you came all the way from Texas to tell me that, you should have saved yourself the trouble."

"Okay, tell me why you should blame yourself."

"Don't ask stupid questions, George. You're too old for it."

"I want to understand why you blame yourself."

"No, you don't. You want to twist everything I say until it sounds like something else. Then you're going to use it to show me I was wrong. I'm not seventeen any longer. It won't work."

"Tell me anyway."

"Hell!" Hen stalked across the wash and through the trees until he stood at the edge of the desert. The distant rain clouds wouldn't reach Sycamore Flats for some hours. The heat from the sun engulfed his body like a wave of fire. He knew what George was trying to do, and he was grateful, but no twisting of the facts could point the finger in any other direction.

"I should have taken Allison's gun right from the first. If I had put him in jail, none of this would have happened."

"Why didn't you?"

"Because I wanted to teach him a lesson. He's not a killer yet. I thought if I could strip away the romance, show him what it really meant to kill somebody. . . ."

"Would he have learned that if you'd put him in jail?"

"No. He'd have come after me the minute he got a chance."

"Will he come after you now?"

"He won't go after anybody."

"Then you succeeded."

"But it cost Hope her life. If I hadn't been so cocksure—"

"You could have been killed."

"He was too drunk."

"He could have shot me, or the saloonkeeper, or anybody else."

"It was my job to see he didn't shoot anybody. Next to that, everything else was unimportant. Go back to the hotel, George. I'm not going to do anything rash, but I've got to be alone."

He turned into the desert. There was nothing out there, but the solitude drew him onward.

* * *

"What did the doctor say?" Laurel asked Horace Worthy.

"He doesn't know what to say," Horace told her. "She should have died within minutes, but she's still alive."

"How's Mrs. Worthy?"

"I can't thank you and Miranda enough, but I don't know what she would have done without Ruth. Grace holds onto her like she would go crazy if she let go."

The normally calm and capable Grace Worthy was still hysterical with grief. Laurel couldn't help but wonder how she would have handled this had it been Adam. Just the thought made her tremble. She was worried about Hen, too. She had never seen him look so desperate. She wanted to go to him, but she didn't dare leave Horace. Hope could die any minute. He would need all the support she could give him.

But even as she went through the motions of making certain everything was ready, her mind remained on Hen.

"I don't think you'd better come in," Horace said to Hen. "Grace has finally begun to get herself under control. Seeing you might set her off again."

"I just wanted to see Hope."

"Doc Everson says no one is to see her."

"Then she hasn't . . . She's still hanging on?"

Horace looked as though he'd aged twenty years in the last few hours. "Doc says she can't last out the night." The admission was too painful to share, and he averted his eyes. "Now you'd better go home. It looks like rain. A gully washer if I'm any judge. You'll get wet through."

Hen wondered why Horace should think he would be worried about getting wet. "Is Laurel here?"

"She's with Hope. She hasn't left her side since they brought her home."

"Tommy?"

"Miranda took him home with her. Now I'd better get back."

A few drops of rain hit the dusty street as Hen turned away from the Worthys' home. But he didn't head toward the jail or his house. Or the hotel. There was nothing there for him.

There was nothing anywhere.

"I don't know where he went," George said to Laurel. "Not even Jordy can find him. And he strikes me as capable of finding anything that walks, creeps, or crawls."

Laurel's smile was weak. She had stayed with Hope until Mrs. Worthy had become calm enough to rejoin her husband at Hope's bedside. After that, she felt she was intruding. Even worse, she couldn't rid herself of the suspicion that the Worthys somehow blamed her. If it hadn't been for her and Adam, Allison Blackthorne wouldn't have come to Sycamore Flats.

There was no question Grace held Hen responsible. Laurel could see it in her eyes. There was no warmth. No friendliness. There was nothing except the dread certainty that her beloved daughter would die.

"Where was he headed when you last saw him?"

"Up the wash toward those mountains."

Like a wild animal, Hen preferred to lick his wounds in solitude. So did she, but tonight was no time to be alone. Not for Hen. Not for her.

The initial fury of the storm had passed, but a steady rain continued to fall. Laurel pulled a scarf over her head even though she knew it would be soaked in a few minutes. She hurried across the muddy street and down one of the alleys until she came to the wash.

Sycamore Creek flowed bank-full tonight.

She looked up toward the mountains that rose abruptly behind the town, to the canyon it had taken several millennia to carve from the stone. He was up there somewhere. She would find him. He would not be alone tonight.

Hen stared out at the meadow with unseeing eyes. He was as unmindful of the deer and mountain sheep that grazed the wet grass as he was of the rain that soaked him to the skin, of the cold that leached the heat from his body until he felt chilled and stiff. His attention centered on the pain that gnawed at his insides until he wanted to rip it out with his bare hands.

For years he had refused to feel anything. That refusal had been his shield, his armor. But it hadn't always been so, and tonight's tragedy brought back memories of a time when he was more vulnerable, when there seemed to be nothing but pain.

Fourteen years ago, he had stood at his mother's grave. Her love, her beauty, her refusal to forget the kinder world that had given her birth had been his shield against his father's cruelty. He had been able to forgive her weakness as long as she lived. But her death, her fervent wish to die, had been the final betrayal. He had buried his belief in the goodness of life in that parched Texas grave along with her frail body. He swore then he would never feel anything again.

But he had changed since he came to Sycamore Flats. He knew it the minute he faced Allison.

He hadn't seen the gun, the danger to himself, the threat to the townspeople and their property. He had seen only a boy much like the boy he had been years ago, teetering on the verge of the abyss, an abyss Allison didn't even know was there. Once you kill, something within you dies. It's impossible to go back to being the way you were before. Hen knew. He had tried. He had seen others try. His only concern had been to keep Allison from crossing that line. But in allowing emotion to cloud his judgment, he had forgotten himself, George, Tyler, everybody. He had nearly cost Tyler his life.

He had cost Hope hers.

He had come up here as much to escape hearing the news of Hope's death as to be by himself. In fourteen years, no one he'd taken under his protection had ever been hurt. Tonight he had failed twice.

He tried to shut out all thoughts of Hope, but it was as

though his mind had been invaded by demons who delighted in torturing him with memories of Hope as she used to be and as she was when he last saw her, lying on the floor, the color drained from her, a ragged, blood-soaked hole in her chest. Memories of Grace Worthy screaming at him, of Horace Worthy looking old and lifeless, rose to torture him.

He started to his feet and lunged from under the protective shelf of rock overhead. The shock of cold rain stinging his face brought him to a standstill. He desperately wanted to run away, to hide until the hurt went away, to stay hidden until he could refortify his soul. But he knew it was useless. He wasn't running away from Sycamore Flats or anybody in it. He was trying to run away from himself.

From that there was no escape.

He was weak. Just like his mother. He had known it all along. He had tried to deny it, but he should have known he couldn't hide from something like that forever. The greatest irony was that he had thought he was strong enough to love Laurel, to take care of her and Adam.

As if by magic, a vision of her appeared on the far side of the meadow. She was walking toward him, almost obscured by the slanting rain. He cursed his mind for playing this cruel trick on him. He closed his eyes, but the image was still there when he opened them again.

Relenting, too emotionally exhausted to block out the cruelly taunting image, he wished the vision could be real, that Laurel was really coming to him. Amid the rubble of his soul, his love for her was the only constant, the only thing that made sense.

It was something to hold onto, to redeem him.

He stared at the mirage as it danced and hovered in the darkness. She was so beautiful. Not just beautiful of body, but beautiful of soul. She was the kind of woman who could make a man better than himself, make him dare things he never dreamed possible. She could make him believe he was worthy of redemption.

She was the kind of woman he wanted to be his wife.

Yet the very moment he knew he wanted to marry Laurel, he also knew it was the one thing he couldn't do. The weakness would always be there. On the surface, things would seem okay, just as they had with his mother. But one day, when everything depended on him, he would fail her just as his parents had failed him.

He couldn't do that to Laurel. She was strong. She could stand alone. But if she ever started to depend on him, that might prove to be a weakness she couldn't overcome. No. If he loved her as much as he thought he did, he wouldn't add to her burden.

The pain of knowing he must back away from the only thing he really wanted was almost more than he could stand. Closing his eyes, he turned away, pounding his forehead with his fists to dislodge the vision that tortured him beyond his ability to endure it. He staggered forward, letting the full force of the rain pummel his body. He must face reality. He must decide what to do, and visions of Laurel would play no part in that decision.

But the minute he opened his eyes again, he knew Laurel was no vision. She was real, and she was coming toward him.

Laurel saw Hen standing in the rain, pounding his forehead, and wondered again if she should have come. He might feel she had no business here. She clutched the oilskin protectively to her chest. She plodded on; the increasingly heavy rain did not slow her steps or dent her determination.

She didn't know what she was going to say. She had no idea what to do. She didn't know what kind of demons he might be fighting, but she didn't want him to have to face them alone. She didn't know why she thought she could help when his family obviously couldn't, but her footsteps never faltered.

The man she loved was suffering. She would do just about anything to help him.

He was watching her now, staring at her. She felt the restraining hand of doubt tug at her footsteps, but she pushed it aside. Hen might turn her away, but nothing else would.

He didn't speak. He just watched. His clothes clung to his body. She had never realized he was so thin. She remembered Hope saying he ate very little. He ought to eat more. It wasn't good for a man to be so thin, especially not a man who demanded so much of his body.

He continued to stare at her. She could barely make out his features. Only the moisture reflecting light off the surface of his skin made it possible to see his expression. His face was blank, but his eyes burned like blue fire.

Laurel felt some answering flame leap within her. The chains were off. The thick leather hide that had encased his soul had cracked wide open, leaving him exposed and vulnerable. If she was ever to know the man she loved, truly know him, it would be tonight.

"I brought you some dry clothes," Laurel said. She held out the folded slicker.

"Why did you come?"

She knew he wasn't asking about clothes. Neither did he refer to his safety. His question went far beyond physical comfort. It reached to the very center of her soul.

"Because I love you."

That was it. All of it. Yet the words left so much unsaid. It was impossible to tell him of the ache deep within her that would never go away. It was impossible to explain how he had won her heart when so many before had failed. She didn't understand it herself. She only knew that she couldn't live without him. He was the part of her she had never found before, the part she hadn't even known was missing.

She held out the slicker. He took it, but his eyes never left her face.

"Why did you come?"

"Didn't you know I would?"

"No."

She could tell he meant it. It wasn't that he doubted she loved him. He didn't believe he was worthy of love.

"I'm a gunfighter, a killer."

"You have fought with guns, but you're no killer."

The two of them stood in the rain, staring at each other. Water dripped from his nose and ran in rivulets over his face, as if someone had emptied a bucket over his head.

"Where's your hat?"

He shrugged.

Laurel put her hand to his cheek. "You're cold."

He put his hand over hers. "You're warm."

She wanted to remain standing like this forever, his hand on hers, him looking deep into her eyes, conscious of nothing and no one else. But she had to speak. She had to find a way to help him through this dark hour.

"It wasn't your fault."

He dropped his hand and turned away. She hadn't wanted to say those words, to intrude on the feeling between them, but she knew why he had come up here. Avoiding it was cowardly. Besides, it wouldn't help Hen.

"I might as well have shot her myself."

She put her right hand on his arm and tried to turn him toward her, but he wouldn't move. She stepped in front of him. The rain hit her full in the face. "Nobody believes that," she said, wiping the water out of her eyes with her left hand. She could see the agony he was suffering. She would have traded everything she possessed to wash it away.

"Things seldom turn out as we expect. Allison could have shot someone else."

"But not Hope!"

"Would it have been any better if he'd shot Scott Elgin? Or Tyler? *Or you?*"

She felt rather than saw the tears in his eyes.

"How would you feel if it had been Adam?"

She couldn't let herself dwell on that question. She had stayed inside because she was afraid Adam would run down the street. She still felt a little guilty about that. But she had to answer him. She had to be as honest as she could.

"I would be crazy with grief. I would be angry at the whole world. I would try to hurt you because of the terrible hurt I was feeling. But no matter what I did, I would know it wasn't your fault. I would only be trying to tear the pain out of my heart."

"You think Mrs. Worthy will feel like that?"

"After a while. The important thing is how *you* feel."

Hen turned away. "I'll leave as soon as they've buried Hope." He stumbled over the words.

Laurel felt him slipping away. She tried to contain the fear of losing him forever.

"Where will you go?"

"It doesn't matter."

"Will you go home?"

"No."

Laurel pulled on his arm until he turned to face her. "Then it matters more than anything."

"Why?"

"Because you can't keep running from yourself, from people who love you."

"How can you love me when you know what I am?"

"Nobody knows what you are, not even yourself."

Why hadn't he been able to see that before? "Aren't you afraid of who I might turn out to be?"

"Are you?"

"Yes." All his life he'd been afraid he would turn out to be like his father. All of them felt like that except Zac, who was too young to remember the bastard. But he was also afraid he would be weak, like his mother. "Nothing good went into making me. How could I be worth anything? Have you ever looked at yourself and been afraid of what you might see?"

"All the time. I'm petrified I might see my own father. He was always chasing dreams and ignoring reality until it was too late. A small part of me will always be like him"—that was why she'd never given up hope of marrying Hen—"but when I'm tempted to do something he would have done, the rest of me helps hold me back. I can't always make myself feel the way I ought, but it helps to have Adam. I can do anything for his sake."

Hen felt more alone than ever. He felt protective of his brothers, but he suspected that Laurel's feeling for her son involved a kind and quality of caring that went far beyond anything he could feel. He thought of the way he had seen George and Rose look at each other. He'd seen it so many times, he took it for granted. Sometimes it made him impatient, critical, even skeptical. But that had come from the emptiness inside himself, the inability to feel, not wanting to feel, of always wanting to distance himself from any emotional ties.

But he didn't feel that way about Laurel. Not tonight, not ever. Even as he had turned his back on the town and the people in it, he had retreated to a place that was hers, a place where he was very much aware of her. For the first time in his life, he didn't want to be alone.

He looked at her with the rain streaming down her face, her raven hair clinging to her head and shoulders. She'd never looked more beautiful. The sheen of water gave her white skin a luminous quality. Pinpoints of light flickered in her near-black eyes. She seemed like an angel sent to pull him back from the brink.

"You think I have a better nature, that I can pull back from the devil inside me?"

"I know you can. You did it tonight."

He held out his hand. Laurel placed hers in it. "Why did you come?"

"Because I didn't want you to be alone tonight."

Hen's need to reach out, to share what he felt, washed over him like a flash flood through a mountain canyon. His life suddenly seemed barren. From that very first day, he had sensed in Laurel a person who could touch the part of him that always seemed to be just out of reach. He had wanted to protect her and Adam, but he'd been selfish as well.

He wanted her to save him.

Unaware of the water that continued to drip from them, Hen put his arms around Laurel and pulled her tight against him. The pressure of her breasts against him, the feel of her in his arms, was balm to his tortured soul. The pressure inside him, the feeling that he was about to explode, gradually subsided. She was his touchstone. As long as he could see her, touch her, he was okay.

He bent over her, protecting her from the onslaught of the rain. He wondered why it had taken him so long to realize that he wasn't strong enough to do everything by himself. He also wondered why it had taken him so long to realize that he wanted this woman, that this need was something apart from his other needs. It was physical, visceral, a need he had buried deep within him but had refused to acknowledge before.

Because he considered it a weakness.

As long as he needed nothing and no one, he was free.

But Laurel had destroyed that freedom.

No. She had destroyed the cage he had built to protect himself, the cage that would have kept him a prisoner forever. She had forced him to feel, to want. To need.

He couldn't tell whether his body trembled from the cold or from fear. He had never been so vulnerable, never felt so helpless. He reached out to Laurel. "I need you."

The words exploded in his brain like white heat. He had always refused to let himself depend on anyone, even his twin. He stood on his own. He wanted it that way.

But if he turned away from her tonight, if he fought the shock and pain of Hope's death until he could feel it no longer, he might never be able to feel anything again.

"I need you, too," Laurel said.

He drew her to him. "Hold me," he said in a hoarse whisper.

Laurel slipped her arms around Hen's waist and laid her head against his chest.

Then he cried. He didn't know he could. He didn't know why. He only knew he needed to.

The tears dissolved the bitterness of years, the accumulated hatred, the unrelenting anger. They dissolved the last of the shell he had built around himself. They allowed him to mourn for all he had lost.

They allowed him to cry for Hope.

Chapter Twenty-two

Laurel's arms tightened around Hen. She wished she could do something to help him, but she realized that his tears were for a past in which she had no part, for things lost that could never be regained.

Then she started to cry for Hen, for all the years when he could only survive by refusing to feel. She had thought her life had been hard, but his must have been even worse. He had been pressed and squeezed until there was nothing left. Then the inside of him had been scorched by fire to make sure nothing would ever grow there.

But somehow he had managed to keep a tiny part of himself safe from the flames. She didn't know if it would be enough.

She held him harder.

He would learn to love. He must. She would help him. And not just for herself and Adam. She would help because she loved him too much to do anything else.

He was calmer now. His arms felt firm around her, no longer rigid. She started to withdraw. His arms fell away from her.

"Do you want to go back?" he asked.

She had thought he might want her to go, that he might be ashamed to have cried before her.

"No."

"Will you stay with me?"

Eternity lay before her in that question. She looked up at him and saw only the face of a man tortured by demons he would never be able to defeat alone. Not even his brothers had been able to do that for him.

But she could, and he was offering her the chance.

"Yes."

"I'm not very experienced."

"I'm not either."

"As a matter of fact, I've never been with a woman."

"You've nev—" She broke off. Surely it was difficult for a man to make such an admission.

"I never thought much of women, but I couldn't just use them. Monty could spend the night with one and forget her face and name before breakfast. That would have haunted me."

Laurel didn't know what to say. She'd never met a man who didn't look at women as something to be used. Men accepted that attitude as a natural thing. So did women.

"I knew someday I'd meet the right woman, and then it would be the right time."

Laurel swallowed hard. To think Hen wanted her to be the first. She knew Carlin had been with other women. Making love to her, creating a child together, hadn't been anything special for him.

But it would be special with Hen.

"Let's get out of the rain," she said, and drew him under the protective shelf of rock. "I brought you a blanket." She picked up the folded slicker and handed it to him.

"You're as wet as I am."

"Only my dress."

"We need a fire," Hen said.

Using some of the wood Laurel kept stacked inside the cave, Hen built a small fire against the back of the cave so it would reflect the heat better.

"Now get out of those wet clothes," Hen said.

They stood face to face, each very much aware of the other.

"Would you help me?"

Hen had never unbuttoned a woman's dress—he hadn't wanted to—but now his muscles grew taut with anticipation. Laurel turned her back to him, but he couldn't take his eyes off her. He found her neck and shoulders impossibly inviting. In the firelight her skin looked incredibly smooth and soft. He reached out to touch her.

She shivered.

"You're cold."

"No." She looked at him over her shoulder. "I haven't been touched by a man in a long time—and never with such gentleness."

He had barely brushed her skin. How could his touch have such a powerful effect on her? He opened his hand until his palm covered her shoulder. She shivered even more violently then.

"You are cold."

"No."

He didn't believe her. He unfastened her buttons, then unfolded the slicker and took out the blanket. "Get out of that dress."

She slipped the dress down past her waist, then stepped out of it altogether.

Moisture made her shift, never more than a poor shield against immodesty, cling to Laurel's body, revealing contours Hen had only imagined. He felt the blood surge in his veins and a prickly heat radiate through his body from his groin. Unsure of his reaction, of his control, Hen hurried to drape the blanket over Laurel's shoulders.

"Now you," Laurel said.

Hen stripped to his underclothes.

"Everything. You're soaked."

"Turn your back."

Laurel smiled, but she turned to look out over the meadow.

The rain had slowed to a drizzle. The sky had begun to clear to the west. She could see a cluster of stars hugging the tops of the mountains. The clouds would be gone in less than an hour.

Hen shed his underwear and slipped under the blanket with Laurel. "You don't have to stay. It was unfair of me to ask."

"Do you want me to go?"

"No."

"Then hold me. It's colder than I thought."

Hen didn't feel cold. He felt deliciously warm. He put his arms around Laurel and drew her to him. He could feel her breasts moving free inside the chemise. The effect on him was electric. The stirring in his groin was abrupt and dramatic. He was afraid that such a graphic sign of his lust would frighten Laurel. He shifted his body to make his condition less obvious.

He kissed her—softly, lingeringly, lips tasting each other, slowly, completely. Aware that his fingers were digging into her soft flesh, Hen tried to relax and ease the tension that made his body hard and rigid.

His success was hardly noticeable.

Tonight he had swept aside barriers he had hidden behind for fifteen years. He had unleashed a part of himself that he had kept on a short, uncompromising rein, a part he had never allowed to get out of control for even one moment. The results were a shock and a surprise. He wanted Laurel so badly, he could barely control himself.

For the first time in his life, he began to understand what Monty meant when he said he had to have a woman or die.

But the jailer in him would not be banished so easily. It wanted to know how he could make love to a woman in a cave in the middle of a mountain canyon. It wanted to know what had happened to his dream of sharing his life and his first experience of love with someone young, pure, and innocent.

But Hen felt no guilt. Laurel had come to him out of love.

She stayed for the same reason. There could be no dishonor in that. She had come to him because he needed her as he had never needed anyone in his life. She had asked nothing for herself. She hadn't even asked that he love her in return.

But he did. He loved her as much as he was capable. He had begun to fear that he was destined never to know love, that he was incapable of feeling anything for a woman beyond appreciation and friendship. His body told him his fears were groundless.

"I wish I could see you better," he whispered.

"Maybe you'll like me better for a little mystery. I'm told firelight is flattering to a woman."

"Not even the brightest sun can dull your beauty."

Spirals of electricity shot through Hen as he unbuttoned Laurel's chemise and slipped his hands inside to caress her back. Her skin was unbelievably soft and warm, the smell of the rain in her hair earthy and cool. He wondered if he was moving too fast. He didn't want to do anything to frighten her. He never wanted her to be afraid of him.

Moving to one side, Laurel slipped her chemise off her shoulder. Then she grasped Hen's arm and pulled until she could reach his hand. Taking it in her own, she moved it up her side and around until it covered her breast.

Hen froze, waiting for permission to proceed.

"Touch me here," Laurel said, guiding his fingertips to a hardening nipple. She gradually fell back until she lay on the blanket, her lowered chemise an open invitation.

Hen had never beheld anything so beautiful in all his life. He was tempted to sit and stare in wonder. But an even stronger need to touch and feel overrode his reverence. Reaching out, he touched her belly. The skin was soft and supple. Her stomach rose and fell with the rhythm of her breathing. Hen moved his hand until he reached the swell of her breasts. Laurel's breathing hesitated when his hand covered her breast, then resumed at a more rapid rate.

"Am I hurting you?"

"No." Laurel reached out. "I want to touch you, too," she said.

A welter of sensations washed over Hen. No one had ever touched him. The sensations were new and acute. Her touch on his chest and shoulders was too distracting; he took Laurel's hands in his own and lay down beside her.

"I'm probably doing this all wrong," he said as he kissed her fingers, "but I can't think with you doing that."

She pulled his hands to her lips. "You think I can, with you touching me?"

"I don't know. I just know your touch is driving me crazy."

"Then hold me," Laurel said.

Hen put his arms around Laurel and fell back pulling her over on top of him. Her damp hair cascaded over his face. Laurel threw it over her shoulder with an expert toss of her head.

"Is this any better?" she asked.

As an answer, Hen took her face in his hands and kissed her long and deep. Then he rolled over on top of her. Even as he kissed her again, his hand instinctively covered her breasts. And once again responding to an instinctive desire, he left a trail of kisses as his lips traveled along her neck, over her chest, until he gently kissed her breast into full firmness.

Fearful of hurting her, of frightening her, he cautioned himself to go slowly. But his long-buried hunger erupted to sweep away gentleness and patience. His hungry assault on her breasts soon had Laurel moaning softly, her body squirming under him. Despite some fumbling, he was able to help her shrug free of the chemise.

"Are you sure you aren't cold?" he asked as his hand traveled over her side and paused momentarily in the small depression in her thigh.

"Not as long as you hold me," she replied.

He wanted to hold her forever. He wanted to touch and taste her, to experience her with his mouth and body, until he knew her as well as he knew himself. An excess of hungers assailed him. He wanted to taste fruit stolen from her lips, to see her helpless with laughter, hear her singing from happiness. He wanted to smell her hair when it was hot from the sun, to nuzzle her body when it was warm from sleep.

His inexperience filled him with doubt. He didn't want to do anything that would make her draw away from him. She had no experience to make her look forward to their lovemaking. He didn't know enough to know how to please her, how to help her forget the past. He was so ignorant, he might even make things worse.

He cursed to himself.

But his emotional heed of Laurel was stronger than his physical need. He had never wanted any woman the way he wanted her. He had never let himself be swayed by such a need. He wanted to hold her tight, to press her against the entire length of his naked body. He wanted to sink into her until he felt lost and safe.

Yet just as powerful was the feeling of awe that this woman would give herself to him, would yield her body to his control, for his satisfaction. For years he had looked upon this act as the ultimate gift, the highest honor. For years it had remained beyond his grasp. For even longer, he had felt unworthy. Yet Laurel had opened her arms and her heart to him, as well as her body.

He continued to shower her with kisses, to caress her body with his hands, to warm her with his nearness. All the while his burgeoning need drove him closer and closer to the edge of desperation.

He felt Laurel start to tremble. Before he could ask if anything was wrong, she threw her arms around him and pressed her leg between his.

Hen's resolution collapsed like a wall of mud swept away by a flood. He grasped her buttocks in his hands and pressed her against him so hard that he knew she could feel the heat of his need pressed hard against her abdomen. His fevered lips forsook her mouth and laid a searing trail of kisses along her neck and shoulder before they buried themselves in the valley between her breasts. Laurel arched against him, driving an agonized moan from Hen.

Laurel's hand slipped between the tangle of their legs, igniting a flame in his loins. Sparks of desire burst in every part of his body until his limbs trembled with desire.

"Please," Laurel murmured.

Hen hesitated, unsure of himself. Impatient, Laurel moved lower along Hen's body until she could take hold of him.

Hen gasped, his body went rigid.

Laurel guided him to her moist heat. When Hen remained rigid and immobile, Laurel pushed against him, driving him inside her.

Hen felt virtually paralyzed by the feeling that flooded through him. The force of his physical desire, the vigor of the animal need, was much more intense than anything he had ever experienced. He could feel his body begin to buck and plunge. Instinct as strong as the need to survive drove him.

As Laurel pressed herself against him, driving him deeper into her body, he was consumed by a need as old as man himself. He began to move within her, and everything receded from his mind except the need to satisfy himself and the woman he held in his arms.

Hen gripped Laurel, drawing her to him. He gave himself up to the swirling feeling that seemed to lift him on a cloud of desire and rush him into a blinding vortex of need, out of control, on a shooting star of feeling that propelled him through space at blinding speed.

He clung to Laurel, but even as he moved faster and deeper within her, as his own body became tense with desire, he became less aware of her. His need gradually blocked everything from his consciousness until he felt he had been melted down into a single shaft of energy, a shrieking kernel of light hurled through space, its vitality straining against the barriers until it exploded in a shower of blinding light.

Gradually the tension left Hen's body, and he felt himself float back to earth on a downy cloud of love.

It wasn't until he realized that the gasping, gulping noise was the sound of his own harsh breathing that he began to understand the magnitude of what had happened to him. Even as he struggled to mute his breathing, he knew his self-control had been shattered beyond mending. Never again would he be able to repress his desire for this woman. Never again would he be able to deny his feelings. Laurel had smashed the dry husk that had grown around him. And the part of him that he had denied and imprisoned had burst forth—strong, vital, and thirsting for life. He would never be able to imprison it again.

He didn't want to.

Laurel felt wrapped in an impregnable cocoon of love. Never in her life had she felt so warm, so safe, so loved. She had nothing to look back on but abuse and neglect. Nothing in her whole life had prepared her for the experience of feeling safe and warm and protected. She had no way of knowing what it meant to lie in the arms of the man she loved.

It was so wonderful that it simply took her breath away.

She thought of the mother she could hardly remember. She wondered if she and her father had ever shared an experience like this. If anyone had ever given Laurel just one minute of the love she felt now as she nestled in Hen's arms, she would never have misunderstood her feelings for Carlin. Nor would she have mistaken his feelings for anything except the desire to satisfy his physical need.

But Hen thought she was something wonderful and precious and valuable and worth risking his life for. She was as important as life itself. He thought she was beautiful. He thought she was the finest, most wonderful, most courageous woman in Sycamore Flats.

Just thinking about it caused her to melt. No one had ever said she was beautiful, not even Carlin. Neither had he ever sat gazing at her as if he couldn't get enough of just looking at her. He had never touched her skin with reverence or kissed her as though he were savoring the nectar of life. He had never cried in her arms or needed to. He had wanted her, but he had never needed her.

She had never felt the closeness she felt with Hen. She had never felt that she shared in their lovemaking, only that she was there. Everything was so different with Hen, it was as though she, too, were experiencing love for the first time.

She gloried in his strength as he held her close. He was too thin, but he still managed to convey the impression of solid strength. Maybe it was the ease with which he clasped her tightly against the hard, taut muscles of his torso. Maybe it was the fact she felt so small and powerless next to him.

But none of the reasons mattered. She felt safe, loved, and protected, and that was all she needed to know.

"You're cold," Hen said. He could feel the goose bumps on Laurel's back. Now that the fires of passion had cooled, the cold penetrated the blanket.

"A little."

Hen leaned out of the blanket to throw some wood on the fire. Then he wrapped their wet clothes in the slicker, and using it for a bolster, he sat up against the back of the cave. He pulled Laurel into his arms and wrapped the blanket around both of them.

But as his body cooled, the protective aura around them began to dissipate. Reality began to intrude, bringing with it doubts and questions. Hen knew he loved Laurel and wanted to marry her, but he didn't know if she could love him enough to forget what he had been.

"What's wrong?" Laurel said.

"Nothing."

"Yes, it is. I can feel you starting to pull away. What is it?"

He didn't want to destroy the wonder of this night, but it seemed to be crumbling already. In a few minutes, there wouldn't be anything left to preserve.

"I was just remembering some of the things you said."

Now it was Laurel's turn to grow stiff and withdraw. "What things?"

"About my being a gunfighter and a killer."

"I shouldn't have said any of those things. I was angry. I was afraid you were like Carlin. I didn't even try to see what you're really like."

"What am I like?"

"You're the most gentle, genuinely caring man I've ever known. I didn't know a man could be that way."

Hen experienced a strange feeling, almost as though something inside him had cracked and broken. It didn't hurt. It just felt as if some kind of pressure had been released.

"I knew it the moment you touched me. Your words were so harsh, your actions so abrupt. But your touch told me there was another part of you hiding just out of sight." Laurel looked up at him. "I needed that part more than I needed your healing powers. Then I fell in love with you, and I didn't care about all the rest."

"Why do you love me?"

Laurel smiled up at him. She looked so lovely in the firelight. He wished they could stay here forever. He wished the magic which embraced them tonight would never end.

"What else could I do when a big handsome man stormed into my life, told me he was going to take care of me, then proceeded to do it? You took care of my wounds, gave my child what only a man could give him, offered me the promise of everything I'd ever wanted."

Hen was stunned. He had never viewed what he did in that light. He just did what he always did, what he would have done for anyone. But it was different this time. Never before had he ended up with a woman in his arms. He had never stood around in the rain wanting to kiss her. He had never felt that if he let her go, he would break apart, dissolve, wash away in the runoff.

"When did you fall in love with me?" Laurel asked.

"I don't know."

He didn't. He had never considered the possibility of falling in love. He hadn't looked for it. He hadn't even recognized it when it was happening. When it finally became too obvious for him to fail to recognize, he'd been in love for some time. "Maybe when you kept fighting Damian, when you wouldn't give up even though he knocked you down."

"You couldn't have loved me then," Laurel said. "I looked awful. You told me so."

"You looked beautiful to me. You always have."

"You must have been besotted."

Hen wasn't blind to Laurel's faults or to the differences between the two of them. He was well aware of the difficulty any man would have being in love with a woman like her. But he liked her toughness, her hard-headed defiance of anybody she thought might not treat her or her child as they ought. It was the same insolent attitude he had shown the world for years. Only he had backed it up with his gun. She had nothing more than her own courage.

"Maybe I was besotted," he said. "I probably still am."

"I never met a less besotted man in my life," Laurel said. "There have been times when I wondered if there was any feeling inside you at all."

So had he, but Laurel had helped to answer his question.

"Will this help make up your mind?" he asked.

Hen kissed her tentatively. He wasn't experienced in kissing. He didn't really know how to go about it. But instinct seemed to be guiding him. Laurel did the rest.

Laurel chuckled softly. He cringed, fearful that his kiss was so poor she couldn't help but laugh.

"When I was young, I used to dream of the man I would fall in love with someday," she told him. "He would ride in on a magnificent stallion or smuggle himself in in a load of hay. I even dreamed of him being brought in with a rope around his neck. But I never expected to be kissing him at midnight in a mountain canyon in the rain."

"George would tell you I'm not romantic. Monty would say something worse."

"Someday I'd like to meet your brothers, if only to tell them they're wrong. You're the most romantic man in the world. You go dashing up a mountain canyon to fight for a woman you've never even seen. Hardly a day passes that you haven't found a way to do something else for me. You tell me that I'm beautiful, that I'm more wonderful than I ever hoped I could be."

Laurel put her arms around Hen's neck, pulled him down to her, and kissed him with very satisfying fervor. "Nothing could be more romantic than that."

"But I don't know the right things to do or say."

"You weren't very bad a short while ago."

"I was clumsy, and you know it."

"Maybe a little, at first, but you're a fast learner."

"I shouldn't have been a beginner. I should have known more."

Laurel kissed him. "I like it. Not many women can have the joy of knowing the man they love has never shared himself with any other woman, that she is his first and his only."

"You really don't mind?"

"I wouldn't have it any other way." She slid her hand down his chest and along one powerful thigh. "But you could use a little practice." Her hand found a more vital location. "Do you think you might be up to it?"

His reaction was immediate and powerful.

Chapter Twenty-three

"Mrs. Worthy won't see you," Laurel told Hen. "She won't leave Hope's side."

Everyone in the Worthy household had been too preoccupied to notice that Laurel hadn't slept in her bed or that no one heard her leave next morning to collect the laundry.

"How is she?" Hen asked.

"She's still unconscious."

"What does Doc Everson say?"

"He doesn't understand how she's held on this long."

"Then he doesn't think she's got a chance?"

Laurel shook her head. "I must go," she said. "No one has eaten a bite."

"I'll get Tyler to send something over from the restaurant."

"He already has. I have to try to get them to eat it."

"I'll come back in a little while."

"Come to the back door."

"I love you," Hen said softly.

"I love you too. Now I'd better go."

"You made a right fair mess of things," Avery Blackthorne said to Allison. "Who put the damned fool notion in your head to go after Randolph?"

Allison wasn't the same boy who had ridden into Sycamore Flats less than twenty-four hours earlier. He'd found he didn't like shooting all that much. The whole time the doc was taking care of his arm, he was telling Allison about the little girl he had killed with a stray bullet. It made him feel sick to his stomach. He had also figured out that Hen Randolph was twice as fast and ten times as good as any gunfighter he'd ever seen. Hen could have killed him any time he wanted.

Allison decided he wasn't the least bit attracted to the idea of dying. He hadn't even considered the possibility when he rode into town. But after looking into Hen Randolph's eyes, he knew death was a certainty if he took up a gun against him again.

"You said you wanted him dead," Allison said, relieved that iron bars stood between him and Avery. He had always been a little afraid of his grandfather. Avery acted calm and reasonable, but he was ruthless.

"If you were going to kill him, why didn't you do it right off? You were a damned fool to go shooting up the town. All you did was get the whole damned place mad as hornets."

"Is she dead?"

"It's just as well if she is. They'll blame Randolph for not killing you first. That'll make it easier to get him in the end."

Allison was reluctant to disagree with his grandfather, but he couldn't remain quiet. "He didn't try to kill me. I could see it in his eyes. He was mad as hell, but it wasn't a killing mad."

"You don't know what you're talking about. Hen Randolph is a killer."

"No, he's not," Allison contradicted, his courage bolstered by the protection of the iron bars. "He could have killed me any time he wanted. He meant to teach me a lesson."

"I hope you learned it. A cub shouldn't tangle with a curly wolf like Randolph. You leave him to me."

"You don't have to kill him," Allison said. "He ain't killed any of us."

"Have you forgotten what he did to Ephraim?"

"Pa's a bigger fool than I am. You said so yourself. We ought to take the kid and forget the sheriff."

"No! Nobody crosses a Blackthorne and gets away with it. He beat up Damian, humiliated Ephraim, and now he's shot you. You let that keep on, and every two-bit nester in the territory will be pulling a gun on us. I'm going to plant that sheriff good and proper."

"He's not like the others. He's smart."

"Maybe, but he'll die just the same."

But Allison didn't want the sheriff to die. He had a feeling that what Hen had done for him was more important than anything that had happened so far in his sixteen years.

"You won't get fat eating like that," Tyler said. He had come to collect the dishes from Hen's lunch.

"What's this?" Hen asked, poking at his food.

"The look of food never bothered you like it did Monty. You got things on your mind. Better get them off."

"I've got nothing to say to you."

"Always were stubborn as a mule. Everybody says Monty's the most stubborn, but he just likes to make a lot of noise. You're the one who thinks he has all the answers."

"Well, if it's any consolation to you, I don't have the answers, and I know it."

"Didn't take two seconds to see that."

"When did you get to be so discerning?"

"Trouble is, you don't know what to do about it."

"And you do?"

"You wouldn't listen if I did."

Hen admitted that was true. Maybe it was just that men never listened to younger brothers, but he couldn't imagine explaining any of what bothered him to Tyler. Even if he thought he would understand.

"I wouldn't listen to anybody who sends telegrams scaring people and spreading rumors."

"Stop trying to annoy me and talk to George. You won't do it."

"Do what?"

"Annoy me. I stopped paying attention to you and Monty years ago."

Hen looked at his younger brother with new eyes. He guessed Tyler had grown up. Strange he hadn't noticed. He wondered what else he had missed.

George was writing a letter when Hen entered his room. "Don't stop," he said when George put down his pen. "I can wait."

"But you probably won't," George said. He covered the inkwell and turned to face his brother. "You've done your best to avoid me ever since I got here."

"You shouldn't have come. You were a fool to listen to Tyler."

"So you told me."

"How's Rose?"

"Just fine."

Hen's gaze narrowed. "She was pregnant, wasn't she?"

George smiled. "She had a girl just before I left. Black hair and the biggest black eyes you ever saw."

"Sounds like she looks like you."

"Probably, but I insisted she be named after her mother. We'll call her Elizabeth Rose."

Hen was honestly pleased. Rose would probably have had a dozen children if she could. After losing a baby a couple of years ago, he had doubted she would try again, but he should have known better. When Rose wanted something, she usually got it.

George leveled a penetrating gaze at his brother. "You didn't come here to talk about your newest niece."

"Hell, I don't know why I came."

"Yes, you do. You just don't want to say it. Talking has always been hard for you."

"I'll be damned if I know how you ended up in this family. You're not a bit like the rest of us."

"I think we can safely assume Ma never played Pa false."

"While he cheated on her all the time."

George didn't answer. He just sat there. Hen knew he was waiting for him to get to the reason he had come. But now he was here, he didn't know where to start. He wasn't sure he knew what he wanted to say.

"Do you think I'm a killer?"

It came out before he could consciously form the thought, but he knew that question was the reason he'd come. Everything else depended on that.

"Of course not."

"I've killed several people."

"So have I, but I'm not a killer."

"But that was in the war."

"I would have killed again if it had been necessary."

"But that's the difference," Hen said. "You would have done a lot of things if they'd been necessary, but you never did. I always seem to be looking for it. It's almost like I don't want to avoid it."

"I always thought you avoided it as long as possible."

Hen looked surprised. "You must be the only one."

"Monty has said the same thing several times. So have the others."

Hen pondered that for a moment. It was natural that his family would try to think the best of him, especially his twin. No one wanted to admit he had a killer for a brother.

"Do you know why this town hired me?"

"No."

"Can't you guess?"

"I'd rather you tell me."

"They were having trouble with rustlers, and they'd already lost three sheriffs. Peter Collins convinced them I could not only shoot faster than the outlaws, but that I wouldn't be too particular about making sure it was a fair fight."

"I wouldn't get upset just because Peter got the wrong notion."

"Did he? Until I shot that boy in the arm instead of the heart, you couldn't have found anybody in this town who would have agreed with you."

"Why didn't you? With all that wild shooting, you knew there was a chance of his doing just what he did."

"He's sixteen."

"Guns don't care about the age of the man who pulls the trigger."

"I saw myself in that boy. What I used to be like before the rustlers caught Monty."

"I wondered about that."

"If I had shot him, I *would* be a killer."

"You aren't."

"This town's paying me to kill. Who's to say I won't start killing because I like it? I wanted to kill Damian that day. If I could have gotten a clear shot, he'd be dead right now. That scares the hell out of me. If I don't stop now, if I kill somebody else, I feel like I'll pass the point of no return."

"Did Damian have anything to do with Laurel?"

Hen didn't know why he thought he could keep anything from George. He should have told him from the first. George had always been able to see into his brothers' heads. That was what made him such a good brother and such a damned nuisance.

"He beat her up and tried to steal her son."

"I don't think anybody would have blamed you if you had killed him."

"That's what they *expected* me to do. That's what they wanted me to do."

"Now you don't want to?"

"Not exactly."

"You don't want Laurel to think you're a killer."

Hen nodded.

"But she does anyway."

"She says she doesn't, but she doesn't want her kid to grow up like me."

"Does that matter?"

"Yes." Silence. "I'm in love with her. I think I want to marry her."

"Does she know?"

"That I love her. I haven't said anything about marriage."

"Why not?"

Why hadn't he? It wasn't just that he hadn't known he loved her until a short time ago. He was afraid of himself. Killing wasn't something he took lightly. He traded on his reputation to prevent it. But when it proved necessary, he didn't hesitate long. It might be only a small step to no hesitation at all.

"I don't know who I am. I thought I did, but now I realize I've been hiding from myself as well as the rest of the world."

"Is it Pa?"

Hen almost smiled. George thought everything was Pa's fault. It made sense for George. They looked so much alike. But he and Monty looked like their mother. And her weakness ran through them like quartz through rock.

"When Ma died and Madison left, Monty and I made a

vow to protect what was left or die trying. It became an obsession, even after you and Jeff came back. But Monty got interested in other things. I never did. Now I want to protect Laurel and Adam, but I don't want to have to do it with a gun."

Quite suddenly, Hen realized what had happened. Each man had a limit. No matter what the situation, there was only so much he could absorb without something going wrong. He had reached his. If he killed anybody else, he stood in grave danger of losing his soul.

Yet he couldn't marry Laurel unless he was willing to do whatever was necessary to protect her and Adam. Knowing the Blackthornes, that would mean using his gun.

"You've turned out to be the family protector, much as I've become its head, but you resent it. That's why you're always running away. But you feel it's your duty, so you come back. We're all protectors, but we're not killers."

"Then why do I think of a gun as part of almost every action?"

"We all use the tools we have until we can find something else. You use a gun. Monty uses his fists. I use family loyalty. If you marry Laurel, you're going to protect her any way you must. You're afraid if you depend entirely on guns, you may destroy the love that's between you. You came here today because you haven't been able to come to terms with that fear."

Leave it to George to put things in a nutshell. But there was more to it than that. He had agreed to protect this town. If he stayed, there'd be a confrontation. Could he leave because of Laurel without feeling that he had run away?

Laurel had accepted his past use of a gun, but could she accept it again? Could she see that though he was willing to use a gun, he didn't like it? Even if she did, could she live with him afterwards?

He didn't know, but from what he knew of Laurel, it was extremely doubtful.

* * *

"She's been asking for you all morning," Mrs. Worthy said to Hen as he followed her upstairs to Hope's bedroom. "I didn't want to let her see you, but the doctor said it would upset her too much if I didn't."

This is how people treat a hired gunman. Everybody wants you when they're in trouble, but nice people don't want to have anything to do with you the rest of the time.

"Hope was my first real friend here," Hen said. "I would do anything to change what happened."

Mrs. Worthy was silent for a moment when they reached the upper landing. "Horace tells me I must apologize for some of the things I said."

"Forget about it."

"I didn't know what I was saying. I was distraught thinking Hope was going to die. I don't suppose you can understand, not being a parent yourself."

"I shot my first man because he had a rope around my brother's neck."

Mrs. Worthy reached out to pat Hen's arm. "Maybe you do." Her smile said that all was forgiven. "Don't stay long. She's still very weak."

"Is she going to be all right?"

Mrs. Worthy smiled and nodded. "The doctor says it's a miracle. She ought to be right as rain in about a month. Your brother's in there now."

"Tyler?"

"He's been tempting her appetite. She can't get well if she won't eat."

Tyler was feeding Hope one of his clear broths when Mrs. Worthy opened the door. Hope's eyes lit up and she pushed the spoon away.

"What kept you so long?"

Her voice was weak and she spoke slowly, but the old sparkle was still in her eyes. Hen felt a suspicious feeling of moisture about his eyes and an unfamiliar tightness in his throat. He had to get himself under control on the double. If Tyler suspected that he was feeling even the slightest bit sentimental, he'd never let him hear the end of it.

"Had to wait until looking at me wouldn't cause you to have a setback," Hen answered.

Hope frowned. "I know mother wouldn't let you come. I heard them whispering. It's not fair, especially when she lets Tyler come."

Hen kept his eyes from Tyler's face. "She was afraid I might tire you out."

"You've got to promise to come every day."

"There's no need. You need lots of rest and—"

"Every day. I never missed taking you lunch or dinner."

"Only if your mother says it's okay. Now I'd better be going."

Hope put out her hand to hold him back. "How's Mrs. Blackthorne? They didn't hurt her or Adam, did they?"

"They're just fine. After what happened to you, any Blackthorne fool enough to come within a mile of this town would get torn apart."

"Aw, go on."

"Mary Parker is a thing of the past. Every boy in town has been bringing flowers to your door."

"I told you I'm not interested in boys."

She glanced at Tyler as she spoke. Hen's face remained expressionless.

Hen got to his feet. "You hurry up and get well. I got spoiled having my lunch brought to me. You know those fools you warned me about?"

"Yeah?"

"They've been worrying me to death. Besides, Jordy wants you back. Your ma doesn't give him as much food as you do."

"How is the little monster?"

"As terrible as ever. If I can sneak him past your ma, I'll bring him by one day. He's been asking about you so much he's about to give me nervous fits."

"I been thinking about him, too. He hasn't gotten into any more trouble, has he?"

"Not a bit. He's waiting for you to help him. He said he never knew girls could think up so much good stuff."

Hope laughed, then turned white. She might be better, but the wound was far from healed.

"I'll be going. You eat your soup and get well soon."

"Tyler says it's consomme."

"Yes, well, Tyler's got a fancy name for everything. To me it looks like something you'd pump out of the bottom of a mine, but I guess it tastes a little better."

"Thanks for the compliment," Tyler said. With an almost imperceptible motion of his head, he indicated that it was time for Hen to leave.

"I'll be back if you promise to keep getting better. Otherwise, you'll be stuck with Tyler."

As he closed the door behind him, Hen felt a great weight lift from his heart. No matter what Laurel told him, he hadn't been able to credit Hope's miraculous recovery until he saw her. He didn't know what he would have done if she had died.

Mrs. Worthy wasn't on the landing. Laurel met him at the bottom of the stairs.

"She looks so white," Hen said. "Are you sure she's going to be all right?"

"She looks wonderful compared to that first day. Your brother brings her the most wonderful soups."

"I'll give Tyler that. He may have the longest nose in Arizona, but he can cook."

"You don't like your brother, do you? I just realized I've never seen you together. Your other brother either."

"We're not a close family."

"Then why are they here?"

"Tyler was afraid the big bad Blackthornes were going to get me, so he sent a telegram to George asking him to come help drive them away."

"You don't think you need help?"

"George shouldn't be here. He has a wife and four children, the last one a brand-new baby. Tyler and I don't have anybody."

He could have bitten his tongue. He didn't mean that the way it sounded, but he didn't have anybody like Rose and the children. Laurel might love him, but she wouldn't want to marry anybody like him.

"I'd better be going. You okay?"

"Sure."

"You're not going to try to move back to the canyon?"

"No."

"Good." He turned to leave.

"I love you," she said softly. "You know that, don't you?"

"Yes. It's something I remind myself of at least once every hour. I still can't believe it's true."

"It is. It will always be true."

He wondered if that meant she would love him even though she wouldn't marry him. That would be a curse rather than a consolation. "We need to talk."

"I can't leave just now. Mrs. Worthy is taking a nap. She sits up with Hope every night."

"I'll come back this afternoon. About two o'clock."

"Okay." She kissed him lightly. "I'll meet you in the wash behind the jail."

Hen started down the boardwalk toward the hotel. He felt better than he had in weeks. Seeing Hope had made a world of difference. Things wouldn't be easy. He knew that. But for the first time he not only knew what he wanted to do, he thought he had a chance of doing it.

He started to step down from the boardwalk so he could cross the street to the hotel. He looked up just in time to see Madison, Monty, Iris, and Jeff ride into town.

The stream of curses he uttered caused Emma Wells to cover her daughter's ears and rush inside the hardware store before the child could hear any more of the disgraceful things the sheriff was saying. But Emma remembered every word. She had to tell her friends. She was certain they would be as shocked as she.

Chapter Twenty-four

"Some welcome after we've come a thousand miles to save your hide," Monty said. He jumped down from his horse and clasped his twin in a bear hug. "I told Madison you'd be running around growling at anything that crossed your path."

"You'd better be in one hell of a lot of trouble," Madison said, as he painfully eased himself out of the saddle. "If I've flattered this nag into thinking it's a horse by riding it over the worst country Monty could find, you'd better have at least a dozen Blackthornes breathing down your neck."

"Sorry. I only got three in jail and another skulking around town."

"Damn," Madison cursed, rubbing his backside without regard for staring eyes. "I should have listened to Fern."

"Where is she?"

"Home, pregnant again, what else?" Iris said, directing a disgusted look toward Madison. "I think he moved to Colorado so he'd have more room for all the children he means to father."

"We didn't pass any Blackthornes on the way down," Monty said. "I hope this isn't going to end up a hoax."

"Serves you right if it does," Hen said. "You ought to know better than to listen to Tyler."

"Who said anything about Tyler?" Monty demanded. "The call came up the outlaw trail. Every man on the place heard it. It went as far as Canada."

"I guess that's why they got so many replies," Hen said. "More than a dozen have shown up already."

"Good!" Monty said. "I haven't had a good fight in years."

"Not since you married me," Iris said. "Go ahead and say it."

"I've had plenty of good fights with you," Monty said, pulling his wife out of the saddle and giving her a brazen pat. "I thought I might like a change of pace."

"You two stop carrying on in the street," Madison said. "You'll give the family a bad name."

"You're just jealous Fern isn't here," Iris said, settling securely under Monty's arm.

"Yes, I am," Madison said with a grin. "Damned jealous."

"You can get accommodations at the hotel," Hen said. "Then, when you get cleaned up and cooled off, you can head back to Colorado."

"I hope they've got plenty of rooms," Madison said, giving Jeff an evil eye. "If I have to share with Jeff, you're liable to have a shooting before morning."

"Getting along just as well as usual, I see," Hen said.

"Madison doesn't like being seen with a cripple," Jeff said. "It embarrasses him."

"If I hear one more word about your being a cripple, I'm liable to shoot your other arm off."

"And if he misses, I won't," Monty threw in for good measure.

"It was a memorable trip," Iris said with a grimace. "Point me toward the hotel before I get violent, too."

"Ask the clerk to tell George you're here," Hen said. "I'm sure he'll be delighted to see you. When you get settled in, you can go down to the restaurant and ask Tyler to fix you something to eat."

"You're not coming with us?" Monty asked.

"You're big boys. If you can find your way from Colorado, surely you can check into a hotel by yourself."

He had no intention of doing anything to make his brothers more comfortable. The more miserable they were, the faster they would leave. That couldn't be too fast for him.

"I don't think he sounds too happy to see us," Madison said. "Reminds me of a time in Abilene when—"

"You bring that up, and you'll get your fight sure enough,"

Hen threatened as he turned to Madison. "Besides, if you hadn't come, you'd be married to Samantha Bruce. I'd lay odds she wouldn't let you keep *her* pregnant all the time. You'd have been allowed two proper little Bostonians, then it would have been out the door, down the hall, and keep your hands to yourself, thank you very much."

Madison made a face.

Iris eyed her brother-in-law with an inquisitive gaze. "I haven't heard about this."

"You won't, even if I have to shoot Hen before the Blackthornes get a chance."

"Look who turned up," Hen said to George when he stepped out of the hotel. "When's the barbecue?"

George offered Iris a hand up the steps. "You must be exhausted. Your hotel room is ready."

With a snort of disgust, Hen turned on his heel and walked away cursing.

"I'm heading for the restaurant," Monty said. "I never thought I'd be glad to eat Tyler's food, but after three weeks on the trail, I'd eat anything he cooked no matter what he covered it with."

"I want a bath," Iris said. "I don't plan to get out until tomorrow."

"I want something to drink," Madison said. "I have a dry patch at the back of my throat just begging for a good brandy." Madison reached inside his saddlebags and withdrew a bottle. George laughed.

"I never depend on other people to know my tastes," Madison explained.

"What about you, Jeff?"

"I'll eat in my room. I don't want people staring at me."

"How did you get along with him and Monty for three weeks?" George asked Madison after Jeff had gone inside the hotel.

"I had two more of these when I started," Madison said, pointing to the bottle of brandy.

"At least Zac's not here," George said. "If he were, *I'd* need a drink."

Hen experienced a most unexpected reaction as he walked back to his office. Even before the last curse fell from his lips, he realized that he was smiling. There was a lightness in his heart he hadn't felt in a long time. He felt good, and he couldn't figure out why. With most of his family in town, he was in for more trouble than ever. George and Madison might have somehow helped to ease the situation, but trouble followed Monty and Jeff the way thunder followed lightning. He didn't even want to guess how many husbands and lovers would be in trouble before nightfall because they stared too long at Iris.

Trouble was gathering around him like snow clouds around a mountain top, and here he was feeling as if he didn't have a worry in the world. His mind must have snapped from the strain.

He was acting like a fool because he really felt truly, honestly, and deeply loved. Five men had dropped everything and traveled thousands of miles because they thought he might be in danger. They were ready to endanger their lives and risk losing all they held dear because of the love they felt for him. He felt something flutter inside him, something embarrassingly close to the desire to cry.

He fought it off.

Before he fell in love with Laurel, he would have accepted his brothers' presence without a thought. Now he understood what a sacrifice it represented. He wanted to tell them he wasn't worth it, that they should go back to their families, that he would rather die than have to explain why they had come to harm for him.

But he didn't. He didn't want them to go. For the first time in his life, he knew what it meant to be loved, and he didn't want to do anything to dispel that feeling.

* * *

"Did you see them?" Grace Worthy asked.

"Everybody has seen them," Ruth Norton replied, more excited than anyone could remember seeing her since the saloon girl stepped out in a high wind and her skirt blew over her head. "If Miranda is to be believed, every unattached female in town is panting after one or the other in the most disgraceful fashion."

"They look so much alike, you'd know they were family on sight."

"Like peas in a pod," Ruth replied. "You couldn't tell the sheriff from his twin if Hen wasn't thin as a rail. That other one looks enough like the older brother to be his double. I declare, I don't know when I've seen so many handsome men in one place. I'm a liar," Ruth said with conviction. "I've *never* seen so many handsome men at one time. Seeing the four of them coming down the boardwalk practically gave me palpitations."

"Ain't none of them a patch on that redhead," Tommy Worthy said. His mother had made him clean up and come sit with company, but he had spent half the afternoon with two of his friends trying to get a good look at Iris. "Sammy nearbout died in his tracks. He hasn't said a word since that we can understand."

"You certain she's married to one of them?" Grace asked.

"The one that looks like the sheriff," Tommy assured her. "It's the first thing I found out. Otherwise half the men in town would be hanging about the hotel lobby."

"Having them in town is bound to cause trouble," Ruth said. "I can understand their concern for their brother, but you mark my words, it will cause trouble."

"But I can't move into your house," Laurel objected.

"Of course you can," Hen said. "It's a perfect solution. Adam and Jordy won't have to move."

"But where will you go?"

"I can sleep in the jail." And he would before he'd move to the hotel with the rest of his family.

"That's absurd. Besides, I couldn't possibly stay there alone. This town would light up with gossip."

Laurel had just decided to move out when Hen came to introduce Iris to Mrs. Worthy. Now that Hope was on the mend, Laurel felt in the way. She had never intended to stay with the Worthys for more than a few days, but in the aftermath of Hope's illness, she had forgotten to think about finding a place to stay.

"You've got an entire house to yourself?" Iris asked.

"The last sheriff was married," Mrs. Worthy explained. "His wife wouldn't let him come unless we gave him a house. Much good it did him. He was killed less than six months later."

"Is there a room for Monty and me, too?" Iris asked.

"Sure," Hen replied.

"Good. We can act as chaperons. Then nobody will have any question. Besides, if I don't get Monty away from Jeff, he'll kill him. Not even George will stay with him."

So a few hours later, Laurel found herself settled in a new house, feeling even more unsettled than ever.

"You don't have to look so worried about putting Hen out of his own house," Iris said to Laurel. "I don't think either he or Monty feels as comfortable indoors as out."

Laurel couldn't tell Iris that her uneasiness had nothing to do with putting Hen out. It had to do with her being in his house. She had thought it would be easier this time, but it was harder.

Laurel tried to tell herself not to despair, but the letter she held in her hand gave her no reason to keep hoping. Once again, no one knew anything of a marriage between Carlin Blackthorne and Laurel Simpson, and they didn't know of anybody who could help her. After years of writing every court house, mission, preacher, or judge she heard of, it was hard not to give up. If in seven years she hadn't been able to find anyone who could prove she'd married Carlin, she couldn't expect to in the future.

The man who'd married them had probably forgotten all about them or moved out of the territory.

"I was hoping I'd run into you," Iris said, practically bumping into Laurel as she emerged from the post office. "I have to confess I don't care to walk by myself in a strange town."

Laurel could understand why. Iris Randolph was so beautiful that everybody stared at her. Even though she had come down the outlaw trail on horseback, she managed to look more smartly turned out than anyone in town.

"Monty tells me we could be here for a while. If that's true, I've got to buy some clothes. I was hoping you would tell me the best place to go."

"You'll have to talk to Miranda Trescott. I've been too poor to buy anything I couldn't absolutely do without."

"You cut right to the heart of things, don't you?" Iris said.

"It saves time."

"And people saying it for you."

"That too."

Iris waited for Laurel to exchange greetings with a local matron. "I know I'm being nosy, so tell me to be quiet if you wish, but is that letter bad news?"

Laurel stared at the envelope in her hand. She didn't want to tell Iris about it. It was none of her business. But the Randolphs would learn about it soon enough. It might as well be from her.

"My husband and I ran away to get married. Unfortunately, I didn't think to ask him where we were going. He was killed a month later, and I've been trying to locate the man who married us ever since. This letter is another dead end."

"In other words, some people don't believe you were married."

"Carlin's family refuses to acknowledge it."

"It doesn't seem to have hurt. Nobody passes without speaking."

Laurel's smile was cynical. "It wasn't like that before Hen arrived. At best, I was the town laundress. At worst—well, I'd rather not think about the worst."

"Now you're afraid Hen's family will kick up a fuss because you can't prove you were married."

"Wouldn't you?"

"Not a chance. Then I'd have to show you the skeletons in my closet."

"But I thought—"

"So does everybody else. And I mean to go on letting them. It's none of their business. But nothing like that is going to stop Hen. I don't understand him very well—he doesn't like me very much, so we don't talk—but he doesn't care what anybody thinks, even George. If he means to marry you, nothing will stop him."

Laurel didn't know if she could believe Hen was quite that impervious to other people's opinions, especially his family's, but it did make her feel more hopeful. She put the letter into her pocket. She had one more name to write.

"You say people here tried to snub you," Iris remarked. "Shall we parade through town, refusing to take notice of anyone, or shall we be ruthlessly condescending? My mother was a terrible woman, but she was absolutely unmatched when it came to convincing people they were something that ought to be stepped on."

Laurel grinned mischievously. "No, but I have to admit it's tempting."

"Well," Iris said, linking her arm with Laurel's, "if you're not going to let me misbehave, let's go buy me a dress. Monty says I look like a vagabond."

So Laurel went off to help Iris buy the kind of dress she'd never been able to afford herself. Iris was right. Everybody nodded and spoke to them. Laurel tried not to feel bitter. She knew her treatment was a reflection of the respect they had for the rich, powerful, and stunningly good-looking Randolph family.

Laurel's pride stiffened her resolve. The people of Sycamore Flats could admire the Randolphs all they wanted, but one of these days they were going to realize that Laurel Simpson Blackthorne was a woman of stature in her own right. They were going to be sorry they'd treated her so badly.

"Whatever you just decided, you can count on me to stand with you," Iris whispered in Laurel's ear. "Hen doesn't know how lucky he is."

Laurel stared at the ruin of her adobe. Much to her surprise, she regretted the loss of that house. It had been a poor, miserable place, but life had been simple when she lived there.

Now the house was in shambles, and so was her life. She didn't know what Hen thought, felt, or wanted. She doubted Hen knew himself.

She looked about the yard at the abandoned wash pot and the ashes already half covered with dust. Everything here represented a distant past, the time before Hen came up the canyon that first time. Since that day, her life had become chaotic. She hadn't been able to understand or control anything. Even her relationship with Adam.

The chute Hen had built to the house lay broken and empty, the flow cut off at the stream, the water evaporated.

She turned away from the ruin. She started toward the meadow.

She had tried not to think of the future with Hen, but she seldom had a thought that didn't include him.

Even when she faced the fact that he hadn't spoken of marriage, that she might have to build a new life without him, she thought of everything in terms of his absence. It would be impossible to find anyone else who could take such good care of her. No one else would make half as good a father for Adam. But it didn't matter. She wouldn't marry again. She'd never stop loving Hen.

Nobody will marry you anyway. They think you're only one step removed from being a whore.

Laurel pushed that thought aside. She had almost forgotten it. Since Hen had been here, everyone else seemed to have forgotten it as well.

The meadow awash with sunlight bore little resemblance to the meadow that night in the cold, pouring rain. Yet it didn't feel half as warm and welcoming as it had then.

Hen was here. You're alone now.

She guessed that was the difference. She was alone. She had always felt alone, but for a short time she had felt comforted and protected.

That was foolish. She hadn't had to worry about Carlin for years, about her stepfather for even longer than that. She'd never really worried about the men in town. She hadn't been afraid until the afternoon Damian tried to take Adam, the same afternoon Hen had walked up that trail with a bag full of linen shirts and changed her life forever.

Laurel climbed up to the small cave. She had come here so many times before. Most of the time she and Adam had come to watch the deer or the butterflies. To pick flowers. To play in the deep grass in the springtime. It was their private place to forget the work and drudgery of their life.

But sometimes she had come alone. Just as she was doing now, she would sit in the shade of the ledge, her arms around her bunched-up legs, her chin resting on her knees, staring out over the meadow lost in thought, wandering through dust-covered, cobweb-hung corners of her mind.

This was no time to torture herself with broken dreams of youth. It was too late to wish for someone to come sweeping through her life and fix everything that had gone wrong. No one could wipe out her parents' deaths, her stepfather's abuse, or Carlin's desertion. Neither could anyone give back her innocence or restore the years that had been lost to despair and hopelessness. The girl who dreamed those dreams was lost, gone beyond recall.

No, she was still alive somewhere deep inside. She was battered by disappointment and a little disillusioned by life, but she was still alive, still hoping.

For what?

"I was hoping I would find you here."

Laurel felt as if her entire existence had been suspended. Everything she had ever dreamed of was embodied in that voice. But as she turned to face Hen, she wondered anew if any of her dreams would ever come true. They couldn't come in pieces. She had to have everything, or none of it counted.

"How did you find me?"

"There aren't many places you go."

"You know me too well."

"I don't know you at all."

"Nothing's stopping you."

Hen lowered himself next to her. "You are."

"Why do you say that?"

"I suppose we both are," Hen admitted. "You don't approve of me, and I don't trust what's happening."

"What's that?" Laurel skipped past the part about her not approving of him. She knew all about that. She didn't know about the other.

"This business of falling in love," Hen explained. "I always thought it was stupid. I wasn't going to let it happen. Then it did."

"And?"

"I don't know. What does it feel like to you?"

What did it feel like to be in love with Hen Randolph? Terrifying. She'd never been more frightened of anything in her whole life. At the same time, she held on to his love with a death grip. "Sometimes I'm even afraid to think about it."

"Why?"

"Because I want it so much."

She tried not to see his silence as a retreat, but he seemed to withdraw into himself, to consider thoughts he wasn't willing to share with her.

"What do you want?"

Laurel swallowed. Everything and nothing. He had already given her so much, yet she felt empty, God, she'd better not say that. He'd swear she was crazy.

"I want somebody to love me. A lot. I don't expect him to do anything out of the ordinary, but I want him to make me feel I'm special, that in his eyes I'm the most wonderful woman in the whole world. I want him to call me his woman. I want him to be possessive, to be jealous. But I want him to be able to forget all that because he knows I would rather die than betray him.

"I want him to think I'm the most precious person in the whole world, to protect me and to guard me. But I want him to know I have a mind and feelings and opinions, that I can think and act and stand on my own. I want to feel free yet bound by his love. I want to feel owned even as I feel I'm the owner."

Laurel wondered if she'd said too much. He didn't react, just sat there looking at her. "Do you understand what I mean?"

"Everything you say seems to be a contradiction."

"Tell me what being in love means to you."

Hen wasn't sure he could. Even though he had thought about little else these last few days, he had come up with very few answers.

"For my father, it was fetters that choked the life out of him. I used to think he hated us. Now I know he wasn't strong enough to hate—or to love. For my mother, love was an obsession that blinded her to the truth. When she finally couldn't ignore the truth any longer, it killed her. The day we buried her, I swore that even if it meant I had to live and die alone, I'd never love anybody like that.

"Then Rose married George. There was nothing destructive about their love. They simply made each other better, happier. There was no mooning and sighing or having to be constantly in each other's company. Sometimes they're in the same room and they don't even seem to be aware of each other. But they are. It's like they're connected. They don't have to say anything or do anything. It's just there all the time. It's like they're part of each other." Hen looked into Laurel's eyes. "That's what I want."

Sighing inwardly, Laurel rested her hand on Hen's. "That's what I want, too. I just didn't say it half as well."

"But don't you want all the rest, the sighing and the mooning and the swearing God never made a more beautiful woman?"

Laurel laughed softly. "Of course I do. I'll bet George tells Rose how beautiful she is all the time, just not where his brothers can hear. That's something he wants to share with her alone."

"I don't care if other people know I think you're beautiful."

"I don't care if the whole world knows I think you're the most handsome man who ever lived, but would you want the whole town camped out in the meadow watching us now, listening to every word we say?"

"Do you think they'd mind very much if I did this?"

Hen kissed Laurel's ear and nuzzled the side of her neck.

Laurel found it hard to think about Sycamore Flats or anything else with Hen firing her senses this way. "I imagine Mrs. Worthy would put her hand over Hope's eyes. Mrs. Norton would drag poor Rachel off to bed."

Hen eased Laurel's dress off her shoulder and planted several kisses on the soft white skin.

"Bill Norton would leave about now. He probably thinks this is conduct unbecoming to a banker."

Which just went to show how mistaken a banker could be. Laurel could imagine few things more pleasing. She imagined Mrs. Norton would be a trifle shocked if her husband suddenly started nuzzling her neck and kissing her shoulders, but she expected Ruth wouldn't have much trouble getting used to it.

Laurel didn't. This was nothing like Carlin's selfish lovemaking. Hen seemed more interested in pleasing Laurel than in pleasing himself. She was sorely tempted to thrust her hand between his legs to see if her presence excited him as much as his did her, but just the thought caused her body to flame with heat. Hen seemed to think it was the result of his kisses and moved his lips to the tops of her breasts.

Laurel decided not to confuse the issue.

She realized that Hen meant to make love to her right there and then, and her entire body thrilled with excitement. Carlin had only wanted her when he was drunk. That Hen should want her in broad daylight, her body warmed by the sun, seemed truly incredible.

Of course she wanted him. She hadn't thought of it that way at first, but today it hit her like a blow to the abdomen. When she had looked up and seen him standing next to her, her view had been first of his powerful legs, then his groin. Only by straining her neck and shading her eyes could she see the rest of him. They were on eye level when he squatted down beside her, but the damage had already been done.

Her body was on fire, and he was the cause.

She let her hands run through his hair. It was so blond and soft. It looked almost white in the sunlight. But the back of his neck was burned a deep brown from years under the Texas sun. She allowed her fingers to slip under his shirt to feel the powerful muscles of his shoulders. Hen's hot tongue found the engorged nipple of her left breast and Laurel nearly forgot about muscles and powerful shoulders.

Nearly.

Even as Hen's tongue laved her nipple with maddening intensity, she pushed her hands down his shirt across his back. His skin twitched and she could feel the muscles as they moved easily under his skin. Soft, warm skin. He smelled good. The faint scent of spices clung to him, made stronger by the heat that coursed through his body.

Without knowing quite how, Laurel found herself naked to the waist, welcoming all Hen's attentions. Fumbling with the buttons, she finally managed to open his shirt and slip it off.

His skin was amazingly white. If it had not been for the collar of tan around his throat, he could have been an Adonis carved from pure white marble.

But though she longed to explore his body, to enjoy the feel of him beneath her fingertips, his attentions to her own body were gradually rendering her incapable of doing anything beyond surrendering to the demands of her own desire. Abandoning her quest to know him as he seemed intent upon knowing her, she buried her hands in his hair and pressed his mouth to her breast.

Even being held in such a manner couldn't slow Hen. In just a few minutes, he had removed her clothes as well as his own. Nor could limited experience check his drive to satisfy the desire that enslaved both their bodies. Yet he didn't immediately enter her. He continued to seek ways to give her pleasure, drawing out each precious minute.

Laurel had never known physical pleasure could be so intense. Even without experience, Hen pushed her well beyond any threshold she had ever achieved. Laurel yielded herself fully, trusting Hen to guide her on this fantastic journey and return her safe at its end.

Hen entered Laurel, and they became as one. She clung to him, teaching him everything she knew, experiencing his raw power, his newly unleashed hunger. He reached his climax before she did but he continued driving her on until she shared the ecstasy.

She lay in his arms knowing that here was a man who would always treat her as a partner. To live with him would be to share everything.

"Your love does make me better," Hen said.

Laurel felt a faint resentment at the intrusion of words into the marvelous afterglow of lovemaking, but as the meaning of the words sank in, she realized the importance of what Hen had said.

She rolled up on her elbow so she could see him. He lay on

his back, his eyes closed, his body soaking up the warmth of the sun.

"Are you sure it's not just physical?" she asked.

"What's wrong inside me has nothing to do with my physical appetite," Hen said. He rolled on his side so the sun was out of his eyes. "If it had, I could have fixed it years ago."

Laurel felt a surge of happiness held in check by the hand of fear. "There's nothing wrong inside you."

"There's nothing right."

"Who told you that?"

"Nobody had to tell me. I knew it myself long ago."

She wanted to argue, to tell him he was wrong, but she didn't even know what he feared. "Are you saying you don't want to get married because there's something wrong with you?"

"No. I'm saying I shouldn't."

Laurel couldn't sort out the jumble in her head. As she and Hen dressed, she tried frantically to see beyond his words to what he meant, what he felt.

"There's not much inside here," Hen said, tapping his chest. "I would never marry any woman unless I thought I could offer her as much as she offered me. Until now, I never thought that was possible. Now I find myself hoping it is."

"That's the most ridiculous thing I ever heard," Laurel said. "Half the women in the world would kill for a husband like you."

"I expect they'd soon be glad to see the last of me. There ought to be a lot more to a man than what you can see."

"I wouldn't."

"But it's not just a question of you and me, is it? There are other people to be considered."

Maybe, but she didn't mean to let them stand between her and Hen. She had found the man she wanted, and she meant to have him.

Chapter Twenty-five

"Adam, you're not listening to me."

Laurel wanted to shake the boy until his teeth rattled. He was becoming more difficult each day. She sat in the shade of a sycamore-and-oak grove along the wash behind the sheriff's house while Adam worked his horse in the glare of the morning sunshine.

"Leave Sandy alone and come here," she said, trying to invest her voice with as much authority as possible. "I have something very important to talk with you about, and I want your full attention."

"I can listen and—"

"Come here!" Laurel snapped. She was as surprised as Adam at the sharpness of her voice, but Adam tied Sandy and came to stand in front of her. He stood stiffly, clearly present under duress. He didn't look at her. That was okay. He only had to listen.

"I'm thinking of getting married again. How would you like a father?"

"No."

"Wouldn't you like someone to teach you how to ride, to take you hunting, to—"

"No!" Adam shouted.

The expression in his eyes when he looked up shocked Laurel. Instead of the anger and resentment, she saw fear.

She knelt down and put her arms around him. He struggled but not enough to break away. "I would never marry anyone you didn't like," she hastened to assure him. "You don't ever have to worry about that."

"I don't want you to get married." The anger and the resentment was there too now, but the fear remained.

"But you like Hen. You've never liked anybody as much."

Adam wrenched himself from his mother's arms. "I hate the sheriff," he said, backing away. "I hate him."

"Don't be ridiculous," Laurel said, impatient at his reaction. "You've been sleeping in his house, eating his food, following him around with Jordy. You can't possibly hate him."

"He doesn't want me to be his kid. He doesn't want you to be my ma anymore."

Adam was so upset that he was on the verge of tears. Laurel reached out to pull him to her, but he backed farther away.

"I told you that's not true. He likes you very much. He thinks you don't like him."

"I don't! I hate him! He wants to take you away."

Someone had been trying to poison his mind against Hen. And they had succeeded.

"Who said that?"

Adam hung his head.

"I want to know who's been telling you lies, Adam. Was it Jordy?"

"He likes the sheriff," Adam said, scornfully. "Jordy thinks the sheriff is perfect. He wants him to be his pa."

"You used to want him to be yours. What caused you to change your mind?"

Again Adam said nothing.

"What did they say?"

Adam remained silent.

"Are you going to answer my question?"

Adam shook his head.

So he meant to defy her. "I'm your mother. I need to know what they said."

Silence.

"Okay, if you won't talk, I guess I can't make you. But you have defied me, Adam Blackthorne, and I can't allow that. I will have to punish you."

She thought Adam looked a bit uneasy, but she couldn't be sure.

"If you can't do as you're asked, you will have to lose some privileges. Having a horse is a privilege. I'm going to take Sandy to the livery stable. You won't be able to ride him or go near him."

Adam looked shocked by his mother's threat, but he held steady.

"If you haven't told me by tomorrow, I'm going to sell him. Now that I can't do much laundry, I need the money. Mr. Elgin has offered me a very good price. He says Danny needs a horse."

"You can't let Danny have Sandy!" Adam exploded. "You can't. He'll let Shorty Baker ride him."

"It's up to you." Laurel walked to where Sandy stood. She untied him and started toward the livery stable. She hated to treat Adam like this, but he had to learn.

"He said you wanted to marry the sheriff," Adam said, looking at the ground.

"What's wrong with that?"

"He said the sheriff wouldn't want me to be his boy, that he'd want you to spend all your time with his babies."

Laurel stopped and knelt next to her son. She tipped his chin up until he had to look her straight in the eye. "I'm your mother, Adam. It wouldn't matter if I had a dozen more babies. I'd still love you just as much as I do now. My babies would be your brothers and sisters. You'd love them just as much as they would love you. We'd be a family. Why do you think Jordy wants to be the sheriff's son? It's because he knows he's a wonderful man who has lots of love to give a little boy, even though he isn't his son."

Adam didn't even seem to be listening to her.

"Don't you remember how he taught you to ride? He wouldn't have done that if he didn't like you. And if he liked you, he would never want me to stop loving you."

Adam's expression remained rebellious.

"I wouldn't marry any man who didn't want to love you."

Adam looked as if he was bursting with something he wanted to say.

"What is it? Is there something more you haven't told me?"

Still the boy wouldn't talk.

Laurel stood up. "I think we ought to go talk to the sheriff. Maybe you will tell him what you won't tell me."

"No."

There was no longer any fear in Adam's voice. Just deep anger.

"Why not?"

Adam could contain himself no longer, and the answer literally burst from him. "Because he killed my pa."

The answer was so unexpected, so absurd—or artfully cruel—that Laurel was momentarily bereft of words.

"Who told you this? Adam, you must answer me. Who told you this?"

"My grandpa."

Avery had been seeing Adam! He could have stolen Adam at any time, and she wouldn't have known who had done it. How could she have been so careless!

"Tell me what he said," Laurel demanded. "Every word."

"He said Pa was trying to catch some bad men, and the sheriff shot him."

"But that doesn't make sense. Hen is the sheriff. He wouldn't kill anyone who was helping him."

"Grandpa said he killed Pa," Adam repeated.

Laurel realized that Adam wasn't capable of reason on this point, and it was her fault. Because she thought a little boy needed to be able to look up to his father, she had done everything she could to make him think his father was a good man. She had decided it was a lie that would do more good than harm. Now she had to decide whether to tell Adam the truth about his father and hope he would learn to like Hen again, or let him go on believing his father was a hero.

She wondered if Adam was old enough to understand why she had told him a lie. She doubted he would be able to accept the truth. Or forgive her. He would someday, but right now he would only feel anger and betrayal. If he believed her at all.

But she had to tell him, for his sake as well as her own. She owed nothing to Carlin. She had lied for Adam's sake. She would tell him the truth for the same reason.

"Come here, Adam. There's something I have to tell you."

It seared her heart to see him reluctant to come to her. Only a few months ago, nothing would have come between them. She had thought she would always have his complete trust. It frightened her that she could have been so wrong.

"I suppose I should have told you this before now, but I didn't want you to have to be ashamed of your father."

Adam tried to wriggle away, but Laurel had him in a firm grasp. "Pa was good. You told me so. Grandpa did, too."

Laurel realized that her task was going to be more difficult than she had anticipated. She could tell from the projection of Adam's lower lip that he wasn't going to accept what she had to say.

"I didn't tell you the truth about your father," Laurel began. "I wanted you to love him."

"I do love Pa."

"The sheriff didn't kill your father. He was killed nearly seven years ago, long before the sheriff came into the territory. Your father wasn't trying to stop rustlers. He was trying to steal a bull. One of the men on the ranch shot him."

"That's not true," Adam protested. "Pa was good. The sheriff's bad."

"No, Adam. Your father was caught rustling."

Adam wrenched himself out of Laurel's arms. "You're lying!"

"Why would I lie?"

"You want to marry the sheriff. You don't want me to like Pa. You want me to like Hen."

"Who told you that?"

"Grandpa. He said you'd try to make me believe Pa was bad. He told me."

Laurel realized that she had walked right into Avery's trap. Now Adam wouldn't believe anything she had to say.

"I won't be his kid. I'll run away if you marry him."

"Adam, listen to me. I don't want you to see Avery again. He wants to steal you. He wants you to—"

"He doesn't! I asked him. He said he could have stealed me dozens of times, but he didn't."

That statement set off a warning bell in Laurel's head. "What does Avery want?"

Adam deflated as quickly as a blow toad. "He don't want nothing. He just wants me to like him."

"He didn't ask you to go anywhere with him, to do anything?"

"No."

Adam was lying. She could always tell. "You're not telling me the truth."

"I am! I am! He just wants me to like him. He tells me about Pa. Pa was good. You said he was."

"I know. I lied because I thought it would be better if you could be proud of your pa. But I see I was wrong because it has made you dislike a man who is truly good."

"You're lying! I won't listen to you anymore."

Before Laurel could stop him, Adam disappeared around the corner of the house in the direction of the canyon. She hated to let him go when he was so upset, but there was nothing she could do for him now. He had to calm down before anybody could talk to him.

She had to make him believe the truth about Carlin. She also had to make him believe Hen liked him. She had to. She couldn't possibly marry a man her son hated.

"She said Pa was bad," Adam told Avery, "just like you said."

Though he was careful to keep a concerned expression on his face, Avery smiled inwardly. Laurel had played right into his hands. Now if he could just coax Adam into helping him. But the boy was proving remarkably stubborn. Just like his father. If Carlin had done as he was told, he'd still be alive today. He wouldn't have married Laurel Simpson. She was a real beauty, Avery had to admit that, but he had known at a glance she'd be trouble in the end.

"You can't blame your mother too much," Avery told Adam. "Women will do almost anything to get a man. Lying ain't nothing to what I've seen some of them do."

"What's that?" Adam asked.

"It doesn't matter now. What matters is you helping me get even with the sheriff for killing your pa."

"Ma said it was a long time ago. She said the sheriff was all the way in Texas."

"Your ma don't know. She wasn't there. Now are you going to help me?"

"Ma said it was somebody else."

"I told you, boy, I'm positive. Now quit worrying about it. We gotta decide on a plan."

But Adam wasn't paying attention. Avery got the definite impression that he was thinking of some plan of his own.

"You don't have to look so hang-dog," Iris said to Laurel. "That big, hard-headed brother-in-law of mine will come to his senses soon enough."

"W-what do you m-mean?" Laurel stammered, startled out of her reverie.

"It's plain for the world to see you're in love with Hen. It's just as plain he's in love with you. That being true, the only reason I can see for all the gloom and moping is that he hasn't asked you to marry him yet. He hasn't, has he?"

"He never said—I never expected—No."

"That's what I thought. None of the Randolph men marry easily. I think they're all slightly crazy. I know Jeff is. And Zac is beyond understanding. The only one who seems to be sensible most of the time is George, and that's probably due to Rose. She's the only person who can do anything with this family."

Laurel was horrified to find her thoughts were so transparent. She wondered if every woman in town thought she was setting her cap for Hen. She blanched just thinking about it.

"Don't worry. He'll get around to it soon enough. He's going around with that haunted look. He won't be able to stand it much longer."

"I don't want him to feel like that."

"The Randolphs have to suffer. There's something about them—Rose says it's their father—that makes it impossible for them to fall in love like normal people. They're a little too protective sometimes, but they make wonderful husbands."

Laurel could tell from the confidences that Iris already considered her part of the family. Maybe Iris understood the other Randolphs, but she didn't know Hen. No one knew him, including Hen himself. That was part of the problem. Falling in love had forced him to look at himself, maybe for the first time ever. Until he had time to get used to what he saw, he couldn't possibly consider anything as complicated as marriage.

Which was just as well, because as long as Adam swore he hated Hen, Laurel couldn't marry him.

"You'll make him a perfect wife. You're just as quiet as he is. I didn't think there was a woman alive who could talk so little. Monty and I can never be quiet."

Laurel believed her. Being around Monty and Iris nearly exhausted her, but it was obvious they adored each other. Monty talked too much and too loud, but he was the kind of man a woman could count on to be there when she needed him. Iris could never sit still. Even though she clearly thought Monty hung the moon, she would occasionally tell him where to put it.

Laurel wondered what people would say about her and Hen. He had been as attentive as always, but he was clearly distracted. At first Laurel thought he was annoyed that his brothers had come to town. Everybody in Sycamore Flats was talking about it. People were taking bets on which family could round up the most men, the Randolphs or the Blackthornes.

She thought he might be worried about the Blackthornes, but he said he already knew what he was going to do. That only left her and Adam. And from the look in his eyes, he wasn't having happy thoughts. Laurel wanted to talk to him, but she held back. Whatever Hen was thinking, it was something he had to settle himself. He would let her know when he was ready.

"You're worried about more than Hen, aren't you?" Iris asked. She studied Laurel a moment. "Is it because they come from an old Virginia family? I overheard some of the women in town talking," Iris explained. "That's part of it, isn't it?"

Laurel nodded.

"Well, you can stop worrying about that. Rose's father was a Yankee officer. You can imagine how that went down with the rest of the family. Fern's father was a Kansas farmer, a Jayhawk at that. I won't tell you what my parents were like. I'm only telling you this so you'll believe Randolphs marry where they want. According to Monty, all that blue blood is getting thin. It needs a good infusion of thick red stuff, the kind you've got plenty of, I'm sure."

"If they're after good, hardy common stock, they've come to the right place. There's nothing else in Sycamore Flats. And I'm the commonest of the lot."

"But the prettiest, and from what I've heard, probably the smartest."

"How do you mean?"

"It's not easy for a woman to make it on her own. I understand you not only did that, but that you're a woman of property."

"Oh, you mean the canyon."

"It's the town's main source of water, isn't it?"

"Yes."

"There's nothing else in this place more valuable, not even gold."

Yes, there was. Hen Randolph. She just didn't know if she'd be lucky enough to stake her claim.

Hen was in a foul mood. He had been for several days. He always felt like rotten snake meat when he couldn't figure something out. Not being able to figure out what he wanted to do about Laurel made him feel worse than ever.

"You're like a bear with a sore head," Monty said. "You'd think we came to start trouble instead of keep you from getting shot to ribbons."

"Believe it or not, I appreciate your coming—at least, I appreciate the *reason* you came—but I don't need the five of you parading about town starting everybody talking about a confrontation. All I need is another crazy fool to shoot some kid. If that happens, it'll be a race to see who gets me first, the Blackthornes or the town."

"I guess that is a little daunting," Monty agreed. "But I couldn't get Madison or Jeff to stay behind. Which is rather stupid, since Madison hasn't been in a saddle for years. I have to give it to the bastard, though. He didn't complain. Of course, Jeff was a big enough pain in the ass for both of them."

Hen didn't care about Jeff or Madison. His future was hanging in the balance, and their saddle sores and feuding weren't going to help him make up his mind.

"But it's something else that's really bothering you. It's that woman, isn't it? The widow with the kid. What's the problem?"

"I'm in love with her, you fool. That's the problem."

Monty regarded his brother for one startled moment before a look of unholy glee shone in his eyes. Then he broke out in shouts of laughter.

"Stop it before I knock you flat!"

"You can knock me down and jump on me, and I won't

care," Monty managed to say between guffaws. "After the way you acted when I was going through hell over Iris, I wouldn't do a damned thing to help even if you were hanging by your balls twisting in the wind."

"I always said you were the meanest son-of-a-bitch in Texas."

"I always said you were."

"If it weren't so juvenile, I *would* knock you down."

"Go ahead if it'll make you feel any better, but it won't solve your problem."

Hen was tempted to take out his frustration on his twin, but he drove his fist into a leather-covered chair instead. It responded with a satisfying thud.

"Won't she have you?" Monty asked.

"I haven't asked."

"Then how do you know there's a problem?"

"I'm the problem."

"How?"

"I won't make a good husband."

"Probably not. Lord knows *I* wouldn't marry you. You've got a rotten temper, you never tell anybody what you're going to do until you've done it, and you can't carry on a decent conversation at the dinner table. You'd probably expect her to sit home nights and watch you frown."

Hen's smile was brief. "It's not just that. You know we're all like Pa. I swore I'd never treat anybody the way he treated Ma."

"I should hope not."

"Who's to say I won't do that to Laurel?"

"You're foul-tempered and morose, Hen. You're not cruel."

"Thanks. I don't suppose she wants a husband like that."

"Ask her. Tell her what a rotten bastard you are. Then if she marries you, you can say she had it coming."

"I don't want to do that, you blinking idiot. I love her. I'd rather walk out that door and never see her again than do anything to hurt her."

"You really do love her, don't you?"

"Of course I do. Do you think I'd give you the chance to crow over me if I didn't?"

Monty's gaze stilled. "Have you made love to her?"

Hen nodded.

"Then it is serious."

"I told you it was."

"I know, but I didn't think you'd broken your self-imposed celibacy."

"I didn't mean to."

"You sorry?"

"No. It's just that now I feel I've committed myself to something I'm not sure I can do. You know what it means to think about getting married."

Monty laughed. "Far better than you."

"But you always were one to act first and think later."

"It's a shame *you* can't do the same once in a while."

"I did, once."

"I forgot."

"Well, I can't. Just because you used to sleep with everything you could get your hands on doesn't mean I can."

"Leave me out of this. You love this woman. Do you want to take care of her, be with her all the time?"

"Of course."

"Then what's the problem?"

"I don't know that I can do it. Be serious. Do you really think I'd make a good husband?"

"The best. You always did understand women better than any of us. But it's got to be the right woman."

"Laurel's the right one."

"Then you've got nothing to worry about. Well, that's not true, but nothing every other married man hasn't had to learn."

"I'm just not sure I'm the right man."

"No man ever is. I got cold feet every time I thought of marrying Iris."

"But you're crazy about her."

"That doesn't change anything. Marriage is a scary thing for a man."

"You're telling me. Especially when she's got a little boy who hates my guts."

"You'll work that out. You always did have charm."

"You were the charmer."

"No. I'm the kind who gets away with murder because I'm good-looking, rich, and not a bad guy when all's said and done. You're mean as sin and smooth as silk. Exactly the kind of man women can't resist."

"I don't know that I like having all of them in town. It might be just the thing to cause the Blackthornes to ride down on us."

"I saw all six of them walking down the street a little while ago. I sure wouldn't want to face them. That sheriff may have the reputation with a gun, but one of those black-headed ones looks mean enough to take on half the territory."

"And his twin is big enough."

"You're getting yourselves upset for nothing," Peter Collins told the men gathered in Elgin's saloon. "The Randolphs always back each other."

"I don't have any problem with that. I just don't want to get caught in the middle."

"Why would that happen?"

"Them Blackthornes might think we're protecting them."

"Aren't we?"

"We hired the sheriff to protect us. Not the other way around."

"I think we ought to get rid of him," someone said. "I don't want him bringing his trouble here."

"But the Blackthornes know we hired him to go after them. Maybe they'll come after us once he's gone."

"Nobody's heard a peep out of the Blackthornes since the sheriff captured those rustlers," Bill Norton pointed out. "Maybe they won't come. Now, why don't you have a drink and talk about how soon before the rains come."

"Fire!" The shout came from the street. "Somebody's set the whole town on fire!"

Chapter Twenty-six

"How many fires were there?" Laurel asked Hen. The blaze at the restaurant hadn't done much damage, but the customers would dine to the smell of charred wood for the next while.

"Six," Hen replied.

"Any of them bad?"

"No. They were set as a warning."

"About what?"

"Someone left a note on the jailhouse door. It said to get rid of me or the town would suffer along with me and my brothers."

"Are you sure it was just a warning?"

"If they'd wanted to burn the town down, they'd have waited until people were in bed and smashed the water tanks."

Laurel had known the confrontation was coming, yet now that it was finally here, she found it hard to believe it was happening. "What are you going to do?"

"Bill Norton has called a town meeting next morning. We'll decide then."

"I'm not talking about the town," Laurel said. "I mean you."

"I'll wait until I know what the town decides."

Laurel grabbed Hen's arm to turn him toward her. "You can't depend on this town to stand behind you. Why do you think the job pays so much? The last three sheriffs were killed, and nobody did anything to stop it."

"I've got my brothers. I didn't ask them to come, but since they're here, they might as well make themselves useful."

"That's only six people. There'll be at least two dozen Black-thornes. Maybe more." He didn't understand the danger, her fear. He never would.

"That's only four apiece. Monty's going to feel cheated."

Laurel stamped her foot in frustration. "Be serious. Don't stand here acting like it's a game. You and I both know they mean to kill you and anybody who stands with you."

"A lot of people have meant to kill me. Nobody has yet."

"These are the Blackthornes. I told you, at least twenty-four would come—"

"Just after George and Jeff got back from the war, we stood off more than forty McClendons determined to kill us for a half million in gold we didn't have. That was eleven years ago. We're a lot better at fighting now."

"They're rustlers."

"So were the McClendons."

"And killers."

"The McClendons killed young Alex Pendleton. Just shot him where he stood."

Laurel couldn't understand why men seemed to think that if they managed to do something dangerous once, they could keep on doing it without getting hurt. They claimed to be logical, but any woman, no matter how emotional, knew you couldn't keep tempting fate. Not even the Randolphs were immortal.

Hen pulled Laurel to him and kissed her lightly on the lips. "People like the Blackthornes don't plan. They think sheer numbers make them invincible. If things don't go as they expect, they don't know what to do. Monty and I survived five years of fighting rustlers, bandits, and Indians when we were Hope's age. George and Jeff were officers in the war. We'll have them out-generaled in no time."

Couldn't he realize she wasn't interested in strategy? She didn't want him fighting at all. The thought of his handsome face, his warm strength, cold and stiff in death made her feel sick with fear.

"You don't have to worry about strategy and mistakes or anything else," she said. "You can leave, now—today, tonight."

Holding her in the circle of his arms, Hen looked at her with suddenly cold eyes.

"I can't run away."

"I didn't say anything about running away."

"Yes, you did. You said I could leave tonight, even before the town meeting. That would be running away."

"Turn in your badge, resign. Then you wouldn't have any responsibility to anybody."

His eyes narrowed, and his arms became hard around her. She wanted to run from his disapproval.

"You can't mean that you want me to walk away from this fight."

"Is it better to stay here and get yourself killed?"

"Yes. If being a coward is the other choice—yes, it is."

"No one thinks you're a coward."

"If I left now, I'd think so. Nobody else's opinion would matter."

Now she understood. However much it might have to do with honor and justice and fulfilling one's promises, when it came down to it, it was Hen's image of himself that would make him stay, make him fight. There was absolutely no way she could fight against that. She fought off a sinking feeling of failure.

"You'll get killed. You and all your brothers."

Hen relaxed slightly, smiled, and kissed her again. "I have no intention of being killed. I have plans when this is all over."

Hen kissed her hard, and Laurel found it nearly impossible to think of anything else. It was difficult to imagine any danger when she was in his arms.

"What plans?" she asked, hoping he wouldn't need to take his arms from around her to explain.

"I want to get married."

Laurel's heart filled her throat. "Have you asked anybody yet?"

"No."

"When are you going to?"

"Right now." Hen pulled his arms from around Laurel and put her at arm's length. "Will you marry me?"

Laurel wanted to say yes. The word leaped frantically in her throat seeking a way out. Her lips moved, trying to form the word on their own, but fear and uncertainty formed an insurmountable barrier. What she had seen as the most wonderful thing that could happen to her was suddenly offered to her at a price she couldn't pay.

"I can't."

Laurel felt as though she had stabbed herself in the heart. She had lived for this day, this moment. Yet now that it had come, she had to refuse.

"Why? Don't you love me?" Hen asked, mystified, his face reflecting shock, surprise, disbelief. "After we made love, I thought—"

"So did I," Laurel said. "I've been wanting you to ask me for weeks."

"Then why did you refuse?"

"I can't face the future knowing there'll be another gunfight after this one. And another after that until some day somebody kills you. I know what it's like to lie awake wondering if you'll come back. Whether you'll be dead, wounded, or injured for life. I love you more than I ever thought I could love anybody, but I can't do that. Maybe it's a weakness in me. Maybe it's a flaw. I don't know. I just can't do it."

"I'm not going to get killed."

"Every man who goes into a gunfight believes the other man will be the one to die. But one of them is wrong."

"A man must do what—"

Laurel lashed out through pain that gripped her in its suffocating toils. "I'm tired of being told *what a man must do*. It always ends up meaning a woman's got to wait, alone, wondering if the man she loves will come back to her, with no one to help her keep her family alive. My father got himself killed arguing over a worthless mine claim because he had to stand up for his rights. All he got was a cold grave. My mother got a husband who beat her. I married Carlin to get away from him, but Carlin got killed and left me with a baby. Now you want me to marry you and get left all over again. I can't do it. I've spent my whole life trying to survive the desertion of people who said they loved me, who said they'd take care of me. Don't ask me to do it again."

"Laurel, listen to me. People can't let bullies steal their cattle and terrorize their towns. If they do, they might as well hand over everything they own and move somewhere else. Even that won't help. A man who will run from a bully in one place will run from any place."

"I don't care about everybody else," Laurel said, wondering why Hen always had to think in terms of towns and families and people in general. Why couldn't he think just of himself, of her, and forget everybody else? "It won't do me a bit of good to know Bill Norton is safe in bed or Horace Worthy is snoring next to Grace if you're buried out there in that cemetery. You may care more about Sycamore Flats than you care about yourself, but I can't."

"I didn't mean that. But you wouldn't respect me if I turned my back on this town."

"What good would respect do me if you were dead?" Laurel demanded. "Can it hold me close when I'm hurt and frightened? Can it put prickly pear on my bruises? Can it fill a heart that's about to dry up from loneliness?"

She didn't know why she bothered. No matter what she said, he just didn't understand. He would never understand.

"There's Adam, too," she added.

"What about him?"

"Do you think I could give him a father knowing he would

be killed? That's already happened to him once. It would be cruel to do it again."

"I told you—"

"I know what you told me. I imagine Sheriff Alcott told his wife the same thing. Now she's a widow with three children to bring up. She *has* to marry again, anybody who'll ask her. Just like my mother. I won't do that to myself, Hen. I love you. I thought I could do anything if you only wanted to marry me, but I can't. I just can't."

She had lost him. She could see it in his eyes. She could feel it in the way he released her and stepped away from her. She could see the barriers going up just as clearly as if they had been pine timbers piled high between them.

It hurt more than anything in her whole life.

She was sorry if she had failed to live up to his notions of what a woman should be, but she could only do what she could do. Maybe Iris could stay home knowing Monty was riding into trouble, but she couldn't.

She hadn't told him about Adam. It didn't matter now.

A sob caught in her throat. She couldn't stand the thought of not marrying Hen. Just thinking about it made her want to kill every Blackthorne in existence. If only she had never married Carlin, if she just hadn't been so anxious to run away from her stepfather, if she hadn't . . .

But she had, and now she had to live with the consequences. She would move away and start over. Losing Hen would break her heart, but she would survive. If she married him and he was killed, she might as well point a gun at her head.

"Please don't argue with me anymore," she begged. "I'll be out of your house as soon as I can find a place for Adam and me to stay."

"Stay as long as you like," Hen said.

He looked dazed, as if he could hardly believe what had happened to him. His eyes looked empty, the way they had when she first saw him. She knew how he felt, as though all

the life had been sucked out of him. She would go on living—
she had to for Adam's sake—but there was nothing for her. It
had all disappeared with Hen.

Hen stared at the closed door as though he expected Laurel
to come out, say everything had been a mistake, and of course
she'd marry him. But it didn't open. Laurel didn't come out.

She wasn't going to marry him.

He'd never considered himself good husband material. He
didn't see much about marriage that appealed to him. He
didn't think he was suited for the parts that did. But he never
thought he'd be turned down because he refused to back
down from a fight. His honor and courage were just about the
only things he liked about himself. He had always believed
that if his parents had only had those qualities, their lives
would have been different. He had held to that belief. Now it
had betrayed him as well.

Hen felt a tide of helpless anger building within him. Why,
after all these years, should he find a woman he could love
only to lose her again? He could have lived the rest of his life
alone. He was used to that. He expected it. But no matter
what happened after this, he would always remember Laurel
and wonder.

He felt a chill begin to settle deep inside him like cold at
the bottom of an ice cave. But this was not the stiffness of
self-imposed detachment. Nor was it the rigidity of temporary
loss of hope. It was the rigor of despair, of the certainty that
all possible chance of salvation had died.

Hen fought off the feeling. He loved Laurel. She loved him.
There had to be a way, and he meant to find it. The cost of
failure was too high. He knew. He'd been paying it most of
his life.

The town meeting teetered on the edge of chaos. Hen leaned
against the saloon wall, his eyes seeming to take in everyone
in the room. Laurel sat at the corner out of range of his pen-

etrating gaze. She didn't dare look him in the face. If he once saw the longing in her eyes, even guessed how much she ached just to touch him, he'd never believe she wouldn't marry him. Even now it was all she could do to keep from shouting out that she'd changed her mind.

Angry voices intruded on her thoughts.

"I say we ought to tell the Simpson tart to move some place else," one woman shouted over the buzz of voices in the saloon. "Those Blackthornes wouldn't be interested in us if it weren't for her."

"You can't throw a woman out of town," a man said.

"Why not?"

"We'd look right fools. Every thief and gambler in the West would know we're ripe for the picking."

"They won't leave us alone until she's gone."

"I think we ought to get rid of the sheriff. He's the one they're mad at."

"We can't throw him out for doing what we hired him to do," Horace Worthy objected.

"Why not?"

"Because I'm not such a yellow-bellied coward."

After a sharp exchange of words, Bill Norton managed to get the room back in order. Laurel wondered if Hen was still determined to stay. He had stuck his neck out for this town, and now they wanted to get rid of him. It made her feel ashamed. She was relieved to see the rest of the Randolphs weren't present. She wouldn't have been able to look Iris in the face after this.

"We could always break Allison out of jail. Maybe then the Blackthornes would leave us alone."

That suggestion was shouted down by townspeople as well as ranchers, but the longer the discussion went on, the less people seemed able to agree. Everybody had his own idea of what to do, and the more they talked, the less willing they were to compromise. Laurel feared several of them would come to blows. They fell quiet when Miranda Trescott got up to speak, although it took some sharp nudges and one well-placed punch to quiet the last of the hotheads.

"I suppose it's only to be expected that each of us should have a different idea about what we think should be done"—there was a general murmur of approval—"but it's essential that we reach a consensus. I doubt the Blackthornes will be so obliging as to postpone their attack until we've had time to complete our deliberations."

Polite laughter.

"I haven't been in Sycamore Flats very long, but already I've come to think of it as my home. So I hope you'll be kind enough to allow me to speak a few words."

"She's had more than a few already, and she's just warming up," one rude soul whispered. He got a sharp elbow in the ribs for his pains.

"The responsibility for law and order in this town rests with the duly appointed head of the police force. It should be up to him to decide which course of action is best. Once that has been determined, it's up to the townspeople to follow his advice. That's the way it is done back East. I don't see how you can consider any other possibility without running the danger of chaos and mob rule."

"Thank you, Miss Trescott," Bill Norton said as Miranda returned to her place. "I'm sure we—"

"That's a damned load of sheep droppings," a shabbily dressed man shouted as he jumped to his feet. "We ain't got no police force. We just got a sheriff. And we ain't dealing with one criminal or even a gang. We got a whole clan of crazy-mad Blackthornes itching to take it out on us that this here sheriff has got some of their kin about to be hanged."

"If we could get the Army to come in here, that'd be something else."

"We don't need the Army," Horace Worthy said, "as long as we stick together."

"You willing to walk out in the street to face those Blackthornes?" the man demanded.

"Of course I am," Horace said. "And I expect the rest of you to be there with me."

"Then you're a damned fool."

Laurel could stand no more. She had put up with these people for seven years. She had hated some of them, she had been furious at others, but she'd never felt so ashamed that she couldn't hold her head up. She strode to the front of the room.

The townspeople stared at Laurel, shocked into silence.

"You make me sick," she hissed, breaking in on Bill Norton's efforts to quiet the room. "Sick to think I ever wanted to be one of you. Sick to think I sat up in that canyon for nearly seven years wondering if you'd ever accept me and my son, if I could ever walk these streets and feel welcome, like I belonged. Now I'm ashamed to say I'm one of you."

"You've got your nerve," a woman shouted.

Turning on the woman with the quickness of a ferret on its prey, Laurel waded into the crowd. "That's right, Mabel, the Widow Blackthorne has the gall to be ashamed of you. The Simpson tart is embarrassed to think anyone would associate her with such a collection of sniveling cowards."

Angry protests rose from several corners of the room, but Laurel didn't falter.

"Yes, I called you cowards, too. You hate that, don't you? You've looked down on me for years, called me names, torn my reputation to shreds, but you can't say a word because you know I'm right."

Without warning, she turned on a saloon owner.

"You let the sheriff go into the street alone after a sixteen-year-old boy while you hid behind your bat-wing doors. I know because I watched you."

Even before the man had recovered from his shock, she had buttonholed a rancher.

"You let him catch your rustlers. Now a little bit of trouble threatens, and you're ready to throw him out, me included, and give up."

A man in the back of the room jumped to his feet.

"You open your mouth, Julius Hatfield, and I'll have something to say about a pair of missing longjohns."

The man in question turned beet-red and dropped into his seat.

"You're weak, silly fools if you think you have a chance against the Blackthornes unless you stand together. They'll cut you down one by one. And those of you who are left might as well be their slaves."

Undaunted by the angry faces turned toward her, Laurel walked from one table to the other, calling one person after another by name, making each feel personally responsible for what the town was trying to do to Hen.

"If you don't have the courage to stand up for yourself, Joe Bailey, you deserve to be despised for the desert rat you are. And you know, Emma Wells, that every petty criminal for hundreds of miles around will come flooding in here to cheat, steal, and murder until you won't have a town to protect.

"The sheriff is the only man among you with any backbone. You lose him and you lose your chance to have a decent, respectable place to live. His brothers came hundreds of miles to stand behind him even though they have nothing to gain. You've got your lives, your property, your children's futures, your self-respect. Isn't that enough to fight for? Or do you have to wait for a woman to lead the way? Well, one already has. Miss Trescott has said she will support the sheriff. I will too."

Laurel looked directly at Estelle Reed.

"I know what some of you are thinking. *It's all her fault. The Blackthornes wouldn't be bothering us if it weren't for her and her little boy.* Well, you're right. Some of it is my fault, and I mean to be in the street with the sheriff when they come. And I won't be hiding behind any bat-wing doors. I'll be out there where they can see me. Even though I'm ashamed to admit it, this is my town. And I mean to defend it."

Chapter Twenty-seven

Hen had never been prouder of anyone than he was of Laurel at that moment. The stunned silence that followed her remarks underscored the power of her words. She looked at him over the heads of the others. If he had ever had any doubts that she loved him as much as he loved her, he had them no longer. She had done this for him, not for the town.

Grace Worthy got to her feet. "You all can do what you want, but I mean to stand with my husband. You might not think we've got anything here worth defending, but I do."

"I do as well," Ruth Norton announced as she got to her feet. "You started this, Miranda," she said to her niece. "Stand up and be counted."

Across the room, people stood amid an undercurrent of grumbling. Here and there a reluctant husband was prodded to his feet by his scornful wife. Soon half the people in the room were standing.

"Good," Bill Norton said, taking his position at the front of the room before the dissidents could launch a protest. "Now that we've decided that, I think we ought to hear what the sheriff has to say."

As Hen headed toward the front of the room, Laurel started toward the back. Their paths would cross. What could he possibly say to make her realize how he felt about what she had done? Maybe she had changed her mind about marrying him. Surely she couldn't have said all that if she hadn't. He walked a little faster, a little more hopefully, his heart beating rapidly.

"Laurel, I—"

She looked at him. One glance dashed his hopes.

"As soon as this is over, Adam and I will be leaving Sycamore Flats."

She tried to hurry by, but his arm shot out and grabbed her. She whipped around to look up at him, startled, a little frightened.

"Don't." It sounded like a plea for understanding and help at the same time.

"I love you," Hen whispered.

Her expression didn't change. "Let me go."

Hen released his hold. He had to with so many people watching. But when this was over, he meant to talk with her again. She obviously didn't understand about fate and the futility of struggling against what was meant to be.

Hen walked to the front of the room. "I have a plan that won't require many people, so anybody who's not willing to stand up for this town can leave now. Just make sure you and your families are packed up and out of town by sundown tomorrow."

There was a lot of shouting back and forth. People said some pretty hard things, but Hen stood firm. Be willing to fight or get out. Pretty soon the dissenters and grumblers and yellow-bellies started to shuffle out. Hen could tell they didn't want to go—they'd be marked forever—but they went. Soon the room was quiet once more.

"Now here's what I want you to do," Hen said.

Hen heard the click of a gun and froze. He guessed he should have taken Laurel's warning about the Blackthornes more seriously, but he had thought they would come in a group, not send someone to ambush him in his office.

He waited, but the person made no sound, gave no instructions. Curious, Hen started to turn in his chair, slowly so he wouldn't startle the intruder.

It was Adam. The child stood barely six feet away, a gun pointed directly at Hen's chest.

"Put the gun down," Hen said.

"I'm going to shoot you," Adam said. His face was white. He looked scared to death. But he looked determined.

"Why?"

"Then my pa won't be bad anymore."

That statement made no sense to Hen, but it obviously made sense to Adam.

"I didn't make your father bad."

"Yes, you did," Adam insisted. He became agitated, and the gun wavered in his hand. The hammer had been drawn back. It wouldn't take much pressure to release it. Hen could feel the tension begin to pool in his belly. He had to find a way to get the gun. The slightest mistake could cause Adam to pull the trigger.

"I don't understand," Hen said. "Explain it to me." If he could understand what Adam was thinking, maybe he could think of a way to talk him into putting the gun down.

"You said bad things about Pa," Adam said. "You made Ma say bad things about him, too."

"So if you kill me . . ."

"Nobody will say bad things, and Pa won't be bad anymore."

Hen would never have thought of it that way, but he could see how a six-year-old could reach that conclusion. "I didn't make your ma say anything."

"Yes, you did," Adam insisted, on the verge of tears. "You made her lie about Pa." The tears started to roll down his cheeks, and it all came spilling out. "You want her to marry you. You want to take her away. You want her to love your babies, not me."

So that was it. It more than explained why Adam had come to dislike him.

"Who told you that?"

"Grandpa."

Hen didn't know which was more important to Adam, that he be able to believe his father was a good man or that his mother not leave him, but he knew the boy was going to have to accept his father as he was, not as he wanted him to be. Even more important, Adam had to stop believing his own self-worth was tied to his father.

Why should a six-year-old boy be able to figure that out when you haven't, and you're twenty-eight?

All his life he had been the victim of his own hatred. It had kept him from being close to his own brothers, from being able to give or accept love. He didn't want that to happen to Adam.

"Adam, I'm sorry, but what your mother said was the truth. Your father was not a good man."

"You're lying. I'm going to kill you."

Adam gripped the gun tighter. Hen felt a drop of sweat roll down his back. He had to keep talking, he had to keep trying to reason with Adam.

"Didn't Jordy say the same thing? Shorty Baker and some of the other boys? Are you going to kill everybody who says things you don't like?"

"If I kill you, they won't say it anymore."

"That still won't make your father good."

Adam didn't say anything, but his grip on the gun never slackened. If things hadn't been so serious, Hen would have laughed at the irony of a famous gunfighter being shot by a six-year-old.

"I suppose every little boy wants a pa he can love and be proud of, but not all of us get one. I didn't. My pa was worse than yours. Worse than Jordy's."

Hen wondered if it ever helped to know someone else suffered the same pain you did. He doubted it. It hadn't helped him or his brothers. Still, it had seemed to help Jordy. Maybe it would help Adam, too.

"I'm sure your father wanted to be a good man. Something just went wrong."

Adam looked as if he wanted to deny Hen's words, but he still didn't speak.

"Not all of us can do what we want or be what we want. My pa was a terrible person, but I'm sure he wanted to be better. I'm sure he tried. I'm certain your pa was the same. You can be proud of that."

You should take your own advice. Can't you at least take pride in the way your father died?

"My pa was good," Adam insisted, but he didn't sound so certain this time.

"I'm sure he was good most of the time. I know he would have loved you very much and been proud of you."

Hen wondered if his father would be proud of him. Or his mother. They might think he had turned his back on them. Maybe he had. And so turned his back on part of himself as well.

"You know, Jordy's pa used to get into trouble. Jordy got in fights all the time. He didn't like people talking about his pa any more than you do."

"Jordy doesn't get into fights."

"I know. We had a long talk. I told him about my pa, and he told me about his. Then we made a promise to stick up for each other. Jordy promised to stick up for you, too."

Adam's expression continued to be mulish, but Hen could tell it was softening. He was starting to accept that his mother had lied about his father being a good man. He had probably kept denying it because he thought if he did, it wouldn't be true.

Hen realized he'd been denying as well. As long as he cut both of his parents out of his heart, he could pretend he didn't hurt. He had tried to be like Madison and Monty, who didn't care, but he couldn't. He had to reach a settlement of his own. Adam needed to reach a resolution, too. And it had to be now.

"Don't you want to know why Jordy offered to stick up for you?" he asked Adam.

The boy shook his head, but his eyes pleaded for some relief from the pain he didn't understand.

"The same reason I stick up for Jordy. He's a great kid and I like him. I'm sorry his pa was so bad. We're sorry your pa wasn't good all the time, but you're a great kid. We like you."

Adam continued to stare at Hen, but the gun had started to waver.

"Everybody likes you. Even Hope. She says you're pretty sensible for a little kid."

Adam's eyes lost some of their burning intensity.

"Your mother loves you more than all of us put together. She loves you so much that she lied about your father. She knew you missed not having a father like all the other little boys. She couldn't bring him back, so she did the next best thing. She told you about a father you could love and be proud of."

Maybe that's what his own mother had been doing when she implored her sons to love their father. Maybe it was her love that had become the enduring strength that threaded the family together. She had been destroyed by her love, but it had saved her sons.

Something inside Hen snapped. All the energy that had gone into building up the barriers that had held back eleven years of emotional overflow fell away and left him too weak to stem the tide. For a few moments he thought he would be swept away, pulled under by the swiftly moving currents.

Then almost as quickly as it started, it was over. It was gone. He had let go.

After eleven years, he had finally let go.

"Your mother loves you," Hen said to Adam. "Jordy likes you. A lot of people like you. I like you."

That seemed to galvanize Adam. His gaze focused on Hen, the gun steadied and pointed in his direction once more.

"You hate me! You want to—"

"I don't. I want your mother to marry me. I want you to be my son."

"You're lying! Grandpa told me to kill you so you wouldn't tell any more lies."

"Don't you believe I can like you? Do you think if your father wasn't good, then nobody can love you? That's not true. My father wasn't good, but your mother loves me. Jordy's father wasn't good, but you like him more than Danny Elgin or Shorty Baker."

"You're lying!"

"Adam, if you believe your grandfather, go ahead and shoot me. But before you pull that trigger, I want you to come here and look me straight in the eye. Come on, come closer."

Adam edged closer.

Hen slipped from the chair and knelt in front of the boy at eye level. "I love your mother, Adam. I love you, too. I want us to be a family."

The words came harder than anything Hen had ever said, but they were the right words, the words he should have said to Laurel. Maybe if he had been able to state things that simply, she wouldn't have refused to marry him.

"I don't want to be a sheriff any more. I want us to have a ranch on the Pecos where your ma will never have to wash anybody else's clothes, where you can help me with the cows. I'll teach you how to rope and dog calves and—"

"Stop!" Adam cried. "Stop!"

Hen froze. Adam aimed the gun straight at him.

Hen stared into the barrel of the gun such a short distance away. What would Adam do? It depended on whether he thought shooting Hen would solve his problems. Hen would have shot just about anybody in the world if it would have brought his mother back or made his father into someone he could love. He couldn't expect Adam to be any different.

Hen heard the door behind him open, but he didn't dare turn around.

"Put the gun down, Adam."

It was Laurel. Hen turned on his knees. She stood just inside the doorway. Laurel didn't take her eyes off her son.

"Put the gun down, Adam," she repeated.

"I'm going to shoot him."

"You're not going to shoot anyone. Put the gun down."

"Grandpa said—"

"Your grandfather lied to you. I lied to you. The only one who's never lied to you is Hen."

Adam stared at Hen, undecided.

"You can't shoot Hen, Adam. He loves you. Even though you haven't been very nice to him, even though I haven't either, he loves us both. That's very rare. You can't afford to waste it."

"Grandpa said you were going to marry him, that you wouldn't love me any more. He said I have to shoot him."

Hen watched in amazement as Laurel walked between him and Adam. She was shielding him with her own body.

"I'm not going to marry anybody, Adam," Laurel said. "We're going away, just you and me. It'll be just like it used to be."

"The sheriff didn't lie?"

"No."

Adam paused. "Pa was bad?"

"Yes, Adam, he was."

Suddenly Adam's face crumpled. "I hate you!" he yelled at his mother. "I hate you." He threw the gun down and raced from the office.

The concussion of the gunshot was deafening in the small room. The bullet struck the desk just inches from Hen's head. It dug a furrow across the surface and sent splinters flying all over the room. Before the last echo died, Hen and Laurel were in each other's arms.

"Are you okay?" Laurel asked, her face buried in Hen's shoulder.

"How long were you outside that door?" Hen asked, holding her tight against his chest.

"Only just now. I was afraid I'd cause him to shoot you if I came in, but I had to." She pulled away so she could look into his eyes. "It was my fault. I should have known something was wrong. If I hadn't been so preoccupied with my own troubles—"

She broke off, but Hen knew what she had started to say.

"Thank you for talking to him," she said, "for what you said. It would never have been the same coming from me."

"It's okay."

"I'm sorry I lied to him. I thought I was doing the best thing. I meant to tell him the truth when he got older. I guess it just goes to show that lying never helps, even when you mean it for the best."

"Laurel—"

"Don't say it!"

"What?"

"Whatever you were going to say."

"But you don't know what it was."

"I don't want to know. It won't do any good. Adam and I will be gone in a few days. I should have left years ago."

"We would never have met."

"Then I wouldn't feel like I'm being torn apart."

Hen stepped toward Laurel, but she shrank back. She was so upset, she was shaking.

"Please don't make this any harder for me. I can't think when you touch me. I can hardly stand it with you looking at me like that."

"I love you. How else can I look at you?"

"Adam may not want to kill you anymore, but he hates you," Laurel said, refusing to answer his question. "How could I marry you knowing that?"

"But you love me."

"It doesn't matter. My first duty is to Adam."

"What about me?"

The office door burst open and Monty, gun drawn, plunged through. George and Tyler followed. "What happened?" Monty demanded. He stared at the furrow in the desk. "We heard a shot."

"Adam fired one of Hen's guns," Laurel said.

"It was an accident," Hen explained.

"Are you crazy? Letting a six-year-old kid play with your

guns?" Monty demanded, incredulous. "You've got half the town grabbing for their guns or looking for a place to hide, thinking it's the Blackthornes."

George's gaze had traveled from Hen to Laurel and back again several times before he spoke. "I don't think Hen was letting the child play with his guns," he said. "Sometimes things happen you don't expect."

"He ought to keep the damned things locked up," Monty said, incensed. "I had to lock Iris in to keep her from following me. You can't imagine the kind of hell she's going to give me when I let her out."

"Then you'd better go back and get it over with," George advised.

"Stop trying to get rid of me, George. I'm no fool. I know there's something going on between them. I just wish they wouldn't do it with me jumpy over these infernal Blackthornes. I came close to shooting myself." He leveled a hard look at Hen. "But not as close as you came."

"I have to find Adam," Laurel said. She refused to meet Hen's gaze. "He's probably not very eager to see me right now, but he's still a little boy. He needs his mother."

"You know what I said," Hen said as she started toward the door. "I'll follow you."

She turned back, her gaze still slanted to one side. "I hope you'll change your mind."

"I won't."

Laurel left without speaking further.

"You going to explain all this?" Monty asked after Laurel's departure left the room in an uneasy silence.

"No."

"I didn't think so. Oh well, if the Blackthornes do show up, let me know. I'd rather face them than Iris."

"I'd better get back to the restaurant," Tyler said.

"What are you waiting for?" Hen asked when George remained.

"I don't know," George answered. "With you I'm never sure."

Hen felt guilty. He always did with George, but he wasn't going to explain anything. Not today. The wounds were too new, too painful.

"If I can't do anything here, I'd better get back to the hotel. I left Madison trying to figure out how the family could put together enough money to start our own railroad." He paused, but when Hen made no reply, he let himself out.

Hen remained standing for a long while after George left, his thoughts consumed by Laurel and Adam. He knew he couldn't let Laurel walk out of his life without doing everything in his power to convince her to stay, but he didn't know what it would take. Maybe he would ask Iris.

But not even the cloud hanging over his future could completely dull his excitement. He felt exhausted yet exhilarated. After years of helplessness, years of not even knowing what was wrong, he had been released from the yoke of his own hatred and guilt. And Adam had helped him do it. The sense of relief was almost overwhelming. He felt stronger. He could come to Laurel as a whole person, a man worthy of her love.

He did want to go to Laurel. More than anything else in the world he wanted to feel her arms about him, to feel her softness nestled in his embrace. At last he was able to reach the love that had been buried so long. Having found it, he couldn't wait to give it all away.

The wagons had been leaving town all day. Some were piled high with furniture. Others contained little more than a family and all the possessions they could carry in their arms. Some people even left town on foot.

"It's a pretty sorry-looking procession," George said as he watched alongside Hen.

"It's not much of a town," Monty observed.

"It's more of a town than you think," Hen said, looking at the pitiful collection of wood-frame buildings huddled in the shadow of the mountain.

"Ought to give the whole damned place to the Black-thornes," Monty said. "It would serve them right."

"Where's Madison?" Iris asked. She stood next to her husband. Apparently he had found a way to placate her, for she leaned on him, his arm around her.

George smiled. "Back at the hotel. He said he could tolerate gunfights, but he'd be damned if he'd get his shoes dusty a minute before he had to."

"I suppose we're getting too civilized for all this scrapping," Monty observed. "Too old, too."

"Too civilized!" Iris exclaimed. "Too old! And this from the man who spent half the winter chasing wolves and grizzlies for fun."

"They prey on our cattle," Monty said.

"Not when they're in Montana."

Monty didn't look the least bit embarrassed. "A friend of mine needed some help," he explained.

"He was bored," Iris said.

"Not as bored as I am now."

"You could have stayed in Wyoming," Hen said.

"When do you expect the Blackthornes?" George asked.

"Probably tomorrow. I figure they won't want to risk a fight with everybody leaving town."

"Will they all be gone by then?"

"They'll all be gone by sundown," Hen said.

"We'll have seven saloons to ourselves, and not a drinker among us," Monty observed.

"I told Allison what you said," Adam said to Avery.

"What did he say?"

"He said you'd better watch out. He said the sheriff is smarter than you think."

"He may be a lot smarter than green boys like you and Allison," Avery said, still angry over the failure of his plan to have Adam kill Hen, "but he ain't smarter than me. Hell, the whole town is leaving. There won't be anybody here tomorrow. We'll wipe him and his brothers out like they never was."

"Allison said he didn't want you to shoot the sheriff."

"Has he forgotten the sheriff ruined his shooting arm?"

"He said the sheriff could have killed him, that he shot him to keep him out of trouble."

"I don't believe that cock-and-bull story."

Adam's silence told Avery that even though Adam might not believe it yet, he would soon. Avery had to accept the fact that he had lost the boy. If he wanted Hen Randolph dead, he would have to do it without Adam's help. In fact, the boy was fidgeting badly. He wanted to be gone. His defection left a bad taste in Avery's mouth.

"What's that thing in your hand?" Adam asked Avery.

"What thing?"

"You were doing it when I came in the barn. You scratched your head, then something appeared in your hand."

Avery didn't want anybody to know about his shoulder gun. It was his ace in the hole. Given Adam's frame of mind, he didn't dare let him know he had been practicing with a concealed gun.

"It was just a trick I was practicing for the horses. I put a piece of apple up my sleeve, then scratch my head. When I lower my arm, the apple falls into my hand. Now you go back and tell Allison to be ready. Come tomorrow noon, Sycamore Flats is going to be a Blackthorne town."

She called herself Miss Katrina Gibbs, and she was the tallest woman Sam Overton had ever seen. He stared at her as she gave instructions on how her trunk should be secured to the stage roof. She seemed very handsome, though a net prevented him from seeing as much of her face as he wanted. She was too tall for his taste, but she filled her dress out like a woman should. Though her determination to see her trunk secured to her satisfaction seemed almost unfeminine, she had a very satisfying way of stammering in a high, breathy voice when he spoke to her.

The rich material of her clothes rustled as she moved. She might be a beanstalk, but this beanstalk had money. That dress had been made to order. It seemed too fancy for riding on a stagecoach across southern Arizona. Maybe she was going to one of those fancy saloons he'd been hearing about in California. People said some of those women were so beautiful you'd think they came from the best families in America. Miss Katrina acted as if she was used to having people wait on her.

"Let me help you up, ma'am," he said taking the expensively gloved hand in his own. "I'm afraid this stage is a lot rougher than you're used to."

"I'm not the least bit frightened as long as I'm in the hands of a big, strong man like you," Miss Katrina cooed.

Sam grew so hot and bothered that he started tugging at his collar.

"It is awfully hot," Miss Katrina said, sympathetically. "Sometimes I think I might swoon clean away."

Sam became positively feverish at the thought of holding this oversized bundle of femininity in his arms. He had his hand on her waist now, a very tidy waist. He hoped for a glance of ankle, but she wore high-top boots and was very careful to keep her skirts low. Her feet were too large to be dainty, but then she was a large woman.

Sam liked the idea of a woman big enough to overpower him. He decided he wouldn't put up much of a fight.

"Are you sure we're going to be on time?" Miss Katrina asked, her enormous black eyes staring soulfully at him. "It's absolutely imperative that I reach Sycamore Flats this evening."

"We'll be there about nightfall. I'll escort you to the hotel myself."

"You're so kind." The vision smiled at him. "I'll be sure to write the company about you when I get home. You've been very helpful."

The lady settled in the corner of the stage and reached inside her large handbag to extract a fan. Sam shouldn't have been startled to see a very businesslike revolver in her purse, but he was. He knew a woman traveling alone must be prepared to defend herself, but he couldn't imagine that anyone but a savage would molest Miss Katrina. Well, she wouldn't have need of that revolver while Sam Overton was her driver. He couldn't imagine why such a bang-up female should want to go to a godforsaken place like Sycamore Flats, but if that's where she wanted to go, Sam would see she got there without a hair out of place.

"You need any help packing?"

Laurel looked up. She was surprised to see Monty Randolph standing in the doorway. Even though they had been staying in the same house, she'd hardly spoken a dozen words to him. "You didn't come to help me pack," she said. "You want to see if you can talk me into changing my mind."

"Hen always said I was no good at lying."

"Did he send you?"

"He never sends anybody to do anything for him. He figures if people won't do things on their own, they won't stick very long."

"I always said Hen was smart."

"Yeah, but he's not an easy one to figure out. Most people are afraid of him."

"That's absurd. Hen is just about the kindest, most gentle person in the whole world."

"You're the only woman who thinks so, which is exactly the reason you ought to marry him."

"What do other women think?"

"That he's some kind of mysterious gunfighter, maybe even a killer. He won't talk much, and he keeps away from them. They don't know what else to think."

He had kept away from her at first too, but she had come to him when he was hurting. He had shared a part of himself with her that he had shared with no other women. She would never forget that. As long as she lived, she would cherish the memory of that night.

"He'll find someone to understand him. Miranda Trescott would try if he would just let her. She's a nice woman. She'd make him a perfect wife."

Monty contradicted her without hesitation. "She wouldn't understand his moods, or the demons he fights when he won't talk for days and goes about looking like he wants to kill the first person to cross his path. She'd probably tell him to have a couple of whiskeys and forget all about it."

"Why do you think I'd do any better?"

"Because you've got your own demons. You know you'll never get rid of them. You'll never be completely happy."

"I intend to be."

"But you won't. Too much has happened you can't forget. Or forgive. You would help Hen."

"What about me? Don't you care about what's good for me?"

"He would help you. Neither of you would ever be as happy with anyone else."

"And suppose I don't want to do this?"

"Iris says you're crazy in love with him."

"You believe her?"

"I always take Iris's word for things like that. I'm not very good when it comes to love and all that."

"But you understand Iris."

Monty's laughter gave Laurel an eerie feeling. He looked and sounded so much like Hen that it unnerved her.

"Iris may be so beautiful it nearly makes your eyes pop out of your head, but she's just as cantankerous and hard-headed as I am. We fit. That's why I had to talk to you. I never thought Hen would find a woman like him. None of us did. But you're perfect for him, just like Iris is for me."

"I'm sorry, but I disagree. Besides, I have my son to worry about. Right now, what's best for him is all I care about."

"But Hen would make a perfect father."

"If he lived long enough."

"So that's it."

"That's it."

"You're making a mistake."

"You're making one as well. Hen would be furious if he knew you were here."

Monty laughed easily. "I've been fighting with Hen ever since I can remember. We had one hell of a fight over Iris. It seems only fair we should have one over you."

Laurel gave up. She would never understand these Randolphs. She didn't have their strength, their ability to absorb pain and defeat and keep coming back for more. She just wanted to go away somewhere and lick her wounds.

"Thanks for coming, even if you are more concerned about your brother than you are about me and my son. I've thought it all out, and I've made my decision."

"This is not the end, you know. George will come. He always does, and George won't be so easy to turn away."

"Please ask him not to. It won't do any good. I won't change my mind."

"I don't know about that, but George will come. He wouldn't come all the way from Texas to save Hen's hide and not walk down the street to save the rest of him."

"Maybe I should put a check list on my door. That way you can all make sure you get a go at me." She laughed ruefully. "I used to think Hen's brothers wouldn't think I was good enough to be part of his family, and here you are doing your best to convince me to marry him."

"Hell, everybody's too good for us," Monty said. "We got blood in our veins a mountain lion wouldn't want."

Chapter Twenty-eight

The stage pulled into Sycamore Flats about an hour after dark. The town looked deserted. Sam jumped down from the box and went inside the hotel.

"Where is everybody?" he asked the clerk.

"They've left town," the man replied. "The Blackthornes are coming tomorrow. Folks figure they plan to kill anybody they see."

Sam hurried back out to the stage. "You can't get down, ma'am. Everybody's gone on account of they're having a war."

"Don't be absurd," Miss Katrina said. "I'm not letting a few criminals force me to change my plans."

Sam helped her down from the stage. He had the feeling she would have jumped down if necessary. She swept into the hotel, pausing only to call over her shoulder, "Bring my trunk."

By the time Sam had wrestled the huge trunk off the stage, up the steps, and inside the hotel, Miss Katrina was engaged in an argument with the clerk.

"What do you mean all the best rooms are taken? I can't be expected to sleep in the lobby."

"I'm sorry, ma'am," the harassed clerk said, "but they've been taken for a week already."

"Move somebody out," she said, with an imperious wave of her hand.

"I can't do that. They're the Randolphs. A whole family of them."

"Who are these *Randolphs*?" she demanded. "I've never heard of them."

"They're from Texas."

"That accounts for it. *Nobody* lives in Texas." She smiled

enchantingly and fluttered her eyes seductively. Sam decided he would have put the territorial governor into the street for Miss Katrina, but the hotel clerk was made of sterner stuff.

Apparently concluding that her wiles were falling on sterile ground, Miss Katrina reverted to her imperious manner and said, "If you won't throw them out, at least give me two rooms. I can't possibly be expected to sleep in the same room where I bathe. And I must have the largest tub you can find filled with hot water as soon as it can be arranged. I shall go to my room now. I will expect my dinner as soon as I have finished my bath."

She sauntered up the stairs with all the nonchalance of a crown princess.

"We ought to send *her* to meet the Blackthornes," the clerk said, mopping his brow. "They wouldn't have a chance."

The Blackthornes were coming.

Hen felt a sense of relief. For far too long, the threat had hung over the town like some kind of curse. The time had come to settle the issue once and for all. Then everybody could get back to their lives. Including his own family. Already they were getting on each other's nerves. Madison swore he wouldn't travel back to Colorado with Jeff. Monty had already threatened to shoot him. Tyler rarely left the restaurant.

Only George remained calm. But George never got upset. Hen supposed that was why they all listened to him when they wouldn't listen to anyone else. It was good they had George and Rose. The family wouldn't have survived without them.

But that started Hen thinking of the family he wouldn't have unless Laurel changed her mind. He had given it a lot of thought. For the first time in his life, he knew exactly what he wanted, what he needed. No doubts, no questions. No hesitation, no second thoughts. He wanted Laurel, and when this was all over, he was going to figure out a way to convince her she needed him just as badly.

"Is everything ready?" George asked.

"Yes."

"Can you depend on them?"

"I have to."

Hen was surprised but pleased when Adam entered the office. He hoped this meant that the boy didn't hate him any more, that they could start to rebuild their relationship, but he wished Adam had chosen a better time. With the Blackthornes on their way into town, he couldn't stop to talk. He unlocked a drawer in his desk and took out several boxes of ammunition.

Adam watched with stoic calm as Hen filled his gun belt with bullets. Hen had concluded that Adam just wanted to watch when the boy suddenly announced, "Grandpa told me a lie."

"So he finally told you the truth about your pa."

"It wasn't about Pa."

Hen didn't have time to listen to a catalog of Avery's lies. He had to get out in the street. He stuffed his pockets full of rifle bullets.

"He said he was doing a trick with apples, but he lied. It was a gun."

"What gun?" Hen asked. He unlocked the weapons cabinet and took down a long-barreled rifle.

"He told me it was a piece of apple for the horses, but I saw it. It was a gun. He scratches his head and he gets a gun in his hand. He said it was magic."

Hen checked the rifle to make certain it was clean. He didn't know what Adam had seen, but his story didn't make sense. Maybe he had made it up just to have something to say. Maybe it was a way of signaling that he wanted Hen to forgive him. Hen hoped so. They'd have a long talk just as soon as this was over.

"Guns don't appear by magic," Hen said, deciding on a second rifle. "I expect he had it hidden on him somewhere. Now I'm going out in that street. I want you to stay in here. Don't go near the window. Remember what happened to Hope."

"Are you going to get killed?"

"No."

"Are you going to kill Grandpa?"

"I hope not."

"Grandpa lied to me. He lied a lot. You can shoot him."

They rode into town like a conquering horde. Two dozen men yelled and fired guns into the air like cowboys careening into Dodge at the end of a cattle drive. They filled the single street of the silent town with their milling horses, strident voices, and thundering guns. One young buck jumped his horse across a wagon. Only good fortune kept him from breaking his neck and his horse's legs.

It was several minutes before the men realized that there was no one about. No faces showed at windows, no eyes peered from behind cracked doors, no children peeped from around corners.

"Looks like every damn one of them has left town," Damian announced.

"Randolph ain't gone," Avery said. "He's here somewhere."

"I don't know," Damian said, looking around. "Why should he stay behind when everybody else has run away? No point in being killed for a town nobody wants."

"I want it," Avery said. "I swore I'd have it or burn it down."

"Let's loot the stores first," one man said. "I bet I could find shoes for every one of my kids."

"Ain't none of your kids that'd know what to do with shoes. Like as not they ain't never seen 'em before."

"You boys shut up," Avery said. "I know Randolph is here. I got to think."

"Let's do something. I'm tired of standing around."

"It's no fun taking an empty town," Damian said.

"It's not empty," Avery insisted. "I tell you, Randolph is here. And his brothers with him."

"Just give me one chance at him," Ephraim begged, the humiliation of that night still vivid in his memory. "Just one chance."

"You sure it ain't his horse you're wanting to get back at?" one of his relatives taunted.

"You boys shut up before I hit you up side the head with my gun butt," Avery threatened.

The men quieted, but their restlessness translated itself to their mounts. The silence was punctuated by stamping feet, jingling bits, and squeaking leather.

The creak of an opening door drew their attention to the hotel. A woman stepped out onto the boardwalk.

Damian let out a low whistle. "Who in hell is that?" he exclaimed, looking as though he didn't believe the evidence of his own eyes.

"I don't know," Ephraim said, "but any town with a female like that sure ain't empty."

"You boys keep your minds on business," Avery snapped.

"Who is she?" Ephraim asked his father.

"Some whore who came in on the stage last night."

"What's a whore like her doing here?"

"I don't know, and I don't care. Now put your eyes back in your head and pay attention."

"She's looking this way!" Damian exclaimed.

Miss Katrina shimmered from head to foot in willow-green silk, an impudent feather curling back over a magnificent mane of black hair. She had discarded her veil. While her heavy makeup might lead some to question her character, none questioned her looks. She was a stunning woman, all six feet of her. The Blackthornes watched, mesmerized, as she strolled down the steps and into the middle of the street. She stopped in feigned surprise. "I never saw so many good-looking men in one place," she said in a seductive, throaty whisper.

"What is this town? Maybe I should stop here instead of San Francisco."

Beginning with Ephraim, she sauntered from one Blackthorne to another. Her murmured remarks caused more than one man to flush with excitement. Using her feather like an instrument of torture, she left a trail of bemused faces in her wake. The heavy scent of her perfume affected them almost as powerfully. She appeared totally unconcerned that the hem of her gown trailed in the dirt.

"What's that woman doing in the street?" Hen demanded of George.

"I don't know. Maybe she can't resist the sight of so many men."

"Tell the clerk he's got to get her back inside the hotel. She could get killed when the shooting starts."

"So could he."

"Tell him we'll keep out of sight until they're inside."

"I don't think he'll go alone."

"Ask Sam Overton to help. He's so besotted with her, he'd do just about anything."

"That's the best-looking female I ever saw," Ephraim sighed in a state of near ecstasy.

"I didn't know they made them like that," said one of his cousins.

"They make them like that for fools like you," Avery growled, fretting that his men would forget the reason they had come to Sycamore Flats before he could figure out where Hen Randolph was hiding. The men had been spread out, but now they rode forward until they practically surrounded Miss Katrina.

"What a nice how-do-you-do," she said in a soft Southern accent. "You boys make a girl feel downright welcome."

"What's your name?" one man asked.

"Katrina Gibbs," she purred, "but you can call me Miss Katrina."

Avery pushed his way through the crush. "Do you know where Hen Randolph is hiding?"

"I don't know anything about anybody named Randolph except they took all the best rooms in the hotel," she pouted.

"Are they still here?"

Miss Katrina fanned herself rather energetically. "It sure is hot in Arizona."

"Are they still here?" Avery repeated.

Miss Katrina let her eye travel from one Blackthorne to another. "I don't see any reason why they should leave."

Avery's eyes narrowed, but Miss Katrina appeared to have no idea she had said anything to anger him. She was tormenting Earle, a cousin of the rustlers.

A very nervous hotel clerk worked his way through the throng. "You shouldn't be out here," he half-whispered to Miss Katrina as he cast uneasy glances at the bemused Blackthornes.

"Why not? These men have been very nice."

"There's going to be a gunfight," he hissed.

"Really? I've never seen a gunfight." She turned to the Blackthornes. "Do you shoot each other?"

"We shoot at the Randolphs," Damian explained.

"The Randolphs you can't find?" she asked, her gaze wide and innocent.

"We'll find them," Avery assured her.

Sam Overton muscled his way through the gathering. He exhibited none of the clerk's nervousness. "You've got no business being out here, Miss Katrina." He took her firmly by the arm. "I should have put you on the stagecoach to Casa Grande the minute I heard there was going to be a fight." Though she resisted with unfeminine strength, Sam and the clerk turned her toward the hotel. "A nice lady like you has no idea what terrible things these boys can do when they get riled."

"But they look so handsome," Miss Katrina protested, looking over her shoulder and winking at Damian.

"Handsome is as handsome does, I always say," said Sam. "And unless I miss my guess, there's going to be some mighty unhandsome things happening real soon."

"You know where that sheriff is hiding?" Avery asked.

"He ain't hiding," Sam answered over his shoulder. "You'll find him soon enough."

One of the men, angered by Sam's rudeness, started to draw his gun. "Don't, you fool," Damian said. "You might hit Miss Katrina."

"Is everybody in place?" Hen asked George.

"They will be as soon as Sam gets that woman back inside the hotel. You sure you want to go out there alone?" George asked. "They might decide to just shoot you."

"They won't, at least not right away. Avery will want his chance to crow."

They waited in silence until the hotel doors closed behind Miss Katrina. Then Hen opened his office door and stepped out on the boardwalk. He paused a moment to give his eyes time to adjust to the sunlight and George time to get to his position. Then he stepped into the street.

Hen smiled to himself. Miss Katrina's appearance had left the Blackthorne ranks in some disorder. But not enough. Avery would settle them down soon enough.

As he walked down the dusty street, he noticed that the town didn't look so miserable as it had that first day. He remembered the times he had wondered to himself why he had taken this job. The answer stood before him. The strong should not be allowed to tyrannize the weak. It wasn't a job every man could do. It wasn't one he could refuse.

But if he survived this day, someone else would have to take up the task from here. He would have done his part.

* * *

"Are you still determined to go out there?" Iris asked Laurel. The two women had listened to the confrontation from inside the sheriff's house.

"Yes."

"Wouldn't it be better if you stayed here? Those men look ready to go to war."

"Would you go if it were Monty?"

"I'm never sensible about Monty."

"I'm the same way about Hen."

"Does he know you're coming?"

"I told him, but I don't think he believed me."

Laurel's hand went to the letter in her pocket. It had come that morning. After seven years, she had proof that Carlin had married her. But it had come too late for her and Adam. It didn't matter that she could go to Hen as an honest woman. It didn't matter that she could prove she and Adam were as good as anybody else in Sycamore Flats. They would be leaving town today.

They would be leaving Hen, too.

Laurel opened the door, walked across the boardwalk, and stepped out into the street. As she headed toward Hen, she thought of the Randolph men. They stood together against the world. She couldn't help but wish she belonged to a family like that. It was almost enough to shake her resolve.

She forced the thought from her mind. She must think only of Avery Blackthorne. Somehow she had to stop the fight. Too many people would get killed. And one of them might be Hen.

She couldn't live with that.

She tried to walk by Hen, but he caught her by the arm.

"I know you're doing this for me, but it's not safe out here."

"This is my fight as much as yours."

"When did you start hiding behind a woman?" Avery called to Hen, his tone mocking.

"Hello, Avery," Laurel said. "I can't say it's nice to see you."

"You got no business here," Avery said, anger in his eyes. "Get out of the way."

"You're the one who has no business here. If you don't ride out now, you'll destroy your family."

"And who's going to do that? Him? You took your time getting here," Avery said to Hen.

"I was waiting until they got that woman off the street."

"Where are all those brothers I heard so much about?"

"Around."

"It won't do you no good. There's more of us."

Hen noticed that some of the Blackthornes were still looking in the direction of the hotel. Apparently they were more interested in Miss Katrina than in him. "State your business, Avery. We want to get this over and you and your crowd out of town."

"We!" Avery crowed with laughter. "I don't see nobody but you." He sobered quickly. "We got a lot of scores to settle."

A man pushed his mount forward. "My name's Barlow. You got my brothers in jail. I want 'em out."

"I want Allison, too," Avery said. "He's just a kid."

"Corbet and Doyle will stand trial for rustling," Hen said. "What you do will determine what I do with Allison."

"Let's kill the sheriff and break 'em out," Barlow said.

"Fire one shot, and they'll be dead before you reach the jail."

Several men had started to reach for their guns. Avery stopped them with an impatient wave of his hand.

"You and that woman can't do it by yourself. We'll cut you to pieces."

"You don't see Sam or the hotel clerk, but they've got guns trained on you."

"I ain't afraid of them."

"They're not guarding your kin."

"Who is?"

"My brother."

Avery looked around. Miss Katrina was watching from the hotel window. She waved to the men, but there was no sign of another living soul.

"Before you decide it's okay to shoot me down where I stand, let me show you something."

Avery's yellow eyes glowed. "What makes you think I'm about to do that?"

"Your eyes. The lids have lowered just a bit."

Avery's body relaxed. He leaned back in his saddle. "Okay, show me."

"Now!" The order was so loud and unexpected that the Blackthornes started in their saddles. Before the echo had died away, a series of rifle shots splintered the morning calm. The Blackthorne front rank was reduced to chaos.

Two shots sent hats sailing through the air. One destroyed a saddle horn. Another splintered a rifle stock. A fifth threw up dust between a horse's front legs, sending him into a frenzy of bucking.

Several Blackthornes drew their weapons, but they looked in vain for targets.

"Tell your men to put their guns away," Hen said. "If they do, no one will get hurt."

"The hell we will," Earle Blackthorne shouted, his horse caracoling in panic.

"Tell them," Hen said.

"No," Avery said. "I—"

"Now!"

The rifle shots sounded almost as one. Several guns were shot out of Blackthorne hands. One man ended up with a bullet in his shoulder.

"Sorry, but Jeff's not the best shot in the family. He only has one arm."

Panic showed in Avery's eyes as he frantically searched for the location of the deadly rifles. Things weren't going the way he had planned, and he felt helpless to do anything about it.

"You ready to order your men to put away their guns?" Hen asked.

"We'll kill you," Avery swore, his face savage with rage.

"We'll find every last one of your brothers and kill the lot of you. Then we'll burn this town to the ground."

But even before the last words were out of Avery's mouth, the thunder of galloping hooves caused everyone to turn. A herd of horses had turned into the street. They came at a gallop, with Brimstone in the lead.

Ephraim Blackthorne took one look, turned white, and spurred his horse forward. Hen caught his horse's bridle as he attempted to ride past. He pulled Ephraim from the saddle. "I hate to do this," he said to Laurel, "but you're not safe here." Gripping her around the waist, he lifted her into the saddle. A sharp slap on the horse's haunch sent him galloping down the street. Clutching the horse's mane to stay in the saddle, Laurel looked back, but Hen had already turned to face the Blackthornes.

Their horses filled the street. There was nowhere for the stampeding herd to go. Within seconds, the street was a milling mass of squealing horses and shouting men. From behind doors, out of windows and alleys, even from under the boardwalk, men materialized, rifles in hand, to charge into the melee. Each targeted a particular Blackthorne. Within minutes, every invader had been pulled from his saddle and forced to sit on the ground at gunpoint. Only Avery was allowed to remain on his horse.

"As you see," a female voice announced, "the sheriff wasn't alone."

Heads swiveled in time to see Ruth Norton step out of the bank looking surprisingly well-acquainted with the rifle she held in her hands.

"I used to shoot coyotes for my father," she announced. "This is like old times."

Grace Worthy stepped out of the restaurant. Estelle Reed came around the side of the bakery.

At the end of the street, Laurel turned Ephraim's horse. She was stunned to see everything over so quickly. She was even more stunned to see that the townspeople had helped Hen.

She pulled up and dismounted.

So this was what Hen had planned. She was glad the towns-people had stood behind him. Even though she was leaving, she was glad she could at last be proud of the town. She watched as Hen's brothers came out to stand in a line behind him. The sight gave her chill bumps. How wonderful it must be to belong to a family with that kind of loyalty.

A lump filled her throat when Iris went to stand beside Monty. She ached to go to Hen, but she knew it was time to leave—before everything was over, before Hen had time to discover she was gone.

The hotel door burst open, and Miss Katrina Gibbs sauntered out. She surveyed the line of Randolphs with a faintly disdain-ful smile. "You must be those Texas Randolphs I heard so much about," she said. One by one, her gaze brazenly raked their bod-ies from head to foot. "Not bad-looking." She strolled up to Hen. She brushed her feather under his chin.

Hen knocked it aside.

"Dear, dear, aren't we grumpy this morning." When Hen's frown only deepened, Miss Katrina sighed fatalistically. "Are all of you Randolphs as bad-tempered as those longhorns you're so proud of?"

"Go back to the hotel," Hen snapped. Turning away from her, he spoke to Avery. "Get off your horse."

His yellow eyes blazing with fury, Avery dismounted.

"If you wanted Allison," Hen said, "you only had to ask. I was just keeping him until his wound healed. Jordy," Hen called, "go get Allison."

During the minutes it took Allison to walk from the jail, his eyes blinking as they adjusted to the sun, everyone's attention focused on Miss Katrina, who didn't let the fact that the Black-thornes were in custody keep her from flirting. She stopped in front of a particularly young and susceptible Blackthorne and started fanning herself with her feather.

"Would you happen to know where a girl could get a drink in this town?" she asked.

Her breathy voice and painted cheeks might have no effect on Hen, but the young Blackthorne turned white, then flushed to his hairline.

Avery watched the collapse of all his scheming in helpless fury. He had planned the perfect gun battle. Everybody in Sycamore Flats was supposed to have fled. He had four times as many men as the sheriff. But things hadn't gone the way he had expected. Now every one of his men was on the ground, helpless. And some of the people who'd done it were women. The humiliation almost choked him.

There was no hope of a rally. Like dumb animals, their eyes followed Miss Katrina as she strolled among them, teasing, flirting, dazzling. They couldn't have mounted a counterattack if they'd been released and handed their weapons.

Avery was still struggling to get his temper under control when he got a look at Allison's arm. "You've ruined him," he shouted at Hen. "He won't be able to handle a gun."

"It'll heal," Hen assured him.

"It doesn't matter," Allison said.

"Where's his horse?" Avery asked. "Did you steal it?"

"Jordy's coming with it now," Hen said. Jordy, looking as proud as a peacock, came riding down the street from the livery stable.

"What are you going to do with me?"

Hen could tell Avery had given up. "I'm going to let you go." A tiny flame flared in the depths of Avery's yellow eyes. "But if you ever set foot in this town again, I'll kill you."

Avery's eyelids sank lower. "And them?" he said, indicating his men.

"We're going to let them go, too. Now they know Sycamore Flats is willing to stand up for itself. I doubt you'll be able to talk them into coming back. One more thing," Hen said as he stepped close to Avery, "leave Adam alone. If you really want to be a grandfather to him, see what you can work out with his mother. But you're not to come near him again without her permission."

"I only want what's best for the kid."

Their gazes met—two unflinching, hard, determined men. "So do I."

Avery flashed a smile as false as it was forced. "I guess there's nothing left but for us to shake hands," he said to Hen.

Miss Katrina's stroll came to an abrupt halt. "Is this how it's going to end?" she demanded. Her feather swished through the air like a brandished sword.

"Looks like it," Hen said.

Uttering a very unladylike curse, she turned on Damian, who had been allowed to get to his feet and gave him a very unfeminine punch in the jaw. Damian tumbled to earth, stunned.

"What was that for?" the injured man asked as he struggled to his feet.

"I didn't come all this way to shake hands," Miss Katrina replied in her husky voice. "I wanted to see some blood."

Confused laughter broke the tension that had held the town rigid for the last fifteen minutes.

"That's the biggest female I ever saw," Avery said, scratching his head, a quizzical smile on his lips. "But I don't suppose I should let her bad temper upset things." Avery's hand fell away from his head as he lowered it to shake with Hen.

Adam's words flashed into Hen's mind. *He scratches his head and gets a gun in his hand. He said it was magic.*

The slice of time froze in Hen's mind—the sun reflecting off the livery stable's new tin roof, the half-assed town struggling to become a place to be proud of. And the small revolver in Avery's hand.

Once again he was being forced to make a decision between life and death. Only this time there was no question of honor, pride, or property. It was his life or Avery's. It was ironic that this should have happened just when he had vowed he would never kill again.

But he felt no hesitation. Avery meant to destroy Adam and Laurel. No matter what it cost him, he had to protect them. He loved them too much to do anything else.

In a movement too fast for the eye to see, Hen drew and shot Avery where he stood.

For a moment everyone waited, motionless. Avery remained on his feet, unchanged, unmoving. Only a small hole in his shirt indicated that the sound of gunfire was real rather than imagined. Then, as a look of shocked fury spread over his face, he sank to the ground.

In the heavy silence that followed, Damian walked forward.

"He has a shoulder gun," Hen said.

Damian bent over Avery and rolled him over. Avery still grasped a small pistol in his right hand.

"Take off his coat. You can see the harness."

"I don't have to," Damian said. "I've known about that trick gun for some time."

"This is the end of it," Hen warned. "The town won't stand for any more hazing and bullying. You ride in here again acting like you're at the head of a private army, and they're going to shoot you to pieces."

"We won't be coming back."

As usual, it was Monty who broke the silence. "I'm in agreement with that outrageous female," he said, indicating Miss Katrina. "This has turned out to be a real letdown."

"It sure wasn't worth riding hell-for-leather down the outlaw trail," Madison complained. "I mean to go back by train."

"It wasn't too bad," Monty said. "It's the first time we've been together since we started the drive to Wyoming."

"All except Zac," George pointed out.

"It's a good thing. No telling what that brat would have done. Probably blown somebody's head off and gotten us all shot."

"He wouldn't do any such thing," Miss Katrina announced in a voice that cracked in mid-sentence.

George took one startled look at Miss Katrina, and his eyes filled with dancing devils.

Miss Katrina sauntered over to Monty, slipped her arm into his, and smiled provocatively. "You're a fine-looking man," she cooed. "Just what I like, big and tough. What say we slip up to my room, and you tell me all about yourself."

As his brothers shook with laughter, Monty tried valiantly to evade the feather that tickled his nose.

Iris was less tactful. She jerked Miss Katrina's hand away from Monty and gave her a very unladylike push. "Get your hands off my husband, you painted tart, before I jam that feather up your nose!"

Miss Katrina accepted her rejection quite philosophically. "Is that one taken?" she asked, pointing to Madison. "He looks wonderfully dangerous."

"He's married and the father of three children, with a fourth on the way."

Miss Katrina tut-tutted. "Such a waste. That one even looks married," she said, indicating the grinning George, "and that one looks like a lodgepole pine," Tyler. "I guess the Randolphs of Texas aren't what they were cracked up to be. Unless you have more brothers."

"One," Monty said, "the worst of the lot."

"I wouldn't say that. He seems to have done his bit to help carry the day." With that, Miss Katrina calmly removed her wig, and bowed to the stunned onlookers.

George applauded in appreciation.

"Son-of-a-bitch!" Monty exclaimed. "It's Zac! I'll break your damned neck for this."

"I'll help you," Iris promised.

Everyone shouted with laughter as Zac took refuge behind George.

"Where did you find that get-up?" George managed to ask when he had recovered enough to speak.

"We had it made for a school play," Zac explained, obviously enormously proud of himself. "I thought it would help if one of us was in disguise."

"It did," Madison said as he headed toward the hotel, thoroughly disgusted. "You have provided us with a suitably absurd end to this farce."

Hope Worthy had come outside to join her mother. "He's the cutest one of all," she whispered.

Mrs. Worthy heaved a sigh. "At least he looks reasonably close to your age."

While his brothers alternately congratulated, cursed, condemned, and threatened to decapitate Zac, Hen turned to look for Laurel. He couldn't find her. He looked up and down the street and along the boardwalk, but he didn't see her. She hadn't come back after he threw her on Damian's horse.

She had said she would leave when it was over. Well, it was truly over now.

Chapter Twenty-nine

"Ma, do we have to go?"

"Yes."

"But I like it here."

"You'll learn to like where we're going."

"Where's that?"

"I don't know."

"Then how do you know I'll like it?"

"Because any place has got to be better than Sycamore Flats."

Laurel didn't look at her son. She didn't want him to see the tears streaming down her face. He wouldn't understand, and she couldn't bear to explain. She had thought she wanted to leave this town, these people, Hen, all the Randolphs, but each step she took caused her tears to flow faster.

"I like Jordy."

"You'll find other friends."

"I like Hope and Tommy, too."

"I'll miss them as well."

Adam was silent for a while. "Will you miss the sheriff?"

Laurel squeezed her eyes to hold back the tears, but they flowed faster than ever. "Yes, I'll miss the sheriff."

"Do you think he'll miss us?"

"Yes, I think he'll miss us very much," she said, her voice a whisper nearly choked by her tears.

Adam hung his head. "I'm sorry I said he killed Pa. Jordy said I was a four-ways fool. He said the sheriff wouldn't never kill nobody who didn't need it."

Now that they were out of sight of the town. Laurel slowed their pace to an easy walk. The dusty road to Tucson stretched before them.

"He said Pa was good most of the time. He was only bad a little. That's like me, ain't it?"

Laurel couldn't speak. The child didn't know he was practically killing her. Every word he uttered was like a dagger thrust to her heart. She had refused to marry Hen because she couldn't live with the certainty that sooner or later he'd be killed, but she had depended upon Adam's dislike to bolster her resolve. She had kept telling herself that even if she was such a fool as to accept Hen any way she could get him, she couldn't force Adam to accept a father he hated.

Now Adam was pushing the weight of the decision onto her shoulders alone. She didn't think she could stand it. She knew she couldn't if Hen caught up with them and took her in his arms. She urged the burro to a faster pace. She wanted to reach the first stage station before nightfall.

"Grandpa said the sheriff didn't want me."

"Hen liked you a lot. He wanted you to be his little boy."

Adam pulled Sandy to a stop. "Do you think he still wants me to be his little boy?"

"I'm sure he does. Why?"

"He said he didn't want to be a sheriff any more. He said he wants to start a ranch on the Pecos and take us with him. Can we go? What's a Pecos?"

Laurel's heart was beating so hard she could hardly breathe.

She felt as if it might explode right out of her throat. "Repeat what you just said."

"I didn't say nothing."

"What you said about a ranch."

"He said he was going to start a ranch on the Pecos. He said he wanted us to be a family."

Laurel jerked up the burro so abruptly that the animal brayed in protest. She slid from the saddle a different woman from the dejected, spiritless female who'd left Sycamore Flats a short time ago. Every part of her body was tense, tight as a spring, ready to explode. She practically jerked Adam off Sandy. She dropped down in front of the startled child.

"Adam Blackthorne, you look me straight in the eye. Do you want to be Hen's son?" she demanded.

"I guess, if he still likes me."

"I don't want any guessing. You say yes, you love him, or you say no, you hate him, but don't you guess ever again."

"I like him," Adam said uncertainly, confused by her unusual behavior.

"You're sure? You're not going to change your mind again? I'll sell you down the river to pirates if you do."

Adam laughed. "There ain't no pirates around here, Ma. We ain't got no river, neither."

"Mount up, Adam," Laurel said. "We've got ourselves a man to find."

Her room was empty. Adam's things were gone as well. They had left, just as she'd said.

At first Hen felt angry. She could at least have told him good-bye. But she had done that the night of the town meeting. Once the threat from the Blackthornes was over, once he was safe, she had nothing to keep her in Sycamore Flats, no more to say to him. She had said it all many times before.

He tried to tell himself that he ought to be glad loving her had taught him how to love others as well as himself. He was, but it would have been easier if she hadn't. People always said you got over things. Maybe they did, but he didn't. He still hadn't gotten over his mother's death. He didn't think he'd ever get over Laurel.

It wasn't really a question of getting over her. She had become as much a part of him as his arms or legs. He couldn't function like a normal person without them any more than he could without her.

He would have to leave Sycamore Flats, too. He could go back to Texas and join the rangers, but he didn't want to do that. He knew when he saw Avery's body lying at his feet that he was done with killing. He didn't regret Avery's death, but he did regret the fragment of his soul killing Avery stole from him. Every bit he lost came closer to turning him into the killer Laurel had first thought him to be.

He was a protector, not a killer. There was a difference and he knew that now.

He wanted to protect Laurel and Adam. Freeing himself from this curse didn't mean anything without them. He would follow her. He knew he couldn't do anything else. But what would he do when he found her? He couldn't force her to do something she didn't want to do, something that would cause her pain. She had suffered too much already. No matter how much it might hurt him, he wouldn't make her suffer more.

Hen turned and left her room. He had to have time to think. There must be something he could do. He left the house and wandered down the dry wash. No solutions came to his mind, only visions of Adam playing with Jordy and working with his horse.

He wandered up the canyon. The remains of Laurel's adobe reminded him of the ruins of his dreams. He turned his footsteps toward the small meadow where he had shared the happiest moments of his life.

It was Laurel's meadow. Did he have the right to be here?

Yes, his memories were there along with hers. He wanted to be close to them. It was all he had left.

Hen saw her the moment she stepped into the sunlight. She seemed to pause a moment as her gaze swept the meadow, then she began to run toward him. He stood rooted to the spot. He closed his eyes and opened them again, but Laurel was still there. Adam, too. Both of them running toward him. It was no trick.

For a moment, Hen couldn't move. The past was like an anchor weighing his feet to the ground. He couldn't believe Laurel and Adam could love him enough to forget everything he was.

Then he realized that it was because of who he was that Laurel loved him. Just as he loved her. He hadn't wanted perfection. He had fallen in love with a woman who needed him as much as he needed her.

He was running toward her now, his arms held out, his heart open. She ran into his embrace. He lifted her in the air and swung her around in his happiness to be holding her once again.

"I couldn't go," she said, between kisses made salty by her tears. "Are you really going to start a ranch on the Pecos?"

"As soon as I can find myself a wife."

"And you're not going to be a sheriff again?"

"Never."

"Then I would very much like it if you would marry me and take us with you."

"Are you sure? Ranching's not all that safe. I could fall off a horse or stumble and break my neck."

"I'll take my chances. However many years we have, Adam and I want to spend them with you. He'll probably turn into your shadow before the week's out."

Hen sobered. "How does he feel about me?"

"Ask him."

Adam stood back, just outside the circle of their arms, waiting, hoping to be invited in.

Hen turned to him. "I want to marry your ma. Is that all right with you?"

Adam nodded.

Holding Laurel's hand, Hen knelt down before Adam. "I've got another question. It's real important you tell me the truth. Will you do that?"

Adam nodded.

"Do you think you can like me enough for me to adopt you? I want you to be my son."

Adam threw himself into Hen's arms. Hugging the boy close to his chest, Hen stood up. Laurel's eyes were swimming with tears.

"I think that's a yes," she said.

Hen put his other arm around her. "There's something I want you to do for me, too. I want to adopt Jordy. He deserves a lot better than sleeping in livery stables and begging meals from Mrs. Worthy."

"Does that mean he'll be my brother?" Adam asked, unburying his head from Hen's shoulder and seeing his mother's nod.

"It sure does."

"Can I tell him?"

"I don't see why not."

Adam wriggled loose, dropped to the ground, and headed for the trail at a run. He stopped and turned back. "Shorty Baker is gonna bust a gut when he hears this."

Laurel laughed as she watched her son disappear into the trees. "You sure you can stand this much family?"

"You forget I have six brothers."

"I tend to think of you as being by yourself."

"I used to be, but not any longer."

Laurel reached into her pocket and withdrew an envelope that she handed to Hen.

"What's that?" he asked.

"Proof Carlin and I were married."

Hen handed it back.

"Don't you want to see it?"

"No. Save it for Adam."

Laurel slipped her arm around her husband's waist. It had taken her a while, but she had truly gotten everything she wanted.

Epilogue

Laurel felt as if she were dreaming. She was getting married. In a church. In front of the whole town. Hen, backed by his six imposing brothers, was already inside. She had asked Miranda and Hope to be her bridesmaids, Mrs. Worthy her matron of honor. They were all waiting for her to get up the courage to start down the aisle.

"Let's get going, Ma," Adam begged. "These clothes are killing me." He wore a suit belonging to Ruth Norton's younger son. He looked so handsome that it brought a lump to Laurel's throat.

"It's easy after the first step," Iris whispered. "I would have walked barefoot over cactus to marry Monty."

"I'm okay," Laurel said.

"You sure?"

She nodded.

"Come on, Ma." Adam begged. "Jordy and Tommy will get all the food if you don't hurry."

Hen had insisted that Adam walk down the aisle with Laurel. *I want everybody to know I'm marrying both of you.*

Laurel still found it hard to believe that she was marrying such a wonderful man, that she had so many friends eager to stand up for her, that the whole town had turned out for her wedding. And it was all because she had fallen in love with Hen. She hadn't wanted to. She'd tried to drive him away.

She smiled to herself. Hen never listened to anybody. He always thought he knew best. Fortunately for her, this time he had. He'd already made most of the decisions about their ranch. She smiled again. Let him. She'd struggled alone for seven years. She didn't have anything else to prove. She was going to let Hen take care of her, and she was going to enjoy every minute of it.

She intended to take care of him, too. She meant to love him a little more each day. She had made a vow to make him believe he was worthy of her love. She hoped to give him children. He deserved a child of his own body. She planned to keep him happy and content, and to put some meat on his bones. He was too skinny. She wanted him to look just as impressive as Monty. She liked Iris, but she didn't mean to let her man have the edge.

And she meant to keep Hen safe. She had made sure to pack her shotgun. Any gunslinger who came looking for him would have to deal with her first.

Laurel reached out and grasped her son's hand. "Let's go."

"It's about time," Adam said, pulling at his shirt collar. "Shorty Baker's making faces at me. I'm going to knock his block off the minute I get out of this coat."